THEY WHISPER

THEY WHISPER

CLAIRE FRAISE

Sabertooth
Press

Published in the United States by Sabertooth Press. McLeod, Montana.

ISBN: 978-1-7372253-4-8 (paperback)

Cover design by Mila Book Covers.

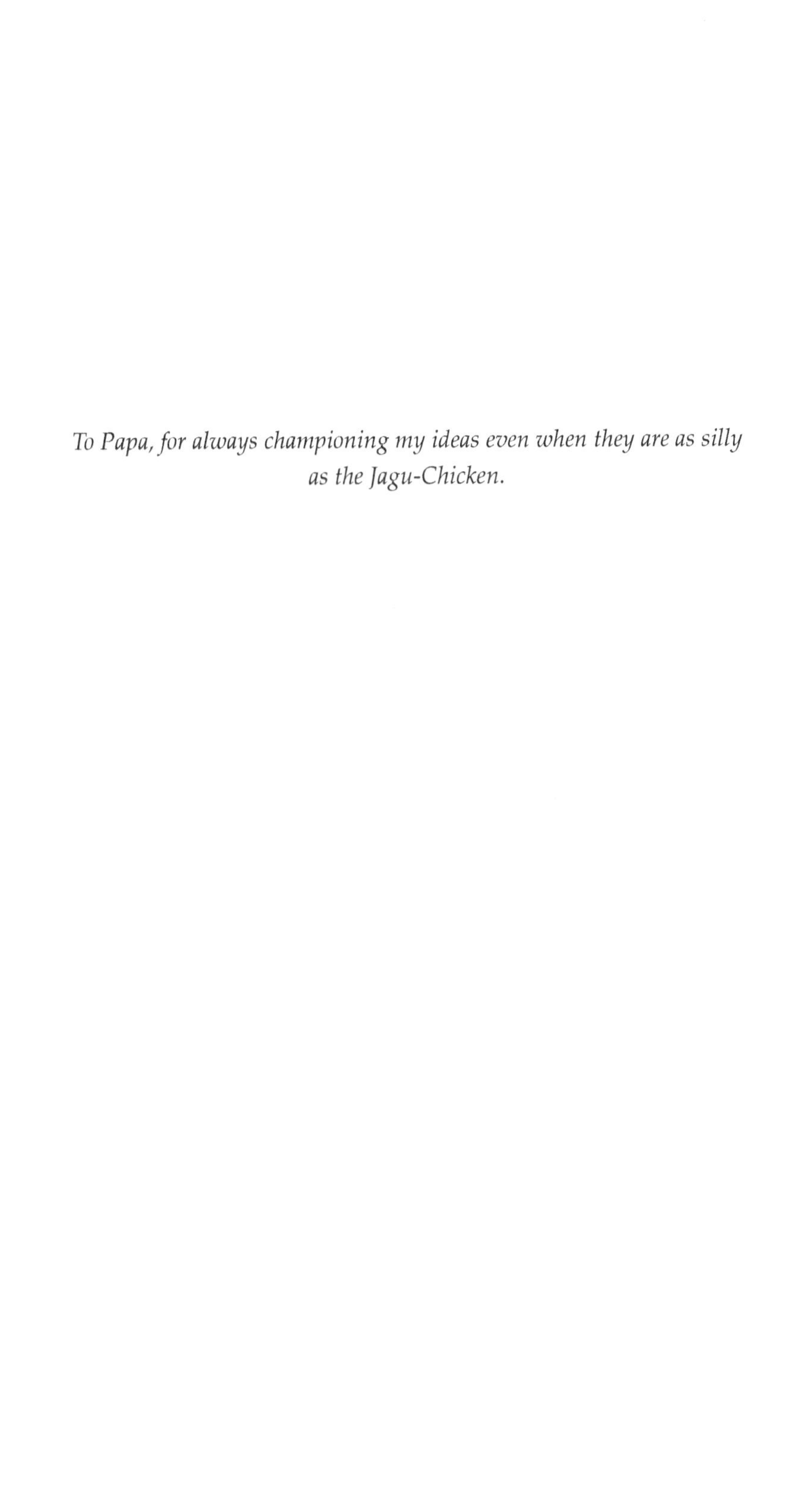

To Papa, for always championing my ideas even when they are as silly as the Jagu-Chicken.

1

Shiloh

"Can we keep the lights on?"

My fingers pause on the light switch. I twist around to look at Max and then at Mom in the armchair in the corner. She's fallen asleep with a napkin from the cafeteria over her eyes. Max is lying on his hospital bed, hugging a balled-up sheet to his chest. He looks small and vulnerable under the bright ceiling lights.

I look up and close my eyes. The lights are strong enough to turn the backs of my eyelids pink. There's no way I'll be able to sleep with them on.

Max pulls the sheet tighter against himself. "Please? I want to keep the bad guys out. They like the dark."

I guess that's fair, considering what he's been through.

"I don't want the bad guys in here either," I say with a sigh, letting my hand drop from the light switch before walking back over to his bed. I take the balled-up sheet from Max's arms and shake the creases out, letting it fall over his body like a shroud. *Stop.* I shake my head to clear it as I tuck him in the way he likes. He laughs, and it gets a little easier to breathe.

I was relieved when Max said he wanted to go to sleep.

We've been in the hospital for five hours, and Max hasn't stopped asking me questions. He remembers nothing about his rescue, but that doesn't stop him from wanting to know all about it.

"Are you cold?" I ask him, careful to keep my voice low so as not to wake up Mom.

Max coughs into his elbow. "I'm okay."

My heart aches. I remember Leonard's enormous hands wrapped around Max's throat, crushing his windpipe and squeezing the life out of him back in the woods. Max is breathing fine now. Coughing every once in a while, but not wheezing or anything. His throat must have healed when Francesca brought him back from the dead.

Dead.

I can't believe Francesca can bring people back to life just like Leonard could. God, I don't even want to think about what would have happened if she hadn't been there tonight to save Max.

Max pulls the blanket up high so it's right under his nose, but I can tell from his eyes that he's smiling. Given the circumstances, he's doing great. His vitals are strong. His doctors ordered a bunch of scans, and I forget the names of all the procedures they're using to check for internal damage, but so far all of them have come back good. The doctor in charge of everything is expecting a clean bill of health, which is a miracle given what Max has been through. He's only got to stay overnight for observation. If everything comes back looking good tomorrow, he can go home.

Wherever that is.

Bits and pieces of the last few days keep coming to me. It's all disjointed, and I'm probably in shock. Dad hit Mom without a hint of regret in his eyes, not even after it was done. I remember thinking Max was dead in the back of Leonard's trailer, and I remember the top of Leonard's head coming off when I shot him. And Miles … he was bleeding so bad …

"You sure you're not too cold?" I curl my fingers around the thicker blanket folded at the foot of the bed. "There's a bigger blanket here."

Max nods. "I'm good."

There has to be something I can do to make him feel like he's not alone, that he's safe, that he's loved, that nothing bad is ever going to happen to him again. But I'm coming up blank. So I say the lamest thing I could say. "Do you want me to stay with you?"

"Yeah," Max says in a tiny voice, and my heart soars. I climb up onto the bed and sit with my back against the headboard. He's turned away from me. It only takes a few minutes for his breaths to slow, and a few more for them to even out.

Sweet dreams, Max. I gently brush Max's hair out of his face. *Dear God, please don't give him nightmares tonight.*

A minute goes by. Ten minutes go by. Pins and needles prickle my left leg, but I force myself not to move in case I wake Max up.

Darkness sloshes into the edges of my vision, threatening to pull me down into it the second I stop fighting. The last time I slept was the night before the homecoming dance. Getting ready for the dance feels like a million years ago. So does getting caught snooping through Principal Orr's office computer, stealing the ghost-seeing monocle from Ella Ruggles, and forcing Connie to lead us to Leonard's trailer. Now that I think about it, I'm going on twenty hours without sleep.

Slowly, I sink down onto Max's pillow, rest my head next to his on the stiff foam, and close my eyes.

Bam. Bam. Bam.

Bullets tear through Leonard's torso and head, splattering blood and brains onto the wall behind him.

My eyes split open. I killed Leonard. I *killed* him. He shot Miles. He killed Max. But *I* killed him. For the first time in my life, I got to do the hurting instead of the getting hurt.

A shaky breath leaves my lips. It's done. Leonard is dead. He can't come after us anymore.

I try to scrape the dry blood out from under my nails. The

dark stain on the front of Mom's yellow homecoming dress swims in front of my eyes. Miles's blood. I'm covered in it. It's clumped in my hair. It's soaked through the thin fabric of the dress and stuck to my skin like glue, dyeing it crimson like a tattooed reminder that Miles had been shot.

And it was all my fault. All of it.

I know the nurse said he was okay, but he didn't look okay when I saw him earlier, thrashing under the sheets like a demon had possessed him. He must be in so much pain.

Because of you, a mean voice whispers in my ear, and I pinch my temples between my shaking fingers. Is it just me or is the room spinning?

Careful to move slowly so as not to disturb Max, I slide to my feet and nudge Mom's bony shoulder.

"Mom," I whisper.

Her eyes snap open, but they're unfocused. She blinks a few times before her gaze settles on me. "Shiloh? Oh God, Max! What's wrong? Is he okay? I'm sorry, I didn't mean—"

"He's fine, Mom. He's sleeping. It's me. I need to go find something to eat." I run my tongue over the dry roof of my mouth. "Can you watch Max?"

With a glance over at Max's sleeping body, Mom nods. The front of her hair has slipped out of her ponytail and looks white under the overhead lights. "Sure. Of course I can."

I chew on my bottom lip before saying, "No, Mom, I mean really watch him?"

Mom blinks at me. After a second, her eyes widen, like she understands what I'm asking. Not just to go back to sleep and wake up if someone comes in. I'm asking her not to take an eye off him because it's our job to protect him. Not mine alone, but hers, too. "I promise."

For some reason, I trust her. I guess I'm too tired not to. "Thank you. Do you have any change?"

A smile tugs on the corner of my mouth as Mom bends to her purse and searches it for change, like she's done all my life.

She gives me a few dollars and a handful of coins, and I step into the hallway and close the door behind me.

The detectives are gone. It's about time. The last time I got up to go to the bathroom, Agent Huang stood by the elevators next to Babin and Finnegan. They were looking dejected after Mom threw them out of Max's room, saying they could question us tomorrow, but now they were going to let us rest. They slinked off back toward the elevator with their ties loosened, slugging back hot coffee because it got so late that it was early all over again.

I'm honestly glad I have more time to figure out what I will say to them, because my brain is not working right now. Do I tell them I shot Leonard? Will that get me charged with murder?

I fired the gun in self-defense. He had just killed Max. I was angrier than I had ever been. But Max is alive now. Will they believe it was self-defense if Leonard wasn't actually trying to hurt me?

A nurse sits behind the long desk in the middle of the suite. She runs her hand over her spiky, jet-black Pixie cut as she hunches over a keyboard.

I walk up to her, clearing my throat softly. "Hi."

The nurse's gaze drops to the blood on my dress, and her eyes widen. "You okay, honey?"

I rub my sweaty palms over the front of my crimson-stained dress. I should have showered when Mom told me to earlier, but it's not like I had any clean clothes to change into, so it wouldn't have made a difference, anyway. "It's not my blood."

"Oh. That's good, hon." She has a kind face, the sort of face you only get naturally and can't pretend to have. But the overhead lights cast a harsh shadow against her cheeks. Dark circles eat away under her eyes, which are only accentuated by her navy scrubs. "Do you need someone to help you?"

"Is there a vending machine around here?"

"Sure is, sweetie." There's another nurse behind her doing files. When she sees me, she gasps. "It's down the hall."

The kind-faced nurse points behind me. She has a tattoo on

her forearm. In the harsh light, I take a second to figure out what it is. "Is that a crocodile?"

A smile spreads over the woman's lips. "It sure is."

The detail on it is insane. Every black scale is distinct. The crocodile's mouth is open, showing off a row of wicked teeth.

"It's cool," I tell the nurse, trying to clear the phlegm that's building up in my throat.

"Thanks, honey," she says with a small smile. "That's sweet of you."

I stare at the mean-looking reptile. I know it's a tattoo, but those teeth look capable of slicing through my skin like a knife through tender meat.

The nurse clears her throat. "Is there anything else I can help you with?"

It hits me that I'm still standing there, staring at her like some sort of dweeb, so I mutter a small "No" and head off in the direction of the vending machine.

The soles of my sneakers squeak against the slick polish on the cream floor tiles. Not going to lie, the hallway is creepy. The strip lights on the ceiling create harsh shadows on the floor and walls that merge into each other as I walk.

A machine beeps from inside a dark room as I pass by it. Lights flash from a patient's bedside through the open doorway. Cold air rushes through me, making the hair on my arms stand up.

Behind me, I hear a steady splashing. It sounds like Dad using the bathroom at night. I glance over my shoulder to see a stream of water pouring from the drinking fountain, but there's nobody drinking out of it.

I stop and walk back toward the fountain. What the hell? It's probably a malfunctioning drinking fountain, but the button looks like it's being held down by an invisible finger.

I reach out to touch the button, and the water shuts off.

Cold air blows past me again. Goosebumps rise on my arms.

Could it …? No, no way.

Is there a ghost in the hospital?

There probably is. Tons of people die in hospitals, so it would make sense. I wish I could see them like Francesca can. I wonder why they don't haunt their own houses. God, I'm still not thinking straight. All I know is ghosts are real. They aren't some sort of weird delusion, and the people who see them aren't crazy like I used to think they were.

What happened to Ella Ruggles's monocle? It came in handy to see ghosts when we were rescuing Max.

I guess it doesn't matter anymore. Now that Max is safe, I'm never going to need to see ghosts again.

I keep walking. The vending machine is around a corner—a black box smack-dab between the women's and men's restrooms.

It's bigger than I thought it would be. Bags of Cheetos, Goldfish, pretzels, and Pop-Tarts in almost every flavor sit behind those metal coils, ready to fall forward at the press of a button. Or get stuck in the coil before they fall. I get a sudden vision of myself trying to shove my hand onto the guts of the machine to get my snack.

Jesus, Shiloh, Jonah would say if he could hear my thoughts. *It's just a vending machine. No need to make things any weirder than they already are.*

What kind of snack do I want? I guess I can buy a Pop-Tart. Lick the sugar off the top to keep myself awake like a crazy person. Licking sugar off a Pop-Tart in a yellow prom dress dripping with blood like the last surviving girl in a Halloween horror movie.

A sick feeling churns in my stomach when I see the Crisp Apple flavor. It's Miles's favorite. Sometimes when he visited me at Rite-Aid over the summer, he'd buy one with his iced tea.

I should go see Miles. He's here in this hospital, two floors up. But something tells me he won't be happy to see me.

I feed three dollars into the flashing mouth of the machine. The black ring holding the blueberry Pop-Tart in place coils backward. I should buy one for Miles, too. It could be my peace offering, as pathetic as it sounds. *I'm sorry I dragged you into this when you didn't want to get involved and you got shot. Here, have a Pop-Tart. Will you forgive me?*

I'm feeding three more bills into the machine's hungry mouth when something clatters behind me.

I spin around, but there's nothing there. The sound came from farther down the hall. It was loud. Like a tray of medical instruments falling over, cascading onto the linoleum floor.

Which is probably what it was. We're in a hospital, after all. But fear creeps up and places its hand around my throat.

Someone's there, a mean voice in my head hisses as I turn back toward the machine. *Someone's watching you.*

Could it be Leonard?

It's not Leonard. I killed Leonard.

Clang. I spin around, only to realize it was my Pop-Tart falling into the dispenser.

I keep my eyes on the glass as I bend over. The pounding in my ears grows louder. Somebody's watching me, I can feel it. My hand curls around the foil. If someone attacked me, I wouldn't have anything to defend myself with, except for my hands, which are useless. What am I going to do? Beat someone to death with a blueberry Pop-Tart?

I pull the Pop-Tart out of the dispenser and stand up.

The foil slips through my fingers.

A nurse is standing down the hall, staring at me. He's close. Close enough for me to see the beads of sweat on his forehead. Sweat soaks his armpits and weighs down the strands of his long, black hair. A large stain darkens the groin of his blue scrubs. His chest rises and falls like he's gasping for air.

"A-are you okay?" I try to keep my voice steady. "Should I go get some help?"

His lips peel back into a grin, revealing a sizeable gap between his front teeth. The strip light above my head flickers. It glints off something in his hand, something metal that his fist is curled around—

He swings a pair of surgical scissors at me. I jump out of the way. The razor-sharp blades graze my skin.

I run away from him, holding my arm. Heavy footsteps pound against the floor behind me. I race around the corner, and my sneakers lose their grip as I stumble to catch my balance, sprinting as fast as I can back into the pediatric ward.

"Call security!" I yell at the woman with the crocodile tattoo. "He's trying to kill me."

The nurse shoots to her feet, concern flashing across her face. "Who's trying to kill you, sweetheart?"

"*Him!*"

I grab the binder from the top of the desk and spin around, holding it out in front of me like it was some kind of magic shield.

But the nurse is nowhere to be seen.

2

Francesca

Miles is certainly dead, as much as I wish he wasn't.

He is transparent. His curls stick up in haphazard directions, the left lens of his glasses has splintered, and there is a large bloodstain on the front of his collared shirt. The stain does not come as a surprise to me. If a person's death is traumatic, it takes time for the marks to disappear. They follow you even after you die, and Miles's death was certainly traumatic.

But two hours ago, he was not dead.

"When did this happen?" I ask, shivering in the frosty morning air.

Miles tries to wring his hands together, but his fingers dissolve into one another like mist. He tries to reply, but his mouth can't seem to form the words, so he buckles over and releases a choked sob.

I attempt to take his slender hand in mine, but it's like grabbing fog and my fingers pass straight through him. "Tell me what happened."

"Jonah," Miles manages. "Jonah was taking me to the road. I was bleeding, I don't know, and my stomach hurt so badly. Next thing I know, I am alone. I'm running … and I …" Boogers drip from his nose and dissipate into nothing. "I'm sorry."

I'm not sure what he's sorry for. It's not his fault that he's dead.

"You were alone in the woods?"

Miles nods. "I couldn't find you anywhere. I heard an ambulance, but then you were all gone. I didn't know where else to go."

How could he have woken up in the woods? In the ambulance, the paramedics used their electric paddles to shock him, and his heartbeat came back on the monitor. I *saw* it.

But if Miles woke up as a soul in the woods, he must have died there. That means he did not come back to life in the ambulance. Bodies only stay alive when souls are inside them. Somebody came back to life in the ambulance—but it wasn't Miles.

Somebody else must be inside Miles's body. But who could it be?

Oh my goodness.

If Leonard could force souls into dead bodies when he was alive, what's to say he couldn't when he was dead?

I curl my fingers around Miles's shapeless wrist. Burning cold shoots up my arm. Although Miles is barely more than a wisp of smoke, he feels heavy and dense. "We must return to the hospital."

"Why?"

"Because we have to stop Leonard."

"What's any of this got to do with Leonard?"

"We are going to the hospital to remove Leonard's soul from your body so that I can put yours back inside it."

This appears to stun him enough to stop him from crying. For the moment, at least.

"Leonard's *inside* my body?" he nearly shrieks.

"Unfortunately, he is."

"You're saying you can bring me back from the dead?" I realize that Miles doesn't know about my necromantic abilities. I imagine it would be rather shocking to learn, and Miles has had enough shocking things happen to him today. "Like Leonard could?"

As much as I'm not fond of being compared to Leonard, I nod. But there is no time to explain everything to him right now, so I drag Miles toward the road, barely dodging an oblivious child whipping past me on his scooter. He rides straight through Miles, who gapes down at the hole in his abdomen. The child stops a few yards away and holds onto himself like something doesn't feel quite right.

"What the *hell* is going on here?" Miles shrieks, dragging his hand over the front of his stomach as it slowly returns to its shape. I'm not sure I've ever heard Miles use a bad word before. "Oh God, my mom's going to be so mad at me."

For being dead? It's not as if he had much control over that, but something tells me his mother isn't in the best emotional place to listen to reason right now.

We reach the entrance to the park. Miles tries to catch his footing, but we're running too fast. His legs flail in the air as I drag him weightlessly along as if he were a balloon.

"You can fix this, right?" he whimpers. "I can't die yet. I've got so much left to do. Francesca, I was supposed to go to college, win a Pulitzer … I don't deserve to die, okay?"

He must be so afraid. I squeeze his hand to console him, although I'm not sure if he can feel the pressure, and I do not want to make promises I cannot keep, so I run to the bus stop. Miles does not stop blubbering all the way to Mount Keenan. I'm so glad none of the other passengers can hear him.

I rush through the hospital's sliding glass doors. As we take the elevator to the third floor, Miles jabbers like a doll with a talking string that someone keeps pulling. His anxiety is growing. I'd like to scream at the elevator to hurry, although screaming won't solve a single thing.

We rush through the heavy metal doors, brush past the soul of a bewildered-looking old woman floating out of one of the wards, and run to his room. In the open doorway, I pause.

The room is empty. There are no sheets on the bed. The smell of antiseptic hits me firmly in the nose, making it wrinkle.

Miles moves his long hair out of his face. "Are you positive this is the room I was in?"

"I swear it was," I whisper.

There's a gray-haired janitor in the room, and he looks up from where he is mopping the floor. "Can I help you?"

"Is this the room Miles Barot-Renaud was staying in?" I ask.

"That's not a question for me, miss, you'd have to go ask the nurse over—"

Before he can finish, I run to the nurses' station. I tap on the shoulder of the first nurse I see. She is a middle-aged woman with dyed pink hair leaning against the counter with a Styrofoam cup in one hand. She appears to be talking about something in a television show.

"Excuse me, ma'am," I interrupt her.

"So anyway, when I saw those leather pants, my jaw *dropped* to the floor. Like …" She stops talking, then turns to look me up and down. Her nose wrinkles. I must be dirty. I haven't changed my clothes since fighting Leonard in the woods. "Can I help you?"

I do everything I can to keep my voice calm. "I'm looking for Miles Barot-Renaud. Could you please tell me where he is?"

At the sound of Miles's name, the annoyance flies off her face and her lips pull into a thin line. "Visiting hours don't start until ten."

"She's hiding something," Miles says beside me, his voice breaking. "Get her to tell you where I am."

"I'm his sister," I blurt out, my stomach churning at the lie.

Miles makes a surprised noise. Neither of the nurses reacts to the loud sound. It's rather funny. No matter how many times I have learned that others cannot see or hear souls, I still have trouble accepting it because I can see and hear them, clear as a bell.

"Why on Earth would you tell them you're my sister?" Miles asks.

Because perhaps they will tell the truth if they believe I am a member of your family, I wish I could reply.

Miles runs his hands down his face in exasperation. "We don't even look a *little* alike."

"I'm his adopted sister," I add, but the pink-haired nurse merely lifts an eyebrow. "Please, can you tell me where he is?"

The nurse raises her eyebrows at another younger nurse with a mole on her chin. "Isn't Miles Barot-Renaud the one who...?"

The mole-chinned nurse steps out from around the counter and places a gentle hand on my shoulder. "Come on, sweetheart, let's go find your parents."

"What's wrong?"

"We should really look for Dr. Pawlowski."

My stomach feels as if it's been set upon a stove, filling my skull with burning hot steam. "Where is Miles?"

"Dead, Francesca." Miles's voice cuts in from behind me. "I'm dead."

The words wash over me like a pot of boiling water. That cannot be. The only way the nurses would believe Miles is dead is if Leonard is not inside his body anymore, which would mean that Leonard's soul is floating around somewhere inside the hospital.

It would mean that Leonard has escaped into someone else's body.

"Ask them where my body is," Miles urges. "You can still bring me back, right?"

"But Leonard—" I whisper.

"Who cares about Leonard?" Miles almost screams. "This is about me. And Jesus Christ, stop talking to me. They're looking at you like you're crazy."

I glance between the nurses. He's right. Both nurses have their eyebrows wrinkled, as if I'm not all there in the head.

"Could you please take me to Miles?" I ask. "I would like to say goodbye. I'm begging you." To appear more earnest, I widen my eyes. "Please, won't you bring me to him?"

The nurse with the mole offers an uneasy nod. "Sure, wait here. I'll go find Dr. Pawlowski."

I let out a long breath as she saunters down the hallway. Miles floats until he is in front of me. The corners of his mouth are turned downward in a deep frown.

"So, uh, Francesca?" he says. "You need to get out of here right now because as soon as my parents get here, they're going to know you're not my sister."

Oh. I had not thought of that.

"My parents won't take you to see my body because they don't know who you are," Miles continues, "which I'm sorry about, but you haven't come up in conversation, you know?"

"It's all—"

"*Stop talking to me*," Miles hisses. "Please, just go scrub the blood and dirt off your face in the bathroom because you look insane."

Swallowing hard, I mumble that I need to use the restroom and slink off toward the single-stall bathroom down the hall. In front of the door is the nearly transparent soul of a disheveled man with a thick mustache. Hospitals are where the lives of so many people end, so it is only natural that this is where so many souls begin their new journey. But I have heard that the first hours one spends as a soul are the most traumatic. Every new soul must process their death, as well as their continuing life. The man blocking the door sobs silently, his shoulders shaking as he buries his eyes in his closed fists.

I wish I could tell him it will be all right, but doing so would only confuse him because I would have to explain why I can see him. I pretend not to notice he is there as I reach through his torso to open the bathroom door.

Miles hovers by the sink as I clean myself up, worry knitting his face together. "We need to get down to the morgue ourselves."

I rinse the soap from my forearms and dry my hands on a scratchy paper towel. "Where is the morgue?"

"How should I know?" Miles freezes, and his eyes grow

wide. "Oh, God. If they do an autopsy, they're going to cut up my body really badly, and then you definitely can't bring me back, so we really have to hurry."

If Leonard killed Miles in order to eject himself from the body, he could have *already* cut Miles's body up badly.

I picture Leonard waiting until the doctors and nurses had left the room before reaching up to turn off the monitors, unraveling Miles's bandage and digging his fingers into the wound, pulling at the flesh, ripping out Miles's intestines until blood poured out of his stomach cavity, soaking through the bed sheets and pooling on the floor before anyone could rush back in and see what had happened. Could that have been what the janitor was mopping up?

If Leonard tore up Miles's intestines, could his body even support his soul anymore?

I clamp my teeth over my tongue. There is no reason to make Miles panic.

But Miles already appears to be panicking. "How are we going to get to the morgue?" he asks as I walk out of the bathroom. "How can we sneak down there with no one noticing?"

A high-pitched laugh soars over the hospital chatter. I glance around for the source of the laughter and pause.

A soul hovers over the water fountain, doing a somersault in the air. She shines more brightly than any of the other souls I have seen today. Certainly brighter than Miles, who is barely visible underneath the fluorescent panels of light above our heads. The soul is a middle-aged woman wearing a high ponytail so tight that it stretches the skin on her skull and makes her forehead appear bigger than it is. Glasses with large black frames magnify her colorless eyes, making her look like some sort of bug.

"I bet the morgue is in the basement." Miles's voice sounds far away. "Morgues are always in the basement. At least, they are in the movies, and always guarded by ginormous guys named Igor." Miles shakes his head as if to tell himself to focus.

"We have to take the staff elevator to get down there, but to do that we'll need a keycard." He points to the identification cards hanging from the left pockets of the nurses' scrubs. "Could I steal one?" He glances at his open palms. "Can ghosts do stuff like that?"

"Not if they died as recently as you." I remember the way Ella Ruggles's young sister flipped books off shelves, and how George Haggarty dislodged the lock to Leonard's trailer. "In order to touch the material world, a soul has to be old. So old that they have already faded to the other side …"

My voice trails off as the bright soul with the large glasses blows air up a passing woman's skirt, making the skirt billow so high it flashes the woman's underwear. I gasp. The woman presses down her skirt as she glances around. The soul erupts into a fit of laughter, rolling and hugging her knees to her chest, somersaulting backward over and over like a playful child.

"Looks like our poltergeist is back," a passing nurse whispers, pointing at the woman still pressing down her skirt.

"Can't keep that damn thing away for long," her companion jokes, laughing like she doesn't truly believe it.

My lips part in astonishment. Perhaps a ghost can help us borrow an ID card after all.

I hurry over to where the soul is still laughing, interrupting her with a soft clearing of my throat. "Hello there," I say.

"*Francesca.*" Miles hisses, and I realize I cannot talk to the soul openly as there are people going up and down this hallway. With sudden inspiration, I pull out the flip phone Jonah let me borrow at the homecoming dance and hold it to my ear.

The soul stops laughing and points to herself as if asking a question. "You talking to me?"

"Yes."

"'Scuse me," she says. While this soul was alive, her eyesight must have been bad because her lenses magnify her eyes so much it makes her look like a button-eyed doll. She doesn't appear to be all that shocked I can see her, which is odd. Usually, people at least raise an eyebrow. "Who're you, and how come you can see me?"

"My name is Francesca, and I have been able to see souls my entire life." The phone is cold against my ear. "Pardon me for asking, but was that you who blew air up that poor woman's dress?"

"What're you gonna do, kill me?" The bug-eyed woman smacks her lips into a smile. "Kitty's gotta do what Kitty's gotta do."

Satisfaction blooms deep inside my stomach. If this woman—Kitty—is capable of blowing air up people's skirts, she should also be capable of snatching an identification card from a nurse's scrubs.

"It's a pleasure to meet you, Kitty," I say. "Unfortunately, we are in a bit of a pickle."

"I always ask for extra pickles."

"See my friend here?" I point at Miles, who is blinking away the tears pooling in his eyes. "He died not too long ago, and we believe his body was taken down to the morgue."

Kitty's eyes widen. "Ooh, I love it down there!"

"Do you know where it is?" Hope creeps into my voice.

"I sure do," she says proudly. "I've explored every inch of this place, and it's not every day I get people to play with. See that guy over there?" She points at an elderly doctor in a long, white lab coat. "That's my daddy. He's a doctor, one of those fancy ones with the coats that have their names stitched on."

"That's wonderful."

"Every time I find a way back here from the other side, which isn't often enough if you ask me, I always come back to the hospital so I can play pranks on my daddy."

I suppose that explains the nurse's comment that the poltergeist was back. Kitty has found her way back to the material world from the other side at least once before.

Miles waves his hand in front of my face. "Can we focus here?"

I nod. He is right. There is not much time. "Kitty, we need

you to lead us to the morgue so that we can find my friend's body and I can replace him inside of it."

"You want to put him back in?" she asks, her face lighting up. I nod. "You're like a … what's the word … a necrophile?"

"Necromancer," Miles corrects, his nose wrinkling in disgust at the thought of it. "Thank the Lord."

"They may take his body away to perform an autopsy," I say, "so we must hurry if I have any chance of saving him."

"Oh, cool! It's like an adventure." Kitty does a flip in the air before landing on the ground behind us. "I'd love to play this game with you."

I shudder. It's a game where if we lose, Miles loses his life.

3

FrANCesCA

I wring my hands together as Kitty bounces on her toes.

"Ivan's got a teeny bladder," she says, referring to the nurse she has selected as our target. "All it takes is a tiny tickle, and he's running to the toilet with his tail tucked 'tween his legs."

I hope she is right. Kitty soars off toward the nurses as Miles sobs beside me. He sure is crying a lot. I would get dehydrated from crying that much.

Down the hall, Kitty titters gleefully. "Come here, you goose!"

Crash. A tray of instruments falls, and a tall man takes the corner at a run followed by Kitty, who is grinning triumphantly.

"Works every time!" she proclaims.

As the man I assume is Ivan opens the restroom door, Kitty blows through him. My lips part as the fabric of his coat wafts forward, his glasses tumble from his face, and his ID card falls to the ground.

Ivan's hand flies to his face. Before he can notice the missing card, I swipe it up and hurry down the hall.

Kitty clacks her teeth together. "I told you, didn't I?" she says. "Didn't I tell you?"

"You certainly did, Kitty. Thank you." I walk with long strides. I do not want to run, because it might make people suspicious of what I was up to.

Kitty points at the door blocking the end of the hallway. With a confident movement, I swipe the key card, and the scanner flashes green.

Yes. I hurry inside. "Where's the elevator?"

Kitty beckons for me to follow her around a corner.

"Hurry, Francesca," Miles says, wringing his hands together. "You look nothing like a doctor."

Around the corner are the double doors of a giant metal elevator. I stab my thumb onto the elevator button five times, lean back on my heels, and wrap my arms around my stomach. In the window to the corridor outside, I can see passing doctors and nurses. I wonder if Leonard's soul is hiding inside one of them.

Miles is hyperventilating, despite being dead. I try to touch his shoulder, but my fingers pass through him and into his chest.

The big metal doors slide open. I run into the empty elevator and press the B button to go to the basement.

The doors close. It hits me that this isn't a normal elevator—it's a freight elevator for people's final journeys. There is no elevator music in here, no paneled wooden walls or a courtesy mirror to check your makeup in. We're in a purely functional part of the hospital now, where the public doesn't go.

The elevator rattles past the second floor but slows to a stop at the first.

I glance at Kitty in a panic. "Why is it stopping?"

Kitty shrugs. The doors peel back to reveal a young woman in a tight-collared shirt and navy pants. She rolls a heavy yellow bucket with a mop sticking out the end into the elevator. Its plastic wheels rattle on the ribbed metal floor. There's a keycard clipped to the pocket of her shirt, partially covered by her side ponytail that falls to the right of her neck.

"Stop looking guilty," Miles hisses at me. "She's going to figure out you're not supposed to be in here."

The woman's eyes linger on me as she steps into the elevator, her hands curled around the mop. She does not press a button so she must also be traveling to the basement.

The doors slide shut, and the elevator lurches. My heart hammers in my chest as I train my eyes on the closed metal doors. The woman's eyes bore into the side of my head like an ice pick trying to find the soft parts inside my skull.

"Oh, this will be fun," Kitty says, crouching down and taking in a huge breath before blowing into the bucket of water. Ripples form in the bucket, sloshing against the edges. Pressure leaves my head as the cleaner glances down at the water in bewilderment.

The elevator slows to a stop. The doors open, and I scurry after Kitty. I hear the cleaner's bucket as it rattles out of the elevator behind us, but I guess she's lost interest now.

"How far is it?"

"This way." Kitty whips around a corner so fast I stumble, trying to keep up with her.

It's dark down here—and gloomy. The theme of functional decor continues as we race past the soul of an old man in overalls. He does not appear to know what has happened to him and is staring at the hand sanitizer, as if it might be capable of dispensing answers. I pass another soul, a younger man this time, with half of his skull flattened like a dropped ball of Play-Doh. Kitty waves at me to follow her. I turn the corner, more confident than ever.

I collide with something firm. Stumbling back, I glance up and into the face of a middle-aged man in jeans and a plaid shirt.

He looks me up and down as he scratches his beard. I notice an ID card hanging from the front of his shirt, but he's standing too far away for me to read his name. "You lost or something, kid?"

He waits for a response. I open my mouth, fighting for the right words.

Kitty soars around the man, pointing down the hall. "The morgue's around the corner."

"Run before he stops you, Francesca!" Miles screams.

With one last panicked look into the man's eyes, I dart around him and run after Kitty.

"Hey!" The man yells. "Where are you going?"

My feet pound against the floor. Or perhaps it's the man's feet, I'm not sure. Kitty stops abruptly and points at a closed door. Before I can lose my nerve, I throw myself inside, grab the nearest hospital trash bin, and jam it underneath the handle. Are there other doors? I run to the other side of the room to jam a supply shelf under the handle of a second door.

The handle wiggles.

"Open up!" yells a deep voice. Those makeshift barriers will not hold the man for long. "Or I'm calling security!"

I turn to face the room, my heart pounding. The morgue is far smaller than I expected. It looks like an examination room with metal sinks along one wall, paper towels in easy-to-access places, and medical instruments lined up on trays beside scrubbed, shiny metal tables. They aren't surgical instruments— at least, I don't think they are. They look like tools found in my school's wood shop, except the saws and drills and knives are clean and glinting. It makes them seem more evil. But at least there's no smell of death hanging in the air, the back-of-the-throat scent of mold and rot, the coppery tang of blood. Everything's been cleaned to within a millimeter of its life. It smells of antiseptic and bleach, like the rest of the hospital.

Kitty spins around the top of the mortuary, making the paper towels flap in her wake. Miles stares blankly at the center of the room. I follow his gaze to a white sheet hanging over a lumpy figure on the examination table.

"The bodies are in here, in the refrigerators," says Kitty, gesturing at the wall of long cabinets stretching floor to ceiling.

I creep toward the figure on the table. If Miles died a couple of hours ago, perhaps he wouldn't have been put away yet.

No blood has stained the white plastic body bag, which is

promising. Perhaps I was wrong about Leonard ripping out Miles's intestines. A thick zipper seals the bag.

I glance over at Miles for permission. For some silly reason, it feels as if I am violating his privacy. "Can I?"

"Of course you can. Hurry," Miles says urgently, glancing at the door.

I pull down the zipper to expose the head.

My breath catches in my throat.

Miles's face looks like it always did, turned up to the ceiling as if he's sleeping on his back, but his skin is waxy—only a couple of shades darker than his soul. The corpse's eyelids are closed like nothing is happening behind them, because nothing is. Miles's face is still the same, except Miles isn't in there anymore to animate its expressions.

I have never seen a corpse look this peaceful. I feel a pang of guilt for disturbing it.

"Oh my God," Miles whispers.

Directly behind my ear, Kitty is slowly humming a child's song, which takes me a minute to recognize as *Three Blind Mice.*

I touch my fingers to the corpse's neck. It is still warm, but certainly cooler than I am. "I have never brought somebody back who has been dead this long."

A fist pounds on the door. *"Open up!"*

"See how they run … See how they run," Kitty intones. I glance up at her and see that she is looking at Miles's body with an unreadable expression.

"Please try," Miles begs. I glance over at his pleading eyes and trembling lower lip. "I can't die yet. There is so much I need to do. This can't be the end of me. *Please.*"

With shaking fingers, I drag the zipper down to the corpse's knees, exposing the yellow paper gown covering its bony frame. I can see the bandage covering the bullet wound through the thin material, but the gauze appears to still be white.

Something bulges inside the corpse's throat. My belly turns as I pry open the stiff jaw. Gauze fills its mouth. Miles's soul gasps as I pull the gauze out through his corpse's teeth like some sick conjurer unraveling a line of flags from a top hat.

"I suppose this is how Leonard must have killed you," I say as the last of the ribbon of gauze emerges from Miles's mouth and I throw it to the floor, where it lands with a splat. An empty metal basin shines like an accusation from its place next to the instruments. In a few hours, Miles's brain, kidneys, heart, and liver will be in there if I fail. "I think I got it all."

"Come on." Miles offers his transparent hands to me.

Behind me, Kitty stops humming as the banging on the door gets louder. "How do you bring people back?" she asks. Her voice is more serious now.

"I'm not entirely sure. I have only done it twice. It's kind of instinctive."

Miles's mouth gapes open. "You don't *know* how to do this?"

With a nervous glance back at the door, I take Miles's hands in mine. My fingers grip onto something cold and solid.

What if I can't do it? Will Miles blame me forever?

Will Shiloh blame me forever?

"Close your eyes," I tell Miles, and he does as he's told. How did I do this last time? In the tent city, I pressed the woman back into her body, which was simple enough as she had not completely risen from it yet. With Max … everything happened so fast that I honestly cannot remember what I did.

"What now?" Miles asks.

I draw in a deep breath, filling my lungs until they ache. I must focus on Miles. Not on the voices outside the door. Not on the fact we could be interrupted at any second.

Pain from Miles's icy hands swirls up my arms. I lift him onto the examination table. He sits down on his corpse. I press him down toward it.

Nothing happens.

"Are you sure this is how you do it?" Kitty asks.

"Perhaps I need to line you up."

"Do you even know what you're doing?" Miles exclaims.

"Just line yourself up with your body right now! Do it!"

Miles lies down, stretching out his arms and legs so they line up with the corpse's. I climb onto the examination table and place my open palms on his soul's chest, pressing down as hard as I can.

"Ow, it hurts."

His soul threatens to leap away from the body, like two magnets repelling each other.

Why isn't it working? I ask myself, my heart thumping in my ears.

Miles cries, asking what I'm doing, but his words bounce off me like rubber balls.

Drawing all my remaining strength, I lean my entire weight on Miles's soul. He screams.

Come on, I think to myself.

I grip his wrists until my knuckles turn white.

A rough sob breaks through Miles's throat. "It hurts."

"Be quiet, Miles. Please," I beg. The sound of fists thudding on the door fades, and Miles appears to be getting more translucent. It's working. I have to keep going.

"Stop it," Miles's soul pleads, his voice contorted as he cries, "Please, stop, I can't do this."

"Be quiet, be quiet, be quiet!" I repeat, gaining strength from the mantra. I lean my full weight onto his soul, using whatever strength I have left to stop him from jumping to the side. "You're almost done, I promise."

"Hurry."

I shove Miles's soul hard and fall forward onto his corpse. My hand pushes against his collarbone, and I throw myself to the side so that I do not hurt him, the cold floor slamming against my knees. Pain shoots up my thighs. I glance down at my palms, then up at the table. I can't see Miles's soul anymore.

Did I do it?

The mortuary swims around me. My eyes settle on Kitty, who is staring at me in absolute awe.

"I never thought magic was real," she says.

"It's not magic," I manage, gripping my head with my hand.

"It's merely something I can do." Kitty's face duplicates, and now there are two of her, staring at me from across the table.

"You 'right?" Kitty asks. "You don't look so good."

Steadying myself on the table, I press my fingers into the fleshy part of Miles's neck.

He's alive.

I did it.

There's an uncommon expression on Kitty's face now. Her eyes are narrow and menacing.

"Do it for me," Kitty says, flying over to a freezer door and pulling hard on the handle. "Bring me back, too."

"I cannot bring you into a stranger's body."

"What do you mean you can't?" Kitty rakes her nails down her face. "I watched you do it." Kitty glows brighter, and the panels of light above us flicker. "I don't care whose body you put me in. Bring me back right now."

I press my hand to my forehead. The lights flicker harder.

"Bring me back!" Kitty screams. "Do it now!"

The light bulbs explode inside the overhead strips, and I hear glass pattering against their plastic surfaces. I cover my head instinctively.

The door bursts open. A hospital security officer barges in, followed by the man I bumped into in the hallway.

I point at Miles. "He's alive. Please, you must help him. He needs …"

The world pulls away from me. A stab of pain shoots through my skull as it hits the hard floor of the morgue. But the men are concentrating on Miles. The man from the hallway checks Miles's neck and shouts something at the security officer, who starts yelling into his walkie-talkie. I feel hands on me, turning me onto my back. Voices sound as if from far away, but their tone is sympathetic. That's the last thing that registers before everything goes black.

4

Shiloh

I hold Max's hand as we walk into our house.

"There is some leftover chili in the fridge," Mom says, closing the door and walking into the kitchen like a nervous realtor. "Do you want any?"

"I'm not hungry," Max says.

Disappointment flashes across Mom's face for a second before she puts the bowl back in the fridge. Max goes out into the backyard, even though it's cold. He picks up the white plastic ball and puts it on top of the Little Tikes batting tee Dad got for him when he first started tee-ball.

I don't know how I was expecting Max to react. I thought he'd be relieved, I guess. But Max only stares back into the house, his shoulders rising and falling underneath the clean dinosaur T-shirt Mom came home to get this morning.

She grabbed a change of clothes for me, too. Peeling off that bloody dress made me cry fat, ugly tears that fell onto the floor and onto my bare stomach. That dress needs to burn, along with all the urine, hay, and rotten food clinging to Max's tee-ball uniform. And I need to shower. For about a thousand years.

I've only been gone from the house for twenty-four hours, but it feels longer. I hadn't expected to come back so soon. We were going to build a new life in the apartment. But Max wanted to come back here. Despite all the bad things that have happened in this house, it's his home.

But it's not mine. Here, every couch, table, curtain, and chair is exactly where it's always been. It's like the house has been sleeping, and by turning the lights on and twisting the faucets, it's waking up again, cranking itself back to life. I turn on the living room lights. All at once, it rushes back to me. Every mark, every stain, and every memory we made in this room. The rug where Max took his first steps as I cheered behind him, the La-Z-Boy's leather still puckered from where Dad used to sit in it. I spot the dimple in the wall where Dad slammed Max's head into the plaster and never fixed it, leaving it as a warning to us never to disobey him again.

The memory of Dad's anger overlaps the memory of Max laughing moments before it happened, and Mom's gentle begging as she asked Dad to stop.

Stop thinking about it.

This house needs to burn, too.

Max comes in through the back door, and I drop to my knees in front of him, taking his small hands in mine. "You okay, buddy?"

Max nods but says nothing. He feels it, too. The memory is bigger than the man, and it stays long after he's gone.

It was like pulling teeth at the hospital this morning when Mom and I tried to figure out what Max remembered from the trailer. He doesn't remember Connie picking him up from tee-ball. The last thing he remembers is sitting on the bench waiting for Dad. Leonard—the big man, Max called him—sang to himself a lot. Fed him peanut butter and jelly sandwiches, but sometimes there was mold on the bread.

Listening to him talk was so upsetting to Mom that she excused herself to go to the bathroom, coming back twenty minutes later with her eyes all swollen.

"Can you take off my shoes?" Max asks.

Relieved to be given something practical to do, I peel back the Velcro straps. Max steps out of his shoes and disappears down the hallway.

"Can you follow him?" I ask Mom, sliding the bolt in place to lock the front door. "One of us needs to stay with him all the time."

Mom wipes her eyes with the sleeve of her cardigan and walks after him.

I lock every window in the living room. The lock on the laundry room window is only half shut, which is irresponsible because that crazy nurse from the hospital could muscle that up if he tried. I imagine him sliding his scissors into the gap, the squeal of surgical steel on metal calling out like fingernails down a blackboard.

He's coming, Shiloh…

I lean against the top of the washing machine with my head hanging between my arms. After the nurse with the scissors chased me last night, the nurse with the crocodile tattoo called security, but they couldn't find any trace of him.

I remember staring at the crushed Pop-Tart on the polished vinyl floor. The man had been real. I still have the graze from the surgical scissors on my arm.

Could it have been Leonard?

No. I killed Leonard. I fired the gun until I couldn't feel my fingers, until my shoulders throbbed with the recoil and I tasted the bitterness of burned powder on my tongue. Besides, Leonard didn't look like that.

So why had the nurse tried to kill me?

I sink to the floor of the laundry room, digging my teeth into my knuckles until they hurt.

Bam. Bam. Bam.

In my memory, the back of Leonard's skull blows open. Clumps of bone and skin slide down the wall. Blood and brain matter sit in his fractured skull like a bowl of tomato soup waiting to be spilled.

Because of me.

If Miles had done it, the guilt would eat him alive, but I don't feel guilty at all.

Is there something wrong with me that I feel a little proud?

"Shiloh!" Mom calls from down the hall, and I rub my groggy eyes. "Can you come here for a minute?"

Shaking my hands out at my sides, I walk to where Mom is standing in front of Max's door.

"Is everything okay?" I ask, glancing through the open door at Max, who is sitting on his bed with Dad's iPad in his small hands. If Dad were here, he'd flip out seeing Max's sticky fingers all over his iPad screen, but Dad isn't here and Max can do whatever he damn well pleases.

"I was thinking," Mom says as her voice quivers. I realize for the first time that she's crying. They're silent tears. Small ones. The kind that don't block her throat or make it hard for her to form words. They drip silently from her red eyes into her lips as she speaks. I'm familiar with those. "It may be best for you to take some time away from school for a while, as well as your job at Rite Aid. You and Max ... you have been through so much, and it would be nice for us to focus on being together as a family right now."

I nod numbly. "So, when can we go to the apartment?"

Mom looks over at Max, who isn't paying any attention to us. "I don't know, sweetheart. Your father is in police custody, so he can't return to the house, and your brother has been through so much. He deserves to be somewhere he feels safe."

"Dad's still here, Mom, even though he's not actually here."

"I know, honey, but maybe we can do something. Redecorate and get new furniture. Get rid of that La-Z-Boy. I've always hated the thing. But I'd also like to talk to you, Shiloh, about the things you told me last night." She glances over at Max, and a hand of dread closes around my throat as I realize what she means.

I killed the guy, I told her in the hospital, tears running down my face. *I said I would if he hurt Max.*

In the moment, all she did was hug me, but I should have known this is not the sort of thing that she would forget about.

"Do you want to tell me what happened?" Mom asks.

Before I can respond, there's a heavy knock on the door.

Mom furrows her brow. "Who could that be?"

She walks past me into the living room, and I follow her like a shadow, peering over her shoulder as she unlocks the door and opens it.

"Good morning, Heidi," says Detective Babin, smiling like I didn't shoot a man in the woods yesterday. But the smile doesn't reach his eyes. Finnegan is standing behind him like he knows he's not the one people like talking to. "Shiloh. Can we come in?"

"Sure thing," Mom says, opening the door wider and stepping out of the way.

Detective Babin shakes Mom's hand and reaches out to shake mine. His fingers are supple and soft, like he moisturizes several times a day and lifts nothing heavy.

"Would you like anything to drink?" Mom asks. "Coffee? I can put on a pot. Sorry, we only just got home, and everything's a little scrambled."

"No thank you, Heidi," says Babin. "This won't take long."

Finnegan takes a seat on our lumpy living room couch. "I guess you probably know why we're here."

With a hand on my back, Mom leads me over to the detectives, and I lower myself onto Dad's La-Z-Boy. The soft cushions hug my body. If they didn't smell so much like whiskey and tobacco, I might even think they were comfortable.

Babin runs a hand over his smooth head. "Shiloh, could you walk us through what happened last night?"

Swallowing hard, I nod. As I tell them about going to the homecoming dance, I am careful to leave out the part about bringing Dad's gun.

"I was torn up by what Principal Orr told me," I say softly, "about finding Max in Akron."

"It was another boy," Mom adds. "Poor little thing had wandered away from his mother in the grocery store."

"Was that when you approached Cornelia Vaughn for help?" asks Babin.

"I wouldn't exactly call it help."

Babin and Finnegan exchange a glance like they're confused.

"Cornelia explained the situation after our patrol found her tied to that tree," Babin says. "Told us you and your friends had come to her house and asked for her help, but before you could find your brother, his captor ambushed you and tied her to the tree. Is that true?"

Red fiery rage simmers in the pit of my stomach. Of all things, I wasn't expecting to hear that. Does she really think she can kidnap Max and get away with it? "She's lying."

This seems to surprise Finnegan. "Lying about what?"

I open my mouth to tell them about kidnapping Max, but the words catch in my throat. Max doesn't remember Connie kidnapping him. I don't have any proof, and Babin and Finnegan probably don't believe in ghosts, so it's going to look like Connie had no motivation to kidnap Max. Not to mention how angry Connie would be if I told them. Right now, she hasn't told the detectives about me breaking into her house and threatening her at gunpoint. If she has any sort of security camera at her house, she could prove it, whereas I can't prove she kidnapped Max. She could prove I had a gun that night, and it would make my claim of not shooting Leonard look a little less believable. I imagine Babin and Finnegan writing about ghosts in their notebooks, taking down my statement verbatim, producing it later in court, and getting laughed out of their jobs.

I curl my fist around the soft leather of the La-Z-Boy. It's not fair. None of this is fair.

Babin clears his throat. "Shiloh?"

"Nothing," I mutter. "I'm sorry. She was telling the truth."

"Good, that's what we figured." Babin writes something in his spiral notebook, and his smile disappears. "Do you know the identity of Max's captor?"

"His name is Leonard Gailis," I say.

Finnegan writes that down. "Do you know who shot him?"

Bam. Bam. Bam.

I remember his heavy body landing on the floor of the trailer with a soft thud. If I tell them I did it, will they charge me with murder? Was it self-defense? He wasn't going after me. He had taken my entire world away from me, and I wanted to do the same to him. I don't regret it. But somehow, I don't think Babin or Finnegan would be very receptive to that.

I glance over at Mom, who gives me a meaningful look. I search her eyes for the answer to what I should do, but her gaze drops to her slippers. I guess I'm on my own for this one, too. Just like I've been on my own for my entire life.

"No, sir."

Babin's eyebrow quirks up. "I know you're a good kid. It's easy to see how, in the heat of the moment, things could have gotten out of hand with no ill intent. If you're honest with us now—"

"I didn't shoot him."

Finnegan stares up at me like he knows I'm lying. Out of nowhere, I'm struck by the memory of him dressing up as Santa during the office holiday parties. He wasn't grumpy when he played Santa. He put on a show for us kids, rubbing his belly and stroking his beard before theatrically guessing what we wanted for Christmas. Most of his guesses were wrong. But there is none of that humor in his face now. "Could you tell us who did?" he asks.

"No. I don't remember."

"You know," Babin says, "the crime scene was tampered with last night."

"Someone went back into the trailer?" I ask, and Finnegan nods. "Did they take anything?"

Finnegan ignores me. "If we find you lied to us, Shiloh, I promise you we will not be as friendly as we are being right now."

This is supposed to be friendly? "I'm telling the truth."

"All right." Babin closes his notebook. "I guess that's enough for now. Heidi, I'd like to speak to you about your husband. Are you all right having this conversation in front of your daughter?"

Mom wrings her hands together. "What's wrong with my husband? What's happening with him?"

"At this point," Detective Babin says, his face twisting and his eyes lowering, "it is likely he could be released on bail sometime this morning, in which case you should file for a temporary restraining order to keep him away from you or the kids."

Mom doesn't skip a beat. "Yes, I want a restraining order."

Finnegan removes the end of his pencil from between his teeth. He doesn't look all that happy. Probably because I was the one who found Max, not him. "Go to the courthouse tomorrow."

"Given the circumstances and the public nature of this scandal," Babin says, "no judge in their right mind would deny the order. But you need to show up in person to file for a temporary order, which lasts until the hearing for your civil protection order."

"Which will happen within seven to ten days," Finnegan grumbles.

"Ernest will be served, and he'll be expected to appear in court." Babin glances over at me, then back at Mom. "I do not wish to alarm your daughter." Both of them are hiding behind legal language, like it's a powerful shield made of logic and fairness. Which is bullshit.

"Taking a month to do your job was alarming enough," I snap.

Babin lets out a nervous laugh. At least he doesn't deny it. "Ernest's court date to resolve the abuse charges will probably be in early November, when his sentence will be decided by a judge."

His words hit me like a brick.

Mom drops her gaze to her hands. "I guess I should go to the courthouse and get that order today."

Babin nods, like he agrees with her. "Unfortunately, in the meantime, he will, in all likelihood, resume his position as sheriff."

Around me, the walls seem to creep closer. The blood drains from my head. "He's keeping his job?"

"Sheriffs are elected, so they cannot be removed, and there is no adequate reason to consider impeachment—"

"No adequate reason? What about molesting his daughter? What about half-killing his wife? Do you want me to show you the dent in the wall where he knocked my brother's head against it when he was two?" I snap, and Mom glares at me. Finnegan looks like he doesn't even know how to begin to respond to that, so Babin leans onto his knees.

"I understand this is hard," Babin says. "He may well be sentenced to jail, but until then, he will remain sheriff."

This can't be happening. "And you guys and Connie will what? Do what he says?"

Babin continues speaking, but I can't understand him. I hear each word as it comes out of his mouth, but they don't seem to form coherent sentences. I knit my fingers into the chest of my sweatshirt. This is not fair. Dad should lose his job and his liberty. He has to pay for what he's done to us, not show up for work in uniform like it's any other day, and he's a good father who doesn't molest his kids in public arcade bathrooms. *Hey, Ernest. Is Heidi still packing your lunch or should we go to McDonald's?* Male laughter. The sound of hands clapping backs. Sympathy, even.

Something sour presses against the back of my throat. Babin is in the middle of asking Mom if he can speak to Max when I cup my hand over my mouth and run down the hallway. I barely have time to lift the toilet seat before the Egg McMuffin I ate on our way home from the hospital rushes up and out of my throat and into the toilet. I puke again, and the chunky brown liquid splashes into the water and sloshes up against the sides of the bowl.

5

Shiloh

I'm resting my forehead against the cold toilet bowl when Mom comes in.

"All right," she pulls the door shut with a click. "You are going to tell me exactly what happened with that man, and you will not lie to me like you did to those detectives."

A thick bubble of air travels up my throat, resulting in a loud burp. "I don't feel so good."

Above me, the sink turns on. A few moments later, a cold compress presses against the back of my neck, and I glance up to see Mom holding a wet hand towel against my skin.

Her actions speak of love and concern, but her voice is cold and low. "Did you shoot that man?" I nod against the fleshy part of my forearm. "Was he trying to hurt you?"

Mom waits for my reply. When she doesn't get one, she exhales sharply. "Answer me, Shiloh. I'm not messing around."

"He wasn't trying to hurt me," I whisper.

Mom makes a disapproving sound, like that wasn't the right answer. "How did you find Max?"

She wants the whole truth, right?

I guess I could try not lying to her.

"Leonard was a necromancer," I tell Mom, who blinks at me like she doesn't know what the word means. "You know, like he brings people back from the dead? He was going to kill Max and bring a ghost back to life inside his body, and Francesca Russo—who sees ghosts—found out that Leonard was going to bring back Connie Vaughn's nephew. So that's what led us to her, and then she led us to Leonard." Mom just stares at me. A far-away look materializes in her eyes, and I bite my lip to keep myself from scoffing. I guess I shouldn't expect anything from her. She spent six years ignoring the guttural way Max screamed when Dad punched the walls. Is she really going to do anything about the necromancer? Or her daughter's perceived insanity?

Mom places a hand on my forehead, but I swat her away. "Shiloh, you're scaring me, honey," she says.

"I'm telling the truth."

Mom clenches her jaw like she doesn't believe a word. She tries a new tactic.

"You stole your father's gun, didn't you?"

I can feel my bottom lip trembling as I nod.

"Where is it?"

"I hid it in the woods."

"This could be catastrophic." Mom pinches her eyes. "If they prove you're the one who shot him, you could go to jail."

"But it was self-defense."

"Not necessarily. You told me he wasn't trying to hurt you."

"I'm sorry," I say, salt dripping through my lips. "I was angry. I thought he'd killed Max. I wasn't thinking."

"We'll figure something out." Mom takes my trembling hands in hers and sucks a quick breath in through her teeth as she pulls me into her arms. I rest my chin on her shoulder. She's breathing heavily. I know she doesn't want to believe what I've told her, but the only other option is to believe her daughter is insane and has killed a man in some kind of alternative reality. "Come on, let's get you to bed," she says.

She's helping me to my feet when the landline rings from the kitchen.

"Who's that?" I ask, and Mom raises her eyebrows and gives me her patented how-the-hell-should-I-know look. For a split second, everything's normal, and I almost laugh.

She walks to the kitchen and glances at the caller ID. Her eyebrows wrinkle as she picks up. "Hello?"

A couple of seconds go by. She lowers the phone and holds it out to me. "Honey, it's for you."

For me? Great. With my luck, it's Connie calling to gloat or Detective Babin calling to say he's already found Dad's gun stashed in that rotting log and he's coming to take me to jail.

I take the receiver from Mom and wrap my other arm around my stomach. "Hello?"

"Hey," says a familiar voice. "It's Miles."

"Miles?" I run over to the couch and jump onto the cushions. Tears press against the backs of my eyes. It's like my body can't decide whether to laugh or cry. "Oh my God, you're alive."

"I am." He laughs a little. The sound is like magic. "Last time I checked, anyway."

"How are you feeling?"

"Oh, you know, like death pretty much." I can picture him shrugging, the thin material of his hospital gown hanging over his shoulders. "Can you come to the hospital right now?"

A smile spreads over my lips. "Sure."

"Cool. Come quickly. Oh, and I'm still on the third floor, but they moved me to room 309."

"Okay. See you soon—"

He hangs up, cutting me off. I lower the phone and press it against my heart.

Miles wants to see me.

He didn't even sound that mad.

I turn around to look at Mom, who is washing her hands.

"Could you drive me to Mount Keenan?"

Mom dries her hands off on the kitchen towel. She looks like she's on the point of saying no, but she lets out a sigh, walks over to me, and tucks my hair behind my ears. "Okay, honey. I have to go to the courthouse, anyway. Promise me you'll get some sleep this afternoon?"

The way she's touching my hair feels nice. I don't even try to shift away from her. "I promise."

"And don't go getting yourself involved in any more of this necromancy nonsense." Her tone is almost joking.

Almost.

"Sure, Mom."

I wring my clammy hands together. Next to me in the elevator, a woman holds a bouquet of red poppies. Their black centers look like eyes, and they're all staring at me, which makes it hard not to stare back at them.

Blood.

If I squint, the poppies look like bullet holes and blood covering the front of the woman's dress, just like the blood that covered my dress the last time I rode this elevator. Or the blood that would have stained the floor if those surgical scissors had sliced through my neck …

I swallow, but my throat is dry. Why would that guy have tried to kill me? He didn't even know who I was.

Will he be in the hospital today? I shouldn't have come back here, but Miles asked me to, so I have no choice.

Ding. The woman carrying the poppies cuts in front of me to get out of the elevator. I follow her out like a weird shadow, glancing around for signs. Which way is room 309?

Dread scuttles up my neck like a small army of millipedes. Why did Miles ask me to come? I was so excited to hear his voice on the phone that I didn't even consider how mad he must be at me right now.

I remember it so clearly, running through the woods with Max's unconscious body in my arms and hearing Francesca's scream. Leonard had a gun pressed to Miles's head. If I didn't give Max back to him, he was going to shoot.

I didn't move, so he shot Miles in the stomach.

I chose Max. I was willing to let Miles die.

I'd never admit it to him, but if I were put in the same situation a second time, I would do it again. How can I pretend that everything's normal?

Walking down the hallway feels like wading through cold molasses. I pass three police officers in uniform with frowns etched deep into their faces. They're standing in front of a supply closet taped off with black and yellow crime scene tape.

I wonder if they're here to catch the nurse. Maybe the guy went after somebody else.

I spot room 309 next to the women's bathroom. Before I can chicken out, I rap my knuckles against the wood three times and sidestep the window. "Hi, um, it's Shiloh," I say.

"Come in," Miles's voice replies, and my heart soars. Here goes nothing. Closing my hand around the handle, I open the door.

I pause. I don't know what I expected to see walking in here. I guess I thought Miles would look tired. Pale. Sick, because he'd recently gotten out of surgery the last time I saw him and didn't look so good and I was terrified he was going to die. But this Miles looks healthy. He's sitting in bed without a shirt on, propped up into a sitting position by pillows. I can see his ribs under his skin and his collarbones jutting out from his shoulders. A thick, clean bandage is wrapped around his abdomen. He's not wearing his glasses, so his eyes are uncovered. They're half-closed like he's high or exhausted, but he's smiling. Dimples cut into his face as he turns to look at me. His skin has a healthy glow to it.

He's okay. He's really okay.

I rush toward his bed and fling my arms around his neck, but he pats my shoulder.

"Okay," he says, pushing me away. "Let's cool it with the hugging."

"Hey, Scooby, where's our hugs?" a voice says behind me.

I spin around. Jonah waves at me from where he's sitting in a folding chair next to Francesca. I blink at them, trying to figure out why they're here, as Francesca rushes toward me and pulls me into a hug I'm not prepared for.

"I am so happy you are here," she says, a dark brown curl brushing against my cheek. She's still wearing her oversized shirt dress from last night, and the smell of sweat, dirt, and antiseptic cleaner makes my nose wrinkle. Usually, I don't like it when people touch me, but something deflates deep inside of me as soon as she lets go. "Thank you for coming."

"Why are you thanking me?"

Francesca frowns. "Something terrible has happened," she says, her voice airy.

I look over her shoulder at Jonah. Like Francesca, he's still in his clothes from the dance last night. Sweat has soaked through the pits of his blood-stained, wrinkled dress shirt. Grease glues clumps of his black hair together, and circles of purple bruises eat away at the pale skin beneath his bloodshot eyes. Unlike Francesca, he hasn't gotten up to say hi. He looks kind of self-conscious just sitting there, like maybe he shouldn't hug me in front of Miles.

He also looks sad. Miles looks sad. Come to think of it, Francesca looks like she's been crying.

Oh God. "Who died?" I ask.

Jonah drops his eyes to the crinkled plastic cup in his hands. "It's more of a question of who didn't."

"What the hell is that supposed to mean?"

Francesca lets out a long sigh as she lowers herself into the folding chair beside Jonah. "I'm afraid we have some bad news."

As soon as Francesca tells the story about Miles and finding his ghost on her doorstep, I shake my head. No. That can't be what happened. She's lying. But I know Francesca well enough to know she wouldn't do that. She's incapable of lying, and if she tried, no one would ever believe her.

She tells me about going down to the morgue. I curl my

hands around the lower railing of Miles's bed. "But I killed Leonard."

"You did." Francesca gestures diplomatically, like she's making a presentation at school. "However, we believe Leonard possesses the ability to enter bodies on his own, as long as those bodies are already dead."

Jonah points the plastic cup at me. "The guy can kill people, kill himself, and hop into new bodies as a ghost."

I turn to Miles. "You were dead in the woods?"

Miles drops his eyes to his hands. "Leonard's ghost entered my body when Jonah was calling the ambulance, so it was him you guys saw at the hospital."

This is insane. All of this is insane. I already saved Max. If I get out now, maybe I can save myself and commit to a future of … of what? Of picking up the pieces and trying to build something resembling a family with Max? Or worse—finishing high school, waiting for the right guy to sweep me off my feet, and ending up exactly like Mom?

What exactly is my future?

I sink onto the foot of Miles's mattress, curling my hand into a fist so tight my knuckles turn white. God, I wish I could hit something right now.

"I hoped more than anything that this would be over," Francesca says, as if she can read my mind. "But unfortunately, it isn't, and Leonard was able to escape."

Miles leans back into the pillows. I can't even imagine how scary it would be to wake up dead. I try to think of something to say to him, maybe something to wipe that look of panic from his face, but all that comes out of my mouth is, "You had Leonard *inside* you?"

Miles winces. "Somehow, that makes it sound even worse than it was."

Jonah lets out a high laugh from the side of the room.

I don't see any blood seeping through the front of Miles's bandage, not like there was last night. I walk over to the edge of the bed and touch his hand, and he smiles up at me a little. "Are you okay?" I ask.

"Surprisingly, yeah. I feel great." He shoots his arms out in front of him like a broken marionette, twisting his lips to do his Pinocchio impression, "I'm not a puppet. I'm a real boy."

How is he laughing right now? I push myself back up to my feet and walk away from his bed, crossing my arms over my chest and leaning against the wall. I look at Francesca. "So ... what, you're saying Leonard could be inside anyone's body?"

She nods. "In all likelihood, his host is somebody from the hospital. Our current working theory is that Leonard, while he was inside Miles—"

"Please stop saying it like that—" Miles wrinkles his nose in disgust.

"—killed somebody who had wandered into Miles's room before killing Miles. He entered this new body and walked away, leaving Miles to ..." Francesca trails off.

Die.

Something hits me like a slap in the face. The corners of my vision spot.

"Leonard's new host is a nurse," I say.

Francesca raises her eyebrows. "How do you know this?"

"Because he tried to kill me last night."

Miles gasps. His eyes get wider than before but are still half-closed. "And you're only mentioning this *now*?"

"How did he try to kill you, Scooby?" Jonah asks, his voice laced with worry. I don't know if I've ever heard Jonah actually sound worried before. Warmth rises to my cheeks.

"He chased me through the hospital with a pair of surgical scissors."

"Oh Jesus," Miles pinches the bridge of his nose. "God, no, this can't be happening."

"In a way, this is good," Francesca says. "If Shiloh saw Leonard's new host, then we may be able to find him and stop him before he escapes and hurts any more children."

"Are you *insane*?" Miles's voice shoots up an octave.

"Leonard almost killed me, and you want to go looking for him again?"

"I do," Francesca says.

"Can't the police look for him?" Miles asks.

I remember how my mom reacted this morning when I tried to tell her the truth about Leonard. "The cops won't believe us if we tell them."

Miles lets out a short laugh. "I'm sorry, but this guy is dangerous. I will not get shot again to save some random kids."

"But it is the right thing to do," Francesca says, like it's simple. "Besides, I rather enjoy solving mysteries with you all."

"It's not our circus," Miles says, "and not our monkeys."

Francesca's brows draw together. "Who has monkeys?"

"I'm with Frankie on this one," Jonah says. "We're the only ones who know what Leonard's doing, so only we can stop him."

It's like they've switched places. Jonah's saying all the things Miles should be saying while Miles lies in his hospital bed wanting nothing to do with it. I guess I can't blame him, but when I look at Jonah, he's looking straight back at me, like maybe he wishes he'd been there to help me fight off the nurse.

Fight off Leonard.

"Shiloh?" Miles raises his eyebrows. "Am I the only one who thinks this is nuts?"

My fists curl around the foot of his bed. Leonard deserves to die for what he did to Max, not escape and keep hurting kids like none of this ever happened.

"We should kill him," I say, and Miles mutters something under his breath. "I killed the son of a bitch once. I want to finish the job."

Francesca claps her hands. "All right. Three against one. I suppose that's settled, then."

Nobody says anything for a second. I clench and unclench my fists on the baseboard of Miles's bed as his heart monitor beeps a little faster.

Francesca breaks the silence by clearing her throat. "Jonah

and Miles, do you remember what Leonard said to us in the woods while Shiloh was rescuing Max?"

Jonah shakes his head. "The whole thing's a blank, to be honest."

"There was that thing he said about wanting to break through to the other side," Miles remarks stiffly. "To find her again."

I blink. "Find who again?"

"Beats me," Miles says. "He just said he had to find *her* again."

"I'm not sure Leonard wants to bring back any more children," Francesca says. "Judging by what he said in the woods, I believe he wants to bring back Evangeline Durand."

It takes me a second to remember who Francesca is talking about. But when I do, my blood runs cold. I remember reading the article from 1944 about how Leonard's necromancy act went wrong, about how he was supposed to kill and reanimate fifteen-year-old Evangeline Durand in front of a captivated crowd but couldn't. That was the night Leonard supposedly killed himself and the circus closed forever.

"Perhaps he feels guilty for killing her all those years ago and wants to atone for it," Francesca adds.

"But to bring her back he's gonna need someone to put her in," Jonah says. "She was, what, fifteen when she died?"

"He's going to go after someone our age," I say.

Jonah nods. "Maybe even one of us."

I wince. Imagining someone else walking around in my body sends a shiver up my spine.

"Hasn't Evangeline been dead for, like, seventy-five years?" Miles asks.

"Yes," Francesca says. "You are right. Evangeline's soul would have already faded to the other side."

I remember sitting on Ella Ruggles's frayed couch last night as she told us about the ghost world and how once ghosts fade from our world, they go to a dimension outside of ours. Ella

Ruggles poked her finger through a piece of plastic wrap. Her thin voice rings in my ears:

Souls can break free on their own and return here. Sometimes, we can help them.

"Can Leonard even get to the other side?" I ask. "Is that possible?"

"I'm not entirely sure," Francesca says. "Perhaps Ms. Ruggles would know?"

I remember the way Ella Ruggles looked at Francesca, like she belonged in some sort of museum. "You're not going back there."

"Who cares how the guy gets to the other side," Jonah says. "All we have to do is find the nurse Scooby saw. He's a nurse here, right? So people have got to know who he is."

Francesca's face brightens. "That's true. Once we capture him, then we can turn him in to the police."

"Or kill his host and kill his ghost," I say. "So that he can't escape, and this is all over."

Miles frowns, like he doesn't like any of this. "Is it even possible to kill ghosts?"

Francesca looks like she's thinking when there's a soft knock on the door and I jump in surprise.

A red-haired nurse with pink lipstick walks into the room, giving us a little smile as she goes to check the bag of fluids hanging on the IV pole beside Miles's bed. Her red ponytail swishes with each step.

"How are you feeling, sweetheart?" she asks him in a dulcet tone, flicking the drip chamber on his IV line.

"Pretty good," Miles says.

She gives Miles a baby-eyed smile. "You're a miracle, you know."

Miles makes a noise like a strangled chipmunk. Jonah snorts. The nurse says everything looks good and to call if he needs anything before walking back around the curtain.

Jonah nudges Miles's leg and whispers, "Dude, are they all as hot as her?"

"Mine are," Miles says. Jonah laughs and slaps his knee. Miles glances at me. "I mean, no. It's not—no, she's not."

"Miles, you're a medical miracle," Jonah mocks, making kissy faces at Miles, who turns an even deeper shade of red.

Ignoring them, I rush behind the curtain and stop the nurse before she can slip through the door, getting her attention with a tap on her shoulder. "Excuse me."

She turns around. "Is everything all right?"

"I was wondering if that male nurse was in today. The skinny one, really tall?" I gesture about a foot over my head. "Had long black hair that looked like it hadn't been washed in a while?"

The nurse grips the clipboard as the blood rushes from her head like she has seen a ghost. "I'm sorry."

She turns to leave, but I grab her wrist.

"Did something happen to him?"

"I really shouldn't say." She glances down at my hand. "You're hurting me a little, honey."

"Please." For the first time, I notice that the dark shadows under her eyes are not just bags. Her eye makeup has smeared and streaked her cheeks like she has been crying. "Is he okay?"

She pulls her wrist out of my grasp and wipes her nose with her palm. "Ben hung himself in the supply closet early this morning. The authorities are calling it suicide, but it wasn't like him. If you'll excuse me …"

The nurse hurries out the door. I stare after her, realization settling in the pit of my stomach like fresh snow.

Leonard hung himself while he was in his new host. That means …

"Leonard changed hosts," I say, walking out from behind the curtain.

Jonah is too busy laughing with Miles to hear me, but Francesca's eyebrows leap up. "He did?"

"The nurse just told me his old host hung himself this morning," I say, "which means Leonard took over someone else's body. We should check who found him, you know, who …

who took him down, but I don't know how we'd figure that out."

This gets Jonah's attention, and his laughter dies down. Francesca's olive skin turns a little green.

"Okay," Jonah says, nodding. "Let's not lose hope. You said he's going to open a gate to the other side, right? If we figure out how to do that, maybe we could stop him from doing it."

"There could be someone from the circus who's still alive and who knew him back then," Miles suggests. "Leonard can't be the only one who knows about the spirit world."

"Didn't the circus shut down in 1944?" I ask. "Everyone alive would be super old."

Miles thinks for a second. "Well, if Leonard was seventeen when he killed Evangeline in 1944, that means he must have been born around 1927, which would put him and everyone else his age in their early nineties. That's old, but it's not impossible."

Jonah holds out his phone. "Columbus, next Saturday at one."

I lean closer to read what it says on the screen. Big green letters announce a performance of the last traveling freak show on Earth. "What is this?"

"Wilma Robinson," Jonah explains. "She grew up in the circus with Leonard telling fortunes. Went to circus school or whatever with him."

What? "How do you know all of this?"

Jonah shrugs. "I looked up that crappy circus website you like. She was in an old black-and-white picture with Leonard, and she was interviewed two years ago for a feature on the circus. In the feature, she mentioned that she still performs with this local freak show, after spewing a bunch of crap about how the circus will be her home forever. I ran a search for the show. It'll be in Columbus next Saturday for the rock festival, so we can go see it at one o'clock."

"The circus is coming to town this week?" Miles asks. "What are the odds of that?"

"Pretty good, since they only do shows in the Midwest,"

Jonah says. "Besides, the Durand Brothers circus was based out of Cincinnati. If Wilma grew up around here, I get why she'd want to stay local."

I take his phone. Opening a new tab, I type in Wilma Robinson and find a grainy black-and-white photo of her with a bunch of other circus types, including a big-eared boy with three fingers on each hand.

Jonah looks over the top of the phone and points at each person in the photo. "Googling Mavis Mills told me she would have been forty-three in 1944, so she's dead. I couldn't find anything on the human frog, but he looks old in that picture so I doubt he's still around. Lionel Hilton was murdered after he joined Barnum and Bailey. The conjoined twins were, like, ten in 1944. They actually got pretty famous, but they died of pneumonia when they were fifty-nine."

"Who died first?" Francesca asks.

Jonah pauses. "How the … how am I supposed to know?"

Francesca's face falls. I understand what she means. Dying beside your sister, confined to a bed beside her dead body, waiting for whatever killed her to take you too, hoping you'd die before the rot set in and your twin started to smell … I can't imagine what that would be like.

"Anyway," Jonah says. "Ella Ruggles said she bought the monocle from a woman who told fortunes. You can bet your ass it's the same person, and I'm thinking she'll be able to tell us how to get to the other side."

I hand Jonah back his phone. "I guess we're going to Rock Fest then."

Miles pulls his lips together like he's stifling a laugh. "I didn't think you had it in you, buddy."

"Basic Googling?" Jonah says, scoffing. His blue eyes are misty and swollen from lack of sleep. Something in my chest tightens. "I'm a man of many talents, but I'll tell you another thing. This feels too convenient. Maybe this was Leonard's plan all along. Maybe there's something at the circus that Leonard needs, and maybe we can get to it first."

6

Shiloh

I'm following Jonah and Francesca out of the hospital room when Miles's voice stops me in the doorway.

"Shiloh, could you stay for a minute?"

His eyebrows are raised in question, but there's no anger in his expression. Only curiosity, like he's wondering whether I'm going to agree.

I cross my arms tightly. I guess I can't avoid talking about what happened in the woods forever.

Swallowing hard, I mutter a hoarse "Okay" and pull a folding chair up to the side of his bed. My heart is beating so fast it's making my chest hurt, which is stupid because it's Miles. It's not like he's going to jump out and hurt me.

But when he takes a long breath in before speaking, it feels like he might as well have. "Shiloh, we need to talk about what happened. I've been thinking about it a lot, and—"

"I'm sorry," I blurt out. Miles drops his eyes to the blanket over his legs. "You shouted my name, and I …" My ribcage seems to draw in, constricting my breathing, but I force myself to keep talking even though it's hard. "I should have tried to save you, too, and I'm really sorry that I didn't."

Miles pulls his bottom lip between his teeth as if he's kneading my words like dough in his head.

"I know you didn't have a choice, Shiloh," he says finally. "You couldn't just hand Max over to Leonard."

A huge breath slips through my lips. "I couldn't do it."

"I understand," Miles says. "I do."

A small smile tugs at my lips. I point at the bed. "Can I sit up there with you?"

Miles sends me a smile back. "Sure."

Being careful not to pull on any wires or lean against his bandage, I climb onto the bed next to him, and he scoots over to make room for me. The rhythmic beeping of his heart monitor plays like an unusual melody. I remember a couple of weeks ago, when we were walking to the labyrinth, Miles asked whether I thought a good song could be made from the sounds of ordinary life. I told him no, even though there are bands out there who've probably tried it, but I can honestly say that no song has ever made my heart sing as much as the sound of his heartbeat does right now.

I fold my hands in my lap. Miles doesn't smell like he usually does, of spearmint gum and earthy cologne. He smells of sweat and hospital disinfectant and something like expired food, but it doesn't matter because he's alive. I want to bury my nose in his chest and breathe until I can't anymore.

"You look kind of weird without your glasses," I say.

Miles laughs a harsh laugh, like he wasn't expecting me to say that. "So do you. You're all blurry."

I point at his bandage. Up close, the gauze is thick and securely taped in place. "Does it hurt?"

"Yeah." He runs his fingers over the clear tape. "But it's better than it was when I woke up. I'm lucky Leonard stuffed cotton down my throat and didn't rip out my intestines with his bare hands, I guess."

Imagining it makes my stomach churn. "Uh-huh."

"Something must have helped heal the wound a little when Francesca brought me back," Miles says thoughtfully. "Probably some of that *mana,* or whatever Ella Ruggles was talking about."

"You got some *mana*-cine," I say, cringing at the quality of my pun. Bad puns are Miles's thing.

Miles stares at me. After a second, he laughs. "Laughter is the best *mana*-cine."

I giggle. His lips are so close. They're flaking, probably because of how dry it is in the hospital. I notice a cluster of raised blisters under his pec. I gently touch the biggest one, and he winces.

"Where'd you get this?" I ask. Behind his shoulder blade, his skin is a deep red color like a day-old bruise. "Lean forward for a second."

Slowly, Miles leans up from the pillow.

The air catches in the back of my throat. "Why is the skin on your back all red? It looks like you were burned or something."

Miles falls back onto the pillows with a grunt. "I guess it aches a little, but it's fine."

"Weird."

"Do you want to know what else is weird?" Miles points behind him at the small bottle of saline solution on the tray by his bed. "That my eyes don't close anymore."

I stare between his squinting eyes. "You can't blink?"

"Nope. Those handy dandy eye drops are the only thing keeping my eyes from shriveling up."

"I'm just happy you're alive."

"Me too."

Offering him a small smile, I touch my palm to his bare chest, feeling his ribs and the tight muscles pulled around them. But he doesn't return my smile and pushes my hand off.

"Sorry," I say, "did I hurt you?"

"No. It's not that."

The words tumble out of my mouth before I can think them through. "I want to be your girlfriend again."

"Shiloh ..."

"I pushed you away when Max was missing," I say. The beeping of Miles's heart monitor is steady. If I were hooked up to that thing, it would beep so fast it would sound like an alarm. "But I don't want to do that again."

Miles knits his face together like he's tasting something unpleasant. "I understand why you chose Max, and I forgive you for doing it, but I can't be your boyfriend anymore."

His words hit me in the chest, knocking the air out of my lungs. I wrap my arms around my stomach and squeeze, hoping that will make the bad feeling go away. "Oh."

"I didn't ask for any of this," he says. "I almost died—I *did* die—and now that I've got this second chance ..." He gestures like he's trying to find the right word. "You know that I love you. I think a part of me is always going to love you, but you don't love me."

"I do."

He tilts his head to the side. "You love me?"

"Yes."

Miles narrows his eyes. "Then say it."

"I already did."

"Say the words."

"I ..." Heat fills my skull. The words stick to the roof of my mouth like peanut butter.

Damn it. What the hell is wrong with me?

Miles raises an eyebrow. "See?" he says.

"It's not that I don't love you," I say, "it's more that I don't know what love is." My voice is high and sounds pathetic. "I care about you more than anyone—well, except for Max. But my dad messed me up and ruined so many things for me, and I can't let him ruin this for me, too."

Miles shakes his head. "I'm sorry, Shiloh."

"I'll get there." I take his hand in both of mine, gripping his long, slender fingers. "I *have* to believe I can get there. Please, I don't want to lose you."

Miles yanks his hand out of mine. "*Tamē mārī vāta sāmbhaḷatā nathī.*"

"Huh?"

"You don't *listen* to me," Miles snaps. "I'm telling you how I feel, and you're not listening to me."

"You speak another language?"

"Gujarati. My mom speaks it at home."

"How did I not know this about you?"

"I'm saying *no!*" Miles shouts. I flinch at the sudden volume of his voice. "No, okay? No. I deserve to be with someone who loves me like I love them, and I deserve more than what you did, even if I understand why you did it. You'd do it again, wouldn't you?"

I stare hard at his face. The down-turned corners of his mouth. His mussed hair. The sadness in his big, brown eyes.

"Yes."

Nothing I say will ever change his mind now. He's gone. My piece of Miles is gone.

I scramble to my feet and stand there, slamming my fist into my palm while Miles stares at me.

"I still want to be friends," he offers, and he looks almost like he's pitying me. "You know, after it stops being awkward."

"Are you still going to help us stop Leonard?" My voice is barely a whisper.

"I'll come to the circus," Miles says. "I can tell it's important to Jonah, but I won't fight Leonard again. I'm not going to go looking for death when I only just escaped it. I was dead, Shiloh. It made me realize all the things I wanted to do if I got a second chance to be alive."

"Okay."

He stares at me. He probably doesn't want me here anymore. But my hand pauses on the doorknob. Hot tears sting my eyes. I blink them away, and they drip into my lips. "What is love supposed to feel like?"

Miles says nothing. I wonder if he heard me, but I don't want to turn around to check so that he doesn't see I'm crying.

"You just have to feel it," he says eventually.

"But I don't know what I'm supposed to feel."

"Shiloh, I'm sorry," Miles says. I need to get out of here. His eyes bore into my back like lasers cutting holes through my skin. "I hate hurting you."

I walk out into the hallway, wiping my wet cheeks with my sweatshirt sleeve. The tears pooling in my eyes blur my vision like I'm trying to see the hallway through the surface of a pool.

All my life, I tried not to feel things so that Dad couldn't get to me. So that Max wouldn't be more scared than he was already. So that I wouldn't have to remember the places Dad touched me in the Fun Palace bathroom. I'd let myself feel things with Miles. But I guess that's not enough.

Am I ever going to feel love for anyone but Max?

Sobs boil up my throat, and I hunch over, crying into my hands so hard that my lungs burn.

7
JONAh

On our way off the bus, I bump Francesca's shoulder with mine. "Want to go get custard?"

Her eyebrows knit. "Custard?"

"Frozen custard. You know, from Chip's Frozen Custard over by the car dealership."

A bright laugh flies out of her. "You've just learned Leonard is alive, and you'd like to eat some ice cream?"

"First of all, it's custard, and second of all, don't judge me. Any more bad news and I'm going to end up like one of those scarecrows over there."

Across the street there's a bunch of scarecrows strung up on the telephone poles. The library does some sort of scarecrow-making competition every year to mark the beginning of the fall. Hay sticks out where their wrists and ankles should be. They stare at us with unblinking buttons for eyes, tied to the poles by their necks.

I jerk my chin toward Chip's. "Come on, Frankie, I've got cash."

Francesca goes along with me.

At Chip's, I order two chocolates. One for Francesca because that's what she wanted, and one for me because I'm not a vanilla kind of guy and butter pecan is the kind of old man's flavor that Miles would get. I take my bowl and slide onto the bench of an aluminum picnic table out by the flickering OPEN sign. It's cold out, but the bench is warm from the sun.

I bite off a gummy worm's head. A powerful burst of strawberry flavor dissolves on my tongue like a sweet bomb. "Mm, it's the little things in life."

Francesca pops a spoon in her mouth. It's still in there when she winces and touches her breastbone.

I quirk my brow up. "You good?"

"I'm not sure," she mumbles, pulling out the spoon. "It's an aching pain, as if something is not wrong at this exact moment but might be later."

That's weird. The sleeves of her cardigan ride up her wrists. Blue veins jut out on the backs of her hands, her thin skin wrinkling around them. Dark brown liver spots speckle her knuckles. They look almost like Aunt Moe's mom's hands, all pale and frail. Old lady hands callused from knitting.

"Aren't you a little young for age spots?" I ask.

Francesca pulls the sleeves of her cardigan down over them, her cheeks flushing red. "I do not have age spots."

The skin around her eyes is crinkling, too. Miles would elbow me in the ribs for saying it, but this girl's gotta moisturize. Shiloh's got wrinkles, too, but hers are from worry. I imagine running my thumb over her forehead, rubbing the creases away like I'm smoothing a patty of Play-Doh—

Francesca's voice jars me back to reality. "Bringing back Max and Miles ... could it be ... *aging* me?"

I want to say that's not possible, but who knows what's possible anymore? Forget all the ghost stuff. Shiloh had me listening to songs from a musical. "What, like, making you all wrinkled and stuff?"

Francesca nods and nestles her spoon into her bowl of custard like she's done eating. "You know, when I was a girl, my mother used to tell me a story about Pinocchio and the curse of Pleasure Island."

I wish I could say I didn't know what she was talking about. "My mom let me watch the Disney movie when I was a kid."

"At first," Francesca continues, completely ignoring me, "the island appears to be a figment of the little boys' imagination. A kind of paradise where everyone is free to do whatever they please. However, if they misbehave badly enough, donkey ears sprout out from their skulls. Each boy's laugh turns to a bray. Their hands become hooves, and most of the children lose their ability to speak, at which point they are stripped of their clothes and sold to the salt mines, unable to warn the other boys arriving on the island as they are shipped far away."

That whole section used to give me nightmares as a kid, but I'm not about to tell her that. "I saw the movie."

"My mother told me to remember I am not my own, and that I was bought at a price." Francesca turns her veiny hand around in the sunlight. "Perhaps it is the same with my gift."

"Or you could just moisturize."

Francesca doesn't laugh. "Everything … everything comes at a price."

"You're gonna have to stop bringing people back from the dead."

Francesca offers me a cheeky smile. "Perhaps you should all stop dying."

"Fair enough. I promise not to die." I hold up three fingers like Miles used to back when he was a Boy Scout, half to make fun of him and half because I want to cheer her up. "Scout's honor."

Francesca hides her hands in the folds of her dress. I've been around girls enough to know that's the look they get when they're done talking, so I scrape my empty custard bowl and stare out at the trucks chugging by. I can identify every make. There was a point when I was a kid that I wanted to be a truck driver. Long distance, all across America. Heading to the West Coast, driving into some kind of endless sunset like the end of some crappy movie. But the dream died after I realized how boring highway driving is.

I wish I could get out of here now. But I'm in too deep to back out of this mess, and I'm not about to leave my friends to deal with Leonard alone.

I pull my JUUL out of my pocket and close my eyes as I inhale. On the exhale, I open them to check that the vapor isn't blowing into Francesca. She's got one eyebrow curved up.

"Don't tell Shiloh about this," I say, breathing in deep. "She's not big on the whole smoking thing."

Francesca's lips curve into a knowing smile. "When are you going to tell Shiloh that you are in love with her?"

For a second, I wonder if I heard her right. She stares at me expectantly. Heat rises to my face.

"What the hell are you talking about?" But I'm no actor, and even I can tell that my words sound half-hearted.

"If you carry on like you did in the hospital today, it's only a matter of time until she discovers the truth."

My stomach drops. "Was it that obvious?"

She shrugs. "It was to me, although I pay more attention to people than others seem to." She nibbles on a spoonful of custard. "It explains why you are looking at me like I have released a secret that you wanted to stay hidden, and it also explains why you continued to help search for Max when you are only Miles's friend and nothing to Shiloh and therefore not obligated to her."

Nothing to Shiloh.

Francesca must have seen me wince, because she adds: "I do not mean to offend you. I was only wondering, because you smile a lot more when you are around her."

"Enough."

"Have you told Miles?" she asks. I take a drag from the JUUL, and her forehead crinkles. "Jonah, I am sorry. It would be painful to choose between hurting Miles's feelings or hurting yours."

"It's not a choice."

"It is possible that Shiloh feels the same way," Francesca says, moving her spoon around. "She certainly looks at Miles with more annoyance than love. I was questioning why she had chosen to be with him until he nearly died. The agony that rushed across her face was pure."

"*Frankie,*" I snap, and she whips her head up. "Just stop talking, would you?"

She puts the spoon of custard into her mouth, her lips twisting into a pitying frown.

"Don't look at me like that."

"I'm sorry, I am not—"

"Say nothing. To her, and especially not to Miles. You understand?"

"I will not breathe a word."

I hang my head. The sun beats down against the back of my neck. Damn it. I didn't think it was that obvious. I hope Francesca pays more attention than Miles or Shiloh.

Shiloh looked so down when she heard the news about Leonard. Seeing her face … man, I can't think of anything I've wanted more than to hold her right there and tell her I'd never let anyone hurt her again, especially after what she's been through. But she would have wanted to hear that sort of stuff from Miles, not me. I can't use words the way that Miles does. Coming from him, a promise would sound powerful enough for her to believe it. To want it. To get lost in his safety and protection. From me, it would sound like empty words. Or the sound of wind whining through wire.

But that doesn't mean I don't mean it.

She wants Miles. I don't blame her. I would, too. Miles was the only person who was there for me when nobody else was, and everything in my life had gone to pot. He's more than my best friend. He's always made me feel like there's a place where I belonged. Even when nobody wanted me or when I hated myself. I won't do anything that would hurt him.

She doesn't care about me the way I do about her, and for Miles to be happy, she never can.

What's stupid is that I thought I was doing a good job hiding it.

"I'm going home." I drop the JUUL back in my pocket and toss my empty bowl in the trash. "Nothing gets past you, does it?"

Francesca stands up from the picnic table, wrapping her hands tightly around her half-full custard bowl. "I try not to let it. But I promise you that your secret's safe with me."

As I turn onto my street, the air catches in my throat. A cop car is parked in front of Ella Ruggles's house. I wonder why that crazy bitch called them. Maybe she finally knocked. Or maybe she got into such a nasty fight with her ghost friend that the neighbors called in a domestic disturbance.

I rub my eyes. God, I can't wait to go to bed and sleep away all the crap that's in my head.

Moe's house looks pretty sad in the golden afternoon sun. White paint peels off the siding like pine bark. Plastic toys litter the front lawn—everything from pink shovels to an empty kiddie pool filled with sand. It's like a carnival game exploded in the sky and all the prizes ended up in our yard. I hope to God Moe doesn't ask me to pick up after Kaylee this morning. She knows what happened last night. As much as I wanted to avoid telling her, she saw it all over the news.

I unlatch the chain-link gate. Bessie jumps against the fence, wedging the pads of her paws through the gaps and barking in my face.

"Chill, Bessie," I say, scratching her head as I close the gate behind me. Bessie licks my hand. "Calm your tits."

I kick off my shoes by the front door. I'm walking to my room when Moe's voice stops me in my tracks.

"Jonah, come over here a minute," she says.

I pinch the bridge of my nose. "Whatever it is, can I do it this afternoon?"

"No, Jonah. Come here now."

I've been here long enough to know nothing good ever happens when she uses that tone. I turn around. There's nothing like guilt, even when you're not guilty of anything.

I immediately freeze.

"Jonah," Moe says, gesturing to the young guy in a cop uniform sitting at our kitchen table. "This is Officer Randall Zweering, and he'd like to talk to you for a minute."

Officer Zweering has to be in his early twenties. He has dark, bushy eyebrows, a gentle face, and too much gel in his dark comb-over. He looks like he irons his uniform every morning and sets his alarm early so he's always got time to do it. I'll bet he polishes his badge, too. I guess he keeps himself the way Miles would if he were a cop. He and Miles could be friends.

I let out a long sigh.

Officer Zweering puts his mug down on the table and stands. "I'm responding to a call from a Ms. Eleanor Ruggles, who reported a stolen monocle. Any chance you know anything about that?"

Oh, Jesus. I don't have the energy for this today. "Are you even old enough to be a cop?"

Moe glares at me in warning. "Watch your mouth."

Officer Zweering waves his hand like he's saying, *It's okay.* "Do you mind if I take a look around?" he offers.

"Yeah. I mind," I say. "Fuck off."

"Jonah."

"There were other kids there, but you come to me," I say. "You come to me first, just like the rest of them. Cops, teachers, social workers: all of you. Get out of my house."

Officer Zweering holds up a hand to Moe but keeps his attention on me. "Listen, kid. Ms. Ruggles probably misplaced it, but she was adamant you had something to do with it."

"I'm going to bed," I say, zipping up my jacket. No need for him to see any of Miles's blood still staining my shirt. "But for the record, no. I didn't steal her monocle."

I walk down the hall to my room and slam the door behind me, leaning my head back against the cold wood. My heartbeat slows. Date Shiloh Oleson? Yeah, right. In my dreams.

Who does this woman think she is, calling the cops on us? I probably shouldn't have stolen the thing, but it's not like that middle schooler in there can prove I took it.

I've only just stripped off my homecoming shirt when Moe barges into my room, her tight ponytail making her forehead look even bigger than usual. Veins stand out on it like the veins on Francesca's hands, and her face is red.

In one abrupt movement, she hits me over the back of the head and spits, "You're out of your mind."

"I'm sorry."

"I know you went through hell last night." Moe's so much shorter than me that it's almost funny, especially when she puts her fisted hands on her hips. If Francesca were here, she'd probably compare Moe to Grumpy the dwarf trying to stand up to Snow White. But Moe's scary as hell when she's mad like this. "I know that. And I know you don't want to talk about it. But you need to dig deep inside your soul and return what you stole from her to poor Ella Ruggles."

"Jesus Christ, I didn't steal it."

Moe jabs a finger at my nose. Hard. I can practically see the smoke coming out of her ears, and I don't feel tired anymore. "*Language.* Oh, I am warning you, you had better not test me."

In the living room, Kaylee wails. I slump my shoulders as Moe lowers her finger.

"Stay in here and keep out of trouble." She walks out of my room. "I love you, Jonah, but Lord help me."

The door slams. I twist the lock and walk over to my closet, digging the monocle out of the Abercrombie sweatshirt Mom got for me, turning it around in my hands before stashing it under a loose floorboard under my bed. I wouldn't put it past Moe to rip through this room while I'm at school, and I don't want her finding it. Not when Leonard's alive, because we're going to need it.

Outside, a car door opens. I peek through the blinds. Officer Zweering is getting into his patrol car. He sees me and narrows his eyes like he knows there's something I wasn't telling him, the way all cops do after talking to me.

Hi, Sheriff Oleson. I'm here to take Shiloh to homecoming.

Not in this world. Not in any world. Zweering gets into his car and drives off.

8

Shiloh

Tomorrow we're meeting the Soothsayer, and tonight, I can't sleep.

The wind is howling around the house. It's blowing so hard that it's making the rain gutters whistle and the walls creak, like an enormous accordion being played wrong. I can hear it in the trees in the backyard. There'll be branches down in the morning.

I grip the edge of my blanket, grogginess muddying my senses. If Leonard were to break into the house right now, I wouldn't be able to hear him coming.

Bam. Bam. Bam.

Across the hall, the door to Max's room creaks open. I lie still, waiting for him to open my door and tell me he's had a nightmare, but he doesn't.

Where is he going?

Is there someone in the house?

My heart hammers in my chest as I kick off the covers and enter the hallway to see a tall, shadowy figure standing in Max's doorway.

Panic closes my throat.

The figure steps into Max's room. I throw myself across the hall, but my movements are slow as if I'm trying to run through tar. Max's dinosaur night light casts a blue light onto the figure's feet, illuminating his white sneakers and the ankles of his scrubs.

No.

No no no.

"Wake up!" I scream at Max. He is sound asleep in his bed with his teddy bear pressed to his chest. "Run!"

The nurse's long, black hair tumbles down his back as Leonard pulls the teddy bear from Max's arms.

"Don't touch him." I try to run at the nurse, but my feet are stuck to the carpet like it's a glue trap. "Or I'll kill you!"

Max's head falls limply onto the nurse's shoulder as Leonard carries him out of the room.

"*Stop!*" I muscle my feet off the carpet and run after them. My arms and legs aren't doing what I need them to. I trip onto my hands and knees, clawing at the laminate floor as I try to stand up. "You can't take him away from me. Not again. *Please.*"

Before walking out the front door, Leonard gives me a little wave.

"Scooter?"

My eyes shoot open. The lights are on in my room. I sit up in bed, glancing around for Leonard, but I only see Max standing next to my bed in his pajamas. His eyebrows knit together in worry.

I grab his shoulder. "Are you okay?"

He nods, rubbing his eyes like he just woke up. "You were screaming a lot."

It was just a dream. Oh, thank God.

Letting out a huge breath, I pull Max into a hug, but his body stiffens like a board and I let him go. Cold sweat clings to my skin.

"I guess it was a nightmare," I say.

Max swings his arms at his sides. "I have nightmares, too."

"Want to stay in here with me tonight?" I ask him. "So neither one of us has nightmares?"

"Not really."

Something churns in the pit of my stomach. Before Max went missing, he would have jumped up here with me and pulled the blanket up over his nose, and we would have listened to the wind howl and made up stories about the man with enormous lungs blowing air onto our brick house.

I'll huff, and I'll puff ...

"Please?" I try, hoping my voice doesn't sound as desperate as I feel.

"No."

"Oh. Okay"

Max walks out of my room, pulling my door closed behind him. I clench my fist into my blanket.

Leonard might not have killed Max, but he took a part of him away to wherever he lives.

And I'm going to make him pay for that.

A girl with blue hair scans my ticket, a man with a graying beard shines a flashlight into my backpack, and I walk into the festival.

"What an interesting group of people," Miles's dad says in his thick French accent, pushing his wire-framed glasses back up his thin nose. We pass a group of biker vests and pink hair, and he looks at Miles as though questioning his sanity. "Please explain to me one more time why you wanted to assist this concert?"

"We wanted to *attend* this concert," Miles corrects his dad gently, "because I read online that the circus performance that comes with it is supposed to be amazing. One guy can swallow swords."

"That's an enviable ambition, I am sure," Miles's dad says, and his mom loops a loving hand over the crook of his arm.

I don't think Miles's parents see through the lie. Miles is a terrible liar. Every time he lies, his eyes twitch, but I guess his eyes can't twitch now that he can't close them anymore.

As if on cue, Miles fishes his eye drops out of his pocket. He holds down his bottom lid and squeezes a drop into it, blinking away the moisture.

That's the fifth time he's done that since we left Bethany. His eyes must be bothering him a lot.

"Are you—" I start to ask but stop myself.

I'm not allowed to ask if he's okay anymore. It's not my job to worry about him now. He saw to that.

Miles looks back at me. His head tilts quizzically before he decides it isn't worth his time, and he keeps walking after his parents.

I was surprised that Miles's parents let him come. He was only released from the hospital on Wednesday, but I overheard Miles telling Jonah in the car that his doctor said his bullet wound was healing exactly the way it was supposed to be, so as long as he doesn't get into any trouble, he'll be fine. Which I'm sure is why his parents said he could only go if they tagged along. It's obvious they're here to chaperone us, and we're getting a few goofy grins.

From the way Miles made it sound in the hospital, this will be the last time he helps us try to find Leonard. I hope it's not also one of the last times I get to see him outside of school.

Jonah lets out a small gasp. His face pulls into an awed expression as he cranes his neck to look at the tall guy with greasy hair who's playing his guitar one-handed on stage, his right arm held high above his head, his fist clenched. The crowd in the mosh pit is going nuts. It must be ear-crushingly loud in there. The guitarist turns toward the speakers and feedback screams out across the field. Miles's parents wince in tandem. The singer leaps into the air, and the band hurls themselves into what might be a chorus, but it sounds to me like a mix of white noise and roaring. Jonah's mouth is hanging open in what looks like wonder.

Miles catches him looking and laughs. "Want to go over there instead?"

"God, yes. Do you know who that is?" Jonah asks Miles, not laughing. "That's Sabertooth." Miles blinks, and Jonah's mouth drops open. "Oh, come on. Local legend? The singer went to our school back in the day, though you'd never believe it. Call-me-Bill would have a field day trying to look cool here."

I imagine our vice principal with his forehead furrowed, wearing his best drugs-are-bad frown, and I laugh. I've heard of Sabertooth. I couldn't name any of their songs, but Brian from Rite Aid used to talk about them all the time—I think he had a T-shirt. He claimed some chance acquaintance with one of the band members. He'd be here somewhere, I guess.

I try to make my voice sound playful. "Come on, Miles, you should know stuff like this."

The words come out all stilted and stiff. Miles lowers his head, and I clamp my teeth over my tongue. *Damn it.* Why did I say that?

Jonah glances at Miles, then at me. Warmth rises to my cheeks. Did Miles tell him about the breakup? I'm sure he would have. But something about the way Jonah's looking at me doesn't make me feel so sure.

A hand rests on my shoulder, and I glance back to see Francesca studying me knowingly.

"It's all right to be sad," she remarks, placing her other hand on Miles's shoulder. "Endings have ways of making us sad, but we must not lose sight of all the ways they allow us to grow."

"*Okay,*" Miles says, shrugging off Francesca's hand. "Let's talk about something else, shall we?"

Wrinkles slice across Francesca's forehead. Honestly, the only thing growing in me since Miles dumped me is bitterness, but I won't say that. Francesca's only trying to help.

I poke her arm to get her attention. "That's a really nice way to think about it."

She smiles like she's already forgotten Miles's comment.

A tall blue and yellow tent comes into view right on the edge of the lot. It's a big top, but not a very big one. I guess that makes it a small top. I laugh to myself for no reason.

Jonah points at it. "That's it over there. It has to be."

We walk across a half-empty field where the grass has been scuffed away by thousands of feet and last night's rain has turned the surface to a few inches of mud. Miles's mom isn't wearing the right shoes for it. Mud squishes around the toes of her red canvas slip-ons.

The line is long. It takes fifteen minutes to get inside. As soon as we walk through the clown's open mouth and into the tent, the baby hairs rise on my arms and neck stand upright.

The air smells of sweat and cigarette smoke. It's steamy, unventilated, and way warmer than outside. Everything is set up like a standing-room-only gig. There are no bleachers. No seating at all. Just one giant pit leading up to the stage that's crammed with enough people to support a crowd-surfer.

We join the crowd and try to press deeper into the tent. They've put cheap matting down, but it's covered in mud that's been tracked in from outside. I lean onto my toes to get a better look at the empty stage. Swords of different lengths stick out from a wooden display block. Scaffolding holds up lights of different colors and a flashing sign in pink neon that reads PARENTAL DISCRETION ADVISED. Miles's dad looks at the sign and then back at Miles. We might be the only kids there.

God, I hate circuses.

"Well, this is horrible," Miles's dad says, his angular face twisted in a grimace. He probably means horrifying. Miles has said before that his dad mixes words up when he's not speaking French. Or maybe he means horrible and hates circuses as much as I do.

Someone bumps into my shoulder, knocking me into Francesca. I turn and glare at a burly man with a huge beard and frosted tips like Guy Fieri's. He's wearing a leather vest, and he shoulders his way through the crowd. An arm brushes against my back. I flinch and glance back to see a red-haired woman with a lime green motorcycle graphic on the front of her T-shirt follow the man closer to the stage. Her shoulders block my view of the speakers. She has to be six feet tall.

Miles grunts next to me. I see someone knock into him as they pass, and my eyebrows shoot up in concern.

"Did they hurt you?" I whisper.

"I'm fine," Miles snaps.

"You sure, buddy?" Jonah asks. "Doesn't look like it."

"It's only some heartburn," Miles says, smiling at him without teeth. "My stomach hurts a little, but I'm fine, I swear."

At least his wound isn't hurting. I'm not supposed to worry about him anymore, but it's not like I can turn it off. He was the one who stopped caring about me.

With some justification, I guess.

On the other side of me, Francesca leans up to whisper in my ear, "I always thought freak shows were against the law."

"In some states, they are," I tell her. "But they also died out naturally in the mid-1900s because doctors started being able to pick up—" I make air quotes "—'medical oddities' before babies are born. The general attitude toward people with disabilities also got a lot better, so freak shows kind of lost their punch. Also, the country has passed legislation supporting people with disabilities to get jobs and stuff, so disabled people are not treated like outcasts the way they used to be, which is progress, of course."

Francesca nods in understanding. I read a lot about that this week. Not going to school and having nothing else to do but watch *Fear Factor* with mom has its benefits.

Jonah clears his throat from the other side of Miles, and I whip my head around to see him point up at the sides of the tent. "Check those out."

Oh my God. Posters like the ones I saw on the old circus website stretch up to the sky, almost three times my height. They've been designed to look like tarot cards you wouldn't want to be dealt. One poster displays THE SWORD SWALLOWER, a man wearing a green tie tilting his head back and lowering a sword down into his throat. Another, advertising

THE TRICKSTER, shows a man with a long, blond braid trailing down his back, carrying two hefty kettlebells from hooks lodged inside his eye sockets. One girl, FIONA THE FLEXIBLE, is shown contorting herself so her head pokes out from between her thighs. THE LIZARD MAN is tattooed all over his body and it looks like he's had body modification surgery to implant ridges above his eyebrows. His face is bright green, his tongue is split down the middle, and on the poster he sticks it out as far as he can.

Goosebumps rise on my arms.

Miles has turned a slightly different color. "I don't know if I'm going to be able to watch this," he says. "I'm sorry, but I won't give myself nightmares."

I raise my eyebrows at him. Leonard literally shot him, and he hasn't already been getting nightmares?

"There's the latest take from Pi Guy, who belongs in here just as much as they do," Jonah jokes. He elaborately pantomimes setting up a microphone. "Giant nerd breaks world record, recites 71,000 digits of Pi."

"I only ever got up to a thousand."

"How embarrassing for you."

Miles whacks Jonah on the arm. Miles's dad looks at Jonah in disapproval. I raise my eyes back to the posters. It's interesting how the performers in this show differ from the ones who performed with the Durand Brothers. Back then, the people who were considered freaks were people with disabilities. But now, performers either have insane skills or have chosen to modify their bodies. Shows like this give people who want to be different a space to celebrate that difference, instead of the old shows where people had no choice but to stand and have people stare at them.

Some of the audience members have their own modifications. The man next to me has a hole in his cheek kept open by a silver circle. On the other side of him is a girl with one leg whose prosthetic looks more like a space-age weapon than something that could help her walk.

"Is that the Soothsayer on that poster?" Francesca whispers, pulling my attention back to the posters.

I notice the long poster of a woman bent over a glowing white orb. I don't know who else it could be.

"Compared to the sword swallower, the Soothsayer is going to be a pretty lame act," Jonah says. He raises his voice as he says, "*In the future, you will die. Come back in twenty years, y'all, see if it came true.*"

Before anyone can reply, heavy rock music explodes from the speakers. Green lights flash. Francesca's hands shoot up to cover her ears as the crowd around us screams in excitement.

"Are you ready ..." a gravelly voice bellows over the loudspeaker, "to *face* your *fears?*"

A man runs onto the stage with his arms raised over his head. Jonah pumps his fist in the air, and Miles looks a little queasy.

"Ladies and gentlemen," the man yells into his microphone. "Welcome to this afternoon's first performance of the infamous Hell's Mystique Circus Freak Show Revue!"

More screams. This guy's wearing a leather vest and has tattoo sleeves climbing up his arms. His long hair is tied in two braids. Black makeup drips from around his eyes, down his cheeks, and into his graying beard.

Jonah leans down to me. His lips brush against my ear as he whispers, "The dude looks like Marilyn Manson's dad."

I laugh.

The guy straightens his top hat. "It's showtime here under the big top. Give it up for our *fear-inspiring* cast!"

The rock music blares even louder as people rush from the back of the tent onto the stage. My eyes shoot open. A power drill whirrs against a blond guy's cheek. He grins as he runs the bit against his skin, then holds it out close to audience members who flinch away from him. A bearded man juggles two roaring chainsaws. A girl runs out in a tight, glossy bodysuit. Shiny black hair swishes out behind her as she bends over and pulls her ankles behind her head. A small gasp slips through my lips. She has to be one of the most beautiful women I have ever seen, and I'm not the only one who thinks so. Jonah's looking at her—so is every guy in here. A man with long dreadlocks juggles batons of fire. Green tattoos cover every inch of visible skin of a performer who could only be The Lizard Man. He sticks his tongue out. It's split down the middle. Another man runs out in a handstand. It takes me a second to realize he doesn't have any legs. He leaps onto a barrel on his hands, turning upside down and walking on top of it as the barrel rolls underneath him.

Holy crap. This is actually pretty cool.

In the corner of my eye, an old woman creeps out from behind the banner, holding a glass ball in both hands. The shawl wrapped around her shoulders looks like an antique rug.

Even from far away, I can tell it's her. The Soothsayer.

Francesca tugs on my sleeve. "There are souls in the Soothsayer's orb," she says.

"Really?" I squint at the orb. In cartoons, fortune tellers always have glass balls with wisps of smoke dancing inside of them that let them see the future. This one looks empty to me, but I guess I wouldn't know if there were ghosts in it. Not like Francesca would.

The ringmaster cracks his microphone cable like a whip. "On this day, and on this day only," he bellows, "come see the amazing Fiona the Flexible survive being *cut in half*." The beautiful girl in the bodysuit mimics sawing her own head off. "And watch the Trickster hold weights by his eye sockets alone!"

The man juggling the sticks of fire puts one in his mouth. Francesca covers her own mouth.

"I don't like this," Miles says, but I can barely hear him over all the shouting. "This is creepy as hell."

The music cuts out. As quickly as they came, all the performers rush off the stage.

The ringmaster breathes heavily into the microphone. "Our first act will *terrify* and *amaze* you." He widens his eyes. Covered in black makeup, they look huge. "In our ranks, we have an amazing woman with a long history here in the circus. After getting her start with the Durand Brothers right here in Ohio, she toured the world with the *freaks* of Barnum and Bailey."

A woman in fishnets walks out and sets up a folding chalkboard sign. I squint to read it:

One volunteer needed for a special reading.

"We should all volunteer," Jonah says, keeping his voice down so that Miles's parents can't hear him.

But Miles hears him. "Are you crazy?"

"Jonah is right," Francesca says. "If each of us volunteers, we have four times as many chances of being chosen, and then we can meet the Soothsayer."

Slowly, the Soothsayer walks up the stairs to the stage, clutching the glass ball as the girl in the fishnets pulls out a chair for her. The Soothsayer places the orb in the center of the table with a *plink*. The ringmaster raises a finger to his lips, and the crowd goes quiet.

"Come on up if you dare. Find out how you're going to *die*," the ringleader says with a pointed smile as he hisses out the last word. "One lucky audience member will get a psychic life reading—but beware!" He points his finger straight out at us. "The amazing Soothsayer has never been wrong." The Soothsayer lays one hand over the orb. A chill shoots down my spine as the ringleader bares his teeth at the audience. "Anyone care to volunteer?"

The burly guy in front of me who pushed through the crowd earlier raises his arm, but the girl at his side pulls it down. Francesca's hand shoots up, as does Jonah's. Miles slowly raises his.

Francesca taps me on the shoulder. "Raise your hand, silly."

I hesitate. What if she says something about my future that I don't want the entire audience to hear?

Could she tell everyone that I shot Leonard?

But we need to talk to her about finding gates to the other side.

"Come on," Francesca urges again. "What are you waiting for?"

Swallowing hard, I raise my hand. The Soothsayer's deep-set eyes travel over the silent and unmoving crowd. She extends a spindly finger toward Francesca.

"Me?" Francesca mouths the word.

The Soothsayer shakes her head and moves her finger slightly to the side.

My stomach drops.

She's pointing straight at me.

"You," she says, her lapel mic blasting her creaking voice through the crowd. "The young girl."

From the stage, the music plays a long, doomy chord. The Soothsayer beckons me to her as heads turn to look at me.

"Go on," Francesca urges, her voice sounding like it's coming from far away. "You can do this."

Crap. I can feel every eye on me as I walk toward the stage. The ringmaster points at the stairs. My knuckles are white on the railing as I climb them, trying my hardest not to trip as I take a seat on a stool at the Soothsayer's round table. We're both side-on to the audience, sitting opposite each other. Fingerprints smear the sides of the glass ball. Up close, the Soothsayer looks old. Wrinkles are etched deeply into dark skin that seems to hang from her cheekbones. A square of lace covers most of her thin gray dreadlocks and falls over her shoulders, and the lights around us glint off her gold earrings.

The ringmaster says something to the crowd, and they laugh. I didn't catch what he said. I try to find Miles, Jonah, and Francesca in the audience, but the spotlights are too bright.

The Soothsayer leans into the tall back of her plush chair. Metal studs line the chair's rim. In a throaty voice, she says, "What a rarity to have someone so young. Relax, darling. There's no need to be afraid."

Someone in the audience snickers, and I clench my jaw.

"I'm not scared."

The Soothsayer reaches a wrinkled hand across the table, palm upward. "Come, darling. Put your hand in mine."

I don't move. The Soothsayer wriggles her fingers. Her

impatience is probably all part of the act, designed to instill fear into whoever sits opposite her. How do I bring this conversation around to Leonard? I can't. Not with an entire audience looking at me. This was a stupid idea. Why did I have to volunteer if I couldn't ask her about Leonard?

Swallowing my nerves, I give her my hand.

Her fingers are paper thin but soft and warm against mine. I'd expected cold sticks, like twigs on a tree in winter. "Oh, my darling, your skin is so dry. It's splitting, like firewood."

I recoil from her self-consciously, but her grip is so strong that she traps my hand.

She places one hand over the empty orb, a shiver traveling through her. "Tell me what you would like to know. What questions form your innermost secrets?" She's playing to the crowd now.

Someone goes, "Whoooo," like a ghost in a bad movie. In the distance, I hear cheering and more noise as another band starts up.

The Soothsayer points at a list on top of the table, hand-written in dark purple ink and hard-to-read cursive. "I am never wrong, you know. I never have been. Never once in my life."

I run my eyes down the list.

Ask about …
Love
Health
Friends
Enemies
Business
Travel
Wealth
Who will you marry?
When will you die?
HOW will you die?

"Uh …" A month ago, I wouldn't have believed any of the

Soothsayer's fortunes could come true, but knowing what I know now about Leonard and how he could do exactly what the freak show said he could, I'm not taking any chances.

My eyes have gotten used to the stage lights, and I can see the audience now. I scan the unfriendly faces until I find Miles's. If this happened two weeks ago, he would have given me an encouraging nod, but he pulls his lips into a thin line.

He dumped you, I remind myself. *He won't comfort you, because he doesn't like you like that anymore.*

Or at all.

"I guess the when will you die one," I say, pointing to the question like I'm ordering a sandwich from a menu.

I'll have a BLT with a side of death.

"Darling, I must warn you, some find my words … upsetting." The Soothsayer glances down at the orb, and I grip the bottom of the chair so hard my knuckles throb. "Understanding how things come to their end can remove the joy you encounter on your way toward that end."

"Why are you saying that?" I ask. "Do you see something bad?" The stage microphone picks up my words, and the personal question becomes a public one.

"Could you handle it if I did, do you think?"

She doesn't think you can, a mean voice whispers in my ear, making goosebumps rise on my arms. *She thinks you're weak.*

I tighten my grip on her hand. "What do you see?"

"Such … *anger*, such rage inside of you. Tell me, darling, what scares you so much? What do you fear most in this world?"

That I don't know what real love feels like.

I look out across the sea of faces, but this time my eyes meet Jonah's. He's watching me intently from where he's standing between Miles and Francesca. He offers me a soft and earnest smile, like he's telling me it's okay.

Is he making fun of me? He has to be. Jonah doesn't do sweet things. He does funny things.

"I'm not scared," I say, still looking at him.

"Oh, but your soul tells me differently." The Soothsayer's

voice pulls my attention back to her. "I feel your energy traveling through your skin, palm-to-palm, and fear is an old friend of mine." The Soothsayer leans closer to the orb. "Oh, yes, you are afraid, and you have been for a long time. There has been a monster in your life, a monster that has done ugly, ugly things."

The Soothsayer hums a high-pitched tune that raises the hair on the back of my neck. I know it from somewhere. It's old, not something I'd remember the words to.

The Soothsayer's humming cuts out. "It appears you have been able to escape that monster, but he is never really gone. As much as you may not want him to, he lives on ... *within* you."

Okay, so that's not true. I might have issues, but Leonard taking over my body is not one of them. "I don't think so."

"Your soul does not lie." She points a bony finger at me, bumpy with age and what looks like arthritis. "The monster is living inside of you, but it's fighting to come out."

I get a sudden thought, and it's all I can do to keep myself breathing.

Could ... is she talking about Dad?

"I am nothing like him," I say.

She looks unconvinced. "Maybe not. Maybe so."

I'm done with this. I yank my hand roughly out of hers. An audience member snickers, and I glare out at the crowd. How dare somebody laugh at me? This is not funny.

The Soothsayer gasps.

The ringleader covers his microphone. "Wilma?" he hisses. "Are you okay?"

The Soothsayer grips the edge of the table, squeezing her eyes shut. "I believe I know why you came here today, and I will not tell you a thing about it. I left that part of my life in the past."

Before I can reply, she yanks off her microphone and throws it on the floor, scooping her glass ball up in stiff hands and walking off stage. The crowd is quiet for a few seconds, then the catcalls and boos start coming.

"Sorry, folks." The ringleader lets out a nervous laugh. "Looks like our Soothsayer saw something so upsetting that she had to leave us for a minute. How about you go sit down, huh, girl?"

He points at the staircase. A girl in fishnets steps toward me. I recognize her as Fiona the Flexible. Up close, her makeup is cracked and she's easily ten years older than she looks from a distance. I can't wait to tell Jonah she's as old as his foster mom.

I leap up and run from the stage, out of the spotlight, and after the Soothsayer as she disappears through the flaps in the tent.

9

Shiloh

"Wait!" I yell at the Soothsayer, running down the stairs and pushing through the tent flaps.

Sunlight hits my eyes. I squint, glancing around to find out where she went, then see her hurrying across the lawn. For an old woman, she moves pretty fast. In the backstage area, the grass is green. It hasn't been churned to mud by thousands of uncaring feet. But it's still slippery, and a woman as old as the Soothsayer could fall and break a hip.

"Please!" I say. "I need to talk to you."

She climbs up the metal stairs to a long dressing room trailer shaded by thinning trees. I run past a splintered picnic table and grip the rusted railing of the stairs as I climb after her.

"Leonard Gailis killed my brother," I say, "and he's coming after me now."

A hand clamps my shoulder. I glance back to find myself face-to-face with Fiona the Flexible. Wrinkles slice through the foundation that's caked onto her face.

"Hey," she says. "You can't come back here."

The Soothsayer whips her head around. "It's all right, Fiona. The girl is with me."

The Soothsayer walks into the trailer, and Fiona drops her hand. I hurry after the Soothsayer.

She points at the groggy boy in clown makeup slumped over on the couch. "You. Out."

The clown leaps upright, collects his coat, and slinks off down the stairs. The Soothsayer goes to close the door, but a hand catches it, pulling it back open. Jonah sticks his head into the trailer. Relief washes over me like an icy stream. It's real enough to make me shiver.

"Sorry, can we join?" Jonah asks, stepping in to reveal Francesca and Miles behind him. It's not a question, and for a second, I feel a pang of sympathy for the Soothsayer. She's just an old woman. She must be so confused.

The Soothsayer looks between us. "What do you want from me?" she demands.

"We want to ask you about Leonard Gailis," I say again.

"Whatever he's done to you, darlings, I don't want any part of it," she says. "Some things are better left in the past."

"We think he's trying to get into the afterlife and bring back the ghost of the girl he killed," I say.

"Evangeline," Francesca adds.

"He's going to kill somebody and bring Evangeline's ghost back to life inside that person's body." My words hang in the air. I never thought I'd end up here, openly talking about ghosts to a fortune teller in a freak show like it's as easy as asking Mom what's for dinner. A lot can change in a couple of weeks.

The Soothsayer wipes her orb clean with a soft cloth and places it carefully into a velvet box. Francesca is staring at it, like she sees things we can't. The Soothsayer sinks into a chair in front of a long dressing mirror. I glance around the room. Crates, chests, and barrels are stacked against the wall, and makeup trays lie open on tables. There's a pair of grotesquely elongated false eyelashes on the table under the makeup lights. I bet they're Fiona's. Surprisingly enough, there are a couple of condoms in their wrappers next to them. I don't want to speculate whose they may be.

The Soothsayer sees me staring at them. "Darling, don't be alarmed. Bruce uses them on his screwdrivers. No reason to allow all that pesky rust and germs to get up his nose."

I offer her an uneasy smile as I move a studded vest off the nearest chair and sit down next to her. Jonah sits on an ornate wooden chest in the middle of the room, and Francesca and Miles cop a squat on the couch the clown was napping on.

"Leonard told us about his plan when we rescued Shiloh's brother in the woods," Francesca says.

I lean back in my chair as Francesca tells the Soothsayer about Max going missing, finding Leonard in the trailer, and discovering her own abilities to bring people back from the dead. It's hard to tell if the Soothsayer is taking any of it in. She shifts in her chair, leans forward, then leans back—all without uttering a word.

"We cannot allow him to kill another child," Francesca finishes. "But because we're not sure who his host is, we do not know how to stop him, and we hoped that you could tell us something about openings to the afterlife so that we can find them and then find him as well."

The Soothsayer says nothing. After a second, she hangs her head and whispers, "That *bastard.*"

"Yeah. You can say that again," Jonah mutters.

"Not Leonard Gailis," the Soothsayer adds. "I grew up with Leonard, you see, and he was a gentle boy. It was Elias Durand who saw the potential in Leonard's gift. Elias forced him to kill. He turned Leonard into nothing more than an act. He made us into performers instead of people. Leonard didn't enjoy killing the animals. The dogs and cats. He brought them back, but they were scared silly, the dear little things. You tell me animals can't see death coming, but I'll tell you they can. It's resurrection they can't see."

Miles readjusts his glasses. "If it was so bad, why didn't he leave?"

"It was not that simple. Not back in those days, at least, and Leonard had no family apart from an uncle who didn't want him, so where would he go? Elias had his claws in us. He took our money, and he told us no one would ever love us because we were poor and broken, but he gave us something that few of us had known before … he gave us a family. Not to mention the drugs."

"Drugs?" I ask.

The Soothsayer twists her mouth into an amused smile. "Oh, yes. You children today think you know all there is to know about drugs, that nobody ever used them before. But I'll tell you, us circus folk had drugs for everything. We had quite a lot of time on our hands. It wasn't exactly a happy life, but we found our ways. We had all the normal concoctions, but we also got creative. Mixing … matching … there were drugs that made you believe your left foot was your lover. Drugs that turned you into a puppet. Elias gave them to the most difficult performers, those who said they wouldn't do what he wanted, and after that they did whatever he told them to."

The thought of someone losing their mind that way makes me shudder. "Leaving had to be better than being drugged all the time," I say.

The Soothsayer pulls her lips into a frown. "Back then, people didn't take so kindly to folks who were different. Even Leonard—it's a heartbreaking story. When he was a child, if you didn't know what he could do, you'd never think he was anything but normal, and the townsfolk hated him for it. You know what they did? They brought him their dead. Animals, mostly dogs and cats that'd been run down. Bunny rabbits that had been torn in two by coyotes. Crying children brought them to him, and he couldn't do a thing for them. He could only bring back what he'd sent himself. Then a girl came. She wasn't right in the head, I'm sure, and we thought 'Oh God, here's another one.' And she opened her shawl, and there was a baby in it who was as cold as the ground. Leonard cried, and she cried, and that poor baby stayed just as dead as it ever was. A group of local boys beat him half to death after that. They held him down and cut off his pointer and ring fingers at the knuckle with a pair of tree shears. Said they were going to help him look more like the freak he was. They were so cruel. Leonard didn't even go to the hospital. We made him up a dressing and Elias gave him something for the pain." Goosebumps rise on my arms. The Soothsayer hangs her head. "After that, Leonard was never the same. You couldn't ever tell what he was thinking or what he was planning to do. I say his gift was more of a curse, but that poor dead baby gave Elias ideas, and I guess you've heard about the rest."

Things start to come together in my head. Why, in old photographs of teenage Leonard, he has three fingers, and why the Leonard we saw in the woods had five. How articles reporting on the events of Evangeline's death said that he died.

My spine straightens.

"He changed bodies, didn't he?" I ask. "The day he killed Evangeline?"

The Soothsayer gives a solemn nod. "I believe he did just that …"

"Whose body did he enter?"

"I don't rightly know for sure," says the Soothsayer. "I haven't seen a photograph of Leonard since that day, but I remember the show like it was yesterday, seeing him gone all crazy-eyed. See, Leonard … how do I put this? He was a little too friendly with one boy who cared for the horses, a boy by the name of Patrick De Beauvoir, who was such a beautiful, beautiful boy, and I believe he was maybe a bit soft on Leonard too, although he would never admit it. You didn't in those days. But Leonard ran off to the stables after he couldn't bring poor Evangeline back while everyone was too busy looking out for her. I saw him disappear in there, but I didn't follow him inside. I figured Patrick would be the one to calm him down." She takes a long inhale through her nose, shifting in her seat like even talking about this deeply upsets her. "That was the last time I saw either of them alive."

"Do you have a picture of them?" Francesca asks, and I nod along with her to support the idea.

"I believe I might." The Soothsayer stands, and I hear bones click as she shuffles across the tent to the wooden chest Jonah is sitting on. She waves her cane, tapping Jonah's shoulder with its golden tip, and he gets out of the way. Her fingers fumble with the silver latches. A cloud of dust billows up from the top of the chest and onto the wooden slats as she reaches into it and pulls out what looks like a photo album bound with cloth.

"I believe this is the right one," the Soothsayer says, twisting it and squinting to read the date on the spine. She flips through the pages, her eyes traveling over them as if in slow motion, taking in all the characters from her past. All the memories. I itch to take the book from her and flip through the pictures more quickly until I find someone I recognize, but I force myself to sit still.

"Ah." The Soothsayer turns the album around and puts it on the table. All four of us crowd around her as she taps a knotty finger against a grainy black-and-white photograph of an elephant standing underneath a tent. A boy poses in front of it. "That's Patrick." He looks to be over six feet tall with muscles bulging out of his black sweater. A newsboy cap sits on his head, lifted enough to show his unsmiling face. The longer I stare into his eyes, the worse the gurgling in the pit of my stomach gets. In the photo, the young man's hair is not gray. No wrinkles stretch his skin, but those eyes are the same.

"Yeah. That's him all right," Jonah says.

The Soothsayer sighs, as if she has heard bad news. "I thought so."

"Patrick is dead now." Francesca jerks her chin at me. "He was shot quite a few times."

The Soothsayer doesn't look up. "Patrick didn't deserve that," she says.

As much as I feel bad for Patrick, I'm having a hard time feeling sorry for Leonard, and in my mind, the two of them are the same.

"Excuse me, Ms. The Soothsayer—" Francesca starts.

"Wilma," the Soothsayer cuts her off. "It's just Wilma."

"All right, Ms. Wilma," Francesca says, scratching her temple. "Do you have any idea how Leonard might try to open a passage to the other side?"

"I'd guess he is searching for the passageways that are already in your town. The borders are thin here."

"You mean like … gates to the afterlife?" I ask, and Wilma nods. "There are gates in our town?"

With a quick nod, Wilma shifts in her chair. "See, darlings, the other side exists over the top of ours. It's kind of like a what-you-call-it? A dimension, that's it. A dimension wrapped around our world, and there's just a thin barrier between the two. It doesn't take much for the barrier to … sort of rub against our world a bit too hard and create a small tear." She sniffles and grabs a velvety handkerchief off her table. She blows her nose, and I can hear the high whistle of snot flying from her nostrils. "I suppose what I'm trying to say," she continues, rubbing the side of her nose with her hand, "is there are small openings to the other side that occur naturally, but they are rare and only remain open for a little while before the barrier heals itself right back up and the opening disappears."

"How do you find these openings?" I ask.

"Well, I have never seen one myself. That is a privilege reserved for those among us who can see the dead. I once had a friend who saw one in the bottom of a teacup, and he described it as looking like a dollar coin made of swirling white fog. From my understanding, not many souls find their way back through them, but those who do fade back to the other side on their own."

"Do souls on the other side see these openings when they form?" Francesca asks.

"Truth be told, I have no clue, darling. I cannot see souls myself. But if I had to guess, I'd say yes, the souls can see them or sense them somehow on some other level as I know of souls who have been able to find their way back through these openings time and time again."

"Like Kitty," Francesca says, glancing at Miles. "Do you remember Kitty from the hospital?"

Miles nods. "It sounded like she came back a lot."

"Ella Ruggles's sister did, too," I say. "Ella Ruggles said she can barely get rid of her sister because she's always finding ways back."

"Ella Ruggles is a crazy bitch," Jonah grumbles.

Wilma chuckles, like she knows something.

I stare at Miles. Sweat stains the armpits of his collared shirt. It beads on his brow, but he wipes it away. His parents are probably going nuts outside wondering where he ran off to. I'm about to ask if he's feeling okay when Wilma's voice snaps me back to attention.

"There are some places," she says, "where the barrier between our realm and the realm of the dead is thin. In those areas, openings are more likely to appear." She takes such long pauses between her sentences. I wish she would hurry it up already. "I believe I have a map here, somewhere. Not a map of the openings, you understand, because they turn up and heal quickly, but a map of towns and parts of the country where they are most likely to be." Wilma leans her hands against the table, pressing herself into a standing position as she taps Jonah with her cane again. "Here, darling, scoot." Jonah scrambles to his feet, and Wilma re-opens her chest, rummaging around for a minute before pulling out an old roll of canvas. "This is not a complete map by any stretch of the imagination, but I got friendly with a man after I left the Durand Brothers who'd spent much of his life searching for openings to the other side. Said that if he could find a pattern, some kind of method to all the madness, he believed he could capture souls for use in the circus. To put in my orb, for instance." She taps on the glass. Francesca's mouth drops open, but Wilma does not notice. "But he could not find a pattern."

I wonder how the souls ended up in her orb. Are they

trapped in there, buzzing around like fireflies? Should I accidentally knock the box the orb is sitting in off the table and smash it to set them free? I meet Francesca's eyes. She must be thinking the same thing as I am, because she gives me a swift shake of her head.

Wilma unrolls the parchment onto her dressing table, blowing a cloud of dust from it. "Roland could never get his ideas taken seriously—he was a circus performer, after all. Who would listen? But kooks like us often see more of the truth than people think."

I lean over to examine the map. The parchment looks yellow in the dim light, and its edges are frayed. The map is of North America, but the only parts that are shaded in are inside the U.S. and the northern parts of Mexico near the border.

"He was a brilliant man," Wilma says. "But like so many brilliant men, his handwriting was appalling." Wilma lets out a cackle as she produces a magnifying glass from a pocket, which she probably needs to help her read. "The areas shaded darker green have more openings, and the wall is thin there. Like I say, gates don't appear in the same place, but they often appear in the same general area. Places rumored to be haunted, like abandoned houses and old hospitals, are good places to start. Graveyards, too, of course."

I find Bethany on the map in a sea of dark green.

"Couldn't you look into your orb thing?" Jonah asks. "If you can see the future, can you see where we'll be able to find a gate?"

Wilma glares at him. "I cannot see into the future. The souls inside my orb only recount what happens in the past."

"So your act is a lie?" I ask, really hoping this means she might have been wrong about me turning out like Dad.

"How can you know that there are souls in your orb if you cannot see them?" Francesca asks immediately after my question.

Wilma holds up a finger. "It's not a lie exactly. You'd be surprised at how often the past can tell us about the future.

Especially if you have more than five senses to see it with." Jonah takes a picture of the map with his phone, and Wilma rolls the parchment back up. "I must say, it doesn't surprise me that Leonard is planning something like this. He had his power for so long. Of course he would want to use it. To take it back. Power can twist your mind in outrageous ways."

Before she can say anything else, a soft wince sounds behind us. I spin around to see Miles standing up and hugging his stomach.

"You okay, buddy?" Jonah asks him.

"I ... I don't know," Miles manages. "I don't feel so good all of a sudden."

"Is it the bullet?" I ask.

Miles buckles over, bracing his hands on his knees as he coughs like he's trying to hack phlegm out of his lungs. "It hurts to breathe."

Jonah presses a hand to Miles's forehead. "Dude, you're burning up."

I step toward him. "Where's the pain?"

"In my stomach," Miles says. "Or maybe in my chest. Like really bad heartburn or like there's something in my lungs."

"Want me to find your parents?" Jonah asks.

Sweat beads on Miles's forehead again, and he's breathing quickly as he stands up from the couch. "I'll come with you. I'm fine, I—"

Miles stops speaking. He sways on his feet for a second before he collapses.

10
Shiloh

"Miles!"

Jonah runs to Miles's side and props him up into a half-sitting position. "Come on, buddy," Jonah says.

Miles's head hangs forward. He groans softly and wraps an arm around his stomach.

Oh, thank God. He's still awake. I drop to Miles's other side.

Jonah looks up at me. "Shiloh, call 911."

"I need a phone," I say. Jonah fishes his iPhone out of his pocket and hands it to me.

My fingers fumble on the tiny buttons as something clinks behind me, like the sound of a spoon against glass.

"I want my mom," Miles says. "Where's my mom?"

"I will go find her," Francesca offers, heading for the door.

Wilma stops her with her cane. She hobbles over to me and hands me a paper Dixie cup.

I glance at the chalky liquid. The sharp smell pricks my eyes and makes them pool with tears. "What is this?"

"It will help your friend," Wilma says.

"Miles needs a doctor."

"Doctors can only help the living, darling," she says, the corners of her mouth turning down. "I'm sorry to say your friend is already dead."

I stare at her dumbly. What does she mean, already dead?

"I'm not dead," Miles croaks, glancing up at Jonah who gives me a panicked look, like he doesn't know what he's supposed to do. Miles looks at Wilma. "I'm not dead. That's crazy."

"Perhaps you're not dead yet, but if I am not mistaken, your body has already begun decomposing." Wilma extends a spindly finger to Francesca. "Tell me, darling. How long was he gone before you brought him back?"

Francesca gets noticeably pale. "How did you—"

"Oh, please. I felt it the second you walked in here. You have his gift." By him, she has to mean Leonard. "You did to the boy what Leonard failed to do with poor Evangeline. I can smell it. He has the same smell as the animals used to get." She sniffs the air in front of her, and Miles glances down at himself. "So tell me, how long? An hour?"

Francesca gives Miles a guilty look. "I believe it might have been closer to four hours."

Judging by the expression on Wilma's face, this is not what she was hoping to hear.

I close the flip phone and pass the paper cup to Miles. His long fingers wrap around it, his face knitted in pain. "Are you trying to poison me?" he says.

"Drink it, darling," Wilma urges.

Miles hesitates. But when he coughs again and tears spring from his eyes, he seems to be more convinced. He raises the cup to his lips. I watch in pure astonishment as he takes a big gulp, his face twisting as the liquid touches his tongue. "Ah, God, that's disgusting."

"Trust me," Wilma says.

Why? I wonder. We just met her. But she knew what she was talking about with the ghosts, so I guess she could also be right about this.

Miles drinks until the cup is empty. He wipes the back of his mouth with his hand and slumps backwards onto the couch.

I'm too shocked to say anything. But I find my words pretty quick. "What is happening right now?"

Wilma walks back around the table to close the lid on the clay pot containing the powder.

"What the hell did you give him?" I ask again.

"Benmjöl," Wilma says, and for a second it sounds like she sneezed. She must see the look on my face, because she chuckles. "I never was good at pronouncing it. One of our old performers —Niklas, I believe his name was. He had a father who came all the way from Sweden. Or Norway. One of those countries, anyhow. It was so long ago, it's evading me. *Bone dust*, it means. Actually, I believe it really means bone meal, which is what farmers use as a fertilizer."

Miles burps. "You fed me *fertilizer?*"

"I did not give you fertilizer," Wilma says. "Benmjöl is a powerful painkiller and a very addictive drug. A bit like morphine, but more potent. Once, I knew a tiny little thing. She took too much benmjöl and fell into addiction. She passed after only three months, the poor girl. Benmjöl destroyed her insides until she couldn't eat or drink. She paid Niklas a small fortune just to die. I believe that's a common occurrence with drugs."

Jonah swallows hard but says nothing.

"I'm sorry," Miles interrupts, his voice high and squeaky. Some of the color has come back to his face. "This might be a stupid question, but why would you give me that?"

"Because it's the only thing that slows the process of decay," Wilma says. "See, this used to happen with the animals if their souls had scurried off somewhere to hide and Leonard waited too long before bringing them back. Elias put him on at the start of the show. Shocked the audience silly, he did, killing an animal right there in front of them. He knew a thing or two about audiences, Elias did. Had 'em in the palm of his hand. Leonard came back at the end and brought those animals back to life. Did it every time. Nobody left during the interval, I can tell you, but sometimes it was more than an hour before those poor dumb things came back, and they came back changed." Wilma moves her knitting off her chair and onto the table, sinking back down in her tall dressing room chair. "The animals were hurting, and they were crazy. I used to walk into the stables, maybe see a dog writhing on the hay, and I'd swear it had rabies, not unlike your friend here. Cats were different, mind. They'd slink off, and you'd never see 'em again."

My brow knits together. "Why were they in pain?"

"Well, waiting caused their bodies to start the process of decomposition," Wilma says. "And you know time for dogs and cats goes quicker. Seven years for every one of ours, they say. So seven hours for an hour of our time. Anyway, livor mortis, I think that's what they call it, would set in. They'd get bloodstains forming on their backs or sides. Rigor mortis followed soon after. Each of their muscles would stiffen, starting with their eyelids, jaws, and necks, and then their insides would go bad, depending on how long they'd been dead." I glance over at Miles and his unblinking eyes. Is that why he has to use eyedrops? "Blisters formed on the skin," Wilma continues, "and on the internal organs. The bodies were pretty near uninhabitable, but Leonard forced them back inside, causing those bodies to … what's the word … *reject* their souls."

"Like a kidney," Jonah mumbles, as if processing.

"Exactly, like one of them organ transplant things." Wilma nods. "It broke poor Patrick's heart, seeing the animals like that. Niklas proposed giving them benmjöl to see if it would help. Sure enough, it did."

"So the drug is a cure," I say.

Wilma holds up her finger. "Benmjöl is a muscle relaxant and painkiller. Swallow some, and it'll take away the pain, and relax your stiff muscles so you can get out of bed in the morning—"

"But it won't stop me from dying," Miles finishes, his voice barely a whisper.

Wilma hangs her head. "There's too much damage been done to your body already, darling, and it can't play host to your soul.

You'll get sicker and sicker until your body gives up and rejects your soul entirely."

Miles squeezes his eyes shut. Oh my God. He can close his eyes after the benmjöl. He opens and shuts his jaw, moving it from side to side like he's trying to make it feel less stiff. "How much time do I have?"

The Soothsayer rubs her arm underneath her tattered shawl. "Without benmjöl, I'd give you another week. But with all the benmjöl in this pot …" She pauses. "I'd give you up to a month."

Francesca covers her mouth. Jonah looks about ready to pass out. The walls of the trailer close in on me, threatening to engulf me in black. I clutch my chest, digging my fingertips into my ribcage as if that might help me breathe easier or help air reach my lungs.

Miles nods slowly, as if he's digesting the information he's been given. Where is his classic Miles skepticism? Where is the anxiety?

"She doesn't know what she's talking about," I say, gesturing to Wilma like she's on display. Jonah has an unreadable, stoic expression on his face. God, for once in his life, can't he show even the slightest bit of emotion? "Jonah, tell him. Tell him she doesn't know what she's talking about."

"I guess she does," Jonah says.

Wilma rubs the heel of her palm against her chest. "You have a painful death ahead of you, darling." Her voice is a flat monotone. "I'm sorry I could not give you better news."

This is not happening. I walk across the room and take Miles's hand. "Come on, get up."

Miles holds my wrist with his other hand. "What are you doing?"

"Getting you to a hospital," I say. "I'm not going to believe a sideshow fortune teller more than I would a doctor. Let's go talk to someone who understands medicine, not some phony circus freak."

"Just stop," Miles mumbles.

"*No.*" Hot tears press against my nose and the inside of my eyeballs, threatening to spring free. "Please, you can't just give up like this."

Miles shoves me off with unexpected strength. I catch my balance on the back of Wilma's chair and stare at Miles, who is looking down at his hands like he's surprised at how easy that was for him to do.

"Are you in any more pain?" Francesca asks him.

Miles shakes his head. "It's gone." He looks over at the pot of benmjöl on Wilma's table. It's only about half full. Miles swallows hard, his Adam's apple bobbing in his throat.

Jonah leans his elbows onto his knees, pointing at the benmjöl. "How much do you want for it?"

"How much do you have?"

"I can give you two hundred," Jonah says. Wilma pulls a face, and Jonah adds, "Three hundred would bleed me dry, but I'll do it."

Miles places a hand on Jonah's arm as if to tell him to stop, but Jonah brushes him off.

Wilma stares at him for a long second before shrugging and reaching under the table to pick up an empty jar. She wipes dirt from the bottom and pours around half of the pot of benmjöl into it before reaching out her hand, palm up.

Jonah doesn't move. "What about the rest of it?"

Wilma laughs a high-pitched laugh. "You're not the only one who needs it, darling. I'll tell you, nothing works better for a lady's monthlies than small doses of this stuff right here. Keeps Fiona flexible, too."

Jonah rolls his eyes and digs around in his backpack.

Miles gives her a skeptical look. "Is that going to be enough?"

"It'll get you through two weeks," Wilma replies, taking the bills from Jonah and tucking them into her shawl. "More or less."

"But you said I had four weeks—"

"*If* you had access to my entire supply," Wilma says, "which I never agreed to give you."

The air is knocked out of my lungs.

Miles has two weeks.

Only two weeks.

"Only take a teaspoon's worth each day," says Wilma. "Benmjöl is extremely addictive. It is easy to take too much, and taking too much will kill the fittest man faster than you think."

"I'm dying anyway," Miles says, his voice just above a whisper. "Probably wouldn't hurt me any more to get addicted."

Wilma shrugs as if in agreement. "I'm sorry I can't give you it all, darling, but it wouldn't save you, and there are others who need it, like I've said."

To her credit, she does actually look sorry, but it doesn't stop me from muttering, "God forbid Fiona doesn't stay flexible."

Miles takes the jar in both hands. Wilma tells Miles how to prepare it, telling him to mix it in water like it's vitamin powder you'd buy at a gas station. I run out of the trailer but barely make it down the steps before sinking into the grass. Mud soaks through my jeans. I fold over myself and dig my teeth into my knuckles to stop myself from screaming.

11

JONAh

I open the door for Miles to find Shiloh crumpled on the grass.

Before Miles can see, I run down the stairs and pick her up by the crook of her arm. She wipes her gummy nose with the back of her hand. Any idiot could see she's been crying. Her skin is soft under my fingers. I glance down at where I'm touching her and quickly drop my hand.

"You've got to pull yourself together." I look back at where Francesca is helping Miles out of the trailer. "We need to be there for Miles right now, so he can't see you crying."

Shiloh's eyes are swollen and dull. She swallows hard before nodding and shoving her hands in her pockets. Her jaw is set like she's steeling herself up for something.

"It's going to be okay," I say emptily.

She glares at me. "How can you even say that?"

"I didn't mean—" But it doesn't matter. She's already walking back over to Francesca.

I'd have been better off keeping my mouth shut. When will I ever learn that lesson?

The others are about to go back into the tent when I jerk my thumb over my shoulder at the porta potty.

"You guys go on ahead," I say. "I'll meet you at the car."

Miles looks worried, which pretty much breaks my heart. I should be the one worrying about him. "You okay?" he asks.

"Just gotta take a leak," I say, turning away from him before he can tell I'm lying and walking into the blue box.

God, it reeks in here. Like every porta potty ever. I watch the others walk back around to the front of the tent through the gap in the door. None of them have to see me go in. Miles will worry, Shiloh will ask questions, and Francesca—well, Francesca will figure out exactly what I'm doing before I even do it, let alone before I get the chance to lie about it. I've got an idea of how this is going to go. It's better for all of them if I keep it a secret.

As soon as they disappear, I leave the porta potty and hurry back up to the trailer.

Wilma's exactly where we left her only now, she's knitting. I've got no idea what it's supposed to be. Some sort of purple blanket, I guess, because it's spilling over the sides of the chair and covering her ankles. When she sees me, her knitting needles fall flat in her lap. Her lip curls up. I can't tell if she's curious or amused. Maybe she's doing a bad Elvis. "To what do I owe the pleasure, darling?"

I take a seat back on the creaky chest. Gold studs press against the backs of my thighs as I point at the jar of bone dust still sitting on her table. "Name your price."

Whatever she wants wont be easy to give her, which is why I didn't say anything in front of Shiloh. I don't want any of them to know I'm doing this. But if it's for Miles, then I have to.

Her smile gets wider. "There's nothing you could give me, darling."

"Oh, cut the crap. Everyone has their price. I know there's something you'd take for it."

"Do you now?" Wilma curls a protective hand around the jar. "I am not an antiquities store."

"I'll bet Ella Ruggles would disagree," I say, pulling the

monocle out of my pocket. I hold it by its small copper chain. "You sold this to her, didn't you? She told us she bought it from a fortune teller who knew Leonard. I don't know how many of you there are, but there can't be that many."

Wilma leans forward to get a better look at the monocle. "What a spectacular old thing."

I snatch it out of her reach and tuck it back into my pocket. "I want the rest of the bone dust."

"Each of my pieces is a one-of-a-kind item I have picked up during my many years in this business. I cannot sell you what I do not have, and I have no more benmjöl."

"I want what you have in that jar."

Wilma leans back in her chair. The wood creaks under her weight. "Darling, you get to see a few things along the way to being my age. I've seen people come and go, and I've seen what they leave behind … well, let's say there ain't much of a market for what we have to offer—and nor do we want there to be. The more people who can do what we do, who have what we have, the less spectacular we'll be. The moment we become, what's the right word … *ordinary* … that's the moment the circus dies."

Wilma's looking at me like she's laughing at me. Showing her I'm scared is going to make her laugh harder.

"I can give you another ninety."

"I'm not interested in your money." Unease tugs at my ankles, like it's reminding me I shouldn't be here, but I ignore it. "Earlier, I took it because I was sympathetic toward your friend, and money is the only language some people speak. But as for the rest of it … I want *you*. You are young, handsome, honorable. Tell me, how badly do you want it?"

Is she …? No. No way she's asking me what it sounds like. She's got to be pushing a hundred. But she maintains eye contact.

"What am I, a hooker?" I ask.

Wilma's eyes fly open. She looks as shocked as I feel, and I'd be lying if I said I wasn't a little relieved.

"I'm not asking to sleep with you, darling," she says. "Even I have my limits. I want something much more than that. What I'm asking for is your soul."

That's not what I was expecting her to say. "My soul?"

"I don't want it yet," she says. "You're a handsome young man, and why should I stop you having your fun? All I desire is that in death, you come and join me." She places a wrinkled hand over the empty glass ball. "In here."

"In your orb?"

"Precisely." She grins. "In here, I have souls I have collected over the years. Souls of others who have made pacts with me. Time does not exist to the dead. Not in the same way it does for us. They whisper the secrets of my customers to me, and they lend me the fates of the curious. Nothing spectacular can be created without borrowing from something else." She gestures up at the light bulbs along her dressing room mirror, and the thin filament inside one of them flickers. There's a high electrical buzz like a fly hitting a halogen lamp and burning to a crisp.

Are there really ghosts in her glass ball? I hold the monocle up to my eye. The orb shines like a spotlight in the dark.

I touch the glass. Gentle fog spins away from my finger, turning dark gray and then black. Wilma wasn't kidding. There are ghosts in there. "Are the ghosts, like, awake?"

"Oh, no," she says. With a faint whoosh, the fog turns white again, moving around itself inside the ball. "That would be inhumane. The confinement puts each soul into a state where they cannot assume their natural shape, and so they are not aware of where they are."

"But they whisper to you?"

"With their subconscious."

The ghosts swish around inside of the ball. "So you're saying you want my ghost to live inside your ball?"

"Once you die, your soul will belong to me," Wilma says. "Yes."

How cozy. On one hand, this whole thing is creepy, but on the other, I don't know. I'd already be dead. "I'd never go to the afterlife?"

Wilma closes her eyes. "Upon your death, your soul would come straight to me and join the others. *You* would belong to me. No afterlife, no purgatory, but let me tell you something, darling. Those places are cold and miserable. Heaven is not what it's cracked up to be."

So when I die, Francesca won't be able to bring me back. I'd just be dead. That would be it.

That's probably better. Francesca wouldn't have to age herself to save me, and Miles wouldn't have to go through my death twice. There would be no fake outs. When it's done, it's done.

"Do the ghosts in there know when I'm gonna die?" I ask.

Without opening her eyes, she waves her hand. "Don't you worry about that."

"You won't take anything else?" It's worth a shot.

Wilma cups her hand protectively over the jar of bone dust, over two more weeks of Miles's life. "That is my only offer."

"Hold on, I'm sixteen and you're pushing a hundred. Chances are you'll die first. What happens then?"

"Don't you think you're being a little presumptuous to assume such a thing, given the way you are putting yourself in danger?" Wilma's top lip curls up. "You would belong to the next owner, whoever that might be."

I don't exactly love the idea of that. But my eyes linger on the pot of dust. Two more weeks of Miles's life. That could be enough time for us to figure out how to save him.

So I give her a small nod. "Deal."

"That's wonderful, darling."

She reaches across the table for my hand, but I pull it out of the way.

"Before you do anything," I say. "Give me the jar."

She cackles like an old witch. "How do I know you won't just take it and run? I am not best equipped to catch you."

"You said it yourself. I'm honorable. Give it to me."

Wilma chuckles at that. With a soft grunt, she hands me the clay pot, and I wrap it in my sweatshirt so the lid doesn't fall off.

I stand up. "So how are we going to do this?"

"Pull up the chest," she says. "You will want to be sitting for this."

I drag her uncomfortable leather chest over to her as Wilma sorts through a bag under her table like she's looking for something.

It'll be okay, I remind myself as she curls her hand around mine. *She won't touch me until I'm dead. And then I'll be dead. I won't even be conscious in that stupid ball.*

Wilma pulls a fat leather-bound book onto her lap, quickly followed by a curved blade with a knobby wooden handle.

Oh no.

"Make yourself bleed, darling, and place one hand onto the orb, here," she says, sliding the knife over the dry leather. I pick up the knobby handle. The reflection of my face is visible against the smoke. I look like I'm about to crap my pants. But I force myself not to move. I have to do this. For Miles. I close my eyes and remember that night in the cemetery, sitting next to Shiloh against that old shed. There was an uneaten carrot stick between her fingers as she hung her head and laughed about me stealing Melissa Mulvey's underwear. The fact that Melissa Mulvey's underwear could make her laugh like that is so dumb. The rumor isn't true. I didn't take her underwear, but Shiloh was laughing so hard about it that I didn't have the heart to tell her it was crap. I could have sat there watching her laugh for the rest of the night.

Even after going through everything that happened with her dad, Shiloh could still laugh like a kid. I don't even want to admit how much I need her strength right now.

Wiping the blade on the side of my pants, I touch the tip of the knife to the fleshy part of my thumb.

"Here." Wilma drops what looks to be chicken bone onto the book's cover. Dried meat clings to the knobs. "You can bite on this."

I sniff the bone and put it right back down on the cover. No chance that's going in my mouth.

Before I can back out, I drag the knife across my thumb and watch my skin peel away. I hiss in a breath. "Is that deep enough? Do I need to—"

Wilma grabs my wrist and places it on the glass ball. Blood runs down the sides of it, dripping onto the table between us.

Wilma starts to talk. It takes a second to realize she's not talking to me and that she's muttering in a language I don't understand.

A sharp sting stabs my chest. "What are you doing to me?"

Wilma chants louder. Her grip on my hand tightens. Something starts to howl like the wind during a storm. Using my free hand, I lift the monocle to my eye as I peer at the orb. Ghosts whoosh around the glass like smoke.

And the smoke is as black as shoe polish.

Red spots flash in the corners of my vision. Pain flares deep inside my throat like thorns sinking into my esophagus. I grit my teeth. I don't want to show Wilma how much it hurts.

But as quickly as it started, the pain disappears.

Wilma lifts my hand from the orb, leaving a bloody print where my hand was. She opens her eyes and blinks the moisture out of them, and it runs down her face like tears.

"Phew, that gets to me more than it used to," Wilma says. "We're not all saplings like you."

"I thought you said magic isn't real."

"It's not." Wilma hands me her velvet tissue, and I try not to think about how she used that to blow her nose before as I use it to stop the blood. "Now, is there anything else I can help you with?"

She says it like teachers used to when they dismissed me, with that superior kind of sarcasm that only teachers know how to use.

Something sharp pricks my gut. I just sold my soul to this old hag. The least she could do is act like it was a big deal.

I double-check that the bone dust is in my satchel before walking out.

Before I can open the door, her voice stops me.

"Remember, darling … you cannot hide from me. Do not try to go back on our deal. I'm not the only one watching you." She gestures to the orb on her table. Drops of blood drip silently from the glass ball onto the table. "The souls see through time, through dimensions, through lies—I'm warning you, they see it all. And they will follow you forever."

I find Miles, Shiloh, and Francesca standing with Miles's parents by the front of the tent. Inside, the show is still going on, but the sound doesn't even come close to the noise coming from the main stage. I'm too freaked out to care who's playing.

"Sorry that took so long," I say, hoping my smile looks as chill as I hope it does.

"All good," Miles says. He looks like he did after bombing his AP Biology exam in ninth grade. He tried so hard to keep it together in front of his parents because he didn't want to disappoint them, but after dinner when we were alone in his room, I've never seen him cry so much.

He's got to be scared to tell his parents. I wonder if he's even going to.

Francesca doesn't look great either. The wind is picking up again, flapping the flags of the tent, and she's looking up at clouds that are streaking across the mid-afternoon sky like ghosts trying to outrun Wilma. I glance over at Shiloh. Her eyes are still puffy like she's had an allergic reaction, and her cheeks are all red. I want to tell her I got more, that we're going to figure something out, but I can't say anything with Miles's dad right there.

Shiloh glances up at me, a worried crease appearing between her eyebrows. "I left my sweatshirt in there," she whispers.

Miles does not react. Francesca's got her head in the clouds.

"With Wilma?" I ask, and she nods. "I'll get it."

"No, it's okay, I'll go—"

"I'll be quick. I promise."

Shiloh manages a smile. "Thanks."

"Please hurry." Miles's dad looks back uneasily at the music blaring from the stage. "I think we should all go home now."

I run back to Wilma's tent. I hope Shiloh's sweatshirt is still there, although I don't know why it wouldn't be. Wilma wouldn't have thrown it away. Not when walking anywhere takes her three to five business days.

I hurry past the hot girl in the fishnets and run up the stairs before she can stop me. I open the door without knocking. If my final resting place is going to be in Wilma's stupid ball, we're past the point of knocking.

It's dark in here. The lights are off. Squinting through the shadows, I can see Wilma's vague silhouette slumped in her chair. She must be taking a nap, but I can't find the damn sweatshirt in the dark.

"You good if I turn on the lights?" I ask. No reply. I scoff. "Quit trying to scare me. Aren't we past that?"

Still nothing. I roll my eyes. Screw it. I flip up the light switch by the door, and the bulbs on the mirrors flicker to life.

Every muscle in my body tenses.

Blood covers the front of Wilma's lace shawl. It drips out of a deep gash running across her neck, mixing with the blood that's running down from the knitting needles that have been forced into her eyeballs.

12

Shiloh

Jonah walks back to the group empty-handed. I'm disappointed until I see how pale he is.

"You look like you saw a ghost," I joke.

Jonah doesn't laugh. He takes my upper arm and leads me out of earshot from the others.

"I don't want you to panic," he says, as if we're not panicking enough already. "But the Soothsayer's dead."

At first, his words don't sink in, but when they do the muddy ground seems to shake under my feet. "What are you talking about?"

"The Soothsayer is dead," he whispers. "I went back to grab your sweatshirt, and she was sitting there with knitting needles sticking out of her eyes."

"She can't be dead," I say. "We were just in there with her."

"I don't know what to tell you, but she is." Jonah shakes his head. His nostrils are flaring. There's no way he could be lying. Not with that look in his eyes. "And she was murdered literally seconds ago. Right after I was in there. Shiloh, we have to get out of here."

Behind Jonah, a burly man with green spikes in his hair looks at me with beady eyes. He walks past us, glaring, then heads into the parking lot and opens the door of his dented silver Prius. Dad's face flashes across my memory, glaring at me whenever tears spilled from my eyes. He didn't like it when I cried. There was always a suspended second between when I started to cry and when he'd swipe up a kitchen towel and grab me by the throat, gagging me with the towel and yanking my head back, repeating, "Crying makes you weak," over and over again, until I couldn't tell if the towel was getting wet from my saliva or tears. Right before he rushed at me, I'd see something shift in his eyes every time. His lip would curl like he was disgusted by me, like this man with the green hair did. Why did he look at me like that?

"Shiloh."

I whirl to face Jonah. His face swims like I'm looking at him through a pair of glasses that is too strong for my eyes. His hair blurs into eyebrows which swim into each other, turning his face into nothing more than a blur of color.

"Shiloh," he says again. "We have to get out of here."

I rub my eyes with shaking fingers, and his face comes back into focus. "Are you sure she was murdered?"

"She had *knitting needles* sticking out of her *eyes*," he snaps. "And her throat had been cut. She's really fucking dead, and we're going to be too if we don't get lost because whoever killed her might also come for us."

Oh no. Oh God.

"It's got to have something to do with us," Jonah says. "Whoever killed her probably wants us dead, too." Jonah cups a hand over his mouth. "I just walked out of there. Someone could have seen me. That woman in the fishnets, she was there. She's going to think I murdered her."

Panic wraps around my throat. He's right. We have to leave before anyone else can see us here.

"Shit, Shiloh." Jonah grabs a fistful of his long, black hair.

"I'm already on probation. They won't need much convincing to think it was me. God, who the hell would kill her like that?"

Before he can say anything else, I grab his wrist and pull him back to where Miles and Francesca are standing with Miles's parents.

Miles's dad is bending one of his arms behind his head. "The girl was elastic. She reached behind here." His fingers brush his chin. "Seized her head all the way with her elbow—"

"Can we go home, please?" I interrupt, hiding my shaking hands in my pockets. "Right now?"

"Sure we can," Miles's mom says gently, with a concerned glance at Miles, who looks like he's on the verge of tears. "Does anybody need to use the bathroom before we leave?"

My knee drums against the floor of the minivan.

Francesca looks down at my bouncing knee from where she's sitting next to me all the way in the back. She leans closer to me, covering her mouth with her hand.

"I promise I will do everything I can to save Miles," she assures me, her breath hot against my ear. "We will not give up on him."

I chew on my lower lip. I am worried about Miles. But how can I tell her about the murder? Does she already know? Could Wilma's soul have floated out of the trailer wondering what had happened?

When I say nothing, she leans over to whisper again.

"You know," she says, "something was wrong with the souls inside of Ms. Wilma's glass ball. I could hear them. They sounded like they were crying."

I guess she doesn't know. I lean over and cover my mouth with my hand. "Wilma's dead."

Francesca whips around to look at me, her eyes widening. "*Dead?*" she squeaks.

I press my finger against her lips. "*Shh.*"

Jonah shoots us a look from where he's sitting in front of us. Miles doesn't look up.

Miles's mom glances back at us through the rearview mirror. "Is everything all right back there, girls?"

I can't make my voice work for a second, and I stare at her in silence. "Sure. Everything's fine," I eventually manage.

She turns her attention back to the car radio, increasing the volume on the classical music station a few points. Francesca lets out a little whimper, like a balloon being squeezed.

"How did she die?" she whispers, eyes watering.

I tell her what Jonah told me. Francesca's face blooms in horror. Guilt pricks the pit of my stomach. I probably didn't need to tell her that, but she deserves to know the truth.

Francesca presses two hands over her mouth as she cries silently. I try not to picture Wilma's butchered body as I stare at the back of Jonah's mussed hair. What did she look like? How much blood was there? I wish I could ask Jonah, but I can't risk Miles's parents hearing me. We'll be home soon. All we have to do is keep it together for a little while longer.

I didn't know the Soothsayer that well, but nobody deserves to die like that.

Miles drums his fingers against the top of the glass jar that the Soothsayer gave him. He doesn't look so good, but not in the same way as Jonah does. While Jonah looks nauseated from more than just the car ride, Miles looks like something inside him has deflated, like a part of him that was alive when he woke up this morning isn't there anymore.

I don't remember how much of that bone dust the Soothsayer gave him, but he seems to be feeling better than he was. Not as sweaty or pale.

I pull one of Francesca's hands off her face and hold it. Nothing I can say is going to make it better, but I want her to know that whatever happens, we're in this together.

I hope Jonah knows that, too. I can see his reflection in the car window. There are worry creases on his forehead. His voice plays in my ear like a song I wish I could get out of my head.

They're going to think I murdered her, he said. *I'm already on probation. They won't need much convincing to think it was me.*

Would anybody have seen him leaving Wilma's tent? Maybe Fiona or one of the performers. But is that enough to get him charged with a murder he didn't commit?

Realization hits me square in the face. I grip Francesca's hand so tightly my knuckles hurt.

One or two people might have seen Jonah leaving Wilma's tent. But the entire audience saw me follow Wilma off the stage.

They already think I killed Leonard. If I was also the last person to be seen with Wilma before she was murdered …

If I don't get out of this, I could find myself in as much trouble as Jonah. Maybe more.

I curse my selfishness as I look over at Miles. Wherever I go, at least I'll be alive.

Miles has two weeks.

If he takes the drug every day, he has two weeks left to live.

How are we going to fix this?

13

Shiloh

I see it as soon as we turn onto my street.

Jonah does, too. "Is that …?"

I can't nod. I can't even breathe because, yes, that is my house and, yes, that is a police car parked right in front of it.

This can't be happening. It's too fast. Even if they have found out about the Soothsayer's death already, they couldn't have beaten me home.

Could they?

Oh my God. *Dad*. Has he done something? Are Mom and Max okay?

I grip the neckline of my sweatshirt. Miles's dad slows to a stop behind the cop car and clears his throat awkwardly.

"It was good to see you, Shiloh," he says, and Miles's mom glares at him. I guess I deserve that. I'm the reason their son got shot. If I were Miles's mom, I'd hate me, too.

I clear the phlegm that's blocking my throat. "Thank you for driving me," I say, climbing past Miles and over Jonah's lap to get out of the car. Miles focuses on his shoes. I can feel Jonah's eyes glued to the side of my head. He's probably familiar with this kind of fear. The kind that is ninety percent paranoia and ten percent resignation. The kind that freezes your bones in place.

I guess it's normal for Miles not to care about stuff like this. If cops ever showed up at his house, it wasn't because he was in trouble. And if I go to jail, what's it to Miles?

Justice, maybe. A life for a life.

"Bye," I mumble, sliding the minivan door closed. Long blades of grass tickle my ankles as I run across the lawn, up the front steps, and into the house.

Mom is in the kitchen. Her arms are clasped around her stomach. There's a nauseated expression on her face.

I flip the lights on, flooding the room with a tired yellow glow. "Why is there a police car outside?" I ask.

Mom rubs her eyes. "It's all right, honey." She walks over and rubs my arm gently. "He isn't here to speak to you. He wants to—"

"He?"

Panic closes around my throat.

It *is* Dad.

Oh, that asshole.

I run down the hallway and throw open the door to Max's room to find him sitting on the floor with a toy dinosaur in one hand.

Max scratches his chin. "Hi, Scooter. Why are you scared?"

"I'm not scared, buddy."

Down the hall, I hear a man's voice. I pull Max's door closed behind me and run into the master bedroom.

I stop running, and all the tension rushes from my body.

A young guy is standing in the closet between the hanging clothes, elbow-deep in Mom's family photos and Dad's shoeboxes of crap. He sees me and steps out from between the shirts. He's got curly black hair, uneven stubble on his jaw, and a beige-collared shirt. I vaguely recognize him from one of the Sheriff's Department holiday parties Dad forced us to go to. The man is not a detective. He's a deputy—and not a very intimidating one. He's a good head shorter than me and looks like he'd be more at home playing video games in his parents' basement than carrying guns around enforcing the law. One glance at his nametag tells me his name: J. ULLE.

Deputy Ulle readjusts the walkie-talkie pinned to his vest. "Oh, Shiloh, hi."

I guess he remembers me better than I remember him. "What are you doing in my mom's closet?" I ask.

"Oh … uh … your dad sent me to pick some things up for him." He points at the canvas duffel bag on the bed, unzipped enough for me to see some folded shirts, a locked ammunition case, and his iPad. Great. Max won't be able to play his airplane game anymore. "But for the life of me, I can't find one thing on his list. Maybe you can help."

"What are you looking for?"

"Your dad said he kept a 9mm Smith & Wesson in a shoebox, but it's not here."

Oh no. I try to keep my breathing steady. "Isn't giving guns to someone who has a restraining order against them a bad idea?"

Deputy Ulle shrugs, like he's just following orders. "You don't know where it is, do you?"

I know exactly where it is. I remember sneaking in here on the night of the dance and stuffing the gun in my purse as Mom's footsteps approached down the hall. As I ran out of the woods with Max, I stashed it in a rotting log and covered it with leaves. It's pretty deep in the log. A thorough search is unlikely to find it. I hadn't wanted to bring the thing home. I'd shot Leonard with it, and I knew enough about forensics to know they'd have no trouble matching the gun to the bullets and both to the owner and then to me.

But I'm not about to tell him that.

"No, sir," I say.

"Hmm." Deputy Ulle puts his hands back on his hips and surveys the closet. I doubt a more experienced cop wouldn't have much of a problem seeing through me, but there's not much going on behind Deputy Ulle's eyes. "Your mom didn't know either. Your dad's so organized, and it makes no sense that he'd misplace a thing like that."

Sweat pricks my forehead. "What happens when guns go missing?"

"Your dad will probably report it missing, which will lead to an investigation." Deputy Ulle must see the blood rush from my face because he lets out an easy laugh. "You don't have to worry. You haven't had any break-ins or anything, have you?" I shake my head. "Good, then it's got to be in here somewhere. I'll check with your dad about any other places it could be."

Deputy Ulle's walkie-talkie crackles to life. A deep voice barks something incomprehensible, and Deputy Ulle turns from me.

I back away from him like he's a snake that I'm trying not to scare, and I steady myself on the wainscoting.

If they do an investigation and find there were no break-ins, they're going to figure out somebody in our family must have taken it.

That *I* took it. I guess I could tell them I stole it because I was worried Dad might use it. That would probably work, given what's happened.

I hid it in a log, officer.

Which log? Where? Every new thing that's happening is backing me deeper into a corner and drilling my feet securely into the ground. The cops are coming for me. Leonard's coming for me. And I don't know if I can run fast enough to escape them.

14

FrANCeSCA

Knitting needles sticking out of her eyes.

Poor Ms. Wilma had *knitting needles* sticking out of her eyes.

My breath hitches in my throat. Did her killer push the needles into her eyes while she was still alive? Imagining how painful that must have been makes tears spill onto my cheeks. I sniff the snot back up into my nose, but it continues to drip, and my skull fills with pressure and heat.

Miles's father pulls up to the trailer park gates, and I climb over Jonah's legs to get out of the car.

"By the light of the moon, raccoon," he says with a smile.

I remember him telling me the same thing as we walked back from the tent city. The creases next to his eyes tell me his smile is forced, like he is trying to make light of a terrible situation.

I try to smile back at him, but my mouth simply will not curve upward. "In a while, crocodile."

The minivan pulls away. I pull my coat tighter around myself as I walk back to the trailer, my stomach sinking as I notice Richie's pickup pulled up on the curb at an odd angle. Our flower bed is crushed underneath his tire. Only one or two of the bluebells' cones are still turned up to the sky.

Richie usually parks his car very neatly.

Something must be wrong.

The stairs wobble underneath the thick soles of my clogs, and I can hear the loud rap music through the door. As soon as I open it, the yelling song crashes over me like a violent wave. Richie slouches on the sofa, pressing a can of beer against his forehead as he drums his foot on the ground. His snapback is twisted backwards, hot rod flames curling around its sides.

I cover my ears with my hands. The rhythmic pounding makes my breathing quicken. "Would it be all right if you turned down the volume?" I ask.

Richie raises his head. Three parallel scratches run down his cheek, red and inflamed like they broke through skin.

I gasp. "Oh, Richie. How did you get hurt?"

He waves the beer can at me. There are four more on the floor, empty. The smell of malt hangs in the air. "Whatever, Psycho-sis, get out of here."

"I was hoping I could have a sleep."

"Well, I'm busy."

Richie guzzles down the beer. On the night that my father left us, I told Richie that I was glad we had each other, but he just rolled his eyes and said he wished we didn't. He could have grown an extra seven feet for how small and unimportant he made me feel.

But I am important. I helped Shiloh find Max, and I am the reason he is still alive.

I deserve to be treated as if I have feelings.

Richie's speaker is sitting atop the refrigerator. I press my thumb on the power button.

Richie throws his meaty arm up. "What the hell are you doing, freak?"

"How did your face get hurt?" I notice glass fragments on the floor under my shoes and an orange stain on the kitchen wall above the microwave. "Is everything all right with Ashley?"

Richie applauds. It's all he can do to get his hands to meet. "Ten out of ten for observation, sis. I dumped her crazy ass. Surprise, surprise, she went apeshit. Trashed the place."

I must say, I was not expecting that. Ashley was always mean to me, but Richie cared about her and it hurts my heart to know he is hurting.

"I'm very sorry, Richie."

Richie hangs his head. "Not as sorry as you're gonna be. I'd look out if I were you. She blames your dumb ass."

"Me?"

"Yep."

"Did I upset her?"

"She thinks you're talking shit 'bout her, and she's pissed no one's calling you names anymore. She's going to come for you, make you pay for turning me against her. Least that's what she said." Richie spits onto the dull carpet. "Serves you right for forgetting who you are. No matter how many friends you get, you're always gonna be a freak." My eyes well with tears. Richie notices and rolls his eyes. "Oh, don't be a bitch. That's so messed up."

"I'm sorry," I say, wiping my tears before hurrying out of the trailer and down the steps.

Once I reach the cemetery, I glance between the pale faces until I find Mrs. Lewis, who is ruffling Gus's hair as he tries to squirm away.

"Hello, Mrs. Lewis." I wipe the snot away from my gummy nose. "I really must speak to you."

Mrs. Lewis's face knits in concern. "Oh, dear, are you all right? What's happened?"

Tears well up in my eyes again, making Mrs. Lewis's transparent figure swim in front of me. I'm not sure what to tell her. So many terrible things have happened that I do not know where to start.

"Something Richie said has rather upset me," I say.

Gus squirms away from Mrs. Lewis, floating over to where his identical twin Charlie is playing pat-a-cake with Henry. Thank goodness Henry has returned to the cemetery. The last time I saw him was when I freed him from the cast iron handcuffs Leonard kept in his trailer.

Concern enlarges Mrs. Lewis's eyes. "Oh, no, sweetheart, what did Richie say?"

"He broke up with his girlfriend Ashley, and she is upset with me about it, but I'm not sure why."

"Oh, honey, they'll get over it." Mrs. Lewis's face glows with warmth and good intentions even in death. "He'll have a new sweetheart by this time next week, and she'll recover quicker than you'd think, you mark my words."

A ball of smoke shoots over me, tumbling into a heap before reassuming human form.

"Francesca!" Poppy pops up between Gus and Charlie, her eyes wide with urgency. "Did you get the evil guy? Did you kill him?"

I glance at Mrs. Lewis helplessly. How can I tell Poppy, of all people, that we failed?

A car revs its engine by the cemetery gates. Headlights glow in the early evening gloom.

"Why don't we go over here and talk?" Mrs. Lewis says.

I can hardly manage a nod before following her to the other side of the cemetery, out of range from everybody's prying ears.

"Do you believe Poppy will be upset we left her?" I ask.

Mrs. Lewis laughs. "I don't believe so, honey. Look." I glance over my shoulder to find Poppy already engrossed in conversation with Sam, the boy in the camouflage print who died a couple of years ago in the army. She is bouncing on her toes as he smiles up at her from where he is lounging at the base of the tree and runs a hand over his buzz-cut. Sam is full of tall stories about how he was killed in Afghanistan, but his soul had to follow his corpse all the way back here because he didn't want to spend any part of his eternity among burned poppy fields, wrecked equipment, and hastily dug field graves. It seems he had quite a few adventures on the way. Poppy's smile reaches from ear to ear as she grins down at him. "I think somebody may be developing a little crush."

A crush? Sam is eighteen. He is at least six years older than Poppy.

Mrs. Lewis must see what I'm thinking because she looks vaguely amused. "After you've been dead for some time, your age on Earth stops meaning as much as it used to, don't you think?"

I never thought of it that way, but I suppose she is right. Once Poppy has been dead for twenty years, she will not be thirty-two, but she won't exactly be twelve either.

"Come on, now." Mrs. Lewis shakes her head at me. "Tell me, what happened with that crazy man? Were you able to save the little boy?"

Tears press against the backs of my eyeballs. I open my mouth to tell Mrs. Lewis about Leonard's return when a car horn blares behind me. I nearly jump out of my skin.

"*There* she is."

I glance back to see Ashley Christensen leaning out the window of her small, silver VW Beetle and hoking on the horn. She climbs out of the driver's seat and walks around the front of the car with her hands curled into fists. Despite it being a chilly day, she is dressed in a skin-tight top and shorts that hug her hips in a way that makes it hard for me not to look at them. She does not look happy.

"I presume that is Ashley," Mrs. Lewis says.

I simply nod. I have told Mrs. Lewis stories about Ashley and the ways she torments me at school, but Ashley has never come to the cemetery until now.

Ashley throws open the gate. Usually, she looks at me with cold amusement, like it's funny how much my existence repulses her. But today her swollen eyes are red, and her face is twisted in hatred.

"I hate you," she screams, "you psychotic little *freak*."

Ashley's best friend Tara gets out of the car's passenger seat. Ever since I helped Shiloh find Max, Ashley has stopped paying much attention to me. There have been no mean notes handed to me in class. No trash poured onto my head in the bathroom. I believe it is because I am now friends with Jonah. He appears to be intimidating enough for Ashley not to want to anger him, but Jonah is not here right now. Additionally, Ashley not being with Richie anymore does not change a great deal, as she was not very fond of me while they were together.

I catch my balance on a marble gravestone. "Is everything all right, Ashley?"

Ashley's face twists as she walks toward me with so much tenacity that I back up even more. "What did you say to Richie, huh?"

"I am not sure what you—"

Ashley slaps me. Pain flares up on my skin, and I cup my hand over my cheek. Eye makeup runs down her face in black streaks like venomous tendrils. Her sour breath fills my nostrils. She has smudged pink lipstick on her chin, as if she forgot she was wearing it when she wiped her mouth with the back of her hand. "What did you tell your brother about me, huh?"

Tara catches up to Ashley, her expression knit into a scowl. If Ashley smiled, Tara would smile. If Ashley put her hands on her hips, Tara would do the same.

If Shiloh were here, she would tell Ashley that Richie broke up with her because she has a face like a horse's rear end. I do not believe Ashley looks like a horse, but imagining Shiloh saying that makes a laugh fly out of me.

With a guttural scream, Ashley lunges at me.

I spin around and climb over the partially collapsed rock wall, running as fast as I can into the woods.

"You can't run from me, bitch." Ashley's feet pound against the dirt.

I weave through the trees, running parallel to the road. Down by the cemetery, an engine starts. Tara must be following me with the car. If Tara is blocking the road and Ashley is behind me …

I am trapped.

I glimpse corn stalks through the trees. I'm not sure if I may go into this plot of land because it is private property. But Ashley will catch me if I stop running.

Before I lose my nerve, I rush into the cornfield.

"You won't get away from me in there," Ashley sneers as I hurry through the dry stalks. They are growing so close together that it's hard to move through them, but Ashley is thin enough to walk between raindrops, so she does not appear to have this problem. I dart to the left, away from her and deeper into the field. My heart hammers so hard I can't hear myself think. Am I breathing? Leaves crinkle. Stalks break. I can hear Ashley following me, and I make another sharp turn into the stalks. She should not see me. I hope she loses me. Everything is beginning to look the same. Every stalk. Every row. Which way was the road? Ashley calls for me. Screams my name. But I do not stop running.

Only when I can no longer hear her do I allow myself to slow down. I come to a standstill, bracing my hands against my knees to catch my breath.

It will be all right, I assure myself. *In the morning, the sun will rise like it always does, and in a week, Ashley will have forgotten how upset she is.*

The wind rustles through the corn, causing the leaves to dance and knock against each other, making a sound like tissue paper being scrunched up into a ball. The air is so cold that it makes my nose tingle. I am careful to make as little sound as possible as I meander through the stalks.

If I can find my way back into the cemetery, I could get to safety. I have played enough hide and seek with Mrs. Lewis in the nearby woods, and I am aware of quite a few good places to hide.

But getting to the cemetery requires me to know which direction it is, and I'm not sure of that. Corn stalks stretch up past my head. It's as if I'm lost at sea amid a storm, unable to tell which way is land. Or to find out where the sea creatures are below.

"Oh, Freaky Fr-*an*-kie," Tara says in a sing-song voice, not too far away. She must have gotten out of the car. "We're gonna *get* you."

I pull a stalk to the side to squeeze through. A face appears in the shadows. I nearly cry out, but I recognize the face in time, and it's not Ashley or Tara.

"Are you okay?" Poppy asks. The wind turns the ends of her hair into wisps of smoke. "Can I help you get away from the bullies?"

I press my finger to my lips. If Poppy is talking, I cannot hear them coming. "Which way is the cemetery?" I whisper.

"Oh, it's that way." She points over her shoulder. "Come on, I'll help you get back."

A hand knits into my hair and pulls me backwards.

"Found her!" Ashley screams. I spin around to face her, my hand flying to my scalp. The smudged, wet makeup around her eyes makes her look like a clown from a childhood nightmare. She is much scarier than anybody we encountered at the carnival.

I try to run.

Ashley grabs my wrist, and her sharp pink nails dig into my skin so hard that it stings. She yanks me toward her. I fall forward, only for my face to collide with Ashley's fist.

I cry out in pain. I'm raising my hand to cover my nose when Tara catches it mid-swipe, pulling my hands behind my back as Ashley laughs.

"Please," I beg them, tasting salt in my mouth as a harsh laugh gurgles out of Ashley's throat. "I promise, I said nothing bad to Richie."

Ashley rakes her nails down the side of my face. I struggle against Tara who, despite being short, is surprisingly strong.

"You might be friends with Jonah Weatherby now, but I don't want you to forget what you really are."

Behind Ashley, Poppy screams at me to fight them. The corners of my vision spot.

"You're a freak." Ashley spits at me. "You will always be a freak. And you're going to pay for what you did to me."

She jabs me in the throat. I let out a choking cough.

"Come on, Francesca," Poppy yells. "Show her what you're made of!"

Electricity sparks in the depths of my stomach, traveling up my spine and down to the end of each nerve.

Ashley throws her fist forward. But before she can hit me, Poppy flies to me, transforms into a ball of white light, and slams into Ashley's chest.

Ashley flies away from me into the corn. The stalks snap under her weight, but she keeps soaring backwards, like a powerful force is pushing her. She collapses on the dirt in an ungainly heap nearly ten feet away.

The ball of light drops to the ground, slowly spinning upward as it turns back into Poppy's shape. She wraps her arms around her stomach, a mixture of fear and confusion written on her face.

"What did you just do to me?" Poppy asks.

I glance down at my hands. They burn like I have pressed them against dry ice, but they look like they usually do.

Did I move Poppy with my mind?

She turned from her human shape into a ball of pure energy, and she knocked Ashley into the corn.

Ashley groans. Tara lets me go and rushes to her side.

"Are you all right?" I ask.

Ashley spits a clump of blood onto the dirt. "Get away from me, you crazy bitch."

Swallowing hard and pulling myself together with as much dignity as I can muster, I turn my back on Ashley and Tara and stumble through the dying stalks.

15

Shiloh

The needle in Max's toy compass swings to the left. I stop and turn in that direction before walking deeper into the woods.

A robin warbles in the trees. Usually, I'm not up early enough to listen to the robins, but I snuck out before Mom woke up this morning and I took the first bus to Mount Keenan. I didn't want her to know where I was going. But if Dad reports his gun missing, I don't want the cops to find it here.

A crisp fall wind cuts through my thin jacket. I can feel the frosty ground crunching through the canvas of my damp sneakers. The sky is still dark blue, but it's wasting no time in getting lighter.

I zoom into the map of the woods on my iPod and double-check the compass. I'm still headed south. Good. I hear the river gurgling like a sleeping monster that I shouldn't wake up.

I'm getting close.

When the trees open into a small clearing, I stop.

Black and yellow crime scene tape flaps in the breeze, tied between trees and surrounding Leonard's trailer. The brown camouflage netting hasn't been moved from where it was on the night we rescued Max. The garish tape is sagging and has collapsed in places now. The earth is moving toward winter, freezing the ground and using the wind to strip trees of their leaves. In the spring, fresh shoots will grow around the tires of Leonard's trailer and vines will push through the gaps in the rusted metal walls. Weeds will fight their way in and overwhelm the place. Nature has a way of healing the things we do to it.

A loose plastic sheet flaps over the mouth of the trailer. It looks like it was once pulled tight, but has since been sliced down the middle.

Detective Babin's voice rings in my ears from the morning he first came to question me.

The crime scene was tampered with last night.

Leonard must have cut the seal when he came back for his things. There was probably stuff in there he wanted. Whatever the police didn't take as evidence. Like his clothes. Or his circus drugs.

I wish Francesca were here with me. If the trailer suddenly came to life and swallowed me whole, nobody would notice.

Bam. Bam. Bam.

The recoil rings in my shoulder. I rub the muscle as my soft tissue aches like a reminder.

A sudden gust of wind tickles the base of my neck and rattles the bare branches in the clearing. I need to get out of here. If there are cops in the woods, they'll find me if I hang around.

I try to retrace my steps on my way to the road. Memories from the night we rescued Max churn my stomach, but I fill my lungs with cold air and push them down. I remember the tree with the peeling bark. Wait, no. That tree was standing, and now it's on the ground. The storm must have whipped through here and pulled it down.

I crouch next to a fallen log, the damp leaves soaking the knees of my pants and sending a chill up my spine. This isn't right. The log I hid the gun in was hollow, but this one's still solid.

I clasp a hand to my forehead, glancing around the woods. Where did I hide it?

The next log looks familiar. Lichen and leaves cover the waterlogged, splintering wood.

I push the mushy leaves out of the way and dig around inside the log, but all I feel is slime.

Come on. I shine my iPod's flashlight into the shadows.

Could the police already have found it?

I slam my palm against the outside of the ground. Then I reach back in to search some more. There's something in there. Something … matted and soft. I pull the stringy mass onto my lap.

My hand flies over my mouth, cutting off my scream before it can escape and echo through the quiet morning woods.

Sitting between my knees is a spool of dark purple yarn, covered in blood that was once fresh and crimson but has dried to a dark, rusty brown.

16

FraNCesca

I knock on Shiloh's front door three times, hiding my trembling hands in the rough folds of my ankle-length skirt.

Somebody pulls back a curtain inside the house, and I see Shiloh's mother peeking out at me. If she were an animal, I believe that she would be a dove. Not a white dove, but a dove with cream feathers—ones that are grayish lilac. She has fine, fair features. There is no denying she is beautiful. In her expression, I can see the face of a radiant young girl, but that girl is tired now. She coos like she's mourning, yet nobody knew she was sad.

Mrs. Oleson's resemblance to Shiloh is undeniable, but Shiloh's nose and jaw are thick, whereas her mother's are not. That must come from her father.

Confusion draws Mrs. Oleson's thin brows together as she drops the curtain, unlocks the bolt, and opens the door just enough to fit her head through the gap she's made. "Can I help you?" she asks.

I should not be surprised that she does not recognize me. I only ever saw her once before, at the hospital on the night we rescued Max. The entire night must have been a blur for her. I wish it were a blur for me. I wish every agonizing detail was not burned into my memory like a brand burned onto cattle, from the buckles on Leonard's crocodile skin shoes to the blood trickling from the corner of Miles's mouth in the ambulance.

I offer my hand for her to shake. My fingers wobble in the air like nervous little worms. "Good morning, ma'am. My name is Francesca Russo, and I have come to see Shiloh. Is she—"

Mrs. Oleson's eyes fly open in recognition, and she pulls me into a hug, wrapping her frail arms around me and squeezing me tighter than I am accustomed to.

"Oh, Francesca, honey, I'm so sorry, I didn't recognize you," she says, her jaw knocking against my collarbone. She draws away and looks into each of my eyes. "You were there that night with Shiloh, weren't you? You helped her rescue my son." I nod, and she steps away, tightening the belt on her silk bathrobe. "Come, come inside. Do you like waffles? Eggos are Max's favorite, but I bought some of the Buttermilk kind at the store yesterday. Oh, I'm so happy you're here. Shiloh hasn't had a friend come to visit in years."

The thought of warm waffles makes my stomach grumble. "Waffles sound lovely."

Mrs. Oleson is taking the cardboard package out of the refrigerator when Shiloh appears from the shadowy hallway.

I gasp at the sight of her. She looks awful. Dark bags are etched into the skin beneath her eyes, almost the color of the gray sweatshirt she is wearing. Although her hair is tied up, half of the oily strands have fallen out of her elastic.

"Oh, thank God you're here," she says, grabbing my wrist and pulling me after her. "I have to tell you something."

"I also have something to tell you." I give an apologetic smile to Shiloh's mother as Shiloh drags me down the hallway and through the nearest door.

I wrap my arms around my stomach and glance around at what must be her bedroom. She has kicked a beige blanket into a bundle at the foot of her mattress. Empty hooks are set into the walls that look like they once held pictures. Photographs of her family, maybe. As far as I can tell, the only decorations she has now are the mounds of dirty laundry on the long-pile carpet. Perhaps that is the cause of the smell. Something musty hangs in the air. It smells the way the trailer does if Richie goes a couple of days without taking a shower, of sweat and hair grease and stinky feet.

"It's quite barren in here," I say.

Shiloh shrugs, glancing around at the empty walls. "I took down all of my decorations after this stopped feeling like home. This room was my safe place once, but not anymore. My dad's going to come back. Maybe not for a while, but he will. I don't have to be a soothsayer to know that."

I remember the day she first told me that her father hit her. We were standing in the girls' bathroom at school, and she lifted her shirt to display long purple and blue bruises like tiger stripes on her back. She has not spoken of her father since that day. I hope he is not hurting her anymore, but I do not want to upset her by asking about him right now.

A cheeky smile pulls at the corners of Shiloh's mouth. "Actually, I do have one decoration." She pulls open the door to her closet, revealing a black and white poster of a distantly familiar boy whose shiny hair swoops over his forehead and frames an unnaturally pure complexion for a teenager. Shiloh beams up at it. "I saw Justin Bieber on tour when I was seven, and it was one of the best days of my life." She sees my hands and points at them. "Uh, why are your hands shaking?"

I glance down at my wobbling fingers and swallow hard, even though my throat is dry. "That is actually why I came to speak with you. I believe I may have developed the ability to move things with my mind."

Shiloh blinks. "Like a superhero?"

"Perhaps." I have not watched many superhero movies, but I know enough to be certain I am no hero. "Ashley Christensen was chasing me yesterday, and to defend myself, I moved a soul telepathically. I knocked the soul into Ashley's chest, and she flew backwards nearly ten feet."

"I bet Ashley Christensen deserved it," Shiloh mutters, sinking onto the corner of her bed.

"Ever since it happened, my hands have not stopped trembling," I say. "They do not hurt, but it's as if I have pins and needles in the tips of my fingers."

"You'd better not be dying," Shiloh snaps, serious now. "I wouldn't be able to handle losing both of you."

Miles and me, I realize.

"I am not dying," I assure her, my voice thin. "I assume it would hurt more if I were."

Shiloh picks up an empty water glass from her nightstand. "Want to try moving this?" she asks. "That way, we know if you actually have superpowers, because it would be cool if you did. You could drop a chandelier on Leonard's head with your mind, and then this whole problem would be over."

"Murdering somebody with your mind is still murder," I say.

Shiloh shrugs like she does not agree and takes a seat cross-legged on the carpet, patting the space next to her to invite me to sit. She sets the glass in front of me.

I focus on the glass. It is narrow and tall, with faint smears on the rim from the Chapstick on Shiloh's nightstand.

"If you start feeling bad, stop trying to move it," Shiloh says. "I don't want you to hurt yourself."

I may do that, but I am too curious not to try. What did I do to make Poppy move yesterday? Everything happened so fast. One minute, Ashley was ready to slap me, and the next, she had flown ten feet backward. I was terrified of what she would do to me, but I am not afraid of anything right now.

Perhaps I must become afraid of this glass. What a silly thought. What could a glass ever do to me? I imagine Ashley Christensen throwing a broken cup at me. It spins through the air in slow motion, end over end, light glinting from the broken shards as it flies toward my face, the jagged edges turning to meet my flesh in perfect timing seconds before …

Tip over.

My temples pound as I concentrate harder.

The glass remains immobile, as if it is taunting me.

"Maybe you have to hold your hand out?" Shiloh suggests, stretching her palm out in front of her to demonstrate. "You know, like they do in the movies? Or point at it, or something."

I don't believe that will help, but I suppose it's worth a try. I copy Shiloh and hover my palm over the glass.

Tip over, I think again.

But the glass still doesn't budge.

"Are you sure you moved her with your mind?" Shiloh tries to untangle the heavy knot in her ponytail. "Could you have just kicked her really hard?"

"I am certainly not *that* strong," I say. "Perhaps I can change souls into energy with my mind, and then use that energy to move objects."

"I guess you could practice next time you go to the cemetery." Shiloh pushes herself onto her feet and rummages through her backpack. "You might need to ask for volunteers. But anyway, here's the thing I have to tell you." Before I have time to prepare, she tosses me a Ziploc bag full of something squishy.

I open the bag, peering inside. The room around me sways, and I gasp. "Is that …?"

"The Soothsayer's yarn covered in blood, yes." With a glance at her bedroom door, Shiloh lowers her voice. "I found it in the same log that I hid the gun I used to kill Leonard. The gun wasn't in there. Leonard must have taken it. He has it, and he's left me the yarn as a message."

"*Leonard* killed Wilma?"

"Who else would do it? He probably watched us walk out of the trailer and then murdered her as a punishment for talking to us."

"Or to take some of her magical possessions," I realize.

"Wilma had several magical artifacts Leonard might find useful. Perhaps even her orb or the rest of her benmjöl."

Shiloh stops breathing for a moment. "I thought you said magic wasn't real?"

"After what we learned from Wilma, I'm not so sure anymore."

Shiloh hangs her head, her blonde hair falling into her face. "Whoever Leonard is and wherever he is, he has my dad's gun. He put the yarn where the gun was to threaten me. To tell me that if we keep trying to stop him, he will make sure the police find the gun and send me to jail. We have to find him before he can do that." Shiloh grabs a stack of papers from her cluttered desk and lays them out on the floor in front of me. "Before my mom got up, I used the computer to find a bunch of places that fit Wilma's description of where there could be gates in the town. Remember how she said we should look for places that are rumored to be haunted?" I nod. "Remember hearing about people from school going to drink in the abandoned farmhouse at the edge of the Monroe property in the summer?"

If I remember correctly, the Monroe family owns the field of corn adjacent to the cemetery where I hid from Ashley yesterday. Their farm is enormous. So is their family. I'm sure there are close to ten children. "I did not know they had parties there."

"Well, they weren't exactly parties. Just hangouts. Nobody invited me, but Miles told me that he went with Jonah one time last summer, and he said it was creepy as hell." Shiloh's voice chokes at the end of Miles's name. She clears her throat a little before continuing. "Miles said the whole reason the popular kids like to go there is because the farmhouse is haunted. It's like a dare, to see who loses their nerve and gets scared first."

"Sounds like the sort of place Richie would go," I say.

"Probably," Shiloh agrees. "Anyway, the Monroes abandoned the farmhouse because they moved into a bigger house closer to the working parts of the farm. But according to the legend, old Farmer Monroe's grandfather hung himself in there, like, a hundred years ago, and his ghost now haunts the place. When Miles was there, he said one of the older kids was messing with them by opening and slamming the doors and the kids that were drunk were crapping their pants. That was before he believed in ghosts. I'm thinking that maybe it is haunted, and that it would be a good place to look for gates leading to the other side."

"But isn't that trespassing?" I ask, discomfort settling in the depths of my stomach. "Will we get in trouble?"

"I'm already in trouble," Shiloh says. "But I don't think we'll get caught. Nobody did last year, anyway. It's far enough away from where the family lives, so they won't hear us. One of us can stay on the lookout while you go inside and look around. Miles has been there before, so he can … he …" Her voice trails off as she appears to realize that Miles will probably not come. Not now that he's dying. Not when he needs to worry about himself.

I place a gentle hand on her knee. "Have you spoken to him at all?"

Shiloh shakes her head. "I want to, but I don't know what to say. I tried to find something on the Internet about benmjöl, maybe about how to make it or something, but it's like it doesn't exist. I spelled it in a bunch of different ways and searched to see if bone meal has any magical properties. Nothing. Do you think you could bring Miles back into someone else's body?"

"I don't think Miles would like that."

"What if we found someone who is already dead?" she asks, her voice rising in volume. "Maybe someone who, like, died an hour ago and whose body hasn't started decomposing?"

"Shiloh, it is wrong to play God. If we play God, we do not differ from Leonard."

"But this is Miles." Shiloh drops her eyes to her lap. "It's different."

"It is only different because he matters to you. Everybody matters to somebody. What makes Miles matter more?"

Shiloh does not reply.

Before I can think of something to say to comfort her, Shiloh's mother calls from the kitchen, "Girls! Waffles are ready."

I stand up and offer Shiloh my hand. She takes it, and I lift her to her feet.

"Let's go to the farmhouse this afternoon," I say as she opens her bedroom door. "If it is abandoned, Leonard could even be staying there. An abandoned place near the cornfields would be an excellent place to hide. If any of his victims were to scream, nobody would be around to hear them."

17
FrANCeSCA

The old farmhouse was once white, but the weather and years of neglect have chipped away at the paint, turning the shingles brown. Nearly half of the roof tiles are missing, uncovering planks holding up the beams over the porch. The rain has gotten in, and the planks are warped. Boards are nailed over every window and empty doorway. The front door leans against the porch railing on a bed of broken glass waiting to slice open the paw of any unassuming possum or raccoon that walks across it.

Jonah scoffs, tugging at the metal NO TRESPASSING sign nailed to a tree. "This place is a dump."

We walk around to the back of the house into a small garden. I rock from side to side, glimpsing a discolored tire hanging from a tree. I imagine a child using it to swing underneath the branches and sticking out his bottom lip in protest when his mother calls him inside for dinner. Now it just hangs, swaying slightly in the breeze that rattles in from the field of corn stalks. This house was once somebody's home. It doesn't stop being somebody's home simply because nobody lives here anymore.

Jonah glances at Shiloh as if he is checking to see if she found his comment amusing.

She does not meet his eyes. Her steely gaze is set on the house like the roof will pop off and eat her up. "How are we going to get in if it's boarded up?" she asks.

"One board is loose." Jonah climbs the rotting stairs to the back porch and pulls the heavy piece of particle board to the side to reveal a window frame. Small triangles of glass stick out from the edges. Jonah points at them. "Someone kicked those in so they wouldn't cut anyone, but I still wouldn't put my hand on there. Oh, and you're going to need flashlights, because it's stupid dark in there."

Oh, rats. "I didn't bring one," I say.

"I figured, which is why I did." He takes a red plastic flashlight from his backpack and passes it to me.

I tighten the safety loop around my wrist. "Thank you."

"Did you bring one for yourself, too?" Shiloh asks.

"Me?" Jonah scoffs. "Not a chance. I'm keeping watch out here. You couldn't pay me enough to go back in there. Unless, you know, you guys need protecting."

Imagining Jonah attempting to protect us from a soul he cannot see or touch makes me giggle.

Jonah's eyebrows pull together. "What are you laughing at?"

Shiloh chuckles, too, and claps him on the shoulder. "Don't worry, buddy. Francesca can fight off any ghosts, and if we find Leonard, well, we all remember what happened last time."

Shiloh pulls a Swiss Army Knife out of her pocket and flips it open. The sun glints off the short blade, and my throat dries. I am not fond of weapons. Shiloh must see the horrified look on my face because she quickly closes the knife and puts it back into her pocket. "Don't worry, I'll only use it if I have to."

I suppose I will be grateful she has it if Leonard truly is living here.

Jonah pushes against the rotten wooden porch railing to see if it would be safe to lean against. It moves and creaks under his weight, and he lets it go. "I'll yell if I see anyone coming, and then you run. None of us want a trespassing charge right now. Oh, and Scooby." He digs around in the pocket of his jeans and pulls out what, at first glance, appears to be a headlamp, but I quickly realize it is Ella Ruggles's monocle fastened to an elastic strap. "Put this on. That way, you don't have to hold it up to your eye. Or, you know, so you can see the ghosts you're trying to stab while you're trying to stab them."

I must admit, that is a good idea.

Shiloh smiles a little and tightens the strap on the back of her head so that it lifts the front of her blonde hair. "Thanks, Shaggy."

Jonah's smile widens so much that dimples I never even knew he had come out. He has never smiled so widely in front of me. I'm not sure if it's because he confessed to having feelings for Shiloh, but I don't understand how Shiloh can look at him right now and not suspect that he does. It is written all over that smile and especially over those dimples, which are cut so deeply into his cheeks that they look like they were made by tiny melon ballers.

I wonder if Miles would notice it if he were here. I feel his absence like a hole, pulling us toward it like a gravitational force. I wonder if Jonah and Shiloh feel it, too.

To get Jonah's attention, I clear my throat. He seems to understand what I mean because he hangs his head and rubs the back of his neck. "Right, well, cool. I'll wait over there."

Jonah walks over to the swing, wedging his butt into the middle of the tire and leaning against it.

I point at the crooked piece of particle board. "Shiloh, are you ready to go inside?"

Shiloh nods and beckons for me to lead the way.

I walk past a rusty steel drum on the uneven ground at the foot of the porch steps, half-filled with what must be accumulated rainwater. I'm not sure how often it gets poured out. Probably rarely.

Shiloh hesitates for a second before grabbing the splintering particle board. The surviving nail squeals horribly as she pushes it out of the way enough for me to climb inside. She follows me, dropping the board behind her and shrouding us in darkness.

A cone of yellow light emanates from the flashlight. It is unnaturally dark in here. Perhaps because the boards prevent any natural light from filtering through from the outside. The smell of wood, mouse droppings, and something musty fills my nose, making it wrinkle.

"I don't know about you," Shiloh says, adjusting the monocle, "but I see no ghosts."

"I don't see any either," I say, creeping forward. The flashlight Jonah gave me is not very good.

Shiloh reaches into her pocket and pulls out her iPod. A beam of bright white light shines out of the front, but it's still too weak to bring much into view, so she turns it off.

A long wooden table stretches almost from one end of what must have been the dining room to the other. A flimsy plastic cup crunches underneath my shoe, probably left behind from one of last year's gatherings.

A slender staircase climbs up into the shadows. I run my finger through the layer of dust coating the banister. "It doesn't seem like many people come through here."

"Hence the 'abandoned' part of 'abandoned farmhouse,'" Shiloh says with a teasing smile. She picks up a crinkled cigarette butt. "I'm going to tell Jonah not to litter next time he parties here."

I remember what Jonah said while eating custard, after blowing a lungful of minty vapor into the wind:

Don't tell Shiloh. She's not big on the whole nicotine thing.

I smile at the floor. I know Jonah made me promise not to tell Shiloh about his feelings for her, but he did not make me promise not to inquire about her feelings for him.

"What is your opinion of Jonah?" I ask.

Shiloh looks at me funny. "Uh, in what way?

"In any way, I suppose."

"Are you asking me if I like him?"

"Perhaps you could interpret it that way."

I'm not sure if this is the best way to approach this conversation. I have never talked to anyone about romantic feelings before.

Shiloh laughs nervously and digs the toe of her sneaker between the floorboards of the abandoned house. "He's my friend. *Only* my friend. But he's fun to hang out with, and I get why Miles is friends with him. Why are you asking me this?"

Jonah would not be very happy with me if I revealed his feelings for her, so I say, "I was only wondering," and continue walking.

I pass through an open doorway. Uneven floorboards groan under my weight as I enter the kitchen. Dead flies lie belly-up on the countertops and inside a deep pot on the stove. The sink is empty. I twist the faucet. No water comes out.

Leonard must not be living here if he does not have a reliable source of water. Besides, whoever he chose as a host probably has their own place to live already.

"Did Jonah say something about me?" Shiloh asks behind me.

"He did not—"

"He definitely did. Why else would you bring it up?" Creases appear on her forehead. "Does he not like me or something?"

"Of course he likes you."

Shiloh freezes. "He *likes* me?"

Oh, I accidentally placed a foot in my mouth. "That is not what I meant."

Shiloh snorts in laughter. "There's no way he likes me." A pause. "Does he?"

Something cracks under my shoe. I lift my clog to display a crushed animal skull. Splinters of bone surround it like a bed of flowers. It looks about the right size for a rat. I shiver.

Shiloh comes up right beside me. "Come on, just tell me. Did he say something to you?"

Plink.

I freeze. Shiloh does, too.

What is that sound? *Plink.* There it is again, like someone is tossing pebbles against a window.

Shiloh points upstairs. She's correct. That is where the sound is coming from. Shiloh opens her knife again and holds it out in front of her as if that tiny thing would protect her from Leonard. It took nine bullets to do that. Even one bullet did not stop him. This is rather impressive because if Leonard was nearly the same age as Wilma, his host would have been older than my grandfather. Perhaps he enhanced his strength with a drug akin to benmjöl.

I sneak back around to the staircase, stepping onto the first stair to see if it's safe.

Shiloh puts her arm out to stop me. "I'll go first."

I watch her take each stair. I'm not sure what lies underneath those stairs, but they seem sturdy enough, because she makes it to the top without incident. "Come on, it's safe," she says.

When I reach the landing, Shiloh has gone pale.

She points down the hallway. "Look."

A soul hovers not too far away from us, glowing like a night lamp in a child's bedroom. My eyes tear up at the sudden change of brightness. The soul has its back to us, but it only takes noticing the Brodie helmet fastened under his chin and the collar on his thick coat for me to realize he is not from our time.

This is an old soul.

He must have come here through a gate, which means that he could tell us where that gate is.

I hurry to the soldier. Shiloh runs after me.

"Excuse me, sir?" I ask. He does not turn to us. "My name is Francesca Russo, and I can see souls. I am searching for a passage to the other side. You would not have passed through one recently, would you?"

The soul still does not respond. How bizarre. I move to the front of his face so he can see me. "Sir?"

My hands fly up to cover my mouth.

Ragged skin clings to the sockets where the soul's eyes and nose should be. His lips are slightly parted and downturned like he is in pain. If I had to make a guess, I'd say he had been shot from the side, and the bullet did terrible damage. My father is a history buff and is especially fond of learning about the First and Second World Wars. He told me once that, when they charged, soldiers ran with their faces down, as if their helmets could protect them from enemy fire. The tin helmet might deflect ricochets, but a direct shot would go straight through. Bullets would strike through the forehead and tear off most of the soldiers' features, often leaving them alive, terribly disfigured, and in mortal agony.

I stumble away from the soul, catching my balance on the wall.

Plink.

I glance down the hall. *Plink.* There it is again. I follow the sound into an empty bedroom to find another soul perched on top of a dresser, throwing small pebbles against a glass cabinet in the corner of the room.

I gasp. I have never seen a soul throw anything with such precision. She must be awfully powerful to do that.

The soul snaps her head up. She shines as brightly as the soldier, but judging by her clothes, she is not as old. A dark form-fitting dress clings to her figure, and her short hair is plastered to her forehead in small ringlets.

"Excuse me, ma'am?" I ask, relieved that she has a face. "My name is Francesca Russo, and I—"

She rushes at me, stopping inches from my nose. "Where is Sheila? Could you take me to her?"

"I'm afraid I don't know who Sheila is."

"You must take me to her," she begs, spit flying from her mouth and evaporating in the air. "I don't have much time."

"How did you get here from the other side?" I ask, working to make my voice sound as kind as possible.

Her eyes fly open in horror. "Don't make me go back there. I barely made it out. No, you can't!"

"I'm only trying to find—" The soul shoots past me, flying down the hallway and out of sight. "Wait, don't go!"

I turn back to Shiloh and suck in a short breath. The ghost with no face stands behind her, playing with her hair. There are shards of bone where his eyes and nose should be. Shiloh has not noticed yet and I do not wish to alarm her, so I keep my mouth shut.

"It's cold in here." Shiloh scratches her scalp, moving her hand right through the soul's fingers. "Do you feel cold?"

"Not really."

The base of my skull tickles, like someone is trying to attract my attention.

"Who are you?" a deep voice says, sounding muffled, as if it is speaking underwater.

I shine the flashlight into the corners of the room but cannot find the source of the voice. "Did you hear that?" I ask.

"Hear what?" Shiloh answers.

I brush past her into the hallway. A spot of light is shining at the end of it.

"Shiloh, do you see that?"

She nods. "It's not human-shaped. Could it be a gate?"

I run to it. Shiloh shrieks behind me. She must have noticed the ghost with the mangled face.

"What brings you to my house?" the deep voice says again. The voice is as muffled as before. It sounds like people do when you've got your head submerged in the bathtub. Perhaps he is speaking to me from the other side.

I reach the spot of light. It pulses rhythmically, like a heartbeat. I lean in close to it, closing one eye as I attempt to peer through it.

An eye meets mine. I jump back. Two eyes swim around inside the spot, as if they are trying to find some kind of shape.

This is not an opening.

It is a soul.

A soul who must have lost its human form and become nothing more than a ball of light hovering in the air.

Shiloh points at it. "Is that what happens to souls who have been on the other side for too long?"

The soul groans again. One eye disappears.

"I'm not sure," I say. "I only know that souls on Earth fade away in time, and then become more powerful once they are on the other side. But perhaps after enough time on the other side passes, they lose their human shape and become an echo of who they once were."

"Get out of my house!" screams the muffled voice.

"I believe I can hear a ghost on the other side," I say.

Shiloh's eyebrows jump up like grasshoppers. "Really?"

"The barrier must be thin here." Concentrating, I pinch my temples, and a jumble of other voices blends in my ears. "I cannot make out what any of them are saying."

"Are you sure you're hearing with your ears?" Shiloh asks. "Because I can't hear anything."

I cup my hands over my ears. Sure enough, when I block the normal input for sound, the voices get louder—loud enough for me to make out the distinct sound of a high-pitched tittering. I suppose I am not hearing these voices. I am feeling them in my mind. "If I'm going to figure out what they're saying, I'm going to need it to be quieter," I say. "It's as if they're underwater."

"Water …" Shiloh pulls her bottom lip between her teeth and then gets an idea. "Hold on, I'll be right back."

She runs down the stairs. A minute later, I hear Jonah's voice and some clanging as footsteps re-enter the house. Shiloh and Jonah walk up the staircase carrying the deep cooking pot. Water sloshes around inside.

"Goddamn stupid heavy thing," Jonah says, readjusting his grip on the handle. Water laps over the edges, spilling out onto the dirty floor.

Shiloh points at the pot. "Stick your head in there."

"In there?" I ask, shining my flashlight at the murky water. Flecks of mud and algae float inside of it. "Why would I do a thing like that? Where did you find this water?"

"In the steel drum outside." She brushes past me and sets the pot down on the edge of an old, dusty mattress. "The water's not that dirty. I picked out all the leaves. It might be a stupid idea, but it might also make things in this world quiet enough for you to hear the ghosts on the other side, and then maybe you could figure out where the gate is."

"Don't drink any," Jonah says, like he's teasing Shiloh. "Talk to the ghosts in your mind without opening your mouth."

I suppose anything is worth a try. It won't be the strangest thing I have done in the last couple of weeks.

Handing my flashlight to Shiloh, I take a deep breath, plug my nose with my fingers, and plunge my head into the pot like people do when bobbing for apples in the movies.

The icy cold water surprises me. I brace the hand that's not holding my nose against the bed frame as the water fills my ears, sending a chill down my spine and making me wish I'd worn a bigger coat. My lungs are already burning. I am not used to holding my breath. I have not gone swimming in years.

Focus.

I can still hear the voices. They are louder than before.

"I heard him today."

An uncaring laugh. *"What is that girl doing, sticking her head into a cooking pot? Here, if you press your face against it closely, you can see her."*

The water is drowning out everything except for the sounds of the souls. Shiloh was right. I can feel a presence now, or lots of presences, touching my skin like a weighted blanket that's been stored in a refrigerator, their cold energy making the hairs on the back of my neck rise—

I pull my head out of the pot and gasp for air, smelly water running down from my strands of hair and back onto the mattress.

"I need to lie down," I say, climbing onto the mattress. Dust billows up around me like a cloud, making me cough into my elbow. "I can feel them. There are many of them. I only have to find the way through. Could you hold the pot?"

Jonah balances the pot on his knee, lining up the rim so it's at the same level as the mattress. I lie down on my back and lean my head off the side of the old bed, back into the pot like it's a deep, uncomfortable pillow.

Cold water covers my face. I try to relax and focus on finding the voices. They are right there, right over the top of me—

I open my eyes and sit up on a dusty bed. But something's wrong. The bed is twice the size of the one I was lying on, and Shiloh and Jonah are gone.

"Shiloh?" I call out, glancing around at the room to see where she went. I feel myself levitating, floating like a balloon half-filled with helium. I grab hold of the bed frame and try to use it to pull myself down. My hands look like they are made of fog as they pass through the footboard. I concentrate and find myself able to get some kind of grip.

I am not inside of my body anymore.

Am I dead? It's not possible.

But I am no longer in my body, and this is definitely not the same room. It looks similar. The bed is in the same place, but it is sagging so much in the middle that the frame must be on the point of collapse. The wallpaper is peeling off the wall in long strips. Particles hover in the air around me like ash before it settles after a fire, but these particles do not appear close to settling. They're hovering, where ash would be dropping slowly, flakes spinning in small circles as they fell to Earth.

A soul whips down the hallway. Then another.

"Where are you going?" I call after them, but they ignore me. Another soul whooshes past the open doorway, cackling maniacally. "Can you hear me?" I ask.

"Get out of my house," a deep voice mumbles, and I recognize it as the same voice I was hearing while I was exploring the house. "You are not welcome in my home."

The soul of an old man with a scraggly white beard walks past, his face knit into a scowl as he wrings his hands together. A swollen rope burn runs around his neck, just like the one George R. Haggarty had.

As if from far away, I hear a familiar voice.

"Do you think she's okay?" Shiloh asks. Her voice

reverberates down the hallway, and my heart aches. "She's been under a long time."

I glide toward her voice. "Shiloh! I'm all right. Can you hear me?"

No reply. How can I get back into my body? If I'm not dead, am I dreaming? I pinch the fleshy part of my transparent arm, but it does not wake me up.

Another soul brushes past, and the wind sends me backward.

"Where are you going?" I scream.

The soul assumes enough of a human shape to look back at me. It's a young boy, his face etched with worry. "I heard we can get through this way! Hurry, before it closes up. I want to see my mom!"

Through? He must mean a gate.

But that would mean …

I am on the other side.

The boy hurries through the doorway at the end of the hall. A large part of me would like to hide underneath the bed, but doing that will not help me learn more about where I am, so I glide after him. This room I enter is as dark as the others, and the floorboards jut out at unnatural angles. But one thing is unique. Over the bed is a thin membrane, hanging like a curtain concealing a stage. The membrane is opaque, as if it's made of thin skin. Cold air radiates off it like dry ice. Distinctly human shadows move on the other side of it. There is a small circular tear near the bottom, like a hole in a sock.

A soul claps its hands together a few times before disappearing through the membrane. Immediately, the membrane heals itself.

"*No.*" The little boy's spirit slams into the membrane. Ripples travel out from the impact, but the hole does not re-open. "Oh, Mom, I was so close." The boy cries.

"I'm going to pull her out," Shiloh's muffled voice echoes on the other side of the membrane. "She's been under too long."

I feel hands on my shoulders, and the world is pulled away from me.

I blink my eyes open, shaking my head to dispel the water. Shiloh's face swims in front of me, concern drawing her eyebrows together.

"Are you okay?" she asks. The monocle is hanging around her neck like an odd piece of jewelry. "You were scaring us."

I glance down at my body. My hands are no longer pale. They are wet, covered in the water dripping from my hair. The walls of the room are the same as before. Standing upright, with wallpaper that is not peeling.

"I think I went to the other side," I say, my voice only a whisper.

"What, like astral projecting?" Jonah asks.

"I'm not sure what that means."

"Like, an out-of-body experience," he explains. "Did you have one of those?"

"I do not know." Cold water drips down the back of my shirt, and I realize my teeth are chattering with shock or cold, or probably both. "But I'm sure I was on the other side. There were souls there, and I saw an opening. I believe it was a gate between this world and theirs. I tried to go through it, but it closed up."

Shiloh opens her mouth to ask me something else when there is a heavy knock downstairs.

"*Police*," a deep voice barks. "Open up, kids."

18

Shiloh

My blood runs cold.

I know that voice. Until he moved out, I heard it every day, ringing in my ears like the aftermath of an explosion.

"Come on out, kids," Dad says, his voice muffled by the heavy boards. "Landry and Talulah here saw you go in. This house is on private property, so if you don't make yourselves scarce, I'm going to have to write you up for trespassing."

"Who are Landry and Talulah?" Francesca asks, drying her wet hair on the end of her shirt.

"Who cares?" Jonah is speaking in his defeated tone—the one he always uses when threatened by authority. He sounds half defensive, half resigned, as he grabs the flashlight and leaps up from the bed. "Come on, we need to get lost."

Jonah doesn't recognize my dad's voice. Why would he? Once, Dad told me he knew Jonah on a professional basis, but Jonah's been around a lot of cops. They probably all blur together in his head. Out of nowhere, the thought makes me want to hug him.

Hug Jonah? Am I crazy?

I imagine Jonah's icy response. Or a careless put-down. *Sure, buddy, get out of here.* Francesca's poisoning my brain with all this talk about Jonah liking me. Jonah doesn't like me. I always thought he resented me for getting between him and Miles, and that he only put up with me because I was dating Miles. Since Miles and I broke up, part of me has been waiting for Jonah to turn on me and push me out so he could focus on saving Miles. That same part of me has wondered why he's stuck around.

What is Dad doing here? I guess he enjoys responding to calls like this. Saving people's cats, kicking out trespassers—calls like this let him be the hero without putting himself in too much danger. He comes out of them looking like a man of the people, which comes in handy at election time.

"*Shiloh*, come on," Jonah hisses. "Let's go."

Francesca picks up the cooking pot.

Jonah rolls his eyes. "God, Frankie, no. Leave that thing on the ground."

"But I don't want to leave a mess."

"There's a *cop* outside," Jonah snaps. "It's a mess in here, anyway. What's wrong with you guys? We've got to *go*."

Pins and needles prick my feet as I hobble after Jonah. He runs back around to the loose board leading out of the back of the house. If we can sneak across the yard and into the corn, we might escape.

A heavy knock sounds against the board. Jonah freezes.

"This is your last chance," Dad says on the other side of the particle board, his voice dripping with bravado. He's a couple of feet away from me. The only thing separating us is a thin piece of wood he could pull back any second. "Come on out, or I'm coming in."

Jonah pulls his hair out of his face in frustration. "Shit. Okay, new plan. I remember seeing cellar doors on the side of the house, and doors like that usually come up through the basement. But the cops are going to see us, so we have to run. Head for the corn and get lost in it, okay?"

Francesca clutches the pendant around her neck. I hear Dad's boots crunching the shards of glass on the porch. Jonah pulls open a creaky door in the dining room. Dust falls from the top of it, revealing a staircase leading down into blackness. The smell of mold pricks my lungs. I'm surprised at how much Jonah remembers about this house. Perhaps he came to more parties here than Miles let on.

Jonah runs down the nightmare stairs. Francesca follows him.

Behind me, the board creaks open. Sunlight rushes into the room.

I dash to the open door, but Dad's voice stops me in my tracks. "Shiloh?"

Crap. He doesn't sound angry. He sounds genuinely surprised, like I was the last person he expected to find here.

I should run to the basement after Jonah and Francesca. But if I go now, Dad's going to chase me, and then he will catch all three of us.

So I turn around. In the open window frame stands an acne-covered boy who looks like he's in middle school and a heavyset girl with freckles and shoulder-length red hair who appears to be about my age. They are peeking in to get a look at me, their eyes wide like they're looking at a gorilla in a zoo. Behind them stands an older woman who must be their mother. She has the same red waves as the girl. Her skin is soft and free of blemishes, like it could be made of pizza dough.

Dad pulls the rest of the board from the door frame and walks in, brushing off the front of his pants. The sun shines on him from the back, casting harsh shadows that conceal half of his face but don't touch the other half, making him look like a stocky Phantom of the Opera. The sheriff's star clipped to his lapel glints. His shoulders bulge out from under his beige shirt.

He stares at me with his mouth open. He looks so trustworthy in his uniform that for a second all I can see is the younger version of him, the version I used to run to from the front steps the second he got home from work, flinging myself into his arms as he lifted me above his head. The version that existed before Uncle Jim died. Before the drinking started. And for a second, I forget what he's capable of. But the second ends fast, and I flip open my Swiss Army knife and hold it in front of me.

The older girl watching us—who must be Talulah—sucks in a breath. She must think I'm either some crazy criminal trying to face down the sheriff or the occupational hazard they warn cadets about on their first day at the police academy. But I'm not the one who belongs behind bars.

Dad shoots an arm out in front of himself. "Shiloh, kid, what are you doing here?"

"You need to leave."

"Does your mother know you're here?"

"Don't talk about Mom," I snap, tightening my grip on the knife. "Don't even say her name."

"I know you didn't come here alone," Dad says, his voice even like it's just another day on the job. "Come on, Shiloh. Put down the knife. Where are the other kids you're with?"

"Like I would tell you."

"There's no need to get emotional."

Emotional? "How *dare* you."

The younger boy with acne—who must be Landry—giggles, covering his mouth.

He thinks you're a joke, the mean voice whispers in my head. Come to think of it, the tone sounds rather like Dad's.

I point the knife at the window, and Landry's laugh cuts out. "What are you assholes looking at?"

Mrs. Monroe places a protective hand on Landry's shoulder, pulling him behind her. If looks could maim, they'd be carrying me out of here in a bag, but I don't know why she's looking at me like that. What Dad did to me was on the news. But she's looking at me like I'm a piece of garbage. Suddenly, I know what it's like to be Jonah, staring into all the dead eyes, the common reaction, the guilty verdict with no kind of trial. Is this what it will be like for me now? For the rest of my life?

"I take it you have it handled from here, Ernest," Mrs.

Monroe says, looking over at Dad with an expression of gratitude. "Please let us know if we can do anything to help."

"You'll need to come back later and hammer this boarding back in place," Dad says.

"That much is clear. Come, children." Mrs. Monroe leads Landry and Talulah away from the window.

Dad thanks her and turns back to me, his jaw clenching.

Ah, there it is. The angry jaw bulge.

"You know better than to speak to people that way," he says. His tone has changed now that his audience has left. "The Monroes are good people, and this was their family home once."

What right does he have to talk about family homes, given the way he ruled his? "You should leave," I say. "Mom got a restraining order against you—"

"I am only doing my job."

"You can't come anywhere near me."

"Can we please be civil about this?" he asks. My stomach feels like it was set on top of a stove. The acid inside it is bubbling and filling my head with steam. "I will not hurt you, Shiloh. Please, just let me take you home."

He offers his hand to me. I stare at his callused palms, the same ones that slid under my shirt in the men's bathroom at the Fun Palace when I was twelve. Mrs. Monroe didn't seem to care. If Dad told her it never happened, she'd believe him without question.

What a spiteful girl! Poor Sheriff Oleson. His own daughter, too.

Dad doesn't care. He probably thinks this is a blip. He'll get to keep his job. People will keep voting for him because he will be the same trustworthy sheriff. He'll come out on election night, wearing his best uniform, grinning his *aw-shucks* grin, thanking everyone in town like every time before. Sure, he doesn't get to fall asleep on his La-Z-Boy every afternoon, but judging from the smug look on his face, he has no doubt that everything will soon be back to normal. And suddenly I understand where Jonah is coming from, because I see Dad cruising to retirement, putting in the years for his pension, running his little town where people live behind the curtains, hiding God knows what inside the lie of a happy life.

Tears sting my eyes. I look up at the dirty ceiling, blinking as I clench and unclench my fists. I want to hit something. I want to hit *him*.

"What's it going to take, kid?" I realize that it's only the two of us in this house. Jonah and Francesca have probably already snuck out through the basement doors and the Monroes are no longer here to witness anything. He could hurt me. "I don't have all day."

I dash to the window. Before I make it to the door, Dad grabs my wrist.

"Let me go!" I say, swinging the pocketknife at his head.

He leans out of the way, knocking the knife out of my hand. It clatters to the floor. "Easy."

His grip is firm. The calluses are rough against my skin. My stomach twists like a rag being wrung out. I throw a punch at his jaw.

He blocks it. "Stop acting like a child."

"I haven't been a child since you stopped treating me like one." I kick him in the foot. He winces in pain, shoving me away from the boarded-up window. I catch my balance on the fireplace. I want to punch him in the face. I want him to hurt the way he made me hurt.

He wipes his jaw, shaking his head at me. "Jesus Christ, nothing is ever easy with you, is it?"

Screaming through gritted teeth, I drive my fist hard into the side of the fireplace. I punch the rough bricks again and again until my knuckles beg me to stop. But I can't stop. Every punch loosens the knot in my chest, quiets the screaming in my head. I throw another punch—

But someone catches my hand before it can hit the bricks. *"Hey."*

My eyes fly open. Jonah loosens his hold, and I glance down at my hand. Blood drips between my knuckles and down my arm, gleaming in the sunlight coming in through the loose board and shining on the torn-up flesh against my bones. My vision spots. I reach out to steady myself on the chimney, and Jonah ducks underneath my arm to hold me up.

"You're okay," he says. "Come on, let's get out of here."

I glance over Jonah's shoulder at Dad. Jonah must have pushed past him to get to me.

Dad lets out a malicious chuckle. After a second, he scoffs and throws up a hand. "Never come back here, you understand?" He doesn't have to tell me twice. "And I'm watching you, Weatherby. If anything ever happens to my daughter, we'll be taking a ride. Do you understand me?"

"Sure thing, Sheriff," Jonah replies in a sarcastic voice. "I'll make sure she doesn't go near you again. Don't worry."

Dad shoves his face up against Jonah's, and his voice drops to a whisper. "You want her, son? You have her. I've spoiled her, anyway." Shame makes my cheeks hot. The pain shooting up from my torn-up knuckles is the only thing that saves him from a punch between the eyes.

Dad leans away from Jonah and crosses his arms over his chest like he's come out on top. Jonah helps me past Dad and drops his arm from around my shoulders to help me climb down the stairs into the yard. Dad swaggers off toward his patrol car. I hear him whistle the tune of a song he used to sing to me when I was a kid, and it makes my stomach churn:

Hush, little baby, don't say a word,
Daddy's going to buy you a mockingbird.
And if that mockingbird don't sing,
Daddy's going to buy you a diamond ring.

"Jesus," Jonah says, tucking his hands in his pockets. "That was so messed up."

I've spoiled her, anyway. Dad's voice bounces around in my head, and the boiling heat is making my face burn like I have a fever.

Is Jonah going to ask me what he was talking about?

Dad did spoil me. Even Miles agrees. I couldn't love him the way he deserves to be loved.

Broken glass crunches under my sneakers as I step down from the back porch. The early afternoon sun makes my head pound. Or maybe it's the adrenaline. I don't know.

I glance around. "Where's Francesca?"

"She wanted to go to the cemetery," Jonah says, walking around to the front of the house. "She probably wanted to tell her ghost friends about her out-of-body experience."

She's safe, thank God.

Jonah gestures at my hand. "Try moving your fingers. Is anything broken?"

I start with my index finger and move down to my pinky. It hurts, but I can wiggle all of my fingers.

"Ten out of ten for air guitar," Jonah says, and I can't help but smile a little.

Dad's patrol car cruises past us, and Dad gives us both that flat-eyed stare Jonah is probably all too familiar with. He blips the gas, and the rear wheels spray out dust and grit.

The corners of Jonah's mouth turn down in concern. Concern for *me*. "Let's go get your hand cleaned up."

"I'm really fine."

"You're going to want to trust me on this one." Jonah's voice is knowing, like he's maybe punched a wall or two in his time.

I guess cleaning it won't hurt. Walking back into my house with blood dripping from my hand is going to make Mom ask questions that I don't want to answer, including but not limited to what the hell was I thinking?

Jonah steps back toward the edge of the cornfield, which is the way we came from. "Come on, I know a place nearby."

19

Shiloh

Jonah ducks into an alleyway off Main Street behind the gun store. A huge rat scurries under a dumpster.

I kick a crumpled pizza box. Pizza grease has soaked into the paper. God, I could go for some pizza right now. "Are we going to have a duel or something back here?" I ask.

Jonah walks onto the step and raps his knuckles on a heavy red door. "Yeah, you still have that gun, right?"

My mouth goes dry. Does he know that the police are looking for the gun? Have they gone to talk to him about it?

But he rolls his eyes. "I'm kidding. Obviously." He jerks his chin at the other wall of the alleyway. "That over there is the gun store. This ... well, you'll see."

The door opens as he speaks, and a heavyset guy in a white apron sticks his head out and scowls.

Jonah throws his arms out at his sides, like he's offering the guy a hug. "*Paulie,*" he says.

"Whaddaya want, kid?" Paulie asks, but he doesn't look unhappy to see Jonah. That's an affectionate scowl, like he doesn't want Jonah to know he's got a soft spot for him.

Jonah definitely knows, though. He hugs Paulie, and Paulie pats him once on the back before letting him go.

"My friend got into it with a wall," Jonah says.

I hold up my fist to show him. It only took fifteen minutes to walk here, but that was enough time for the blood to congeal and turn brown. Paulie wrinkles his face.

Jonah points at the multicolored band-aids on Paulie's fingers. "I guess you've got a first-aid kit in there?"

Behind Paulie, pots clang and clatter. I try to remember the restaurants around here, but for the life of me I can't figure out if the steak house is on this block or the next. There's no signage back here. There's just the blue dumpster, and an enormous rat's tail sticking out from under it, twitching occasionally like the thing's found something good to eat.

Paulie steps out of the way. Jonah makes an *after you* gesture to me, and I follow Paulie inside. Jonah closes the door behind us.

I was right. This is a restaurant kitchen, but it's small. Bright white lights glare above our heads. A long stove lines one side wall, and a huge metal counter runs up the middle. A girl in a white shirt with her blond hair tied up pours oil onto a pan with a satisfying sizzle.

One sniff of the grease and beer tells me exactly where we are.

Duncan's Restaurant & Pub.

Dad used to come home reeking of this place. If he's pissed off after finding me at the farmhouse, he might even be here now, licking his wounds. This is his go-to bar to knock back a few too many cold ones and watch his old college football team. But I don't think the Buckeyes are playing today because it's Sunday, and I'm pretty sure they play on Saturdays.

I grab Jonah's arm. "I can't be here."

"Don't worry, we aren't going out to the bar," Jonah says, as if he knows exactly why I'm worried. I don't think I've told him about Dad frequenting Duncan's. But I remember Jonah saying how they don't card him here because he shovels the owners out when it snows, so he must come here a lot, and if he's here a lot, then he's probably seen Dad here. "Nobody's allowed in the back except for staff."

Paulie pulls a heavy first-aid kid from the top of one shelf and shoves it into Jonah's arms. "No blood in my kitchen," Paulie says, pointing down the hall. I didn't notice outside, but his eyes look bigger than normal. They bug out of his head, making him look like he's always a little surprised for no reason. "Go do your business in the restroom."

Jonah goes in for another hug.

Paulie pushes him off. "Get out of here."

Jonah grins, all triumphant. "Come on, Shiloh."

I give Paulie a grateful smile as I follow Jonah to the bathrooms.

"Who was that?" I ask as soon as we're out of earshot.

"Oh, that's Paulie," Jonah says. I have already gathered that much. "He's the cook—and an old friend. He's had to carry me out of this place more times than I'm going to admit."

I recognize the bathrooms. These are the ones the customers use, too, but they're tucked away enough that I can't see the bar from here, and they're single stalls, so once we're in there's no chance of being found.

The signs have changed since I was last here. On one door, there's a beer bottle and the word MEN, and on the other, there's a martini glass and the word WOMEN.

Jonah frowns at the martini glass. "I don't know why they think martinis are a girly drink. I mean, James Bond drank them, and nobody's more of a man than him. They're basically straight liquor."

"That's probably why they had to label them," I say, opening the door and letting Jonah in after me.

It's a little cramped with both of us in here. The familiar smell of almond soap makes my stomach churn, and the dim orange lighting hurts my eyes. I don't care that Duncan's is a sports bar. It's also mid-afternoon, and I want to see the toilet when I have to pee.

Not that I'm going to be peeing in here. Not with Jonah standing next to me, anyway.

He sets the first-aid kit on the edge of the sink and peels open the Velcro top.

I pull up the sink handle. Cold water rushes from the faucet, and a small stream shoots horizontally and sprays Jonah as he takes the hydrogen peroxide out of the red and white bag.

"Easy, there." He brushes off the front of his peace sign shirt. "Any lower and you'd have had me looking like I'd pissed my pants."

I hold my hand under the stream of water and hiss in a breath. It hurts like a bitch, but I don't want Jonah to think I'm a coward.

"Use soap, Scooby." He pushes the plastic Dial dispenser closer to me. "None of that just water shit."

I squirt a glob of soap onto my knuckles. A fresh stab of pain races through my hand, and I can't conceal my wince.

"You've got to rub it in," Jonah says, like he knows what to do and has to stop himself from doing it. "Otherwise, it won't do much."

Being as gentle as I can, I do as he says. The pain is hot and searing, like the cuts are all being reopened.

"Is it bad?" I ask.

"Yeah, 'fraid so," Jonah says. "You're probably gonna die."

I know he's trying to be funny, but the comment knocks the air out of me. Jonah seems to realize what he said because his face falls, and he drops his eyes to the ground.

Miles.

His name hangs between us like an unspoken secret. I'm not dying, but Miles is, and where am I? In a single-stall bathroom getting cleaned up by his best friend.

A stab of longing reverberates through my stomach. I miss him. I wish he were here with me right now, helping me patch up my hand instead of Jonah. He'd probably think the orange lighting makes the bathroom look like the Mos Eisley Cantina and compare Paulie to a fatter version of Greedo, with his friendly eyes that are too big for his head. No matter what Miles and I talked about, I know he would have me laughing so hard that I'd forget my hand ever hurt at all.

Being here with Jonah feels wrong. But it doesn't matter how much I miss Miles. He's never going to forgive me, not after I showed him that I'd sacrifice him for my brother.

Not even now that he's dying.

Jonah smiles as if to make things a little less weird, and I glimpse his straight, white teeth in the half light. I shut off the faucet. A single droplet of water falls onto the sink stopper. Slowly, another one builds, growing heavier and plumper but holding strong to the end of the spout.

Punching the wall was so stupid. I don't know what came over me. Every logical thought flew out of my brain.

I remember what the Soothsayer told me when she read my fortune on stage.

It appears you have been able to escape that monster, but he is never really gone.

She was talking about Dad.

Punching the wall is something Dad would have done. There's a flap of skin hanging from a knuckle. I try to fold it back into place, but some things don't mend that easy.

"Can you tell me something funny?" I ask Jonah.

He snaps his head up to look at me. "I'm not a funny guy."

"Can you try?" I do my best to ignore the throbbing in my hand. Jonah might not have Miles's knowledge of Star Wars or his talent for puns, but he can be funny without trying. In a sort of sardonic, I-don't-care-about-stuff way. "Just no stories about the moms you've hooked up with in this bathroom."

"It's not … well …" He rubs the back of his neck. "Whatever. Fine. Well, I don't know if this is funny, but one time back in middle school when my sister was still living with me at Moe's, she used to bring her friend Rachael around all the time. They would sit in her room to … I don't know, paint their nails or something." There's a wince on his face, like telling me this is actually making him uncomfortable.

"Wasn't your homecoming date named Rachael?"

Maybe it's the orange lighting, but Jonah's face looks bright red. "She's an old friend, but she wasn't my date. That doesn't matter. Anyway, Catherine and Rachael would do their girl shit, and I'd come in and sit on the bed to talk to Rachael because she was pretty or whatever, and it used to make Catherine so mad."

Imagining myself getting annoyed with Max for wanting to spend time with me makes a lump form in my throat. I would give anything for him to want to hang out with me again.

"This is a boring story," I say.

"Just wait." Jonah unscrews the cap from the Betadine bottle and pours the yellow liquid over my skin. It looks like the pulp of some rotten fruit clinging to my knuckles.

The liquid stings. I swear under my breath.

"I know." Jonah pours on some more. "I'm sorry." The golden-brown Betadine dyes the porcelain sink. "But anyway, one afternoon after school, I'm in my room when I get a knock on the door, and it's Rachael. She's acting all weird, telling me Catherine told her that I had a crush on her—"

"Ah, so you had a *crush* on her."

"I did *not* have a crush on her." He's lying, but it doesn't matter. "Catherine just said I did to embarrass me."

"Isn't your sister a lot older? Rachael, too?"

He screws the cap back on the Betadine and puts it back into the first aid kit. "Four years."

"I know you're into older women, and I hate to be the one to break this to you, but when you're in middle school, a four-year age gap is pretty serious."

"You're messing up my story."

"You haven't even gotten to the punchline."

"So, long story short," he says, fighting and failing to keep a smile from creeping onto his face, "I was so mad at Catherine for lying to Rachael that when they went out to grab dinner, I pissed in her humidifier."

His words take a second to sink in. He's looking at me sheepishly. A thick laugh bubbles out from the pit of my stomach, rising from my throat and surging out of me. "Your sister came home to a cloud of piss?"

"Walked straight into it," he says, which only makes me laugh harder. "Moe walked in there, too, and lost her shit at me. Chased me around the house with a flip-flop."

"A flip-flop?"

"Yeah. Thank Christ it was summer, or she'd have been after me with a boot."

I don't know if I'm in shock or if it's actually the funniest story I've ever heard, but I can't stop laughing. Jonah's eyes crinkle as he grins. He's looking at me weird, with a gleam in his eyes that makes my stomach flutter and floods my face with warmth.

I wipe the tears pooling in the corners of my eyes. "I can't believe you vaporized your own pee."

"Catherine kind of deserved it."

He's standing close to me. I guess he doesn't have a choice since it's a tiny bathroom, but he's close enough that I can smell him. I used to think Jonah stank. Like a mix of dirty clothes and cigarette smoke and bad breath. But now he smells like laundry detergent.

"Have you started showering?" I ask.

He hands me a paper towel to press against my hand. "I always used to shower. I just started using soap."

I pretend to gag. Jonah shakes his head like the entire conversation is dumb, but not like he doesn't want to be having it. What Francesca told me about Jonah liking me tugs at the back of my mind, and I search his face for any sign that it might be true, but I don't know what I'm supposed to be looking for. He's holding his bottom lip between his teeth as he takes a bottle of Neosporin from the first aid kit and puts it on the edge of the sink. Based on his reputation at school, I'll bet a lot of girls think he likes them and are disappointed when they find out he's not interested. I always thought he was a player, but the kind of player who flies under the radar and isn't a player for the sake of making conquests, but is just too stoned to consider the idea of committing to anyone. According to Miles, he's never had a girlfriend. Also, according to Miles, he meets older women at Duncan's and sleeps with them before sending them home to whatever husbands or partners they have.

Jonah slides the bottle of Neosporin to me. "You're going to want to put some of this on there." He rips open a package of gauze with his teeth, spitting out the strip of paper off the top. "And then you'll want to hold this onto it before wrapping it."

I glance over my shoulder, up at him. "Could you do it for me?"

Jonah pauses. I can see his spine stiffen, like he doesn't know whether to say yes, but he eventually steps closer to me. He curls his fingers as if to tell me to give him my hand. I do.

He squeezes a dollop of clear ointment onto my knuckles and rubs it in with his pointer finger. I'm surprised by how gentle he is. His palm is smooth. Callus-free. He wipes his finger on his pants and presses the gauze against my mangled skin.

I hiss in another breath. "Ow."

He cups his hand over the gauze, holding it there for a second. "I hate that he did this to you," he says.

"My dad didn't do this," I say. "I was the idiot who punched the wall."

"You know what I mean." Jonah lifts his hands away from mine. He unwraps the bandage from its roll with his bottom lip pulled between his teeth like he's concentrating, and then he wraps my hand. "What he said back there, about spoiling you … he didn't … did he do more than hit you?" The question closes like a hand around my throat. "You don't have to answer."

I don't know what's wrong with me, but there's a pressure in the pit of my stomach like I actually want to tell him. "Once, when I was twelve, in the bathroom at the Fun Palace," I say. Jonah pulls his lips into an angry line. "He told me not to say anything to my mom, and it didn't happen again, but every time I think about it, I feel this suffocating shame like something died in me that day, you know?"

Jonah nods, like he knows. "I'm sorry that happened to you."

I shrug, because what else am I supposed to do?

"I …" Jonah continues, "I know what it's like to feel that kind of shame, but he's the one who should be ashamed, not you."

"It's not that simple."

"It never is." Jonah wraps the feathery gauze around my fingers and back around my thumb. "But it should be."

He tapes the bandage in place. I expect him to drop his hand to his side, or maybe pack up the first-aid kit, but his finger stays there.

Sweat pricks my forehead. Is it hot in here, or is it just me?

"I'm sorry that somebody made you feel ashamed," I say. "You don't deserve that."

"My mom didn't mean to." Jonah hangs his head. "I mean, she was sick. She couldn't help it. But I still blamed myself, you know? After we lost the house, she promised she'd stop, but I kept finding needles in her stuff. I got rid of them whenever I found them, but she got pissed at me and started hiding them, and Catherine told me to stop looking for them, and I don't know … I remember sitting at the hospital after she OD'd wishing I'd done something. Or that maybe if I hadn't broken her needles, my mom wouldn't have left me here."

I remember Miles telling me that Jonah used to live in the tent city before they met and that he got put in foster care because his mom survived a heroin overdose before moving down to Florida without him.

Miles met Jonah in seventh grade. So if this happened when they were in the tent city …

Jonah must have been around eleven.

Picturing him as an elementary schooler snapping syringes in a camping tent makes my heart ache for him.

"It wasn't your fault," I say. "You can't blame yourself for her addiction."

He smiles, misty-eyed. "Like you said, it's never that simple."

"And like you said, it should be."

Even in the orange lighting, Jonah's blue eyes gleam. They are full of understanding. Not pity, because he knows better than to pity me, but the look is familiar. It takes me a second to realize where I have seen that look before.

It was the way Miles looked at me that night in his bedroom right before he told me he loved me.

Oh God.

Guilt closes around my throat. Miles may have broken up with me, but none of that matters right now. He needs us, and he deserves more than me standing in the bathroom of my dad's favorite bar trying to figure out whether his best friend has a crush on me or not.

I pull my hand away. Jonah snaps back to reality, turning away from me and tucking his hands into the pockets of his bomber jacket.

"I, uh, I'm going to go to Miles's house," I say. "I need to see how he's doing."

"Sure, cool. That's a good idea." Jonah takes his hands out of his pockets and closes the first-aid kit. "Call me if he needs anything."

"I don't have a—"

"Right. I knew that."

"I have an iPod. I can text through my email—"

"Sure, let's do that."

I give him my email address, and he types it into his phone without looking at me before tucking his phone back into his pocket.

"I sent you a text with my number," he says.

"I'll probably get it when I get WiFi."

"Well, let me know if he needs anything."

"Jonah …"

"Yeah?"

"Thank you."

But his face is closed now. Heat rising to my cheeks, I fumble with the bathroom lock and brush past an annoyed looking woman back toward the kitchen, giving Paulie a grateful smile. Paulie raises an eyebrow, like he knows Jonah all too well and is wondering what we got up to in there. I hope he can't tell how red I am as I half-run out the heavy door.

20

Shiloh

Gripping the greasy paper bag I'm carrying, I flip up the latch and open the gate to Miles's front yard.

The gardener glances up at the sound, and I stop like I've walked into a wall. Francesca's brother Richie wipes away the sweat beading on his forehead under the visor of his ugly Hot Wheels snapback. He's holding a rake and piling fallen leaves onto a wide square tarp.

"What are you doing here?" I ask.

Richie blinks at me like there's nothing going on behind his eyes. There probably isn't. "Gardening."

"Since when do you garden at Miles's house?"

"I answered an ad," he grumbles. "Since when is it any of your business?"

"Miles's parents thought hiring their son's bully was a good idea?"

"It's not like Dead Boy can do it." Richie digs the end of his plastic rake into the pile of leaves on the tarp. "He's not been at his best since he died and came back to life." He makes a wide-eyed face, like a cheap Halloween mask.

I tighten my grip on the paper bag. I wonder if Richie knows about the benmjöl. Probably not, or he'd steal it on general principles. It's drugs, after all. Francesca definitely wouldn't have told him. And besides, I bet there are a ton of rumors going around school about Miles, me, and how we rescued Max in the woods. Neither Miles nor I have been to school in weeks, and I'm sure that people are coming up with many crazy explanations for why.

"Dead Boy?" I ask. "Is that what you're calling him now? Real creative."

Richie starts raking again. "Eat shit."

"It'd be better than talking to you."

If I hadn't busted up my hand so bad, I'd punch him in the face. But Richie could snap my wrist with a single twist.

Jerking my chin up, I brush past him, go up to the front door, and knock. The sugar cookies from Ethel's are heavy inside the paper bag. Miles bought them for Max and me the day we first kissed. I don't know if he's feeling up to eating right now, but hopefully he will accept it as a peace offering.

As a promise that I will save him.

The door opens, revealing Miles's dad looking like a tired mad scientist from an eighties movie. His mouth pulls into a small frown.

"Hi, Mr. Barot-Renaud," I say with a friendly smile. "I'm here to see Miles. Can I come in?"

He shifts between his feet. "Miles is not feeling well."

Something sharp digs into my heart. "What's wrong? I mean … apart from not feeling well …"

"He has not come out of his room yet," he says. I notice his apron for the first time. The lenses of his glasses are splattered with something, and his eyes look a little crazed. "His mother is asleep as well. I believe she caught something at the hospital. Her teaching assistant was here again to drop off her students' papers, but the young man brought the wrong group. I am making them soup, and I cannot find our teaspoon measure." Broth drips from the soup ladle in his hand onto the glossy floor. "Can you come back another day?"

"Please," I beg him. "I will only stay for a couple of minutes. I really want to see him."

In the kitchen, something clangs, like a stainless steel lid jumping up from a cooking pot. Miles's dad pinches his eyes underneath his glasses as he nods and steps aside. I hurry through the door.

He looks down the hallway, like he's waiting for someone to come out of nowhere and yell at him. Probably Miles's mom. She didn't seem happy with me in the car yesterday. God, was it only yesterday? So much has happened since then. If Miles is worse today, she will blame me for it. Part of me is glad she's in bed and not the one opening the door.

"My mom used to tell me a teaspoon is a third of a tablespoon," I say. "But I'm sure it's going to turn up."

Miles's dad nods in acknowledgment and walks back into the kitchen, and turns down the stove.

I hurry down the hall toward Miles's room. His door is shut. I close my hand around the knob, but I pause.

I can't just open it. Not anymore.

"Miles?" I ask. "It's Shiloh. Can I come in?"

Something clatters, and I hear Miles curse under his breath.

He didn't say yes, but he also didn't say no. My heart pounding, I open the door and slip into the room.

Oh my God.

It's only been a day since I last saw Miles, but he looks like he hasn't slept all night. His bed has been stripped of its sheets, and his usually well-kept room is torn apart like a storm has blown through it. His blankets and pillows are on the ground, next to piles of papers and electrical cables.

Miles is hunched over his desk. His curls are heavy with grease and sweat, and they fall into his face. I run my eyes over his shoulder blades and the vertebrae jutting out of his skin. Oversized fleece pajama pants hang over the gauze bandage wrapped around his bony hips.

"Miles?" I put the bag of cookies on his nightstand. Cold liquid soaks through my sock, and I lift my foot to find I'm standing in a puddle. I don't even want to think of all the things that it could be. "I came to see how you were feeling."

Miles's ribcage expands and contracts like an animatronic robot. As I get closer, I notice the open jar of benmjöl on his desk next to a cup of water and a spoon coated in white powder. Miles is reaching into the tall jar with the teaspoon measure his dad was looking for, but his curled fingers are having trouble gripping it. The spoon clatters against the glass.

The suffocating smell of rot clogs my nose. I gag and close my hand over my mouth.

Is that smell coming from Miles?

The spoon wobbles. Guilt closes around my throat, and I point at the jar. "Can I help?"

Miles lifts his head. I gasp.

His eyelids are half-closed. His lips are parted, and a stretchy glob of saliva hangs out of them.

He tries to get the bone dust out again, but his fingers look like they're frozen in carbonite.

I rush over and take the teaspoon from him, scooping some powder into the cup of water. I stir until it's all mixed in and offer the concoction to Miles.

He's reaching out to take it when his stomach gurgles. Before I even know what's happening, he grips a pink hospital bucket with BAROT-RENAUD written on it in Sharpie. Clear liquid sprays out between his parted lips, sloshing up the sides.

I rub the space between his shoulder blades. His skin is burning hot and slick with sweat.

Miles shakes his head to dislodge the spit clinging to his bottom lip. It makes a splash in the swirling bucket.

"'Enmjöl." Miles tries to grab the jar, but his hands can't close around it. "I 'eed 'ore."

"The Soothsayer said to only take a teaspoon every day and that you have to be careful not to take too much." I hold the cup out to him. "Come on, just drink this."

He holds the cup between his wrists, and I steady it as he raises it to his lips, gulping it down.

He bends over the desk. Every tick of his alarm clock grates on my ear. After one minute passes, his breathing evens out. He squeezes his eyes shut. Opens and closes his jaw.

He snaps his head up. His eyes are wide and staring. His pupils are the size of pinpricks.

I rock back and forth between my feet. "Does the benmjöl make your eyes look like that?" I ask.

"Get out, Shiloh." His voice is hoarse, thin, and barely recognizable.

Goosebumps rise on my skin like a bunch of small spiders are walking along my arms, their legs brushing against my hairs and making them stand up.

He puts the pink bucket back on the desk. Seeing an opportunity to help, I pick it up and take it over to his bathroom.

Miles makes a disapproving grunt. "Don't touch that."

I dump the puke out into the sink. The chunks catch on the drain. I scoop them up with a piece of toilet paper and walk them over to the trash, trying not to let any spill out—

Miles knocks the paper towel out of my hand, sending the vomit onto the glass shower door. "Get out of my house! What is wrong with you? What don't you understand about me not wanting you here?"

The words hit me like a slap across the face. Every one of my muscles is frozen in place. "But I want to help you."

"*You* did this," he snaps, tears spilling over his cheeks. "You dragged me into this. I was in those woods because of you. If it weren't for you, Leonard would never have shot me."

I try to swallow the lump growing in the back of my throat. "I'm so sorry, Miles, I didn't mean—"

"It should have been you," he hisses. "You should be the one who's dying, and I wish you were."

Water pools in my eyelids, making Miles and his entire room swim. "I'm so sorry."

Miles walks into his room. He stands there, completely still for a second, before he grabs his debate trophy from last year and smashes it into the desk. The golden man snaps off.

"*Miles!*" I cry. "Miles, stop! You're so proud of those trophies."

"What does it matter?" he snaps. "I'm dying. I'll be gone by the end of the month. A stupid trophy won't change that."

"We're going to save you. I won't let you—"

"Shiloh, *get out*," Miles screams. *Slam. Slam.* He throws a heavy leather book on the floor. It lands with its pages splayed open on the ground. "I never want to see you again. Get out, Shiloh, go!"

I wipe my runny nose with the back of my hand as I mutter one last "I'm sorry" and do as I'm told.

21

FrANCeSCA

I fumble to close the cemetery gate behind me before hurrying over to Reverend Guessford.

"I traveled to the other side," I tell him, my lungs burning as I attempt to catch my breath. I am not fond of running, but I cannot believe I saw the other side, and I couldn't wait to tell my friends in the cemetery what I did.

Reverend Guessford looks up. He is sitting against the peeling pine tree, the spot where he usually sits around this time in the afternoon. The Reverend once told me that when he was alive, he was an avid reader, and if I remember correctly, he was fond of John Irving, as one of his books had a commentary on religion that he found rather interesting. Most souls cannot touch books, so I imagine life is rather boring for him, especially now that he has been in the cemetery for twenty years. I remember the soul in the old farmhouse throwing pebbles. It strikes me that if you can learn to throw stones in the afterlife, you can probably also learn to turn pages. Ella Ruggles's sister could throw books from Ella's bookcase. I remind myself to tell the

Reverend about this and assure him one day his soul will be powerful enough to read all over again.

The Reverend straightens the small white collar that denotes his former occupation. "How in the Lord's name did you manage that, my dear?" he asks.

"I put my head into an old cooking pot full of rainwater and went to the place where souls go after they fade away," I say, tucking my still-soggy curls behind my ears. They have dampened the fabric of my jacket, making my skin an easy target for the wind. "I had an out-of-body experience."

"Good heavens, Francesca. Where did this happen?"

I point over the waving stalks of corn beyond the cemetery wall, toward the Monroes' old farmhouse. Ensuring that I keep my voice low so that not everybody can hear, I tell Reverend Guessford how I felt the presence of souls on the other side, about being able to hear them, and how I stuck my head into the cooking pot Shiloh found for me. He listens patiently, scratching his bushy mustache until I have finished speaking.

"I continue to discover new abilities I did not know I possessed," I say. The skin on my open palms is wrinkled like the outside of a prune, the way hands get when you have been in the bath for too long. This is quite odd, as my hands have not been underwater. "I am hopeful that these abilities may be the key to finding and stopping Leonard."

Behind the Reverend, a ball of light bounds over to us, assuming the shape of a smiling Poppy.

My heart drops into my stomach. Poppy is paler than she was the last time I saw her, as if she is getting closer to fading away. She appears to be happy, and I do not wish to alarm her, so I pretend not to notice that she seems to be starting her own journey to the other side.

She points a finger at my wet curls. "Did you go swimming?"

"Not exactly," I say.

Mrs. Lewis glides up beside her, concern etching wrinkles into her forehead as she reaches out to touch my face. She often does this, as if she forgets that she cannot make contact.

"Francesca, sweetheart." Her fingers pass through my cheek. "You are all flushed."

"I'm all right," I say. "I have only been running."

"Oh, my dear, take more care."

Her words warm my body as if a hot towel has been wrapped around my shoulders. On the days that feel like nobody on this wide Earth cares, Mrs. Lewis is always there to ask me what's wrong, and she has seemingly endless patience for me.

"Why would you go running?" Poppy asks, the corners of her lips turning down. "Exercising sucks."

I'm about to tell her she's right when I realize I have not told the souls in the cemetery about throwing Poppy into Ashley Christensen. I turn back to Reverend Guessford. "Oh, and I also believe that I can move souls with my mind, as I moved Poppy yesterday when someone tried to attack me."

Mrs. Lewis sucks in a breath and clutches a hand to her chest. Poppy nods, as if backing me up. "She turned me into a ball of energy and threw me across the cornfield. It was awesome."

"I could use the energy that Poppy is made of to affect things in the material world," I say.

Reverend Guessford swallows this information like he's swallowing a large wad of gum. "While projecting yourself into the other side, you mentioned you saw some kind of opening. A gate, perhaps," he says.

I nod, remembering the small tear in the membrane I saw in the abandoned house.

"If what you say is true," he continues, "and you can manipulate the energy of the deceased telepathically, do you think you could open a gate of your own?"

I consider it. The barrier between the other side and our world appeared to be made of a thin, membrane-like material and crackled with energy in the same way souls do when I touch them. If I can move the souls with my mind, I suppose it is logical that I could also move the barrier—although I worry that doing so might take something from me that I could never put back.

"I'm not sure if I will retain my telepathic abilities while projecting," I tell him. "I may not be powerful enough."

Yet.

The Reverend hesitates for a moment before asking, "Could you try? I would like to pass over to my judgment. I was a man of God. I would like to be a soul of God, as well."

I wrap my arms around my stomach and try to press the guilty feeling down. After what I saw on the other side, I'm not sure if there is a judgment.

Heaven ain't all it's cracked up to be.

Who said that? Ella Ruggles? The poor Soothsayer? It may even have been Leonard.

My mother used to worship at the church in Mount Keenan where the Reverend was a pastor before he died twenty years ago. I remember little from my religious education because she died when I was six. But she was the one who introduced me to God, and my beliefs surrounding the afterlife must be similar to the Reverend's. I grew up with the belief that after we die, our soul passes on to either Heaven, Hell, or Purgatory, and the place we end up depends on how many times we have sinned or how badly. Despite my ability to see souls, I always believed the cemetery was a sort of landing place, a waiting area perhaps, and that once souls faded away, they faded to one of those three places to be purified or live out the rest of eternity.

As a man of God, the Reverend's disappointment will be worse than mine when he reaches the other side and sees the warped floor tiles, the colorlessness, and the unsettling differences between this world and theirs. I wonder if our Heaven has its own Heaven and if heavens exist around each other like our world and the other side, with gates pushing through to the next one like worms burrowing through the infinite layers of an onion, traveling through some kind of three-dimensional maze. I do not want to believe that what I saw is all that is waiting for us after we die. The last thing I wish to do is say anything that might upset him.

But a mixture of hope and vulnerability pools in his eyes. Reverend Guessford has been a steady figure in my life ever since I was first able to see the dead, telling me all the ways I could honor God in my life after my mother passed away and my father began his new family when I felt more alone than I ever had before. He has never asked me for anything in return. He is as much a member of my family as Richie is, if not more.

If he wants me to open a gate, I owe it to him to try.

"All right," I say, "but I cannot do it here, as the only way I could reach the other side was by submerging my head into water." I glance between the gravestones for a deep puddle or a bucket somebody might have left out overnight to fill with water, but there is nothing here.

"You could go to the swamp," a small voice suggests.

Gus appears in front of me, standing beside his identical ivory-haired twin, Charlie, and looking up at me through enormous eyes. Their mother, Esther, bounces her seven-day-old daughter on her hip, soothing the cooing baby to sleep.

My eyebrows draw together. "There's a swamp?"

"In the woods," Charlie explains, glancing at Gus. "We play there all the time."

"And there's water there."

A memory gnaws at me of a place I have not gone to in ages. Through the trees behind the cemetery is a large dip in the ground that becomes waterlogged after rainstorms. When I was a girl, I used to play hide and seek there with Mrs. Lewis, climbing over the patches of moss and being careful not to step on the skunk cabbage sprouting from the soggy dirt. In the winter, my feet would break the icy surface of the puddles, and I knew not to go out into the middle where the water was deep. When midwinter came and I was more confident it would hold me, I would walk out onto the ice, treading carefully with my arms held out for balance, looking down at the waterweeds frozen into place as my breath turned to clouds of steam. There have been quite a few rainy days this month. The marsh would have turned into a swamp, and I'd have to be careful. Shiloh would not be here to pull me out.

"You could get in there," Gus says, as if he has been reading my mind.

I'm not too fond of the idea of swimming in the murky standing water, not to mention that the water will be frigid, but I could put my head under it if I lay down on a clump of grass. I remember the souls playing with me on the icy winter pond, dressed in whatever they'd died in, sometimes pajamas or shorts and a t-shirt. Silly things such as temperature don't faze the dead, but they complicate matters for me.

I glance over at Reverend Guessford, whose eyes are brimming with hope. I have never seen him like this before. He's normally a serious man who keeps his emotions in check. He is counting on me.

I cannot let him down. "The swamp should work," I say, and Gus and Charlie high-five. "Could you take me there?"

Mrs. Lewis glances at the boys, frowning. "Are you sure that is such a good idea?"

"It's all right," I tell her. "I can do this."

"This way!" Gus calls, gesturing for me to follow as he leaps over the partially collapsed rock wall at the back of the cemetery.

Steadying my nerves, I climb over the uneven stones and walk deeper into the woods.

The leaves under my shoes are damp. My feet are the only ones that make a sound.

I glance over my shoulder. Only a few souls have followed us, for which I am grateful. I'd rather not have an audience. I see Mrs. Lewis, Poppy, Gus, Charlie, Esther, and of course, the Reverend.

Do you think she can do it? I hear Esther whisper, most likely to Mrs. Lewis.

I am worried about her getting into the swamp, Mrs. Lewis replies. *It is not safe there.*

I hope what she's saying is true, because I'd really like to see my

I remember that little boy on the other side, bursting into tears when the opening closed before he could return to his mother. Is this all we are, spirits in corporeal or other forms who long to be somewhere other than where we actually are?

Perhaps we all just want our mothers.

Gus points ahead, and Charlie bounces up and down. "It's right through those trees!"

The ground under my feet is getting soggy. Dark mud rises over the toes of my clogs, and I dread the hour later on today when I will have to clean them off.

When Richie was in middle school, he kept a toad as a pet. It did not move often. It just sat underneath its lamp, waiting for crickets to inch close enough for it to gobble them up. One day, the toad died, but Richie did not notice for nearly two weeks and continued feeding it crickets until they overran the terrarium and started trying to leap out of it. Such a horrible smell had started leaching from the tank that he had to throw the whole thing away. The toad's tongue had swollen up and forced its mouth open, and it looked as if the creature's body was about to explode like a gremlin in a microwave.

The swamp smells similar to the terrarium that Richie had before he discovered that his toad was dead. The water is so murky that it's nearly black. I cannot tell how deep it is, but if I lie on my back and tilt my head backwards, I will at least be able to plug my ears.

I glance at Mrs. Lewis, who scowls at Reverend Guessford.

"This cannot be good for her," she says to him.

"If you do not wish to do this, you do not have to," the Reverend says, but his voice is thin.

"I can do it," I assure him. "Do not worry."

I pull off my clogs, jacket, and sweater, and I hang them from the low branches of a tree. The decomposing leaves are slippery against my bare feet. It is hard not to think of the leeches that could be wriggling underneath my toes as I wade out into the water. A stick pokes the sole of my foot. The water only comes up to my ankles.

I glance over at the souls standing between the trees. It's bewildering how out of place they seem in the forest, their pale figures barely visible against the bright green and dark brown hues. The Reverend is looking at me with a hopeful expression fixed on his face. My heart hammers in my chest, and I search for Mrs. Lewis, who glides over to me with a reassuring smile.

"I am here, honey. You're all right," she says. "You are not doing this alone."

Warmth radiates through me

I am all right. This is all right.

Slowly, I lower myself into the icy marsh water, and the air leaves my lungs in a gasp. Concern flashes across Mrs. Lewis's face, and it's the last thing I see before I close my eyes.

Murky water plugs my ears, making my head feel like a bell that's been stuffed with cotton wool. The soft bed of leaves presses against my back as I try to remember how I did this while I was inside the old farmhouse. There, I heard the voices before I even tried to listen for them, but I do not hear any voices here.

I wonder if I have to do this in a place where the barrier is already thin, rather than somewhere where there is water. I should have thought of that before, but I will never understand my strange abilities unless I practice them. For a moment I wonder where they came from. Why I was chosen for this, if indeed I was. Should I even think of myself as chosen for this ability like the Soothsayer or Leonard were for theirs, or does everything come down to chance?

A far-away buzzing sound reverberates in my ear. A bug tickles my face, and I sit up, turning my head so that the water runs out of it.

Mrs. Lewis hurries over to me. "Are you all right?"

My jaw chatters, but I clamp my teeth together so that she does not see I am cold. "Yes, it was only a bug."

"How about you come out of there?" Mrs. Lewis says. "We can try this on a warmer day."

I shake my head and lean back into the black water.

The surface closes on top of me. I lie absolutely still. The bug must be gone because I cannot hear it buzzing anymore. A numb tingling creeps over my body, and my lungs burn from lack of oxygen. It feels as though dozens of tiny pins from my mother's old pin cushion are being stabbed into the pores in my skin. I resist the urge to wiggle my fingers or toes and allow myself to sink deeper into my consciousness, allowing myself to forget that I even have a body—

Do you hear that girl crying?

A clear, undeniably female voice bounces around my ear canal, and my chest blooms. I made contact with the other side. The voice is talking about a girl, but I'm not sure which one. They cannot mean me, as I am not crying.

A soft sob follows. It appears to belong to a child.

Above the surface of the water, I hear Mrs. Lewis saying something in a worried tone. I do not want her to worry. I am really not very cold anymore.

I lift my face out of the water, making sure my ears stay under, and extend my hand. Perhaps I could do it like this, just holding my ears below the surface while keeping my mouth and nose above it. I could stay on the other side longer if I could breathe in this world. But although I can't hear, my other senses distract me. I can taste the dirty water on my lips, smell the horrible swampy mud, and see the souls hovering around me, waiting for some kind of answer. I must put my entire head under if I want to cross over.

Perhaps holding my hand will make Mrs. Lewis less worried about me. "Mrs. Lewis, may I hold your hand?" I ask.

She glances down at the murky water dripping from my palm. "Sweetheart, your lips are turning blue. I believe it's time for you to get out."

"I promise I'm all right," I assure her. "Please, will you hold it?"

Pulling her lips into a thin line, Mrs. Lewis agrees, and I wrap my hand around hers, wincing as a burning cold sensation melts through my skin. Keeping a tight grasp on her, I sink back underneath the surface—

Immediately, I soar up from my body into the air. I turn my hands over in front of my face and let out a victorious yip.

I made it.

I am on the other side.

I glance around. The forest had been full of the oranges and browns of autumn when I walked down to the swamp, but now everything is gray, like all the color has been sucked out of the world by a vacuum cleaner. The trees are stark and leafless against a slate-gray sky. Skunk cabbage sits in shriveled, black clumps, looking like it died a long time ago. The dried-out swamp is covered in a web of dense roots and sticky black mud that looks like tar.

"Where are we, dear?"

I turn to find Mrs. Lewis standing beside me, her face twisted in fright as she glances around.

I glide through the air for a moment before catching myself on a clump of dead vines that dangle from a tree. "Did you cross over with me?"

"Perhaps so. Are we in Heaven?" Her voice breaks on the word.

I'm not sure how anyone could believe this is Heaven. Not when it is so barren and cold.

I grab her hand, and her wispy fingers entwine with mine. "Come, Mrs. Lewis, let us try to open a gate for the Reverend."

"A-all right, dear."

I search for something resembling the membrane from the abandoned house, but I sense nothing. But that is likely because there are no openings to sense.

"Is anybody there?" I ask. What a silly thing to ask. A bubble of laughter escapes from me.

I glide forward through the woods. The shadows are dark in

here, hanging between trees. The swamp is much drier in this dimension, and it's hard for me to get my bearings.

"I don't like it here, Francesca," Mrs. Lewis says. "I'd rather like to go back now."

I spot a glimmer of crackling energy at the bottom of the tree.

"Oh, Mrs. Lewis, look!" I get down on my belly and scoot up close. It's a membrane, exactly like the one I saw in the farmhouse. Through the veil, I make out the vague outlines of trees and the tall fronds of growing ferns sprouting up from between their roots. I realize I'm looking back into the world of the living from the other side. I can see my body still half-submerged in a pool of water in the bog as Reverend Guessford looks on, rubbing his beard in his anxiety. But in that world, Mrs. Lewis is no longer hovering over me.

I train my eyes on the small gateway. I concentrate the whole of my mind and the power of my will into my vision and imagine miniature invisible hands reaching out toward the membrane, reaching through toward Reverend Guessford. Electricity burns beneath the surface of my skin and presses against the backs of my eyeballs the way tears do before I cry.

"Please open," I whisper.

The membrane quivers. Ripples radiate through it as if from a pebble dropped into a pond, but no tear appears.

Open, I shout inside of my head. *Please, open!*

Larger ripples move through the membrane as if I am punching it with my mind. But no opening appears.

"Could we leave this hideous place now?" Mrs. Lewis says, shuddering as she inspects a mass of sticky slime running down the side of the tree. "I don't want to stay here."

"Hold on to me. I will try to return now."

Mrs. Lewis squeezes my hand. I glance down at our interlocking fingers and remember what it felt like to lie down in the water. My toes must be numb by now. I focus on the bugs floating around me or the leeches lurking underneath the soggy leaves—

My eyes fly open. I sit up, dirty water running off my body.

The Reverend appears in front of me, his expression widening in hope. "Did you open a gate?"

"I was so close," I say, fighting to get the words out through my chattering teeth. His face falls. "I'm so sorry, Reverend, but I was not powerful enough. Mrs. Lewis, I am so glad you were holding my hand, because you came along with me. Without you there, being on the other side would have been scary."

Poppy's voice is small and sounds far away. "Where *is* Mrs. Lewis?"

I glance behind myself to where Mrs. Lewis had been, but she is nowhere to be seen.

22

JONAh

It's quiet in the computer lab, except for the tick of the clock as the hand inches toward 3:25. This is only my second week in detention, and already I want to kill myself. Don't ask me how I'm going to survive this until the end of the year.

But they had to punish someone for breaking into Principal Orr's office. Because Miles and Shiloh are out of school, Francesca and I are the only ones left for them to take it out on. Shiloh also hit that janitor with a mop, which they weren't happy about, but I was the one who got the lecture about how I'd end up in juvie if the guy pressed charges. *But there were circumstances*, Principal Orr said. A missing child, loyalty, and friendship. Emotions were running high. There was the usual bullshit from Call-me-Bill, who did his friendly uncle act and told us he had to punish us for what we did, but it hurt him to do so, and if anything was on our minds, we should talk to him man-to-man. I got out of there as fast as I could.

Francesca is sitting two rows ahead of me with her notebook open. She wasn't the one who jabbed the janitor's beer belly with a mop, and she wasn't caught like Shiloh, Miles, and I were. She wouldn't have gotten detention if she'd kept her mouth shut, but she confessed to having been involved, telling Principal Orr that she was "as guilty as Shiloh." She's too good a person to be put through so much crap, but hey, here she is.

I glance down at my phone. It's tucked under the table, out of sight from Mrs. Dunsenberry, who seems more interested in her crossword than anything I'm doing. My text to Shiloh swims on the glowing screen.

> Any bruises?

That's a dumb thing to say. I want to ask her how she's doing, but if I ask if she has bruises, then she's going to think I'm laughing at her because her dad hits her, which I'm obviously not. But if I don't text her, am I an ass?

I'm an ass for asking if she has bruises, that's for sure. I slide my phone back into my pocket.

She asked me to wrap her hand. She could have done it herself, but she asked me. Every part of me wanted to kiss her. If she hadn't turned away, I'd have done it. Because I'm a stupid, self-destructive bastard.

I should have minded my own damn business and told her to wash it out at home.

The second the bell rings, I grab my bag and head over to Francesca, who's got a death grip on her pencil and is digging the graphite so hard into the paper that it's flaking.

I nudge her shoulder. "You good there?"

Francesca drops the pencil onto the desk and sniffles like she's crying. Hold on. Is she crying?

"I'm sorry," she says. "I'm all right, I promise."

"Clearly you're not."

She zips up her bag and hurries out of the classroom with her head down.

I follow her, but on my way to the door Mrs. Dunsenberry side-eyes me. I side-eye her right back and raise both eyebrows, making Mrs. Dunsenberry drop her gaze. Teachers are like cops.

Some want to do a good job, but others prefer to mark time until their pensions arrive. Mrs. Dunsenberry is pretty old. She's been at this school since the dawn of time.

I catch up to Francesca. "What happened?"

A tear drops from her eye, and she wipes it away quickly. "I can't believe she's gone."

Oh. She's got to be sad about the Soothsayer's death. Don't get me wrong, it was definitely sad. This might make me sound like a selfish asshole, but every time I think about the murder, I wonder where her orb is and who is going to end up owning my soul. When I found her body, I should have stolen that thing. I don't know why I didn't. I saw blood, and I panicked.

Every time someone knocks on Moe's door, I keep expecting it to be a cop asking me about the Soothsayer's murder. But I've heard nothing about it. Nothing on the news … nothing.

But that won't comfort Francesca. I try to think of something that might help her.

"What happened to her really sucks," I say.

Francesca lets out a low whine, drawing the attention of a group of drama kids clumped by the door to the gym. They look at us, nudge each other, and start whispering. "I'm the reason she's gone."

"Uh …" This is news to me. "You're telling me you were the one who stuck the knitting needles in her eyes?"

Francesca glances at me in confusion before she gasps and shakes her head. "Oh! No, not Ms. Wilma. I'm talking about my friend Mrs. Lewis. I made her disappear. She held my hand while I projected to the other side. I believe I must have brought her over with me and left her behind, because she was gone when I woke up." New tears tumble out of her eyes, as if she's reminded of what happened. "The last thing she said to me was 'I don't want to stay here.' And I abandoned her."

"I feel like I'm missing something here."

Francesca tells me about astral projecting again down at the cemetery and her ghost friend going to the other side with her.

"She stayed there?" I ask, trying to figure out why she's crying. "Isn't that where she'd go anyway?"

"But she was not happy over there, Jonah," she says. "She kept asking if I could take her back. Her husband hasn't faded away yet, you see, and now she's on the other side without him. She's all alone."

I'm about to say that it changes nothing, that Francesca shouldn't be crying because it's not like she killed the woman—Mrs. Lewis was dead anyway, and she just went where she was going to go. But Francesca's clearly upset about it, so saying something like that won't make her feel better. The ghosts are as real to her as people are.

"This is all my fault," she sobs.

Before I get the chance to think about what I'm doing, I stop walking and pull her into a hug. I drape my arms over her shoulders and rest them on her backpack. I'm too tall for her to do the same, so she holds the sides of my backpack like it's a pregnant stomach. I'm pulling away when she grabs hold of me, letting out a heavy sob into the front of my T-shirt.

I pat her on the backpack because I'm bad at comforting people. "You're okay."

"I didn't mean for it to happen," she says, her voice muffled against the dirty fabric. I've worn it two days in a row now, and it probably doesn't smell that great. "She was the only person I had."

"The only person?" I say, a smile easing its way onto my face. "Not anymore, Frankie. You've got us." I hope that doesn't sound weird.

I feel her nod against my shoulder. She's not crying as hard now, so I've got to be helping a little.

"We aren't going anywhere," I say. "Unless, you know, we kick the bucket, and that'll still be okay because you can be friends with our ghosts."

Francesca laughs. The thought of her being buddies with my ghost makes me smile, too, until I realize that she'll never meet my ghost because I'll be stuck in Wilma's creepy orb.

"I always knew I would lose her one day." Francesca's voice shakes. "But I wasn't ready to say goodbye."

"No one's ever ready," I say. Kelsey, a blonde I got with last year, walks by with a group of soccer players. She snickers at us, and I flip her off. For someone who cries after sex, she's got no right to judge. "One day, hopefully a long time from now, you'll see her again."

"Unless I astral project again, then perhaps I can see her sooner."

"Or that, sure." I give her an encouraging shoulder pat. "Come on, let's get out of here. Want to grab custard again or something?"

"I'd prefer to be alone."

"Yeah, that'd work, too." Either way, I'm ready to leave school.

Outside, I squint for a second as my eyes adjust to the mid-afternoon glare. The days are getting shorter, so it's already inching toward sunset. Because school got out an hour ago, the only people still here are the kids in clubs or on sports teams and the only cars left stick out against the empty parking lot. Especially the patrol car with the cop leaning against its hood.

Oh, that smug bastard.

Officer Zweering waves me over.

I do a theatrical look around, then point to my own chest. "Me? Surely not, officer," I say, and Francesca giggles.

Officer Zweering gives me a flat-eyed stare that belongs in a cop show.

"That police officer is looking at you like he is getting ready to eat you up," Francesca says.

She's got that right. He's wearing the look of a cop who has something on you, who is preparing to wave a fat *gotcha* finger in your face.

"Go home," I tell Francesca. "I'll handle this."

"Are you sure? I can wait."

"I'm good."

Francesca wipes her eyes before walking off down the road. I guess she's tired, and not in the headspace to ask questions.

I head over to Zweering. "What, are you stalking me now?"

"You know," he says with a smirk, "something didn't sit right with me after our first conversation about Eleanor Ruggles's stolen property." I steel my face. "You say you didn't take her monocle, but she assures me you did. And the fact is, you were at her house *hours* before a man turned up dead."

"How many times do I have to tell you? I didn't steal the damn monocle."

"I got to thinking that it might be connected," he continues, as if I said nothing. "So I started keeping tabs on you. Kids like you"—he says *kids* like he isn't recently out of his teens himself —"They don't think the rules apply to them. I understand. Life has dealt you a rough hand. But the rules apply to everyone. You can't decide right from wrong just because you believe what you're doing is okay." He pauses, as if for effect, and I try to figure out where he's going with this. "You know, the detectives are looking into who killed that old man out there in the woods, but I think there's more to this than one dead man. I know he kidnapped a child, but the law would have dealt with him. And it won't stop at one man, will it?"

"What are you talking about?"

"I saw you take that girl around back in that alley yesterday, the same girl who murdered that old man." He raises his eyebrows like he's trying to get me to tell him something.

I can't believe this asshole is following me. I hope he doesn't see my surprise. "Oh, that was you trailing us? I didn't recognize you without the giant stick up your ass."

Officer Zweering pulls his sunglasses off his face, revealing sharp eyes that look capable of pinning someone to the floor. I bet he practices that expression in the mirror at night. Underneath it, he's the same unsure recruit who was in my house the other day, but his eyes glint like he knows he's onto something, and suddenly I picture him in high school—the scrawny, overeager, unpopular teachers' pet who loved the rules, cared too much about appearances, and hated the older kids who got away with breaking the rules *and* pulled the girls he was into. Back in school, he was the guy who told on the guys lighting up under the Upside-Down Tree. He's going to grow up to be the kind of adult who confuses right and wrong with lawful and unlawful because he doesn't have the imagination to think for himself. In other words, he'll be a perfect cop.

He must hate everything I stand for. I'm no psychologist, but maybe he thinks making my life hell will stop him from feeling so jealous.

"I can't pretend I know what's going on here, but I will figure it out," he says. I've got to hand it to him, he's not all stupid. "I have plans, and big ambitions. I will not stop until I get to the bottom of this."

"You'd be better off leaving it to the grownups. You're out of your depth and you haven't learned to swim without armbands yet, Officer Zweering."

If he's trailing me and taking pictures, he might be annoying enough to be a problem. God knows I'm putting myself in enough trouble. Sooner or later, he'll catch me in some deep shit, and depending on what it is, it might even be enough to put me away.

But I can't let him know that he's gotten to me. That's my rule, the one thing that lets me keep my dignity.

I never let them see they've got to me.

"Aren't you a patrol officer?" I say. "How about you stick to giving parking tickets and let the detectives do the actual work?"

I head off. But before I reach the sidewalk, he's calling after me:

"A word of advice, Jonah," he says. "Start saving that drug money. After I'm through with you, you're going to need an excellent lawyer."

I cut through the woods to go back to Moe's. If Zweering is following me home, he can't drive his car through here.

I take a long drag from my dab pen and hold the vapor in my closed mouth for a second before breathing it in. Zweering's a crazy asshole, scaring me like that. But I wouldn't be scared if the threat weren't real, and if he didn't have an actual chance of finding something on me. I'd say he's deluded or has bad instincts, but he's right about one thing.

This is more complicated than a missing kid who got found again.

But Shiloh and I aren't the bad guys.

I wonder if he'll put it together with the ghost thing. I breathe out, laughing on the exhale. Zweering's got no imagination. The only way anyone could ever figure out the connection is if they also believed in ghosts and knew that Francesca could see them, and something tells me Zweering will have a tough time doing that.

I crank up the volume on the Cobain song blaring through my headphones. There are no trails out here. It's all untouched woods, which is a pain in the ass when you're trying to walk, because there are roots and rocks and hidden logs lurking under the leaves ready to trip me.

I'm raising the pen to my lips for another hit when something yanks me backward.

I land on my back. The breath flies out of me. My pen tumbles to the ground. So do my headphones, cutting the music off and replacing it with the sound of crunching leaves.

A hooded figure in a rubber face mask stands over me. A backward snapback secures a long black nun's veil to its head. Flames decorate the sides of their cap. They've got a knife in one hand.

I scramble to my feet. "The hell are you doing—"

The nun swipes the blade at me. I duck under his thick arm—he's got to be a he, because no girl I know has arms that big. He plunges the knife toward my stomach.

I leap out of the way and run. I barely make it two steps

before he yanks my backpack a second time. The nun swings me around and tries to stab me again, but I stop his arm. He presses the knife down. I strain against him. That stupid Nirvana song plays from my headphones on the ground, barely audible, like a pathetic action soundtrack.

I shove the knife away with all my strength. The nun drags the blade across my shoulder.

Pain shoots through my back. Blood runs down my chest from the gash. Before the crazy nun tries to stab me again, I turn and run toward the road as fast as I can.

23

Shiloh

I chew on the end of my pencil, spitting a chunk of eraser onto the living room carpet. Mom and Max aren't home. Max has his first appointment with his trauma specialist today, and while I desperately wanted to be there, I needed to use the computer, and I needed to use it while Mom was not home to see what I was using it to do.

But I can't find anything about benmjöl on the Internet. It makes no sense. From the way the Soothsayer talked about it, it sounded like a common enough drug, but there's nothing online that tells me how it's made or how to get more of it.

Not that getting more would save Miles, but it might buy him more time.

I scroll through the online forum I'm reading about slowing the decomposition of a human body.

Stan Citron: *Eating alum before death might stop you decomposing, but it won't stop you from dying. It might even kill you sooner.*

Eva Abidan: *The body of Napoleon Bonaparte remained in good condition for many years following his death. This is because he was poisoned with arsenic. The arsenic in his tissues preserved him and kept bacteria from growing.*

Stan Citron: *I heard he died because his wallpaper had arsenic in it or something.*

Eva Abidan: *Actually, there is good evidence that many people from his time suffered from low levels of arsenic poisoning, both from the wallpaper, which as you mentioned contained arsenic, and also because some women used arsenic as makeup, to make their complexion fashionably pale.*

Stan Citron: *Wow. That's interesting!*

No, it's not interesting at all. One Google search for alum tells me that it's a chemical compound that would kill Miles as fast as formaldehyde if we pumped him full of it. Another search on Napoleon's slow decomposition only brings up articles detailing his penis, which wasn't properly preserved. Apparently, it has been compared to a piece of leather, a shriveled eel, and a strip of beef jerky, which I quickly add to the list of images I never needed in my head.

This is pointless. None of this is going to save Miles.

The only thing that will save Miles is getting him a new host.

I don't think there's any other way. Miles's body has already decomposed past the point of saving, and taking benmjöl will only mask the symptoms of decay. Opioids or morphine will do the same thing—they'll cure the pain, but they won't solve the problem. They might even create additional problems in the form of addiction or dependency. If he has time to get addicted to anything.

I flex my fingers inside my gauze bandage. Jonah was right about my hand, but the pain's got nothing on the itching. Blood repeatedly seeps into the torn-up skin. Punching something would hurt a lot right now, but maybe it would stop me from hearing Miles's voice in my head.

You should be the one who's dying, and I wish you were.

I blink away tears as I stare at the screen. I didn't mean for any of this to happen, but that doesn't mean it's not my fault. So I'm going to save him. He might never forgive me, but at least he'll still be alive.

One note I made on a piece of scrap paper stands out to me. *The hospital.* That's where we will have to find Miles a new host. The funeral home is out of the question because the bodies would have all been dead for too long, and killing someone is also not an option, for obvious reasons. Enough people die at hospitals that Francesca might sneak Miles's soul into a newly dead body before anyone notices. Looking at Miles yesterday, I'll bet his parents will rush him to the hospital soon, where all the doctors and experts in the world won't be able to figure out what's wrong with him.

I know it's a stretch. Jonah's going to say it is, but I don't know what else to do.

The eraser pops off the end of the pencil and into my mouth. I gag briefly and spit it out into my bandaged hand.

What came over me at Duncan's yesterday? Why did I ask Jonah to wrap my hand for me? He probably thought it was weird. I would have thought it was weird if he'd said it to me. But … I don't know. I have no excuse for it except for how close he was standing to me.

And what Francesca said about him liking me.

Would he have taken me to Duncan's if he didn't like me? He hung back to make sure I was okay after Dad came into that farmhouse. I know what he thinks about cops. And he actually looked worried about my hand.

I don't know. But I know that I have to tell him about my idea for saving Miles, because I can't do it alone and I'm not going to suggest it to Francesca before we have a plan.

Collecting all the scraps and notes from around the keyboard so that Mom doesn't find them when she gets home, I pull on my boots and head out the door.

There's a chain-link fence surrounding Jonah's yard. As I go to unlatch the gate, an enormous dog bounds up to me, barking so loudly that I flinch. The dog's eyes are cloudy and unfocused, darting around like it's trying to find what it's barking at. It doesn't look aggressive, just old and pretty much blind. Fading away as it creeps closer to death.

Like Miles.

"Hey, there," I say, so the dog doesn't think I'm a threat. Max has been begging to get a dog for years, but Dad never let us have one because of how much they shed. I'm glad he didn't cave. Our house would not be a safe place for a dog. But if Dad never comes back … who knows, maybe we could get one.

I want to reach through the fence to pat it on its thick head, but I don't know if it would like that very much.

The door to the house swings open.

"Bessie."

I glance up to see a short, middle-aged woman with bronze skin and a tight ponytail pulling her hair out of her face. Her eyebrows draw together in confusion. "Help you?" she asks.

This must be Aunt Moe, Jonah's foster mom, who whacked him with a flip-flop after learning about the pee in the humidifier.

"Is Jonah home?" I ask.

There's a flash of movement as Jonah appears behind her, looking as surprised to see me as Aunt Moe was.

The surprise doesn't last long, though. He turns to Aunt Moe and says, "It's okay, she's my friend."

Moe mutters something to Jonah before heading back into the house. Jonah gestures for me to come in.

I point at Bessie. "Is she friendly?"

"Totally harmless," he says. "Just blind and dumb."

I let myself in through the latched gate and hold my good hand out, palm down, to the dog. As soon as Bessie smells me, she stops barking and starts licking my fingers. I laugh a little. It tickles.

"Come on in," Jonah says, waving me inside. His voice is thin and urgent, like something's wrong.

"Are you okay?" I ask, walking up the creaky, unpainted stairs.

He says nothing and waits for Bessie to trot in before closing the door behind me.

I glance around Jonah's house. I don't know what I was expecting it to be like in here, but this isn't it. My house has dark wood, deep red rugs, and flickering yellow light bulbs, but his house is saturated with color. Potted plants with giant, heart-shaped leaves hang above the front entrance. The couch in the living room has plump magenta and orange striped pillows on it. Dad would have lost his mind if Mom brought those home, but I love them. The armchairs next to the fireplace look like they're made of fake cow's hide, all white with brown spots on them. The air smells like the cinnamon-scented candles Mom used to buy before Dad said they gave him a headache. There's a scruffy old dog bed by the sofa, covered in white hairs.

"Come on, Shiloh," Jonah says.

A multicolored playpen sits on the carpet, and a red-faced toddler in a hot pink onesie grips the side of it as she stares out at me with enormous eyes. A single tuft of hair sticks up from the top of her head.

I glance up at Jonah, who hasn't lost the panicked look on his face, and back at the baby. "Is that your sister?"

"No, well, kind of," he says. "That's Kaylee. She's Moe's biological daughter."

"They're all my kids," Aunt Moe says warmly, walking over to lift Kaylee out of the playpen and nuzzling her nose into hers. "Not one more than the others, and don't you forget that. Jonah, keep your door open."

"Yep," he says, heading down the hall.

I wave bye to Aunt Moe before hurrying after Jonah and through the door he holds open for me. He closes it most of the way, leaving a gap of about an inch, and hits the light switch.

Unlike the rest of the house, this room looks a little more like where I'd expect Jonah to live. His twin bed is unmade. There's a full hamper in the corner, and it smells kind of like my room does, like sweat and hair grease and unwashed laundry. But it also smells strongly of men's deodorant, which my room doesn't, and there are decorations on his wall. A framed Nirvana poster hangs above his desk, next to AC/DC and some blonde woman playing a battered-looking bass. He's got some CDs on his nightstand and a Led Zeppelin album on vinyl hanging on the wall, the iconic black and white one with the burning airship.

"It's the Hindenburg," he says.

"What?"

"The airship on the record cover." He points. "It's not the band's original artwork. It's a picture of when the Hindenburg caught fire in 1937 near New Jersey. Heavily processed, of course."

"You sound like Miles," I say, meaning it as a compliment, but Jonah shrugs and rubs his arm.

Jonah doesn't look like the kind of guy to frame his posters. I wonder if Aunt Moe got that done for him. Maybe to make him feel at home after he moved in.

"The walls used to be purple," Jonah says, almost as if he's reading my mind, "but Moe let me paint them after a year."

Imagining how much young Jonah must have hated having a purple room makes me smile. I wonder what he would say if he saw the Justin Bieber poster in my closet.

I notice a guitar half-tucked under his bed. "Do you play?"

Jonah crosses the room to swipe a JUUL and a few other things into his nightstand. He stares at me, standing in front of the drawer, before whispering, "We have a big problem."

"Another one?" I ask, and he nods. "What kind of problem?"

Jonah glances at the open door and lowers his voice even more. "I got attacked by a nun."

I picture an old woman in a black habit swinging a knife at his head, but the image is so ridiculous it's all I can do not to laugh. I shouldn't laugh. Maybe I didn't hear him right. "A what?"

"A *nun*," he repeats, louder this time. "Or a guy disguised as a nun. He had a mask on. I couldn't see his face, but he jumped me on my way home from school and tried to kill me." Jonah strips off his sweatshirt and tugs up the sleeve of his peace sign T-shirt, revealing a wad of blood-stained gauze taped to his shoulder. Oh God. "He only got me here. But I thought I was going to die."

"This happened just now? Right out there in the street?"

"No, I took a shortcut through the woods. The guy was waiting, or he chased me in, I don't know. I was cleaning it out when I heard Bessie barking, and, you know, I didn't want Moe to see it." He drops the sleeve of his T-shirt. "Shiloh, I think Leonard's trying to kill us."

Jonah is breathing fast, his eyes wide and panicked like he really did run for his life. I am overcome by the urge to walk over there and hug him.

I force my feet to stay where they are. "He wasn't trying to kill us before. Why start now?"

"I don't know," Jonah says. "But I'm telling you, this guy was aiming for my throat, and the knife was easily four inches long."

"Maybe he's pissed that we're trying to catch him?"

"He's definitely pissed about something."

"Could this be a good thing? I mean, if he's going after us, all we have to do is get his disguise off to find out who his host is."

"And then what?" Jonah asks bitterly. "We kill him? Is that the plan?"

"I ..."

"If we do that, we'd only be killing whoever's acting as his host. Not him."

"Well, *we* wouldn't have killed that person. Leonard had to kill them before entering the body."

"The cops won't know that. It'll look like we killed some innocent guy. I've got some kiddie cop with his eye on me as it is." He rolls his eyes. "He's trying to make his name by solving the Mystery of the Monocle."

I start to reply, but it hits me that he's right. We have been so focused on catching Leonard that we haven't made a plan for what we'll do with him if we catch him.

Jonah pinches the bridge of his nose. "Listen. We need to talk to Frankie and make some kind of plan. In the meantime, you shouldn't walk around alone. I'm going to tell Miles and Frankie, too."

This is all so messed up. I walked here alone. I didn't even think about Leonard trying to ambush me.

"I can ask Francesca if she wants to sleep at my house," I say. "I don't like the idea of her living alone in the trailer. Maybe you could look out for Miles."

"Miles isn't going to school right now."

"Well, maybe Francesca and I can meet up with you and then we can all walk to school together?"

"That could work."

I wonder if Leonard has turned Dad's gun in to the cops. That wouldn't kill us, but it might get me charged with murder, and getting me put in jail has the same effect as killing me. I haven't heard anything yet. Babin and Finnegan haven't come to talk to me or Mom. But Leonard's got the gun, so we don't have much time.

"Until this is over, we should all stick together," I say. "I couldn't live with myself if something happened to … I wouldn't want you to …"

He gives me a small smile. But unlike his usual smiles, there isn't a hint of sarcasm embedded in it. "I don't want anything to happen to you, either."

Warmth floods my cheeks. I give him a dutiful nod and sit on the edge of his bed. A pile of bloody gauze is piled on his sheets from when he was wrapping his arm. I glance back up at him. "You should probably finish cleaning your arm."

The sarcasm returns, twinkling behind his bright blue eyes. God, his eyes are so blue they look artificial. Only heavy doses of food coloring could create that color. "Could you do it for me?"

I freeze. That's what I said to him in the bathroom at Duncan's. Butterflies flap around in my stomach as I try to figure out if he's serious.

But he laughs, shaking his head and dispelling my nerves. "I'm kidding, Scooby. I can do it myself."

He climbs onto the bed, pulling up his shirt sleeve so it bunches up above his shoulder muscle. He's sitting so close to me that I can smell the rubbing alcohol he probably poured onto his arm. There's a wet patch on the neck of his shirt. I bet he spilled some on it.

I become hyperaware of how close to him I am. It sends little shivers through my body, but I can't bring myself to scoot away.

He holds the cap to the bottle of disinfectant between his teeth as he pours some out onto a clean cotton ball. I glance at the gap in the door. I hope Aunt Moe doesn't walk by and see the pile of gauze, but there is a clanging coming from down the hall that sounds like Kaylee is playing with something, so she's probably still in the living room.

Jonah peels the gauze off his shoulder. Seeing the sliced-through skin, I gasp. The cut is longer than I thought it would be, but not so deep that he'd need stitches. Blood is still leaking out from between the flaps of skin. One drop runs down to his elbow like a crimson tear, leaving a trail of blood behind it.

I pick up a tissue and reach forward to wipe it away. He jerks in surprise.

"Did I hurt you?" I ask.

"You just surprised me, that's all," he says, his voice tickling the hair on my arm. He takes the tissue from me and tosses it onto the ground. "Here, I got it."

He pours some disinfectant onto a cotton ball and dabs it

against the open cut. He tries to get to the end that snakes back over his shoulder, but he can't quite reach it.

"Want me to do it?" I offer.

Scowling in pain, he hands me the cotton. I scoot a little closer to him and squeeze the cotton ball so that some of the disinfectant drips into the wound. His scowl deepens. He glances down at where my fingers are holding the cotton, not touching him but touching something that is touching him. My heart double-thumps.

I'm hit with the memory of him doing this to me yesterday, except he poured the Betadine onto my knuckles and now here I am, squeezing rubbing alcohol onto his shoulder.

"I guess we need to stop getting into so much trouble," I say.

Jonah laughs a little, but it's cut off by another wince. I want to clean the trail of blood that runs down his back, but it disappears under his T-shirt, and I feel like if I get any closer to him all the molecules in my body will explode and turn me into a gooey mess that would be difficult to scrub out of his comforter.

Jonah turns to look at me, glancing down at the dark cotton ball in my hands. "Shiloh?" he asks. "What's wrong?"

"You've got some dirt on your face." Dropping the piece of cotton onto the ground, I reach up and wipe the smear from his chin.

Jonah catches my hand. His crescent-shaped lips are parted, and he breathes through them. "Leave it."

I glance down at where his long fingers are curled around my wrist. "What are you doing?"

Jonah stands up from the bed, crossing the room and pushing the door closed. The latch bolt clicks.

I blink at him. "Jonah, why are you closing—"

I don't have time to finish my sentence. He closes the space between us in three long strides, taking my face in both hands and kissing me.

I stay still. At first, so does he. His lips brush across mine, and his fingers touch my earlobes.

He pulls away by a few inches and raises his eyebrows as if to ask, *Is this okay?* A hazy look of longing swims in his eyes. My heart is thumping so fast that I'm scared it's going to jump out of my chest.

I knit my fingers in his dirty black hair and pull him back toward me. His eyelashes flutter down as he closes his eyes.

This time, there is no hesitation. His lips crash against mine, moving urgently as if something inside of him has burst free. Something stirs inside of me that I'm unfamiliar with, like a chill or something stronger. Jonah climbs onto the bed. I gasp as his arms go around me, pulling me hard against him as his hand travels up my body, through my ponytail, and around the back of my neck. He gathers me even closer, and I press into him until it's hard to breathe, but I can't stop. I want him closer. He holds onto me tightly, like he has no plans of letting me go.

Jonah's lips part. He breathes against my mouth for one suspended second, before deepening the kiss. He kisses my bottom lip and runs his tongue over it like he's tasting it. It's like he knows what he's doing, not just mashing his mouth against mine and hoping it feels good. He tastes of toothpaste and apples, and his touch is gentle, like he doesn't want to touch me too much or kiss me too hard. I can feel the muscles in his good shoulder through the damp material of his T-shirt, all lean and hard and smooth. Veins bulge out of his forearms. A thin layer of muscle covers his back, cresting and dipping around his shoulder blades.

In one swift motion, he lifts me higher onto the bed and climbs on top of me, pinning me against the mattress with his hips.

"Is this okay?" he whispers against my lips, his voice thick and soft with desire.

"Yes," I say hoarsely, and I feel his mouth curve into a smile.

He laces his fingers with my unbandaged hand, holding it over my head. We roll sideways, and my legs scissor around his. I can't stop touching him. He doesn't seem to be able to stop touching me. He pulls away from my mouth, bending down to kiss the soft skin at the base of my jaw, my neck, my collarbone. A tingling sensation radiates through my chest all the way to my fingertips. But the tingling is quickly replaced by an ache, like there's an emptiness inside of me that only kissing him can fill. The ache is so powerful it's almost painful. My toes curl in my socks.

Jonah pulls away, his eyes twinkling in the dim indoor light. "I don't mean to sound corny or whatever, but you are literally the most beautiful girl I've ever seen."

A small breath escapes my lips.

Beautiful.

Nobody has ever called me that before. I want to tell him that's stupid but don't want to make him feel like he has to compliment me again, so I smile. He has the most amazing eyes. They're sharp like nothing gets past him, but right now, they're filled with kindness and vulnerability.

"You're beautiful, too," I say. He rests his forehead against mine as he laughs. Oh, no. "I'm sorry. Was that a weird thing to say?"

"No," he says, mid-laughter. "I've just never gotten that before."

"Well, it's true." His pillow melts around my head. "You are."

He tucks a stray hair around my ear. "I can't believe this is actually happening."

A wave of nerves makes my heart race. I remember his unbandaged shoulder. He's lying on his side on the bed, which can't be good for it.

"Does your shoulder hurt?" I ask. "Should we stop?"

"I don't care about my shoulder," he says, climbing back on top of me and cupping my face in his hand, staring into both of my eyes so long that I feel a little dizzy. "I don't care at all."

24

Shiloh

I call Francesca on Jonah's phone to ask if she wants to stay over at my house.

"Would that be all right with your mother?" Francesca asks after she's gotten over her abject horror when I told her about the nun attacking Jonah. "I do not wish to be an imposition."

"You're not," I say. Jonah rubs his finger around my ankle in small circles. Each one sends a shiver up my spine and makes it hard for me to concentrate. "Pack a bag and bring it to school tomorrow so you can come straight back to my house after."

I can hear the smile in Francesca's voice when she asks, "What should I put in my bag?"

"Clothes, I guess," I say. "Your toothbrush … some underwear."

"I am extremely excited," Francesca says. "Nobody has asked me to sleep over at their house before."

"Well, I've never had anyone come to stay over, so it'll be the first time for both of us."

Jonah's fingers pause on my ankle. This can't honestly surprise him, knowing what he does about my family.

"I will pack my bag tonight," Francesca says.

I hang up the phone and give it back to Jonah. He's lying on his stomach on the foot of the bed, his finger still on the skin above my sock.

"I need to get you a burner," he says. "So that you can call me if anything happens."

"Or if I walk by a convent and someone looks at me funny?"

"Exactly." He grins and props himself up on his elbow. "I'll run out to get one later."

Imagining him going out and buying a phone for me because he's worried about me makes my heart squeeze like it's being wrung out, but one whiff of rubbing alcohol pulls me back to reality.

"Only go on the main roads," I say, and he rolls his eyes. "I'm serious. You should walk to school with Francesca tomorrow, and then Francesca and I can come to walk with you to and from school every day."

Jonah pauses. "You shouldn't walk alone to come get us. That defeats the purpose."

"I'll take main roads. No one's going to jump me in front of Duncan's."

"I got away from the guy today." He flashes me a cocky smile. "Who's to say I can't do it again?"

"I am." I can feel the corners of my mouth turning up, but I force myself not to smile so he knows I'm not messing around. If that crazy nun had cut more than just his arm today, I … I don't even want to think about how horrible that would have been. "Please, don't be an idiot."

"Sure thing, Scooby."

He's looking at me like he's having to stop himself from closing the space between us on the bed and kissing me again, and the thought makes me let out a nervous laugh.

But before he can do anything, there's a knock on his door. I jump, and Jonah whips his head up.

"Open door, Jonah," Aunt Moe says from the other side

before muttering a couple of curse words under her breath and wandering off down the hall.

Jonah gives me a sheepish shrug before crossing the room and opening the door just an inch.

"I have an idea for something that might save Miles," I say as he walks back over to me.

Jonah stops walking. His face falls, and he puts his hands in his pockets. "You do?"

I explain my plan about the hospital and how it might be possible to find Miles a new body.

Jonah's face darkens. "He's never going to go for something like that."

"I know he won't like it, but I don't see any other option."

"Miles won't want to be someone else, and I can't see him wanting to lie to some random person's family just so he can live."

I can picture exactly what Miles would say. If your whole life is a lie, it's not really your life. It's all very poetic, but it won't save him.

"Also," Jonah continues, "Frankie has to stop bringing people back. It's hurting her. Or aging her, making her hands look all old."

Guilt creeps in. "It is?"

"Yeah."

"She never told me that."

"If we ask her to bring Miles back, she's gonna do it. But it's not right to put her in that position."

"I won't sit here and watch Miles die."

Jonah rubs his forehead and shrugs like maybe we can. Or maybe we don't have a choice.

"None of this is good, but we can't sit around and do nothing," I say. "Miles won't listen to me right now. Could you talk to him?"

After a long pause, Jonah nods.

"Thanks."

He pulls his lips into a thin line, and his eyes harden. An

uneasy feeling creeps between us, and I'm suddenly conscious of the fact that I'm sitting on his bed. He probably doesn't want to kiss me anymore, not now that I brought up Miles and reminded him that I'm the reason his best friend is dying.

Uttering a quiet, "See you tomorrow," I grab my backpack and head out of his bedroom door.

He doesn't follow me.

Crossing the school parking lot the next afternoon, my steps slow to a stop. Being back here feels weird. Wrong, almost, like I'm a criminal on a Most Wanted list going back to their hometown where everyone will recognize them. But it's after the final bell, so not many people will still be here.

Golden mid-afternoon sun glares into my eyes as I sit on a wooden bench by the entrance. I'm actually pretty excited about having Francesca stay at my house. I've never had a friend sleep over before, for obvious reasons. Not that I ever had that many friends to invite over. Sleepovers were such a big thing in middle school, and I had so much fun going over to Kirsten Doi's house that time she turned twelve and invited the whole class. Her mom must have bought out the snack aisle at the grocery store because she had every snack imaginable laid out on the table in giant glass bowls, everything from Lay's chips to Goldfish to fruit snacks. That was the last sleepover I ever went on. A couple of months later, Dad slammed Max's head into the wall.

The memory rises in my throat like sour bile. I can still hear the dull thud in my ears.

It's crazy how one moment can freeze time. One horrible thing happens, and I stay twelve forever. Inside, I'm still the same as I was that day, holding a screaming Max in my arms and promising I'd protect him. That if Dad was going to hurt him again, he'd have to get past me to do it.

The school doors open. I raise my head, my heart soaring for a second before I realize it's Tanya from gym class holding hands with a junior whose name I don't remember. They head off toward the Upside-Down Tree, probably to hook up or maybe to smoke, like I was trying to do with Jonah a couple of weeks ago before we found Max and everything went sideways.

I want to kiss Jonah under the Upside-Down Tree.

The sides of my mouth curve upward. I couldn't sleep last night because every time I closed my eyes, his face appeared against my eyelids and my lips tingled with the memory of kissing him.

And the way it set me on fire.

I wonder if it's going to be weird today when I see him. Until I brought up Miles, everything was so good.

But it doesn't take a genius to know this is bad. Jonah must feel guilty. Miles is his best friend. And Miles is dying.

But you know what? Miles broke up with me and told me he never wanted to see me again. Going and kissing somebody else wasn't wrong.

Except for the fact that it was Jonah.

I shouldn't be kissing Jonah. So why can't I stop thinking about it?

The door opens, and my heart double-thumps in my chest.

Jonah walks out, one strap of his backpack slung over his shoulder. He glances around for a second before his eyes fall on me.

Dimples cut into his cheeks as he smiles.

"Great, my security detail's here," he says, heading over.

All the nerves and worry I had just been feeling melt away. "Where's Francesca?"

"Taking a leak. She's got her overnight stuff packed in this dorky, purple thing." He gestures as if trying to demonstrate a lumpy object about the size of a microwave. "It's hideous. But I've got to say, she's growing on me."

I laugh. Francesca grew on me a long time ago.

"Oh, I got you this," he says, digging around in his bag and pulling out a flip phone wrapped in thick plastic. "It's got ninety minutes on it. I already saved Francesca's and Miles's numbers. Mine, too. Try to call instead of text if you can."

I can't believe it. This phone is mine. I've wanted one of these for so long. Dad used to give me so many lectures about the dangers of social media, telling me I couldn't get a phone because Instagram would rot my brain or make me compare myself to Ashley Christensen and then feel bad about myself— like that would ever happen. What Dad really wanted was to control me. But now, he can't anymore.

"Thank you," I say. "Seriously, you have no idea how much this means to me."

"Sure thing."

The golden light frames his head from behind, glinting against his jet-black hair. He changed his shirt. It's white with some kind of band logo on it, and I can see his shoulder bandage through it. I don't think I've ever seen him in a shirt that wasn't black. Or at least dark gray.

I'm about to ask whether Aunt Moe asked him about the bandage when a scream sounds from over by the dumpsters.

A small freshman with floppy red hair races across the parking lot, wiping the tears streaming down his face as he runs back through the doors of the school. I hear a low, growling laugh.

The hair on the back of my neck stands up. I know that laugh.

Richie walks around the corner with his friend Davey, who is flipping a glinting metal thing shut. Oh, that asshole. Did he hurt that kid?

Richie has a menacing smirk on his face. I should go follow that kid to make sure he's okay, but if he's still here, he's probably part of some club or other, and he'll have some friends to comfort him.

Davey sees Jonah and me. He nudges Richie and points at us. Keeping his focus on me, Richie twists his snapback around so the visor shields his eyes from the sun. Flames that mimic the packaging of a Hot Wheels car curve up the sides. It's the same hat he was wearing when I found him raking the leaves at Miles's house.

"God, he thinks he looks so cool," I say, glancing up at Jonah, whose face is white as a sheet.

"It's him," Jonah says. "Richie was the nun who jumped me in the woods."

What? "How do you know?"

"Because he was wearing that hat. Stop staring at him." Jonah moves my shoulder away. "I swear it was him. He was the same build, too. Oh my God, that means Leonard's host is *Richie*."

The realization hits me like a gut punch.

Richie is friends with bullies.

Richie was raking the leaves at Miles's house.

Richie goes to our school.

Richie lives with Francesca, so Leonard could have known about our trip to meet the Soothsayer and followed us there to murder Wilma.

Has Francesca been living with Leonard this whole time?

I grab Jonah's arm. "You said Francesca was in the bathrooms?" I ask.

He nods. "Yeah, she should be out any minute."

I let go of him and run into the school, hearing his feet pound against the beige tiles as he follows me down the empty hallway to find her.

25

Shiloh

There's no sign of Francesca in the hallway, so she has to still be in the girls' bathroom.

Jonah pauses in front of the door. "I guess I'll keep watch out here."

I hesitate, knowing how important it is that we all stick together, but if Richie were to attack Jonah right outside the door, I'd hear him. So I give Jonah a nod and push into the bathroom to find Francesca drying her hands on the front of her long denim overalls. A chunky knitted scarf with every color of the rainbow hangs around her neck, falling to her knees. Every bathroom stall is open, so there's nobody else in here who could overhear us.

"Oh, hello, Shiloh. I'm sorry if I'm a bit late. I packed all my things like you said to do, although I could not for the life of me find my embroidery cushion. You don't think I'll need it, do you?"

I glance down at the purple duffel bag by her feet. A bunch of bumble bees have been sewn onto the sides of the bag, buzzing around a brightly colored flower in small circles. She must have embroidered it all herself. Jonah was wrong to call this bag ugly. It's beautiful.

Francesca sees me looking at it and smiles. "If a little work can transform an ordinary object into something you will treasure, then it would be silly not to do it, don't you think?"

I snap back to reality. There's no way of breaking it to her gently, so I come right out with it.

"Leonard's host is Richie," I say.

Francesca stops drying her hands and absorbs the information. "You mean Leonard is living inside my brother?

"Jonah recognized the hat Richie was wearing as the same one the crazy nun wore when attacking him yesterday. The one with all the flames?" Francesca nods like she knows which hat I'm talking about. "Richie is exactly the kind of host Leonard would want. He's big, strong, and literally lives with you. He knows we wouldn't suspect him of acting weird because we all know Richie hates us and he acts pretty weird, anyway." Francesca's face falls, and I wish I could take the words back. "He doesn't hate you. I meant he hates the rest of us."

"It's all right," she says. "I would like to think Richie doesn't hate me, but I'm not convinced he likes me very much either."

Francesca falls silent. I wait for her to say something or react in some way, but she doesn't.

"Francesca?" I urge, my heart hammering in my ears. "What are you thinking?"

"I'm thinking that I'm not sure you're right."

"You don't think Leonard is Richie?"

She shakes her head. "I am certain it isn't."

"Francesca …"

"Yesterday, he went to the store and bought me a pack of chocolate pudding."

I pause, trying to figure out what she could mean, before replying. "So?"

"Well, chocolate pudding has been my favorite snack since I was a little girl, and Richie sometimes buys it for me when he goes to the grocery store. If he's in a good mood. He did that yesterday, and Leonard would not have known to do this if he were the one inside of Richie."

Uneasiness churns in the pit of my stomach. I don't know if such a simple gesture is enough to prove that Leonard's host is not Richie. "Could he have found a grocery list?"

"Richie doesn't make grocery lists," Francesca says, wringing her hands together. "My father sends Richie money every month, and Richie does not give me much of a say in where it goes."

A sharp ache pulls at my heart. I can't imagine how frustrating it must be not to have any say in the money that's coming in for you, but Francesca doesn't have an ounce of frustration on her face. Only a pensive look, like she's trying to solve a puzzle.

"Could Leonard have tuned in to Richie's memories when he entered his body?" I suggest.

"No, it doesn't work like that. Do you remember going to visit Natalie Dorado when she was inside Poppy's body, that day at the laundromat?" she asks, and I nod. I was so sure Francesca was lying about ghosts existing until I saw the determination in that twelve-year-old girl's eyes. "Natalie did not know who Poppy's parents were, or even who Poppy was, despite being trapped inside her body. I believe that the body is little more than a puppet. It's the soul inside that gives it humanity."

I guess Francesca has a point. If Leonard is inside Richie, the groceries Richie was bringing home probably would have changed. Even subtly, like buying Munster instead of Gouda.

But none of that's important right now. "Jonah said it was the same hat. How many people could have that hat?"

"Perhaps it is a popular hat."

"It's definitely not a popular hat. It's freaking ugly. Besides, Jonah told me the guy who attacked him was the same height and build as Richie, too."

"Numerous people fit Richie's description. If Leonard is trying to kill us and is using Richie as a host, why hasn't he already killed me?"

I open my mouth to reply, but the words don't come. She's right. If Richie is Leonard's host, Francesca would have been the first target—unless he has a use for her abilities. I go to point that out.

But Francesca is on a roll now. "Richie would not have been in the hospital on the day that Leonard left the body of the nurse."

"You sure about that?"

"I don't see any reason why he would have been." Listening to her say all this is turning the hat into a pretty flimsy piece of evidence. "I *know* Richie is not Leonard's host. There is something that we are missing. I can feel it in here." Francesca jabs her finger into the knitted fabric of her scarf above the top of her overalls. "Please, will you trust me?"

Every single pump of adrenaline coursing through my veins screams at me not to, but Francesca's never led me wrong before. Her eyes are wide and pleading, just like they were on the day she told me that Poppy's ghost could help us find Max. If I didn't believe her then, Max would be dead, and some other kid would be walking around in his body.

So I nod my numb head. "Yeah, I trust you."

Francesca smiles and picks up her purple bag. "I trust you as well. So, are you ready to go back to your house?"

26

Shiloh

I can tell from the wrinkles on his forehead that Jonah doesn't agree with Francesca. His frown is still etched in place when we get to his house. He doesn't come right out and say anything, probably because, like me, a part of him wants to think that Francesca has made some good points. But also like me, something isn't sitting quite right with him.

Francesca only comments on it when Jonah is about to walk through his front gate.

"I am growing impatient, too," she says. "But if we want something to be true badly enough, our minds will play tricks to convince us that it is."

"I don't get why Richie would have the same hat as Leonard," Jonah says. "It's an ugly hat."

Francesca drifts into thought. "Perhaps if we close our eyes and think very hard, then the picture on the puzzle will reveal itself to us."

I guess it's worth a try. I close my eyes and think until my temples throb, but no picture or puzzle appears.

"That didn't work for me," I say.

"Me neither." Francesca frowns. "Which is quite odd. Solutions frequently reveal themselves to me that way."

Jonah gives me an uneasy glance. "Just … don't be wrong," he says.

The creaky stairs give under his weight as he walks into the house, saying hi to Bessie who greets him at the door.

Francesca drops the bag at her feet and stretches her arms up over her head. I reach for the bag's handles, and her thin eyebrows draw together in question. "Is there something inside my bag you would like?"

"I want to help you carry it. We still have a long walk to my house."

"It's all right, I will—"

"I can help," I assure her. "Please let me help." A grateful look flashes across her eyes as I swing the bag over my shoulder. "Come on, let's get off the street."

Francesca's bag lands with a thump on the rug in the spare bedroom. Mom sets her laundry basket on the desk chair and pulls out a crumpled fitted sheet.

"I'm sorry, Francesca. I lost track of time." Mom shakes the sheet out in front of her and lifts the corner of the stiff mattress. "Usually, I'd be a bit more organized, but these sheets have only just come out of the dryer."

Francesca rushes to find the matching top sheet from the hamper. "Please don't worry, Mrs. Oleson. You don't have to make the bed for me. I can do it."

Mom takes the purple bundle from Francesca's arms. "Honey, no. I insist. Please, make yourself at home."

Redness fills Francesca's cheeks, and I realize that it's probably been a long time since anyone did this for her.

I nudge her with my shoulder. "You okay?"

A small smile fights its way onto her face. "Yes."

"Good."

I help Mom tuck in the top sheet, and then I drape a heavy comforter on top of it. The air is crisper in here than it is in the rest of the house, and it feels a couple of degrees colder. Years ago, this room used to be Mom's painting studio, but it became a storage space when she lost inspiration after things with Dad started getting bad. I wonder if she's ever going to get back into it. She used to do lots of watercolors of flowers, the vibrant greens and yellows standing out against the eggshell paper. Some of them are still hanging in the mudroom.

Mom and I step back as Francesca sits carefully on the edge of the mattress, running her hands over the down puffs as a smile stretches over her face.

"This is a beautiful place to sleep, Mrs. Oleson," she says.

Mom gives her a warm smile. "You always have a bed here, sweetheart."

"You are also welcome at my home, although there is not quite as much room there. But I am used to sleeping on the floor."

Mom reaches out and touches Francesca's shoulder, her face full of care and compassion.

I jerk my thumb over my shoulder, back toward the living room. "Want to watch a movie?"

Despite my protests, Francesca insists on doing homework for an hour. I'd have thought she wouldn't still care so much about school, given that we're running from a murderer and everything, but she's insistent that she doesn't want to fall behind.

When I knock on her door at six, she opens it dressed in a matching pajama set and mismatched knee-high socks.

"I usually put on my pajamas in the house," she says. "I have no reason to wear outside clothes when pajamas are more comfortable."

"That's why I like sweatpants," I say. "You get maximum comfort while still looking socially acceptable."

"I stopped caring about what was socially acceptable when I learned that nothing as simple as clothes would change people's opinions of me," Francesca says. "They will dislike me no matter what I wear, so I might as well wear something comfortable."

"I'm sorry that people have been so mean to you. You're a good person, and you don't deserve that."

Redness creeps onto her cheeks. She shrugs and then smiles at me. "Are we still watching a movie?"

I had *The Princess Bride* already cued up on the TV because I had a feeling it was something Francesca would like, but she asks if we could watch *Pinnochio* instead. I have never seen it, but I don't have any objections to it so I rent the movie and we watch it while eating tuna casserole on the couch.

Francesca's eyes are glued to the screen. She stays quiet during the film just sits there chewing. When we get to the part about Lampwick turning into a donkey, the casserole churns in my stomach. The donkey-boy kicks the mirror and brays.

"Why is that donkey so upset?" A voice sounds behind me.

I twist around to see Max standing in the kitchen and pointing at the TV. Mom watches him like she's getting ready to rush forward and cover his eyes, but he only looks curious.

"Want to sit with us?" I ask.

Max nods. My heart soars as he plops down next to me on the couch. Pinnochio and Jiminy Cricket dive into the ocean and escape from Pleasure Island.

"Rest in pieces," Max says, and I laugh.

But Francesca doesn't. "It all comes at a price," she whispers.

I want to ask her what she's talking about, but Max points at my bandaged hand.

"Did you get hurt?" he asks.

I flip his blond cowlick to the side. I never told Mom about seeing Dad at the abandoned house. Doing that would mean I'd have to tell her what we were doing there. Apart from the trouble I got into and told her about, she thinks my life consists of sleepovers and relaxing afternoons with friends as I recover from the trauma of searching for Max, and I want it to stay that way. "I got into a fight with a velociraptor," I say.

"No, you didn't." He giggles, just like the old Max. His big kid teeth are poking through his gums now. "Dinosaurs are extinct, silly."

"You're silly."

I glance back at Mom, who is looking at us like she's about to cry as she brings Max his bowl of tuna casserole.

Mom lets Max stay up and watch the rest of the movie with us. After it's over, Francesca says she's ready to sleep. I hold Max's hand as I double-check the locks on the doors and lead him down the hallway toward his room.

"Good night, Shiloh," Francesca says, standing with one hand on the guest room doorknob. "I really am having a pleasant time. It is like having a family."

"You have one," I tell her, as Max lets out a long yawn. "See you in the morning, okay?"

Francesca smiles and nods twice. "See you in the morning."

I pull the covers over my head, willing myself to go to sleep. But I can't stop thinking about Miles.

Jonah must have already talked to him about changing bodies. He promised he would. I'm going to ask him about it when I walk him and Francesca to school.

The memory of Miles's tiny pupils flashes against my closed eyelids. His hands were curled like the dried bird's foot we found in the labyrinth the day he took me there. He doesn't have much time. Even one day after meeting the Soothsayer, he was almost unrecognizable.

I can't tell if I miss him or if I feel guilty for what I did to him, or if it's a confusing mix of both. I feel guilty about so many things. About Jonah. About Miles, about my obvious choice of Max over whatever feelings I had for Miles. About the fact I didn't hide it. Sometimes, answers are worse than questions.

On the other side of the wall, there's a faint scraping sound, like a window opening. My hands curl around my blanket.

Maybe Francesca got too warm and is just opening a window. But why would she do that if the spare room is already cold?

Thump. Something heavy falls. It sounds like boots on the wooden living room floor.

Oh God. Someone's in the house.

Dad.

That's my first thought, but even he wouldn't be that stupid.

It has to be Leonard.

I climb out of bed, my heart pounding in my ears. If someone climbs in through a window in the living room, I have enough time to get into Max's room without them seeing me, but I have to hurry.

I glance into the shadows that engulf the end of the hallway as I dash into his room.

"Max," I whisper.

He sits up with a start and opens his mouth to scream.

I cup my hand over it before any sound can escape. "It's me, it's okay." Max's brown eyes get huge as his scream tapers off. "Climb onto my back."

Max nods. I bend over to let him get on. He wraps his small arms around my neck as I poke my head out of his door. No one's there. I quickly let myself into the spare room and almost collide with Francesca.

"Is everything all right?" she whispers. "I heard voices through the wall."

I pull the door closed behind us. "Hide in the closet and call the police." Max's breathing hitches in my ear, but he doesn't make a sound. "Tell them someone's in the house. I'm pretty sure they're in the living room, so we can't leave through the front. Be super quiet."

Francesca's eyes widen, but she nods dutifully. "What about your mom?" she asks.

"I'm going to go warn her," I reply.

I lower Max to the ground and drop to my knees. "Stay with Francesca. No matter what happens, don't come out and don't make a sound, okay?"

"What's happening?" he asks.

I pull him into my arms and kiss him on top of his head. "I love you."

Francesca takes Max's hand and draws a flip phone from her pocket. She pushes Mom's dresses to the side in the closet and leads Max in behind them. He shoots me one last panicked look as the door pulls shut.

Steeling myself for what I might see on the other side, I open the spare room door and step into the hallway.

Mom is already up, her hand hovering above the doorknob like she was about to come inside. "What's happening, honey?"

I raise my eyes to the hulking, shadowy figure behind her. A nun's habit spills over its shoulders like a veil. The blue glow from Max's room glints off a long knife in his hand.

Mom searches my face. "Shiloh?"

I push Mom to the side, away from the coming blow. I duck under the nun's knife and run down the hallway. Heavy footsteps follow me into the kitchen.

I hit the light switch, squinting through the sudden dazzle as I run to the knife block on the counter.

A hand grabs my hair and yanks my neck down. I yelp, staring up into the deep-set, beady eyes behind the gaping sockets of the silicone mask.

I grip the eyeholes, pulling the mask up to reveal stubble on his jaw. "Who are you?" I scream, yanking the stretchy disguise higher and knocking his hat to the floor. "What do you want from me?"

I can't get the stupid thing over his head. My eyes run from the unforgiving brightness, making it hard to see.

"Are you Leonard?" is all I can say, as if I'm expecting him to come out and tell me.

He thrusts the blade at my stomach.

I drive my foot into his meaty hand and the knife tumbles out of his grip. He grabs my arm, and there is a harsh *pop* in my shoulder as he flips me around and locks his elbow around my neck.

I grit my teeth to stop myself from screaming so I don't scare Max. My knees buckle as I writhe against the nun's tight grasp.

"Get away from my daughter!" Mom shrieks.

There's a dull thud. The nun's arm loosens, and I spin around to pull the mask up with my good arm.

Richie looks at me for a second with dead eyes. The blow Mom struck on the side of his head is gushing blood, and the skin is split. A tuft of hair falls down over his right ear, hanging from a flap of flesh. Then he tugs the mask down and glances at Mom, who is gripping Max's tee-ball bat in both hands like she's hanging on for dear life, and runs through the open front door.

I rush after him, but my arm isn't hanging right and my legs wobble like Jello. Under the sodium glow of the streetlamp, Richie disappears into the darkness as police sirens ring out through the night.

27

Shiloh

I bite down hard on the neckline of my T-shirt, unable to stop the wail from pushing through my teeth as the paramedic pops my shoulder back into place.

"All right." The paramedic lowers her hands. "You're all done. How do you feel?"

I flex my fingers. Everything seems okay, but the paramedic slips my arm into a canvas sling. She's talking, but her voice sounds far away, and my shoulder starts to throb like it's bruised, but not broken. I catch a few phrases—*dislocation, adrenaline, take it easy, going to be sore*—but all I can think of is how glad I am that Leonard injured the same arm I punched the fireplace with, leaving me with one good arm to stab his evil heart straight through his ribs.

Over by the front door, Max is sobbing hysterically into Mom's shoulder as she gives her statement to the police. Each cry digs into my heart like a red-hot poker. Angry tears press against the backs of my eyeballs, and I blink a few times before looking over at Francesca. Blue and red police lights flash against her frizzy hair as she sits on the lawn, a heavy blanket

227

wrapped around her shoulders. The lights seem to find new lines on her face, and I remember what Jonah said about how her abilities were aging her.

I slide off the back platform of the ambulance and sink onto the soft grass next to her. The ground is damp, and moisture seeps through the fabric of my sweatpants. It's going to look bad when I stand up.

"You feeling okay?" I ask.

She nods before glancing over at me, her eyes swollen and wet. "Is the pain any better?"

It's my turn to nod, even though I can feel the bruising starting to spread through my shoulder.

"I saw his face." I glance over at Mom to make sure she can't hear us. But she's far away and still talking to a young cop with gelled hair, who's acting with inappropriate enthusiasm in the circumstances. This is probably the most serious thing he's seen in his short career. "My mom didn't see him because he pulled his mask down quickly, but it was Richie."

Francesca's face falls. She opens her mouth to respond but hesitates, rolling her words over with her tongue for a moment before asking, "Are you sure?"

"I wish I wasn't," I say. "But it's your turn to trust me."

Francesca pulls the weighted blanket tighter around her shoulders. As uneasy as I was about believing Leonard's host was someone other than Richie, a big part of me hoped it wasn't him because that would mean he was dead. Leonard would have had to kill him before entering his body. I watch as the realization dawns on Francesca. Her bottom lip quivers, and tears pool in the bottoms of her eyelids before running down her cheeks onto the rough fabric. I scoot closer and curl my good arm around her, resting my chin on her shoulder.

"He wasn't very kind to me most of the time," she says, sniffling, "but I never wanted him to die."

"I'm so sorry, Francesca."

"I hope he is in a better place now." Her voice breaks as she presses her face against my shoulder. "I try very hard not to hate people, as they often have a reason for acting the way they do. But right now, I believe I hate Leonard."

Nothing I could say can make things any easier. I hold on to her as she cries until the police finish talking to Mom and go inside to poke around the house.

Francesca wipes her hands down the front of her face with shaking hands. "We must stop Leonard."

"We really don't need to talk about this now—"

"The things we run from always find ways of catching us up in the end, so it is better to be brave and face them. I like to think I am brave." There's a beat of silence. "Shiloh, if we are going to stop Leonard, we will need to make him a soul, which will require *ejecting* him from Richie's body."

I side-eye the paramedic standing by the ambulance, but we're sitting too far away for her to hear us. "Wouldn't that mean killing him?"

Francesca gives me a small nod. "We would not be killing Richie, as he is already dead." Her voice is small, but she powers through. "Once Leonard's soul leaves Richie's body, I will take him across the barrier to the other side."

"Couldn't he just get back here through the gates?"

"Perhaps," she admits. "But I believe it is our only option. We cannot kill Leonard's soul because spirits are made of energy, so I'm not sure it's possible to destroy one."

This reminds me of something I learned in physics class. "The law of conservation of energy."

"I remember that, too," Francesca says. "Energy can neither be created nor destroyed. It can only be converted from one form to another. I do not know how to convert souls into something different. I only know that I can move them. I believe some objects can trap souls, such as the glass orb that the Soothsayer kept hers inside, although trapping Leonard may not be such a good idea, as we would have to keep a careful eye on him to make sure he never escaped."

"But there's still a big problem. If we eject Leonard's soul from Richie's body, the police will think we murdered Richie.

I'm really sorry to have to ask, but what can we do with Richie's corpse?"

Francesca thinks for a minute before a melancholy sort of smile turns the corners of her mouth. "I believe we ought to have a conversation with Miles about that."

I call Jonah as soon as the sun rises. Francesca is sitting on my bed while I do it, chewing on her fingernail as the ring echoes through the phone.

Jonah picks up, his voice thick with sleep. "You okay?"

"Yes," I tell him, trying to ignore the ache pulsing from my shoulder. Sleeping for a couple of hours gave it just enough time for the bruise to grow, and a splotch of deep maroon covers my collarbone like a nicotine patch. "Richie is Leonard's host. We're sure of it now."

He groans like he's sitting up in bed or stretching his arms over his head. "Did something happen?"

"I'll tell you later. But you can't go to school today."

"Moe won't let me stay home unless I'm sick. She gets on my ass about stuff like that."

"Well, make yourself barf because you're not going to school. Francesca and I made a plan for how we're going to save Miles, and we're doing it today."

This wakes Jonah up. "Today? Why are you—"

"We'll come to your house and tell you everything later. But stay put for now. Don't do anything stupid."

Before he can say anything else, I end the call and stare at Francesca, whose eyebrows are drawn into a concerned line.

"Should we call Miles, too?" she asks.

"I'm not sure that's a good idea," I say. "This is a conversation we need to have in person."

I can hear Miles's voice already. *Richie Russo? Is that some kind of sick joke?* But if Francesca ejects Leonard from Richie and brings Miles back quickly, Richie's body will not have any time to decompose, so Miles will have a viable host that he can stay in for the rest of his life. How people will react to a respectful, caring Richie who understands calculus and enjoys poetry is anyone's guess, but we'll cross that bridge when we come to it.

There's a soft knock on my door.

I snap my head up. "Come in."

Mom pokes her head around the door, looking like she hasn't slept at all. Tufts of her hair stick up in every direction, and deep wrinkles are etched into her forehead like they've been chiseled into stone. "Shiloh, can you come look at something?" she asks.

I know that tone. That's her scared shitless tone. The tone she uses when Dad comes home drunk and wants to talk to me about leaving my dirty dishes on the coffee table.

It means that something's really wrong.

My arm sits heavily in its sling as I follow her into the kitchen where Max is eating a bowl of cereal at the counter, and then through to the computer in the living room. There's no blood left on the floor. Mom's gotten pretty used to cleaning up after Dad, and she must have seen to it last night while we were lying in bed pretending to be asleep but not being able to stop listening for any more creaks in the floorboards that might indicate Leonard was back. I got up four times to double, triple, and quadruple check the locks on every window in the house.

Mom leans over the keyboard and points to the article on the local news website. I lower myself into the rolling chair.

Bethany Police ask for help in locating missing 16-year-old girl
October 2, 2019
BETHANY, OH: Bethany Police have issued a missing person alert and are asking for the public's help in locating a 16-year-old girl who hasn't been seen in two days.

Talulah Monroe, 16, was last seen in the vicinity of 300 Holbrook St in Bethany on September 30, 2019 at 4:30pm and was said by her

brother to have been on her way to the Bethany Community
Library.

Police describe her as a female, Caucasian, about 5'2" tall with red hair.

Anyone who sees her or has any information is urged to call
Bethany Police at (740) 693-4533.

Above the article is a picture of a round-faced girl with almond-shaped, sea-green eyes and dark red hair that falls far past her shoulders. She looks vaguely familiar. Probably because she must go to school with me. But then my eyes scan over the words again, and I figure out why.

Monroe.

Talulah's family owns the abandoned farmhouse. She was with her brother, looking over Dad's shoulder as he yelled at me for trespassing. And now she's gone missing.

Did Dad do something to her?

Behind Mom, Francesca walks over to us and scans the article. Her eyes widen as she reaches the end. She doesn't have to say anything for me to know what she's thinking.

It's not Dad, it's Leonard.

Leonard is going to bring back Evangeline.

He must have discovered a gate to the other side or found Evangeline's ghost, because he just kidnapped Talulah to act as her host. It has already been two days since Talulah was last seen, so that means …

He will bring Evangeline back soon.

The sound of the doorbell echoes through the house, and Max whimpers from where he's sitting hunched over his cereal bowl. Before Mom can even move, I rush over to the window to check who it is and see Detective Babin in a blue dress shirt bunched up at his elbows.

I rub the nape of my neck. This can't be good.

"It's okay, Max," I say, keeping my voice steady. "It's not a bad guy. Only a detective coming to talk to us." I give Max a reassuring smile as I slide back the bolt and open the door.

"Good morning, Shiloh," Babin says as Mom walks up behind me. His eye drops to my sling, and he nods at it. "I heard what happened last night, and I'm so sorry that your family had to go through another ordeal." He sounds way too formal, and my senses move to high alert.

"Can we help you, detective?" Mom asks. "This is not a very good time."

"I'm going to need Shiloh to come down to the station," he tells her, and I tighten my death grip on the door handle as he turns to me. "A new piece of evidence has come up, and I'd like to ask you a few questions about the death of Patrick De Beauvoir, as well as the attempted murder of Miles Barot-Renaud."

The bottom falls out of my stomach because I know exactly what they found. Part of me knew as soon as I saw him standing at the door, looking uncomfortable in the early morning sunlight.

"Am I under arrest?" I ask.

Babin shakes his head. "You're not. Out of courtesy to your dad, we could have this conversation here, but I want to show you the evidence and that's still back at the office."

No part of me wants to go with him. But something has changed since the last time I saw him. Even though he said I'm not under arrest, he's staring at me with deadness in his eyes like I might as well be.

So I give him a small nod. "Okay."

"Is that really necessary?" Mom asks, holding my shoulder as if to hold me back. "I mean, she's only sixteen. If there's something you need to tell her, she should have a parent present for it."

"It's okay, Mom." I take her hand off. "I'll go. I did nothing wrong."

But Mom knows just as well as I do that's not true.

At the Sheriff's Office, I follow Detective Babin through a side door and straight to the rear of the building, where he ushers me into a small, cold room and closes the door. The fluorescent tube above us casts a harsh shadow on Babin's usually friendly face, deepening the lines on either side of his mouth and making him look more serious than he already is.

I take a seat in a stiff, rolling chair. Babin disappears through the heavy green door for a couple of minutes, and as I wait, I roll the gauze around my bandaged knuckles between my fingers. I expected the mangled skin to hurt as it healed, but what I didn't anticipate was the itching. It's constant. Unforgiving, like a colony of ants is chomping away at my skin with their many mandibles.

Babin comes back with Detective Finnegan, who is holding a cardboard box. Finnegan puts the box on the square table in front of me, and both detectives sit down opposite me.

"Shiloh, I want to show you something," Babin says. "One of our detectives found this on her front doorstep on Monday evening."

Her. Connie's the only female detective here. Leonard knew which door would be best to leave it at. Someone with a grudge against me, and my dad's closest supporter.

Finnegan takes the top off the cardboard box. I lean forward to peer inside.

Sure enough, it's Dad's gun. Dry dirt is caked into the grooves in the barrel and the grip, presumably from where I stashed it in that log. The nine impulsive gunshots ring in my brain like an alarm clock I can't turn off.

Detective Finnegan searches my face. He points at a small slip of paper next to the gun which I hadn't noticed before. "This note was left along with it."

I read the messy scribble on the note:

I can't breathe. I picture Leonard bending over the scrap of lined paper, holding his bottom lip between his teeth as he focused hard on every dot and loop that made up each letter. Babin and Finnegan surely can't believe this is a serious piece of evidence. Anyone could have written that note, and it reads like it was written by a twelve-year-old.

But there's a mean gleam in Finnegan's eyes, so the gun is probably evidence enough without the note.

"I'm not sure who left this for us to find or what their relationship is to you," says Babin, "but we ran the gun's serial number, and we can confirm that it belongs to your dad." A chill shoots up my spine. I'll bet Dad is feeling pretty smug right now. For him, watching me get in trouble probably feels good, like some kind of payback for dirtying his name and telling the FBI about the abuse and turning Mom against him.

"Your father was in police custody at the time of Patrick De Beauvoir's death. You were there on the night that Patrick was killed."

I remember the Soothsayer showing us a faded black-and-white picture of Patrick and remarking at how much he looked like a younger version of Leonard's original host. Babin or Finnegan must have figured out his identity, either through forensics or evidence pulled from the crime scene. All I can hear is my heart beating so quickly in my ears that it sounds like it's buzzing.

"This man is presumably the one responsible for kidnapping your brother," Babin continues, "so you had good reason for wanting him dead."

"Means, motive, and opportunity." Finnegan ticks three points off on his fingers. "See where we're going with this?"

I shake my head, even though I know exactly where they're going with this.

Babin leans forward, bracing his arms on the table. "I'm sure that it all happened fast. You were desperate, or overcome by your emotions, and it all got out of hand."

"We're sending the gun to forensics today, along with the bullets we pulled from our Patrick De Beauvoir and your friend Miles, and I expect to find a match." Finnegan can barely hide his smile. "We will then have enough to arrest you for Patrick's murder and attempted murder of Miles Barot-Renaud."

Attempted murder of Miles? That's ridiculous. There's no reason I'd shoot Miles, who was not only my boyfriend at the time but was also helping rescue Max when he got shot.

If Babin sees the shock on my face, he doesn't let on. "This is not a joke, Shiloh. You need to tell us exactly what happened, and then we might help you out here."

I sit on my hands. I want to run. But I force myself to sit still. Babin is saying he can help me, but I don't buy it for a second. He means he can help me go to jail for murdering Leonard because, like he said, the narrative makes sense.

I look Babin straight in the eyes. "I don't know what you're talking about."

"Stop lying," Finnegan says. "You lied the first day we came to talk to you, when you told us that a man by the name of Leonard Gailis was the one who kidnapped Max. The only record we have of a Leonard Gailis is someone who died back in 1944."

Sweat pricks at the palms of my hands and armpits. I want to ask if I can plead self-defense and explain what really happened, but the look in Finnegan's eyes is cold. He's older than Babin, and he's probably friends with Dad.

Couple of cold ones after shift, buddy?

Sure thing, boss.

This isn't fair. Leonard kidnapped Max and had just killed him when I shot him. What reasonable person would let him walk away from that? But something tells me they might be even less forgiving if I started talking about the supernatural at this point.

A ghost did it? Sure. You're going to have to do better than that if you want to claim insanity, Shiloh.

"I did not shoot that man, and I didn't shoot Miles," I say with as much confidence as I can muster. "Can I go now?"

Babin widens his eyes a little, shaking his head. He must have expected me to crumble and is disappointed. "I'm not sure you understand the severity of the situation, Shiloh. When the results come back with a match, we will have no choice but to arrest you on felony murder charges. Do you hear me? Because of the violent nature of the crime, you will be tried as an adult."

He stops talking, but what he's saying sinks in.

If the bullets match the gun, I'm going to jail.

28

FrANCesCA

I'm about to doze off for a mid-morning nap when a loud chime sounds from the phone that Jonah gave to me.

I must have gotten a message. Nobody has ever called me on my own phone before, and I am certain no one is calling me now, as it was only one sound and not a long, sustained ring. I pry open the phone. An envelope icon fills the screen, and I read the instructions before pressing the top corner button.

A message pops up.

> Hello Francesca. I am Miles. You will meet me at the Oren's Field Labyrinth at 9 a.m. Please reply

How peculiar. I'm surprised Miles is asking for me. I would have expected him to reach out to Jonah or Shiloh first. Shiloh once told me that the labyrinth is Miles's favorite place. I suppose if something bad was happening, the setting might offer some sort of comfort to him.

I glance up at the wall clock. It is approaching 8:15 in the morning, and Shiloh has not come back from her meeting with the police officers yet. She made Jonah promise not to go anywhere by himself today, and I presume the same rule applies to me.

Typing on this phone is tedious business. Each letter takes a few seconds to type. I imagine it would be a test of patience for somebody like Shiloh.

> Hello Miles, may Shiloh and I come see you at 10?

The phone chimes again.

Come alone at 9.

I'm not sure about this. Shiloh will not be happy when she finds out that I left the house alone, but Miles is our friend. If he needs me, I must go help him.

So I send another message.

> All right, I will come

Once I am with Miles, I'll no longer be alone, and we will have safety in numbers against Leonard. I'm not sure Miles and I would be successful trying to defend ourselves in a physical confrontation with Richie, but perhaps a small part of Richie's memory might still remember who I am and would resist Leonard if he tried to harm me. I'd like to think so.

I pull up the blanket on the bed and put on my warm coat. I can hear Mrs. Oleson and Max talking in his room. Max's voice is high-pitched and inconsolable, and my stomach turns. I'm not sure if I should interrupt them to tell them I am leaving the house, especially since I will come back shortly.

So I hurry past Max's room, pull on my shoes, and head out the door.

I have never been to the labyrinth before, but I believe it's only a little way past the police department. The good thing is that I can walk most of the way on big roads where many people are out and about.

The clouds have quite a lot to say today. Most of them assume the shape of some small animal or another, and each of the animals appears tired. There is a donkey with droopy ears nearly dragging down by its legs, rather like the unhappy donkeys in Pinocchio, and there is also a sleeping cat curled up in a ball with its tail stretching out behind it. Perhaps all the animals look tired because I feel tired. I spot a crocodile creeping slowly closer to me in the wind, and my blood chills. Its teeth are bared like the crocodile brooch that was pinned to Leonard's coat the night I first saw him at the cemetery. It twinkled in the light of the moon and spun in front of my eyes as my head recovered from being slammed into the bark of the oak tree. The crocodile makes me feel like I'm a lost girl in Neverland, with Leonard taking the role of Captain Hook. I can almost hear the echo of a ticking clock, but I know it is only my imagination playing tricks on me.

I pass the police department, and the buildings thin out. I cross a tall bridge. The river roars underneath me, curving and dipping over the slippery rocks. Many parts of the Coshocton are calm enough to watch the striders skate across the surface, but this part is not. Any hapless insect who wanders to this part would be sucked under the water and drowned.

I glance over my shoulder and notice that the woods have grown dense around me. There are not as many people here. The labyrinth must be getting close.

A small sign beside the turnoff to the hiking trail points me toward Oren's Field.

I am almost there, Miles.

I follow the trail until it narrows and ends, opening into a meadow.

A gentle shiver courses through me from nape to navel. This place is like something out of a fairytale. One of the Grimms' fairy tales, not one from an animated film. In this field, the queen is forced to dance to death in hot red shoes, the wolf is cooked in boiling water, and the witch falls into her own oven and screams herself hoarse as she is slowly roasted. The harsh fall winds have stripped the trees of their leaves, reducing them to intimidating skeletons keeping watch over the meadow of dying grass. Their spindly, crooked fingers are stark against the gray clouds. I notice the maze-like pattern in the grass and the tall, abandoned telephone pole in the center of it all. A gentle breeze rustles the bushes and the yellow grass. Perhaps it is simply a gray day, but this meadow does not appear to be full of life. Quite the opposite, like it's a place where living things come to die.

Goosebumps stand up on my arms underneath my coat. I look around for Miles, hoping to find him quickly so we can go someplace else.

"Excuse me, miss," a voice shouts behind me.

I turn to see a portly young man with long, straight black hair and a pair of round glasses walking over to me, his hand raised in a half-greeting. He appears to be in his mid-twenties and is wearing a maroon collared shirt with the top button undone. I have never seen him before. "Could you tell me how to get back to the road?"

"Oh, yes. You go right down that trail, there." I point in the direction I have just come from. "Are you lost?"

He does not slow down. I realize that he isn't walking to the trail.

He is walking straight toward me.

I back away from him. A pattern of inflamed pimples decorates his forehead and cheeks. Cunning malice fills his wide eyes. My foot snags on a root poking out from the dying grass.

"I'm sorry, I don't believe we have met before," I say. "What are you—"

The young man rushes at me. Rough fabric encloses my head. A drawstring tightens around my neck, and I cough as I'm dragged backwards by my arms, screaming and kicking at the empty air.

29

Shiloh

Detective Babin drives me home. I don't ride in the front this time. I've graduated to the back where the guilty people sit.

Babin turns onto my road, and I notice Jonah sitting on my front steps. What is he doing here? I told him to stay put.

Babin glances back at me through the rearview mirror and offers a disapproving "tsk."

"Keeping good company, I see," he says, and it takes all my self-control not to flip him off.

He parks in front of the driveway. I climb out of the car without looking back or thanking him for the ride home, hurrying up to Jonah, who is fingering the hem of his black bomber jacket. There's a stunned sort of expression on his face as he looks at my sling, then up at the police car, and then back at my arm.

"What happened to you?" he asks.

"It's not broken."

Behind me, there's a screech of rubber on asphalt, and Jonah narrows his eyes at the car. "What did he want?"

I run my tongue over my dry teeth. For a second, all I can do is stare at him. I consider lying to him, but what would be the point? Jonah, of all people, would understand the tightness in my chest that's threatening to drag me down like a heavy weight.

"They have the gun I used on Leonard," I say. "Said if it matches the bullets, they'll arrest me for murdering Leonard and trying to kill Miles. I'm going to …"

Jail.

Saying it makes it feel real, so I don't want to say it, but I don't have to. Jonah's eyes widen in understanding.

"You're not going to jail," he says. "They can't prove anything."

"They said they have enough evidence." There's a tremor in my voice. "My fingerprints are all over that gun—"

"Along with Leonard's, your dad's, and mine. I shot the gun, too, remember?"

The memory comes rushing back. I was holding Max and making a break for it, but Leonard yanked me to a halt. He was trying to pull Max out of my arms when his back arched and he fell onto his knees, revealing Jonah looking down at the gun like it had fired itself.

I guess he has a point. He did also shoot it. But there is still one difference between the two of us.

"You weren't the one who killed him," I say. "I was."

Jonah hangs his head like he doesn't know what to say. My bones calcify as I imagine Babin and Finnegan clamping handcuffs on my wrists and shoving my head down into the back of that same police car. Getting charged with second-degree murder could get me locked up for years with no chance of parole, and being tried as an adult would mean going to adult prison. I'd have to watch Max grow up through panes of glass, seeing him every month or so when he came to visit me, talking on the phone through the bulletproof glass until time chipped away at our bond and he only started coming out of obligation. Birthdays … milestones … I would miss everything. Meanwhile, prison life …

So I heard your dad's a sheriff ...

This can't be happening. Leonard killed so many kids. He deserved to die. I knit my fist into the neckline of my sweatshirt, the gray fabric warming in front of my eyes to a fluorescent orange color.

Jonah's voice jars me back to reality. "You won't jail, Shiloh, okay? It's not going to happen."

The wind tickles the base of my neck. It's a cold wind, the kind that doesn't bother moving around you but blows straight through you instead. The kind that tells you winter's coming.

Jonah didn't see the way those detectives looked at me, like I would belong to them the second the results came back.

If I'm going to jail, I need to make sure Leonard dies while I still can.

"I don't want to talk about it anymore," I say, opening the front door. "Let's go find Francesca."

"Your mom said she was sleeping," Jonah says, following me. "I know you told me to stay put, but Moe didn't believe I was sick. I guess I'm a bad actor. So I told her I was going to school and came here instead. Your mom let me wait inside for a while, but I couldn't listen to more of that dinosaur show. That little green one has the most annoying voice ever, I swear."

In the living room, Max is sitting in front of an episode of *The Land Before Time*. I actually like that show, but I don't have it in me to tell Jonah that right now. Mom is passed out on Dad's old La-Z-Boy recliner, her head to one side and her lips parted.

Max sees me and starts walking over to Mom, but I press a finger to my lips and motion for him to stay where he is. He copies me, pressing his fingers to his lips, too, as he sits back down. Mom probably told Max to wake her up the minute I got back. But I don't want her asking me a million questions about what the detectives wanted, which honestly might make me cry because I'm so scared.

I make a beeline for the spare room and knock on the door.

No response. I guess Francesca really is sleeping. But she can't sleep all day, so I let myself in.

The bed is empty. The blankets are rumpled like she rushed to make it, but other than that, everything looks the same as it did last night.

I dart around Jonah and poke my head into the bathroom, but the lights are off. I hurry back to the front door to check for Francesca's clogs, but they aren't there.

"She's gone," I whisper to Jonah. "Why would she leave? Where the hell would she go?"

Jonah pulls out his phone and raises it to his ear. But a few seconds later, he shakes his head. "She didn't pick up."

My mouth goes dry. Francesca wouldn't leave without at least taking her phone with her. If she's not picking up …

Shit.

I wave goodbye to Max before pulling Jonah outside. It's mid-morning now, and the sun warms my shoulders despite the biting wind.

"We need to find her," I say, my voice returning to normal volume. "Call her again."

I hear a sudden buzz, and I glance down at Jonah's pocket where he's just put his phone. His eyebrows pinch together as he takes it out again, but his expression quickly turns to worry.

"It's Miles," he says as he picks up the phone. "What's up, buddy?"

A loud voice explodes from the receiver. I strain to hear what it's saying as the blood drains from Jonah's face.

"*Run,*" he yells. "Run as fast as you can. Don't let him catch you, okay? I'm on my way. Miles? *Miles.*" He grabs my hand. "We've got to move."

"What's going on?"

"Richie's got Miles," he says, pulling me across the front lawn, "and they're at the bridge."

I race through the trees after Jonah, trying not to slip on the soggy leaves. He said this was the fastest way to the bridge.

"I thought Miles was feeling too sick to leave the house," I ask, lungs heaving from running. "Did Richie pull him out of bed?"

Jonah makes a frustrated sound. "Miles has been going to the community park, or to that stupid labyrinth. He gets high on that bone dust stuff and takes advantage of his legs working to get out of the house. Told me that if he's going to die, he's going to die in nature."

"But he shouldn't be going out alone." I leap over a rotting log. "You told him about the attack, right?"

"He obviously didn't care."

I hear a harsh laugh deeper in the woods. Jonah and I run uphill onto the asphalt road, where I see Richie holding Miles half over the bridge's railing, a long drop above the rocky bed of the Coshocton River. Davey and his other henchman, Skip or Scotty or whatever his name is, are flanking him.

Davey sees us first and points. He has a composition book in his hand that must be Miles's. It's the kind he writes poetry in. Skip or Scotty rolls his eyes as Richie pulls his upper lip back into a sneer.

"The fuck are you doing, Richie?" Jonah snaps, casting an uneasy glance at Davey and the other guy. The way Jonah made it sound on our way here, I had imagined Miles trying to run away from Richie, who would be wearing his nun disguise. But this is the Richie we know from school, along with his band of mean friends. They clearly don't know that the real Richie is dead, and there's a raging 90-year-old lunatic animating his corpse.

Davey waves the composition book in the air. "We caught Dead Boy over here jacking off to the sounds of nature. Isn't that right, Dead Boy?"

Richie shakes Miles out against the bridge's railing, holding him by the scruff of his shirt. Imagining Leonard's soul inside of him, commanding his limbs like he's controlling a puppet, is enough to make my fists curl.

"Put him down," I snap.

Richie ignores me and shoves Miles farther over the railing. Rust has eaten away at the flimsy poles. Miles's hips brush against them as he squirms, hanging over the murky, green river that foams as it roars beneath us. If Richie were to let go, Miles would fall off the side of the bridge and into the rushing water, and there would be nothing I could do to stop it.

Richie lets out a low laugh as if he's enjoying every second. I gulp. If it is Leonard in there, which I'm convinced it is, he's dangerous. He shot Miles in the stomach. Who's to say he wouldn't drop him off a bridge?

The corners of my vision spot. I won't let him hurt Miles.

Not this time.

I run down the road. Richie cocks his head at Skip or Scotty, who walks toward me like he wants to snap my neck. He takes a swing at me, but I duck under his fist in time for Jonah to clock him in the face. I see a chip from a tooth fly through the morning air like some kind of surreal comedy accessory from a fight scene.

"Jesus, Scotty," Davey says, which solves one problem at least.

Davey charges at me and grabs my sling, pulling my bruised ligaments hard. I grit my teeth and drive my sneaker into his knee. He yells and lets me go.

I grab Miles's backpack from the asphalt and swing it into the side of Richie's head as hard as I can.

He drops Miles, who yells out and flails his hands, trying to grasp the slippery guardrail.

I shove Richie out of the way and reach over the edge to catch Miles's wrist.

He takes hold of my elbow and looks up at me. The air catches in the back of my throat as time creeps to a standstill.

Up close, he looks even worse. Veins pop in the whites of his eyes behind his drooping eyelids, and the bags under his eyes are so dark that his face looks bruised. Red blisters cover his forehead, and his papery skin is pulled tight over his cheekbones. But he's still Miles. The same Miles who came to the Rite Aid counter every day this summer to buy things he didn't need while coming up with puns about dinosaurs.

I don't need all my strength to pull him back up to the surface of the bridge. He was thin before, but now it's like handling one of those scarecrows hanging in front of the library. Maybe it's the adrenaline pumping through my veins, but right now I feel I could pick him up with one hand and carry him home.

He grabs hold of the metal bar, his chest heaving as if he's finally realized he's okay and not plummeting to his death. "Thank you."

I give him a small smile in response, but it quickly disappears. "What are you doing here?"

"I was reading on the sand by the pond," he says. "These guys came out of nowhere."

"You could have gotten hurt."

"I'm dying anyway, Shiloh," he says. "I won't spend the time I have left stuck in my room."

Behind us, there's a clinking sound, like metal against glass. I twist around to find Richie unzipping Miles's backpack and dumping out the contents. Out falls his pencil case, a plastic water bottle, and a heavy leather-bound book that lands open on the damp, muddy ground with the pages bent. A stray pen falls out, along with a crumpled gum wrapper. Miles's current book, some poetry anthology with a giant nose on the cover, is next. Then the jar of benmjöl crashes onto the asphalt. The white powder shifts as the thick glass strikes the surface of the road.

It doesn't break. I throw myself at the jar to catch it before Richie can pick it up, but someone grabs me from behind, bracing my throat against the crook of his elbow until my vision blurs.

The jar clinks against the ridges in the pavement as it rolls. Richie stops it with his boot.

"The hell is this?" he asks, picking up the jar and turning it over in his hand as he runs his thumb over the Soothsayer's handwritten label. "This your drugs or something?"

"Drop the act, asshole," I spit, hoping my voice doesn't tremble. Richie wouldn't have the slightest idea what it is, but Leonard would know immediately. He's just having fun with us. "Give it back."

He doesn't. I struggle against Davey. He's strong for someone who's built like a stringy ape, and he holds me immobile with little effort. Miles climbs over the railing and reaches for the benmjöl.

Richie punches Miles in the nose. Blood sprays from it like a tube of Party Depot fake blood has been squeezed out of each nostril. Miles cups his hands over his face and crumples to the road.

"Miles!" I cry.

Richie unscrews the top and lifts the jar to his nose. He's having way too much fun with this.

"Jonah, where are you?" I scream.

Sneakers squeak behind me, as if in response.

Richie takes a whiff of the bone dust and coughs. "You gonna tell me what this is?" he asks Miles, who is rigid with fear now, staring at his life-saving powder.

"Put it down," I say. "I swear to God, I'll—" Davey increases pressure on my airflow so hard that I can't say anything more.

Richie huffs at me like an angry bull. "You'll what? Do this?"

He holds benmjöl over the side of the bridge and tips it upside down. White powder pours down from it, falling into the river like a ripped open bag of flour.

Miles lets out a horrified groan, and I open my mouth to scream, but no sound comes out. Miles collapses on his side as Richie throws the jar. It spins end over end as it performs its final desperate arc toward the riverbed, where it hits a rock and shatters into a thousand pieces that fall into the water and disappear with a splash.

Richie's mouth curls into an evil grin. He knows exactly what he just did. He knows exactly what Miles lost. Davey laughs hysterically behind me, sounding like a hyena celebrating a kill.

Red hot rage pours through me. I drive my leg backwards with a strength I did not know I had and connect squarely with his knee. He cries out as he drops me. I spin around, kicking him in the knee again. Davey is on the ground, cradling his leg. I jump and land with all the force I can, putting my full weight behind the blow as both feet hit his joint one last time. I hear a pop like I heard when my shoulder came out, and Davey squeals. His leg is on wrong now, and the sneaker is pointing off at an unnatural angle.

See how you like a bit of dislocation, asshole.

Scotty has started to wake up, but Jonah has him in a chokehold. Jonah looks at me with undisguised admiration.

I turn to Richie. His beady eyes glare up at me from under his snapback. The flame logos on each side of the hat lend his face a strong sense of evil, and a shiver runs down my spine. It's like there's nothing behind his eyes. No thoughts. No feelings. Not even a glimmer of fear. No humanity at all.

Do it, a mean voice in my head urges. *Kill him.*

I kick Richie in the chest. He tries to grab my ankle, but I pull my foot back and throw my sneaker into his shin, and he stumbles back against the guardrail. His body is much heavier than Miles's. The pole creaks on impact. One more blow, and the whole thing will go.

His doughy hands grasp to find his balance. "You want me to kill you, bitch? I almost got you last night, and I can do it again."

But there's a hint of wariness in his eyes now. I take a step forward, my arms outstretched to shove him off the bridge once and for all.

Police sirens sing out through the quiet woods. I whip my head around to find a patrol car sliding to a stop behind Jonah and Scotty.

"Put your hands above your head," an electronic voice bellows from the speaker in the car.

I glance at Richie, who wastes no time before running down

the road and away. Davey is sitting on the pavement, one leg out in front of him and the other to the side. He's crying quietly as he puts his arms over his head.

Jonah drops Scotty to do the same, looking into the patrol car and rolling his eyes. "You again?" he says, like he recognizes the cop. "Are you kidding me, Officer Zweering? You know, if we keep meeting like this, the whole town's gonna start talking."

Jonah sounds annoyed, but fear has wrapped a sharp tendril around my throat. I can't get caught by the police. Not when I was about to force Richie off the side of the bridge.

I rush over to Miles and pull his stiff arm over my shoulders. "You feeling good to run?"

Miles wipes the blood pouring out of his nose with the back of his hand. "If I have to."

Jonah appears out of nowhere, holding Miles up on the other side. The police officer barks something at us, but my heart's hammering too fast to hear him. Jonah and I drag a stumbling Miles down the hill through the woods, and we disappear into the trees as the cop yells at us to stop.

30

Shiloh

Once we're out of sight from the bridge, Miles taps me on my good shoulder.

"Stop, stop, stop." He shakes his head like he's trying to get rid of bad thoughts. One lens of his glasses has a small crack across it, which I imagine is annoying to see around. "I need to breathe."

Jonah and I stumble to a graceless halt. Carrying Miles isn't hard. Even though my adrenaline rush is over, it still feels like I'm carrying a scarecrow. A scarecrow whose face is gray with nausea and whose lips are covered in the blood from his nose. Sweat clumps his dark curls together.

"Need to lie down?" Jonah glances around at the dirt and the damp leaves around us, and the corners of his mouth turn down. "Or sit, maybe?"

Miles shakes his head, pushing Jonah and me off him and bracing his palms on his knees. "Just … give me a second."

Jonah glances over his shoulder as if he's expecting the cop to follow us down here, but he's probably got his hands full with Scotty and Davey. Scotty and Davey are going to come out of this looking like victims compared to Jonah or me. The cops won't care that they were the ones who started it. Davey's knee is probably broken, and I'm wanted for murder.

Jonah touches Miles's shoulder, and I notice that there's a damp patch on the black fabric of his bomber jacket. I realize it's the same shoulder that Leonard sliced two days ago. Brawling with Scotty must have opened the cut.

Small teeth gnaw at the lining of my stomach. I want to ask if he's okay, but Jonah meets my eyes, glances at his shoulder, and shakes his head as if to tell me not to say anything. He probably doesn't want Miles to know he's hurt.

So I say something else instead. "We need to go find Francesca."

Miles looks up, wrinkles etched deep into his forehead. "Where did she go?" he asks.

"If we knew that, we wouldn't have to go *find* her," Jonah mutters, leaning against a tree to catch his breath.

"Leonard must have attacked her before he found Miles," I say.

Jonah rubs his temples with one hand. "Frankie's not stupid. She wouldn't leave the house for no reason."

"Especially since she was there last night when Leonard broke into my house," I say.

Jonah's eyebrows jump up. "That's how you hurt your arm?"

Did I not tell him that? I give Jonah and Miles a short walkthrough of the break-in, and Miles's mouth forms a small O.

"How about we call her again?" I ask. "In case she really isn't with Leonard, and we're panicking for no reason. I saw Leonard run away. I have no clue where he was going."

Jonah takes out his phone. Miles does, too, I guess because he wants to be helpful, but after a few seconds, he narrows his eyes at the glowing screen.

"This is weird," he says. "Here, Shiloh, look at this."

He passes the phone to me. I try to figure out what I'm looking at and realize it's an open text thread between Miles and Francesca's burner.

"I didn't send that text," Miles says. "I don't think I've ever sent a text to Francesca in my life."

My eyes skim over the text that Miles didn't send.

"I would never write 'I am Miles' or 'Please reply,'" Miles says, turning up his nose. "If someone doesn't want to reply, that's up to them."

I scroll down and see a message from Francesca saying that she would come to meet him with me, and then another text from Miles telling her to come alone. I glance back up at Miles. "You didn't send those either?"

"No."

I let out a huge breath. "Francesca must be at the labyrinth. I'm going to go rescue her."

Jonah waves his arm to tell me to stop. "Woah, there, Scooby. Hold your horses. These were sent from Miles's phone. You know what that means."

"It means Leonard must have used it to send it," Miles says. "Could Richie—or, uh, Leonard have taken it when he first found me? Right after I called you, but before you got to me?"

"Okay, and then what?" Jonah asks. "Did he leave you with Davey and Scotty to go meet Francesca?"

"No, he was with me the whole time," Miles says.

"So, if Leonard didn't leave you during the attack, who sent the text?"

I close my eyes to think, just like Francesca said to do yesterday, but no answers come to me. "Was Richie at your house this morning raking leaves?" I ask Miles.

"Nope," Miles says. "The only person who came by was Todd, my mom's teaching assistant, dropping off some papers to grade. I saw him briefly before getting into the shower. By the time I got out, he was gone."

Well, that's not very helpful. Jonah reaches out his hand, and I give him the phone.

"Here, look," he says. "The text was sent at 8:12 this morning. Miles, where were you then?"

"Still at my house," Miles says. "Or maybe getting a tea at the Grind."

Jonah looks at me, and what he's saying hits me.

Holy crap.

"Leonard is working with someone," I say, and Jonah nods. "He couldn't be in two places at once."

"Someone else used your phone," Jonah says. "Sent the text, then put the phone back before you noticed it was gone. Maybe while you were waiting for them to make your tea at the Grind."

"Maybe it's someone Leonard knew from the circus," I say.

"Or a serial killer he found during his many years in the business," Miles adds.

"I bet someone younger sent the actual message," Jonah says, "because, let's be honest, would Leonard even know how to text?"

Imagining Francesca going to the labyrinth, all wide-eyed and ready to help Miles in her chunky rainbow scarf, makes my heart pound so fast that it lodges in my throat.

Miles glances up at me, like he's afraid to say what he's about to say. "This text was sent an hour and a half ago. Do you think Leonard's accomplice lured her there to … you know …?"

The blood drains from my face.

Jonah points at me. "No, no, hold on. Frankie can't be dead. Not if Leonard lived with Francesca as Richie for over a week. He'd have killed her already if he wanted her dead."

I blink at the sky so that the boys don't see that even the thought of Francesca being scared and alone somewhere in the woods is enough to make tears pool in my lids.

"He's got to need her alive for something," Jonah says. "I bet he wants her to find a gate. To bring back that circus girl he liked."

"Can Leonard not do that himself?" Miles asks.

"I guess not," Jonah says. "He wouldn't keep her alive if he could do everything she can."

In the morning's chaos, I almost forgot that Leonard has kidnapped the Monroe girl, too. Mom showed Francesca and me the article, but Miles and Jonah don't know about it. Jonah has to be right.

I tell them about Talulah Monroe quickly. "We have to find them," my voice sounds weird, all tinny and strained.

Jonah holds up a finger. "Still one problem with that heroic rescue plan. Leonard probably just ran back to the labyrinth. If we want to rescue Francesca and Talulah, we'll have to go through him *and* his accomplice. He was going to kill Miles a few minutes ago. He'll definitely try to kill us if we rescue Francesca."

He's right. When we rescued Max, there were four of us. We had a gun, and Leonard was inside the body of a ninety-year-old man. Miles died. The rest of us almost did, too.

"Not to mention, you and I are cripples," Jonah continues, flicking his chin at the blood seeping through his shirt and then at my sling. He nods at Miles. "And don't get me started on you." The two of them grin at each other the way they used to, way back before any of this started.

I chew on my bottom lip, trying to think of a way to get out of this, but Miles speaks up before I can.

"I'll help," he says.

My heart drops into my stomach. "No."

"Why not?"

"Because … *no*. No way. I almost got you killed once, and I won't do it again."

"You aren't doing anything." Miles's bloodshot eyes fill with hard determination. "I want to help."

"But … what you said to me in your room … about wishing I was the one who … you know."

"I shouldn't have said that."

I gesture at him. "This is all my fault."

"It's not." He sits down on a fallen log, folding his hands on his lap. "I mean, sure, you wanted my help finding Max, but that doesn't mean I had to give it to you. I could have said no." He screws his face up like he's tasting something sour. This is almost the opposite of what he told me that day in his room. I wonder what changed? "It doesn't matter whose fault it was. I don't want to waste any of the time I have left feeling angry." He smiles up at me, but his expression is sad. "I am going to help you guys."

Everything inside of me wants to push back against him, but he's not asking my permission.

Jonah clears his throat, and I turn to see him lean up from against the tree and walk over to us. "Will you even be able to fight if it came down to it? I mean, no offense, man, but you've looked better."

"The benmjöl won't wear off for another hour," Miles says, his voice trembling a little like he remembers that Leonard poured the whole jar into the river. Without benmjöl, he won't have any way to relieve his symptoms. He seems to realize this at the same time as me, and he swallows hard. "So we just have to move quickly."

"Oh yeah, about that," Jonah says. "I actually have more of the stuff."

Miles looks at him funny, and so do I.

"More *benmjöl*?" Miles asks. "How?"

"The Soothsayer gave it to me," Jonah says, like it's no big deal.

But it's absolutely a big deal. The Soothsayer didn't want to give Miles more benmjöl when he asked. She said she wouldn't take money. I narrow my eyes at Jonah. "What did you give her for it?"

"That doesn't matter right now," Jonah says. "All that matters is that I have it back at my place."

"Okay," Miles says, side-eyeing him. "Well, we're definitely not done talking about this, but if you have some, I want to take more before we go fight Leonard to make sure my legs don't give out halfway through." Miles takes off his glasses and cleans the specks of dirt from the lenses. The material of his shirt snags on the cracked one. "I can't believe I'm actually saying this, but don't we need some kind of weapon or something if we're going to kill him?"

"Only rope or something to strangle him with," I say. "We can't damage the body too badly or else Francesca won't be able to put you, Miles, into Richie's corpse."

Miles's eyebrows fly up. "Excuse me?"

I glance at Jonah, who is looking at me like I've lost my mind. "Did you not talk to him about switching bodies?" I ask.

Jonah shakes his head.

"*Richie's* body?" Miles almost shrieks. "Like, Richie Russo who has been trying to kill me since elementary school?"

"Francesca suggested it," I say. "It would save your life and also not get me charged with another murder, although that doesn't really matter at this point. Jail is jail."

"I'm in," Miles says, his voice breaking with desperation.

I exchange a glance with Jonah. I thought Miles would put up more of a fight, or at least feel uncomfortable with the idea. "Are you sure?" I ask.

"I'm not ready to die." Miles scoffs. "Richie freaking Russo. I hate to say it, but it's better than dying. So what's our plan here?"

31

Shiloh

To kill Leonard and end this for good, we're going to need a couple of things you can't find at Walmart. Which is funny, because Walmart is the first place I go after getting off the bus in Mount Keenan.

Jonah didn't like the idea of us splitting up, but we had no other option. This is our best chance of getting Francesca back and rescuing Talulah Monroe, who doesn't deserve to be caught up in all this. Miles couldn't make it all the way to Mount Keenan without taking more benmjöl, which he would not do until right before we went to rescue Francesca, so he and Jonah went back to Jonah's house to pick up the monocle and let Miles rest while I went to Mount Keenan to get the other stuff we need. I'd be more nervous about splitting up if I hadn't seen Leonard head off toward the labyrinth. What's he going to do? Get on the bus and follow me? I picture us sitting there for half an hour in our separate seats, looking out the window while elevator music plays in the background, and I have to stifle a laugh.

The Walmart sign is stark against the ugly beige building. Climbing the hill to the parking lot makes my lungs burn, but the temperature has dropped a lot since I left Bethany. Clouds have crept in, concealing the sun and making my temples pulse like it's about to rain. I'll have to move fast if I'm going to get in and out of the woods before the storm starts.

I hurry through the store, putting Saran Wrap, latex gloves, rubber bands, and Duck Tape into my basket. On my way to check out, I grab a plastic poncho from the camping aisle.

I hope the haul doesn't look suspicious. As I load it all onto the belt, the hairs on the back of my neck stand up like someone's watching me, and I glance over to find Zach, Jonah's friend who helped us look for Poppy Rooney, bagging my items. He definitely recognizes me. He wouldn't be looking at me like he's staring down his worst fear if he didn't.

I wonder if Jonah told him that the Poppy who the cops found is a different person from the one who went missing. Zach probably thinks Poppy is still alive. Maybe he's disappointed that she hasn't come to see him since she got home.

Leonard really believes killing kids with hard lives is doing them a favor, but if he actually asked them whether they wanted to die, I bet they'd all say no. There's hope embedded in even the deepest suffering, that things will change or someday get better. But death takes away the chance that it will.

Zach averts his eyes and gives me my bags. "Have a nice day," he mutters before hurrying off toward the bathroom.

Swallowing hard, I take the bags and walk out of the store.

I climb over the bent metal bar and enter the tent city.

Coming here feels wrong, like I'm invading others' privacy, so I stick to the path. A thin fog clings to the spaces between the trees, making it hard to see anything past their trunks. Spindly branches look like skeleton arms reaching out to grab me, to block my path, or to prevent me from running away from anything that's lurking deeper in the woods.

This wasn't the way I entered the woods when I went to find the gun. Instead, I walked forty-five minutes to the edge of town so that I could get to Leonard's trailer the same way we did the night we rescued Max. But I don't have an hour and a half to spare today. Not when Leonard has Francesca. He could force her to help him bring Evangeline back. I have to go the shortest way.

Even though that means going through the Coshocton.

Stay away from that river, Shiloh, I remember Dad telling me once. *You never go swimming in there, you hear me?*

Wading across the river doesn't count as swimming. At least, that's what I tell myself.

People swim safely in here in the summer. It's the only way to get out of the heat sometimes.

But there are also places where the current can take you down. Principal Orr's grandson went swimming on a balmy summer afternoon. I imagine the warm breeze playing through the leafy branches and rippling the surface of Coshocton as it ran through the town like a cool, green snake. Nothing bad could have happened on an afternoon like that.

But nobody ever found his body.

I hear the river before I see it, gurgling like a giant gargling mouthwash. The fog pulls back to reveal the black water snaking through the trees, and I wander off the trail to stand on its banks.

The air snags in my throat. The river's banks are tall, and the water races over the rocks, turning to white foam that rises and dips according to its own rules and not anyone else's. It's like the water was below the bridge. Not even a full jar of benmjöl could calm it down.

I walk along the bank for a couple of minutes to see if I can find a place where the current gets any slower and where there's no white water. I grab a long branch half-covered in leaves and stick it into the river, holding it steady as the water threatens to pull it out of my hand. But it's not that deep here. It'll only come up to my knees. I can't drown in water that shallow, can I?

I wrap my burner phone in the plastic poncho and put it into my Walmart bag with my sling and the rest of my haul. Gathering my strength, I spin it underarm and fling it across the river.

It lands on the bank in a heap, and I let out a shaky breath.

My turn.

Careful not to slip on the slimy rocks on the riverbed, I shuffle down into the water. The current pulls at my ankles. It's strong, but not as strong as I was expecting it to be. I step forward. Moss or waterweed coats the rocks, and the soles of my sneakers slide around as they try to get a grip. I'm up to my knees now. Every muscle in my legs is ready, bracing my body against the unyielding push of the current. I hold out my arms to balance myself and so the gauze wrapped around my torn-up knuckles doesn't get wet. I feel like a tightrope walker heading out across Niagara Falls.

Wrong time for those kinds of thoughts.

On the other side of the river is a thin, straggly tree. It's reaching out to me. All I have to do is grab onto one of its branches and pull myself up onto the bank.

Don't slip, I will myself. *Please, God, keep me from falling.*

The tree isn't far. A couple more steps. I reach for the outstretched branch—

My foot slips. Icy water closes over my head. The current tosses me sideways, and I thrash out for something to grab onto. Something hard smashes into my bad shoulder. Pain shoots up my neck. I force my eyes open. Everything is dark. I don't know which way is up. My skull crashes into a rock, and I cry out. The sound comes out in bubbles, sinking past me. Hang on—they can't be sinking. Air rises to the surface.

Gathering all the strength I have, I flip over. Uneven rocks twist my ankles at weird angles, but I push up as hard as I can.

I break through the surface and grab the nearest branch. Splinters slide into the flesh of my palms as the muscles in my swollen shoulder flare. I drag myself to shore and scramble onto the dirt.

I stay there for a few seconds, on my hands and knees,

gasping for air. Pulses of pain reverberate out from my bruised shoulder like rocks being rhythmically dropped into a still pond. The wind blows through the sweatshirt that's clinging to my skin. A chill enters my bones.

I haul myself to my unsteady feet and go upstream to get my stuff and put on the poncho. I just need to reach the trailer. Get in, get out, and get the hell out of the woods to somewhere warm.

River water squishes between my toes, and my sneakers squelch as I run through the woods. It isn't long before I glimpse some flimsy yellow crime scene tape tied between trees.

I made it.

Ducking under the tape, I race up to the trailer. In the daylight, it looks a lot less menacing. There are no camouflage blankets draped over the top of it anymore. Rust gnaws at the bolts holding it together. The giant circus elephant painted on the side glares at me, like it's warning me to stay away.

I dump out the Walmart bag and wrap my shoes in Saran Wrap before putting on the gloves. I don't want anyone to know I was here in case they charge me for tampering with evidence and give me even more jail time.

There's a loud clang as I push through the loose plastic sheets, open the doors, and slip inside.

My nose wrinkles. It's warmer in here, but it smells worse than I remember. Like urine, sweat, and old furniture, or a carpet that hasn't been washed for a hundred years. I blink rapidly, trying to get my eyes to adjust to the shadows. It's pretty empty, probably because the cops bagged and removed most of the evidence. There are no lamps, no padlocks. I open the chest, and the hinges give out a soft whine. Could there be any benmjöl in here? Doesn't look like it. The only things left are some dirty rags and an old tobacco tin full of sewing needles.

I wander deeper into the trailer, revealing the handcuffs still on the wall. Next to them is a long stain that goes down until it reaches the floor. Leonard's blood. From where my bullets hit him. I remember the top of his head coming off like the lid on a jack-in-the-box, a great spray of bone and blood and brains hitting the wall and sliding down.

At least the cuffs are here. Thank the freaking heavens.

One cuff is open. The other is closed around a ring on the wall, but the key is still in the lock, which makes sense. No ghost could release themselves from it on their own. Leonard probably got the cuffs from the circus. They have some kind of special power like the monocle does, something old and dark that held prisoners fast no matter what dimension they were in or what form they took. Once, Francesca mentioned that cast iron repels ghosts, which is why cemetery gates are traditionally made from it.

I release the locked cuff and tuck them both into my dripping pocket. On my way out, I notice a photo frame hanging on the wall. The photo looks vaguely familiar and so does the short blonde girl with ringlets beaming into the camera. One archived news article I read about Evangeline's death and the circus accident had a picture of her in it, and this is definitely the same girl. The hair's a different color, but she has the exact same face as Talulah Monroe.

32

Shiloh

On my walk to Jonah's house, a raindrop lands on my nose.

Crap. The storm must be starting. Not that it will make much difference now. I'm still soaked from falling in the river. My teeth still haven't stopped chattering. I almost cried in relief when the bus had its heater on. It's probably the only thing that staved off hypothermia. The driver and some passengers stared at me at first, but they've probably seen stranger things than a soaking wet girl on a wintry day, so nobody said anything.

I run down Jonah's street in anticipation of the warmth. A car is parked in the driveway, so I knock.

A few seconds later, Jonah opens the door. He's in the same clothes as he was earlier, but fresh gauze pokes out of the neckline of his shirt, so he must have redressed his wound. His eyes drop to my dripping clothes. "Why are you all wet?" he asks.

I slip past him and into the house, sighing as warmth melts onto my skin. "I fell into the river."

"Seriously?" He snatches up a crocheted blanket from the couch and drapes it over my shoulders. As much as I don't want to get it wet, the heavy knitting feels good. "Come on, let's get you out of your clothes."

I pull off my soggy sneakers. He goes to his room and comes back with a T-shirt and a pair of his pajama pants. I go to the bathroom to put them on. My shoulder hurts from pulling myself out of the Coshocton, so I take my sling from my bag and put that on, too.

Originally, I asked to borrow some of his actual clothes, but he pointed out that his legs are a little longer than mine, so I'd trip over his pant legs chasing after Leonard and that would be a pathetic way to go. So my best bet is to throw my own clothes into the dryer.

Jonah's Nirvana T-shirt has a yellow smiley face logo on the front, but the eyes are just crosses and the mouth is a wobbly line. It's kind of funny and typical Jonah. I'm pulling it over my head when the smell hits my nostrils, and I press my nose harder into the fabric, inhaling the same smell that clung to Jonah's sheets that day he kissed me on his bed.

I close my eyes. My fingers tingle even from the memory of his hands lacing with mine.

"You good in there?" Jonah's voice is urgent and a little thin.

I finish pulling on the T-shirt. "Sorry, one second."

I unwrap the waterlogged bandage from around my knuckles, revealing a web of soft scabs and yellow-green bruises. I'm not going to bother re-wrapping it. It's healed up enough at this point.

I toss the gross gauze into the trash and open the door.

The side of Jonah's mouth curves for a second when he sees me in his shirt. He has a pillowy comforter in both arms. "Here, this might help you warm up."

He reaches over my head to drape the comforter around my shoulders, pulling both corners to the front of my body and holding it there. The soft down tickles my neck, and I glance up and look at his eyes. He doesn't let go of the blanket. He's standing so close to me that I can feel his breath on my cheeks, warming my skin like small puffs out of a hairdryer.

"Is that better?" he whispers.

"Yes." The word sounds like a tiny gasp.

Jonah's eyes flit down to my mouth for a split second. Oh my God. Is he going to—?

The door down the hall opens, and Jonah springs away from me. I scramble to grab the comforter with the arm I'm using to hold my damp clothes as Aunt Moe walks toward us with a finger pressed to her lips.

"The baby's sleeping," she hisses, pointing at Jonah as she walks past us. "You. Kitchen, now."

Her tone is firm. Jonah gulps. It hits me that he told Aunt Moe that he was going to school today. I guess I wouldn't be too happy seeing him come back halfway through the morning, either.

"I'll throw these in the dryer." Jonah takes my clothes, and somehow my face gets even redder. "Go wake up Miles. We have to get moving."

"Okay."

Pins and needles prick my stomach as I open the door to Jonah's room. The idea of being alone with Miles, or even being the one to wake him from a nap, feels wrong, but Jonah's right. It's time to head out.

Miles is curled up on his side in Jonah's bed, the covers only pulled up to his belly button, showing his bare chest and the top corner of his bandage. I inch up to the base of Jonah's twin bed. A floorboard creaks under my foot, and Miles jumps in surprise.

"Is everything okay?" he croaks, then winces like he sat up too fast. His eyes aren't opening all the way.

I forgot that he's a light sleeper. He shot up in bed when I woke him up a couple of weeks ago, the night I snuck over to his house after Dad had one of his episodes. I was hurting and scared, and I ran to Miles because there was nowhere else I could go that would feel safe.

The night he told me he loved me.

"Sorry," I say. On Jonah's desk is the monocle attached to the same elastic strap I wore at the abandoned house and also a clay pot. That must be the benmjöl. I vaguely remember it from the Soothsayer's place. "We have to get going, so it's probably time for you to … to …"

"To take the benmjöl?" He pronounces it with the confidence of someone who knows how to. He probably learned some basic Swedish. He probably already knew some basic Swedish before all this happened, and that is yet another thing about him that I don't know. "You can say it, you know. It's not a bad word."

"I can't pronounce it as good as you."

Miles scoffs. "When it's all you can think about day in and day out, not knowing how to pronounce it gets annoying. Even right now—you're standing right in front of me, and the only thing I can focus on is grabbing that pinch pot and dumping the whole thing down my throat. No water or anything. It's, like, screaming at me." I drop my eyes to the crisscrossing stripes on Jonah's PJ pants, and Miles cringes. "I'm sorry, is that too much?"

"No."

"I guess it won't matter after tonight," he says. "You know, my mom's a neuroscientist, so her don't-do-drugs talk was basically an academic lecture on how drugs affect your brain's chemistry. But if I take over Richie's body, then I'm going to have a different brain, so it seems logical that I won't be addicted to this stuff anymore. I'll be free."

I remember what the Soothsayer told us about Leonard and how he was never the same after getting beaten half-to-death and getting his fingers cut off. I'll bet most of the people who knew him chalked the change in his behavior up to the trauma he'd been through, but if what Miles is saying is true, then it was more than that. Injuries to one's soul are the hardest to repair.

"Or you'll suddenly want to beat the crap out of kids by the dumpsters.

"Or that, true." Miles gestures to the clay pot. "Could you bring that over here and help me take some?"

I hang the comforter over the back of Jonah's desk chair and sit on the edge of the bed next to Miles. He props himself up against the pillows. A sharp, tangy smell hits my nose, like sweat and something murkier. It's not coming from the benmjöl—it's coming from Miles. As hard as I try, I can't stop looking at the swollen blisters on his face. The one on his cheek is almost as big as a quarter.

I take the lid off the benmjöl. The powder is so white it makes snow look gray, and the bitter smell makes my eyes water.

"How much do you want?" I ask.

"Only a teaspoon," he says. "Or maybe a little more. The Soothsayer said not to take too much, and I don't want to OD yet. Not until later, after we rescue Francesca and I have to."

Oh God. I didn't think of that. He's going to have to die right about the same time as Leonard leaves Richie's body so that none of his organs can decompose. That won't happen by itself. What's the alternative? That one of us strangles him like an animal in Leonard's circus act?

"How long does it take to OD?" I ask.

"Usually takes a few hours if you're not found, but because this is a creepy circus drug and I'm taking approximately forty-eight times the recommended amount, I'm hoping it'll be quick."

I hope so, too. I mix a teaspoon into some water and support the glass as Miles wraps his stiff fingers around it. He drinks it all in two gulps, letting out a long sigh as he leans back against the pillows.

I'm sitting close to him. Much closer than I should be. I stand up, but he opens his eyes and grabs my wrist.

"Stay," he says, his pupils shrinking fast. "Please, sit with me for a second."

"Okay."

Miles doesn't pull his hand away. I glance down at where his fingers are clutching my skin.

"I need to tell you something," he half-whispers, closing his eyes again and leaning his head back against the pillows. "Until a few hours ago, I was sure I was going to die. I looked like crap. I couldn't get out of bed, so my parents took me to my doctor two days ago, who gave me some medication that made me throw up everything I ate. I thought the Soothsayer was crazy, but the benmjöl is the only thing that lets me keep food down. I can walk and leave the house, and if I lie completely still on my bed and look at the glow-in-the-dark stars on my ceiling, it makes me feel like I'm floating. But anyway, I kept going into the woods, because if I'm going to die, I want to spend every day I have left doing things I like to do. I started going to the community park to read. I even took my mom to the labyrinth yesterday, and while I was walking it, I realized that some of the happiest times of my life were the ones I spent with you."

His words take a second to sink in, and when they do, I forget how to breathe for a second. "Miles—"

"Not after Max went missing," he says quickly, "because, let's be honest, that wasn't great. I'm talking about before. Do you remember the day I asked you out?"

The memory brings a smile to my face. He came to my house with a bag of sugar cookies from Ethel's, and I almost peed my pants when Dad answered the door. Luckily, Dad didn't get too mad. He just looked at the greasy paper bag for a long time and told me that next time I wanted some of those to ask him to buy them instead.

"Or the time I came over and we watched *The Empire Strikes Back* in your basement," I say, my smile getting wider.

"Nobody has ever let me talk about Star Wars for that long." Miles opens one eye. "Honestly, it was a miracle I didn't tell you I loved you right then."

Loved you. The words make my chest feel tight, but not in a bad way.

"My point is," Miles says, squeezing my hand, "that I used to have so much fun with you before all of this happened, and life is too short for us to deny ourselves the company of the people who make us happy."

"I had fun with you, too," I say, surprised at how easily the words come out.

"Okay, Scooby," Jonah's voice sounds from the other side of the door. "Here are your clothes."

The door opens, and I whirl around to find Jonah holding my dry sweatshirt and pants against his chest. Miles drops my hand. In the doorway, Jonah pauses. I watch his eyes move from Miles to me and then back to the pot of benmjöl, and I see his lips pull into a flat line. The look on his face shifts in a way that I recognize. It's the way Mom's used to when Dad came home drunk or raised his voice when he didn't have to. Like she was bracing herself for whatever happened next.

"We have to go," Jonah says. "Get changed, Shiloh."

I don't think he's ever called me Shiloh. Ever since he yelled at me that day in school for getting Miles involved in the search for Max, it's always been Scooby.

"Okay," I say.

"She's just finished drugging me," Miles says, laughter embedded in his tone.

Jonah doesn't laugh. "It's raining pretty hard, so I'll leave you some raincoats." He snatches up the monocle from the table. "I'll wait for you guys outside."

Something's wrong. I grab my mostly dry clothes and pull them on in the bathroom before hurrying out to the front room where Aunt Moe is sitting on the couch, her feet kicked up on the coffee table. Two raincoats are lying on the bench by the shoes. I figure the pink one is probably for me, so I take the sling off and thread my bad shoulder through a sleeve and zip it up to my chin. Unfortunately, my sneakers are still pretty wet.

Jonah was right. It is pouring out. The rain has picked up from when I first got here, and there's nothing we can do that will stop us from getting wet. Even though it is barely noon, the clouds have turned dark gray, making it look like night is falling early. The heavy drops splat against my hood as I open the door and hurry over to where Jonah is standing in his black raincoat, scratching Bessie on her head. I'm glad I crossed the Coshocton when I did, because it'll be roaring even harder later.

I pull the hood tightly over my head. It's a little small on me. It must be Aunt Moe's. "Are you okay?"

Jonah keeps scratching Bessie. I remember how strong his

hands felt wrapped around my hips and how sure his long fingers felt in my hair. They look delicate, but fingers can be deceptive that way.

"How did you get the rest of that bone dust?" I ask.

Jonah stands straight. Bessie trots toward the front door, scratching it once. "The Soothsayer gave it to me."

"But she didn't want to give it to us."

"Turns out I had something she needed."

"Like what?" I ask. Jonah looks over at me, and for a second, he looks a little misty-eyed. Out of nowhere, I get an intrusive thought, and it's like I can't breathe. "You didn't …?"

He raises his eyebrows like he can't believe I implied that. "Jesus, no, I didn't have sex with her. Believe it or not, I can be useful for other things."

There's a bite to his words that makes me flinch. I probably deserved that. "I only meant she's ninety, and it would be gross."

Jonah mutters something under his breath that I don't catch. I want to ask why he seems mad at me, but then I remember Miles's plan for how he's going to die, and it hits me that Jonah will have to watch Miles OD. Miles is going to do it on purpose, but it doesn't matter. Jonah has to be thinking about his mom. As different as each situation is, it would be hard not to.

"I'll be there the whole time," I say.

Jonah wrinkles his brow and glares at me. "What are you talking about?"

Oh, so maybe I was wrong. "I'm just saying, I can't imagine how hard it must be for you seeing Miles like that."

"Why would it be?"

I don't want to say it. I didn't think I'd have to because he'd understand what I was talking about. "Because of your mom."

Jonah narrows his eyes at me, and I instantly regret saying anything. "You don't know what you're talking about," he snaps.

"I'm sorry." This is all coming out wrong. I reach down to take his hand, but he flinches, jerking it out of reach. My heart stings like a needle is being driven into it. "Did I do something wrong?"

"Just because we kissed one time doesn't mean you're my girlfriend," he snaps.

"I never said I was your girlfriend, but I thought—"

"That you were different? Oh, please."

I open my mouth to say something, but no words come out. Where is this coming from? This isn't how he was acting earlier when he wrapped the puffy blanket around my shoulders to warm me up, and it definitely isn't how he was acting a couple of days ago when we were kissing on his bed.

I don't mean to sound corny or whatever, his voice echoes in my head, *but you are literally the most beautiful girl I've ever seen.*

"You said I was beautiful." What a stupid thing to say. I sound like a whiny baby who wants attention.

Jonah blinks at me. For a second, it looks like maybe his eyes are softening and he's not mad anymore, but then he shoves his hands in his pockets and stares out into the street. "Well, you aren't the only one," he says.

"I was only asking if you were okay."

Jonah makes a frustrated sound. Behind us, Miles walks out in a bright blue raincoat. I swallow hard, trying to ignore the tears pressing against the backs of my eyeballs.

Miles pulls a crinkled plastic water bottle out of his pocket and swishes the cloudy liquid around. "The rest of the benmjöl is in here," he says. "When it's time, I'll chug this and it should take care of business. But if something goes wrong and Francesca can't get me back, I don't want to go through this again. So you have to promise me, no heroics."

Jonah gives him a nod. "No heroics."

"Okay." Miles zips the Poland Spring bottle into his deep pocket. "Come on, we have a friend to save."

33

Shiloh

My eyes open into darkness.

"Help!" I cry, but the sound catches on something soft lodged deep inside my throat, pressing against my uvula and making me gag. I choke against it, but it does not budge.

There's a squishing sound like feet on wet leaves. I rub my face against my shoulder, trying to displace the blindfold as the footsteps grow closer, but rough hands shove my head down and untie it.

The blurry face of a young man is staring down at me. Raindrops cling to his thick, fogged-up lenses.

"Gee, girl," he says in a clear falsetto. "It's about time you woke up."

Woke up? All at once, the memories rush back. I remember receiving a text message from Miles telling me to meet him at the labyrinth and arriving to have this young man throw a sack over my head.

"Who are you?" I try to ask, but the gag in my throat turns my words into something garbled and inhuman. My saliva soaks into the smelly fabric in my mouth, causing tears to pool against my eyelids.

"I have a mind to cut you a deal." The young man leans so close to me that I can feel his hot breath against my face. The smell is foul, like he has not cleaned his teeth in several days. "I'm gonna take the gag off, and you ain't gonna act all ugly and scream or nothing. Understand?

I nod my agreement and stay absolutely still as he puts a hand behind my head and unclasps a buckle, releasing the pressure on my jaw. He reaches between my teeth to pull out a long piece of fabric. Globs of saliva stretch between it and my lips like spiderwebs.

Once my windpipe is clear, I gasp for air, coughing and swallowing as I try to relearn how to breathe.

He folds the square handkerchief and places it beside himself on the mud. "See? I'm not tryna hurt you."

A harsh shiver courses through me, making my body quiver like a spasming puppet. Cold wind brushes against the exposed skin on my ankles and glues my sopping wet coat to my skin. My scarf hangs like a saturated towel around my neck. I look over the man's shoulder and see that we are in the woods and it's pouring with rain. The water is pooling around me, turning the dirt into mud and hammering against the top of the plastic bin I am leaning against. A crinkled brown tarp covers most of the bin, and it must also have been covering me before I woke up. The other end of the tarp is draped over a girl who is sitting upright, shaking uncontrollably with her face buried in her knees. Long hair cascades over her shoulders like orange ropes, and shackles are clasped around her wrists.

I glance down to find an identical pair of cuffs around my own wrists.

The young man offers me a crooked smile. "Ain't no cause to worry 'bout her." His chin-length hair is wet and sticks to his forehead like it's held there with glue. "The tarp should keep her dry. Dry as she can be in a storm like this." He looks to the heavens and raises an eyebrow like he's apologizing to me for not being able to control the weather.

I glance back at the girl, who raises her head to look at me, her glassy sea-green eyes bulging out of their sockets. A piece of duct tape covers her mouth. Despite her haphazard appearance, I recognize her.

Talulah Monroe.

Black spots prick the corners of my vision. "Are you Leonard?" I ask.

"I never meant you kids no harm," he says, and my breathing becomes shallow. I remember Leonard having a bit of a twang to his speech, sounding rather similar to my great grandmother, who had grown up in New Orleans. He does not have the same accent anymore, but he still runs his words together like he used to. "If you'da kept your nose out of my business, none of this would'a happened."

"But …" I struggle to parse all the questions that rush through my brain at once. "If *you* are Leonard, why did my brother Richie try to kill Shiloh?"

"That girl stuck her damned nose where it don't belong," Leonard says, his voice deepening. I don't know how I ever believed for a second that Richie was Leonard when I can see Leonard's face inside this poor man's features. Everything from the downturn in his mouth to the deep wrinkles in his forehead. "That gosh-darned brute shoulda killed her already."

Gosh-darned …? "You cannot mean—"

Leonard presses a finger to his lips. "See, you an' me, we're the same in all ways but one, and the difference is a real important one. You can do something I can't, and I reckon we could enter a sort of partnership, you an' me, where you do somethin' for me, and I do somethin' else for you."

Leonard pulls a glinting crocodile brooch from his pocket. Rain runs over the clear crystals covering the reptile's back and tail. Golden ridges define its nose and nostrils. Each of the gemstones that represent its eyes is black.

Leonard holds it in both hands as if it is precious to him. "This here belonged to my friend, Eveline. She gave it to me for luck, which kinda didn't go like we planned, but I'm guessin' you could use it to find her on the other side." He offers it to me, but my hands are in the cuffs so I cannot take it. Leonard frowns and shoves the crocodile into my palm, anyway. "I fashioned this for you." He pries open the lid of the plastic crate, pulling out a bulbous helmet with its visor glued shut. It looks like an old brass diving helmet that would probably act as a weight and drag me down head-first if the water was deep enough. There's a large rubber opening on the bottom, and I realize Leonard intends to fill it with water and put my head into it. The seal will not be fully watertight, but it'll be enough if I'm lying on my back with my head angled backward like I was in the old cooking pot Shiloh found. It also means I'll need Leonard to be there to take me out of it or I'll drown. I imagine myself lying down with my hands tied, attempting to rid myself of the helmet but unable to move it. I see my movements getting fainter as the other world gets brighter, like it's going to be my home from now on.

"That old preacher said you needed to be in water, but I thought this might do for convenience's sake."

"What old preacher?"

"The fat old goat from the cemetery. Said you can take people to the other side, so I figure you can bring 'em back, too." Leonard twists around. "That's what you said, ain't it?"

I follow Leonard's gaze to figure out who he's talking to. A transparent glimmer pokes out behind a tree. Slowly, the soul glides out from its hiding place, revealing itself to be Reverend Guessford, whose chin is quivering. A chain joins his ankle to a heavy iron ball on the ground, like the ones prisoners wear in old black and white movies.

"Reverend Guessford?" I ask, my voice breaking on his name. "You were working with him this whole time?"

"He p-promised to help me c-cross over," the Reverend stutters. "I didn't mean for any harm to befall you."

I cannot believe this. "*I* could have helped you across the barrier. All you had to do was *ask* me."

"I did ask you, if you recall, but you took dear Mrs. Lewis instead and she didn't even want to go. I thought perhaps it was beyond your control, and this man—this *demon*—he said he would take me if I helped him. Before I knew it, it was too late," the Reverend says. "I had made an agreement. I couldn't—"

"Hush your mouth!" Leonard throws the wet handkerchief at Reverend Guessford. It flies straight through him and hits a tree trunk with a splat. The Reverend returns to his hiding place back behind the tree as Talulah whimpers, the sound distorted by the tape. Leonard turns back to me, forcing the corners of his mouth to turn upward into something only he would call a smile. "See, you're the one I need. You will bring Eveline to me from the other side … please." He says that last word like it's a stranger to him.

Leonard's cold eyes are trained on me as he tips the helmet upside-down into the downpour. The rain is heavy enough to fill it quickly, but Leonard's muscles tremble with the effort of holding it at arm's length.

My heart pounds in my ears as I look at the crocodile brooch in my hand. I'm not sure if I can return souls from the other side. I have never tried. But if I try, and if I succeed … I turn my gaze to Talulah. Her nostrils flare as tears stream down her cheeks. Returning Evangeline's soul would mean Leonard would have to kill Talulah, and I cannot allow that to happen. She does not deserve to lose her life simply because Leonard wants his friend back and needs a body to put her into.

Something occurs to me that makes my breath hitch.

I may not know how to bring souls back from the other side. But neither does Leonard.

I may be able to trick him.

Swallowing my rising tears, I clear the phlegm from my throat. "I will help you," I say, "but I'm afraid this beautiful brooch will not be enough to locate Evangeline on its own."

Leonard pauses, contemplating my words. "What do you mean?"

I briefly close my eyes in thanks. He is listening. "In order for me to locate a soul on the other side, I must bring along somebody who knew them during their time on Earth."

I watch Leonard's face as he figures out what I'm asking him. "But I can't go over there inside my head like you can. I can bring people back like you can, but going to the other side is something only you're able to do."

"You could accompany me if you were dead," I say. "It would only require dying for a moment, as I would bring both you and Evangeline back with me and you could re-enter your host's body as soon as you return."

Leonard appears to consider this. Something flutters in my belly. If I can convince him to kill himself and come with me, then I can abandon him on the other side and still have a new host body for Miles, if Richie is still Richie. Talulah would not have to die, Leonard's soul would be trapped on the other side, and all that would be left to do is bring Miles back to this new body before too much time passes.

His eyes narrow and cold malice creeps onto his face as his fist curls into the runny mud.

"Do you take me for a fool?" he nearly whispers.

"Of course not," I tell him. "I simply—"

He slaps me across the face. I cry out as a hot stinging sensation cuts through my cheek. He grabs my shoulders, and his fingers dig into my skin as he shakes me so hard my neck whips back. Talulah utters another soft whimper, as if it was her who Leonard hit.

"You thought you could lie to me?" He shakes me harder. "That's precious. That's precious, indeed."

"I wasn't ..."

"I asked you *nicely*. I said *please*."

I drop the crocodile brooch into a puddle. Leonard yelps and rushes to feel around for it, rubbing his thumb over the dirty diamonds as if to clean them.

"I refuse to do what you are asking," I say.

Darkness shifts over Leonard's features. "I ain't asking."

"You say we are alike, but we are not," I spit at him. "I would never take an innocent life to save another."

"So then who gets to decide?"

"God."

"Oh, God don't exist," Leonard says, rain running down his cheeks like tears as he grins at me. "I'd know better than all the preachers in the world. 'Specially old Judas over there. But there ain't nothing stopping anyone from taking God's place." Leonard takes something from behind his back. My mouth dries up as he flips open a pair of pruning shears. "You say we ain't alike, you an' me, but you better watch your mouth 'cause I got ways of making us a lot more alike than you'd dare to dream."

He holds up his hand and bends his pointer and ring fingers down. Remembering what Ms. Wilma told us about those evil people cutting off his fingers when he was thirteen, I gasp.

He takes my wrist and presses the ring finger of my left hand between the rusted blades. He takes up the slack on the shears, and I try my hardest not to whimper as the skin breaks under the pressure.

"One squeeze," Leonard says, curling his lip into almost a snarl. "That's all it's gonna take, and everyone will see you for the freak you are. Believe me when I say you don't get over things like that."

I glance over at a cowering Talulah. It is only a finger. Surely I could lose a finger if Talulah gets to keep her life.

"Talulah does not deserve to die," I say strongly.

Leonard curls his upper lip and shrugs like he doesn't care either way. "Then this is on you."

With one swift motion, he jerks the shears closed. There's a clip as the blades come together like they have severed a troublesome branch and a loud snap as my finger flies from my knuckle, falling into the puddle by my foot. Cold air hits my exposed nerves and tendons. Raindrops land on the stump where my finger was, hitting my flesh like little bullets. Blood pours out of the stump. Burning pain jolts up my arm like my knuckle is being pressed against a hot stove.

There is no empathy in Leonard's face. None at all, despite the fact that he has done to me what was so cruelly done to him. There is only mild satisfaction, like a wrong has been righted, or an imbalance evened.

Leonard lets out a high-pitched giggle. "Hoo, boy, see, the pain doesn't set in right away, now does it? Wait for the shock to wear off. You going to help me now?"

Blinking away tears, I shake my head.

His face swims in front of me, and my vision gets fuzzy. He picks up my bleeding hand and shoves the shears deep against the knuckle of my pointer finger, and I imagine the faeries in my belly morphing into brilliant angels.

Please, angels, help me be strong.

But just when he looks ready to cut it off, he drops my hand into a puddle. The ragged flesh covering my knuckle disappears into the mud. The cold numbs all feeling.

"Know what," he says, tossing the shears and turning his attention to Talulah, who kicks her tied-up feet out to get away from him. "I know somethin' that could change your mind."

Gripping the heavy chain, Leonard yanks Talulah toward him. Talulah lets out a low groan that probably would have been a scream if the tape had not muffled it as Leonard closes his enormous hands around her head and forces her face down into the mud. He holds her there.

The realization of what he's doing hits me like a knife in my stomach. "Stop it! Don't hurt her!"

Leonard ignores me. Talulah's legs thrash out. I throw myself against the chains Leonard has wrapped around my arms and legs, but they won't allow me to move. Blood from my stump splatters across the front of my waterlogged scarf as I try to pull my hands out of my cuffs. I lurch forward to gain momentum, but I fall backward into a heap and the corners of the world gray out once more.

"Stop it!" My voice breaks into sobs. "Kill me instead. Please, you cannot do this to her."

But he does not listen. Talulah's movements grow weaker, and her legs stop kicking. Leonard shoves her down into the mud one last time, and the rain falls onto her unprotected head and runs in rivulets through her red hair. He grabs the back of her dress, pulls her head up, and flings her onto her back. I wince because that appears to have been painful, but I realize it no longer matters. Rain washes the soil from her face, and her mouth is ajar. There are flecks of dirt against her teeth, but the heavy drops quickly wash them off, too.

Leonard stands up from Talulah's body. He holds his hands out into the rain like a religious supplicant washing them clean after a ritual. He tries to dry them on the front of his shirt, but like everything else it is soaking wet.

"How could you?" I scream at him, tears tumbling from my eyes and snot streaming from my nose. "You are a *monster*."

Leonard simply shrugs. "Folks die all the time who don't deserve to. It's part of life."

A wispy soul rises from Talulah's body, taking the pale shape of the same harried young girl as the one lying dead on the ground. Seeing Leonard, her eyes shoot open and she whooshes through Leonard's plastic bin of oddities before curling up into a ball next to me.

Leonard leaves Talulah's body lying face up in the rain and turns his attention to me. "Lookie here, now. Don't be sore at me. I need you to find my Eveline 'fore this girl gets too much colder."

I am shivering so hard I cannot speak. Talulah's soul sobs silently beside me. I wish more than anything that I could tell her it will be all right, but it is not all right. None of this is all right, and it doesn't feel like anything is ever going to be all right ever again.

"Come on, now. If you don't help me, it will be too late to put anyone inside that poor girl, and that'd be a waste of good flesh. I'd just have to get me another girl. And another, and another, right up until you said yes." Leonard picks up the shears. "I could do some more convincin' if you feel the need. But there'd be no point in it. Not now that the clock's started tickin'"

Small pumps of pain pulse up from my knuckle, and the woods spin around me. He will not allow me to say no. What is the point of fighting him now that Talulah is already gone?

I give him a defeated nod.

He smiles, but really it's a show of teeth. "I knew you'd see sense." Leonard presses the brooch into my hand. I stare down at the crocodile. The eyes seem to glitter. Or maybe that's a result of the tears pooling against my bottom lid, making the brooch look like it has a life of its own.

Leonard picks up the helmet and holds it in front of me.

"Go on, now," he says. I take a long breath and hold it. "Go on and find her."

He brings the helmet down over my head and drowns my senses in icy rainwater.

34

Shiloh

Long grass bends with the wind over by the edge of the labyrinth. The rain is coming down so hard I might as well not be wearing a coat.

"Francesca!" I call, scanning the tree line in case Leonard comes rushing out of it in Richie's burly body. "Francesca, where are you?"

I'm standing alone by the telephone pole that marks the center of the field. I figured this would be the best place to stand because here Leonard will see me no matter which direction he comes from, and I'm going to look like an easy target. Miles and Jonah are hanging back, hiding near the mouth of the trail and waiting for Leonard to take the bait.

The bait being me.

"*Francesca!*" I scream even louder. "I'm here to rescue you."

Snap. I whip around, expecting to see Richie's huge work boots trampling the undergrowth as Leonard pumps his legs through the trees, but it's just the wind breaking off a naked, spindly branch.

In the labyrinth's clearing, the storm is fierce. Low clouds scud across a sky that's unnaturally gray, and water fills the pattern of the labyrinth that's been cut into the surface. You could sail a paper boat across the center clearing, but the rain would turn it to mush before you could sail it back.

I curl my fingers around the garbage bag and the coil of rope in my pockets to stop them from shaking.

Come on, Leonard, we're ready for you.

I remember the long knife Richie had when breaking into my house. That thing almost found its way into my stomach. Even with Miles and Jonah here, there is a real chance that Leonard will end up stabbing me or slicing my neck like he cut the Soothsayer's.

But as long as Leonard dies, too, this all will have been worth it.

Should I go into the woods? Leonard has to be keeping Francesca somewhere in there, but I don't know which direction to walk in. From the way Miles described it on the walk over, the surrounding woods are part of the Cardinal Preserve, the Whitetail Lakes past the community park, or they belong to the Oren family. The boundaries aren't clear, but the Orens' farm is on the other side of the trees to the north. Leonard wouldn't know or care about the farm, so he could literally be in any of the directions. The woods stretch on for a while before hitting anything. It's basically woods and cornstalks from here to Mount Keenan.

I'd suggest splitting up to go in all directions to find Francesca, but we need to stick together if we're going to have any chance of killing Leonard. Richie's body is twice the size of Jonah and three times the size of Miles or me. For a second, I try to do the math to see who has the advantage if we take him on at once, but the wind howls harder, blowing the grass almost flat in front of me.

I brace against it. *"Francesca!"*

By the entrance to the trail, I see Jonah's raincoat as he adjusts his position behind a rock. Warmth creeps onto my cheeks. Why did Jonah say all those mean things earlier? I genuinely thought he was going to kiss me after wrapping the blanket around my shoulders. I guess he wasn't, and I misinterpreted it because I don't know how things could have changed so much in twenty minutes.

I'm stupid for thinking he meant it when he called me beautiful. And I'm even dumber for agonizing over it. If I get stabbed, the reason Jonah stopped liking me will stop mattering real quick.

A grunt like an expelled breath sounds behind me, followed by heavy footsteps. I spin around to see Richie barreling toward me, his meaty hand clasped around the handle of a long, jagged hunting knife. Drops of water fly from the tip of the knife and Richie's face.

Oh crap. Okay. It's happening. I spring into action and sprint across the rest of the labyrinth to the path on the far side.

Footsteps pound against the short grass, breaking twigs with a snapping sound like the bones of small birds. I glance over my shoulder to see Richie lumbering after me. He doesn't look as if he's actually awake. I imagine Leonard inside him, driving him and striving to control his body with nothing else going on in his mind other than how much he wants to bash my head in.

"Catch me if you can, asshole," I say.

I crash through the long grass at the edge of the labyrinth and run as fast as I can to the mouth of the trail. Miles's blue raincoat flashes in my peripheral vision as I brush past his hiding place and lead Leonard down the hiking trail, further into the woods.

But before I reach the bend, a rough hand grabs the back of my coat and yanks me backward.

"I'm going to kill you, you fucking bitch." The words are slurred, like he's being possessed by something. I guess that's exactly what's happening.

I struggle to get out of Richie's tight grasp. He drives the knife toward my hip. The air catches in my throat as the tight coil of rope in my pocket stops the blade. He winds back to try again.

Jonah comes out of the stunted trees and pulls a bag over

Richie's head. There's something in Jonah's face that tells me that even the combined weight of Richie's strength and Leonard's obsession won't stop him this time. The knife splashes into a muddy puddle as Jonah pulls Richie backward.

"Miles, get his hands." Jonah's voice is curt as he holds the bag firmly over Leonard's head. "His feet, too."

A ripping sound breaks through the roar of falling rain as Miles duct-tapes Richie's wrists together. Richie's hands struggle against the restraints, and I tie Miles's rope over the tape to make sure he can't break free.

We do the same thing with his ankles. Richie tries to hop away and falls onto the trail with an uncomfortable grunt. I take the garbage bag out of my pocket and pull it down over his head, and Miles does the same with his. Richie is triple-bagged, like a dead raccoon I picked up from the backyard or something I don't want leaking before it gets to the trash.

Richie screams inside the bag, making the plastic pucker. I see the outline of his mouth, wide open as he struggles to find some oxygen.

The hairs on my arms stand up. "Got the monocle?" I ask Jonah.

He pulls out the headband and fastens it to his head. The lens covers his right eye, making him look like some strange steampunk scientist in his long coat.

"What about the handcuffs?" I ask.

"Got those, too." He takes them out of his pocket. As soon as Leonard's ghost rises from Richie's body, Jonah's going to clasp the cuff around him. Jonah can't touch ghosts, but the monocle will help him see them and the handcuffs will do the rest.

Miles and I roll Richie onto his stomach in the mud. Miles's cheeks fill with air as I climb onto Leonard's back, loop the rope around his neck, cross my arms, and pull as hard as I can.

Richie's bagged head flails from side to side. Raindrops pitter-patter on the plastic and run down the sides, joining the larger puddle behind his neck as he gags. Bile presses against my throat, like I'm going to be sick. My temples throb. I force myself to yank harder on the rope.

A high-pitched, throaty whimper comes from the bag as Richie's body weakens. It's such a scared, human sound that the rope slackens in my hands. What the hell am I doing? I'm hurting him. He has hurt me and my friends many times, but that doesn't justify premeditated murder.

I snap out of it.

This is not Richie. Richie is dead already.

This is Leonard.

And Leonard deserves to pay for what he's done. If I don't do this, how many other kids will die? If I don't do this, who else will?

I yank on the rope as Richie's enormous frame thrashes around, trying to free himself. Jonah has the monocle trained on Richie. He shakes his head as if to say he doesn't see a ghost yet. I pull harder, as if pressure alone will force the remaining air from Richie's lungs, as if Leonard will leave a few seconds earlier. Slowly, the strength drains from the body. Just a few more seconds, and then he'll be—

Click.

What was that sound? I glance up at Miles, whose eyes are trained on something behind me. Jonah pulls the monocle from his face and lowers his hands to his sides. He looks defeated. Guilty. Like Aunt Moe's caught him peeing in his sister's humidifier. What's going on? I release the pressure on Richie's neck and twist around to find the same police officer who interrupted us at the bridge, holding a gun in both hands. The hands are not exactly steady, as if the young guy can't believe what he's seeing. He's pointing his gun at Jonah.

"Stop!" Officer Zweering yells, spit and rainwater flying from his lips. His uniform is soaked, and the water makes his golden badge glint even in the shadows. "Take the rope off this man and put your hands behind your head."

35

FrANCeSCA

I float up from my body and onto the other side, shooting my arms out to steady myself. I hope I'll grow accustomed to the feeling soon and stop bumping into my surroundings. But like all things, I will improve with practice.

I glance down at my transparent hands. A fragment of bone juts out from the open knuckle on my left hand. The mark must have transferred over to my soul. The throbbing from the raw flesh of my open knuckle pulses up my arm like a numb reminder of my missing finger, but it does not hurt.

At least I do not feel pain in this world. I cannot complain about that.

Butterflies are making my stomach tingle. I glance around at my surroundings. Small particles hover around me in the air, like the ones that did last time I was on the other side, but I am no longer in the forest where I came from. Before me stands a three-story mansion in a wide garden set on a street corner. In real life, I imagine the house was magnificent once, made of dark red bricks, but in this dimension, the colorless façade is crumbling and it appears as if the entire structure would fall to pieces in even the gentlest breeze. Moorish archways protect the entrances from the elements, and circle-top windows line the second floor. Balconies stretch out from the upstairs rooms. Overlapping clay shingles form the gabled roof, and the chimneys rise even higher than the apex of the roof. The houses on the street have encroached upon the quiet corner on which the splendid old building once stood. These houses are narrow and crammed in against each other, vying for space and barely one fourth of the size of this mansion. Pale outlines of horse-drawn carriages sit frozen in time on the unpaved road beside automobiles and modern vehicles. But the trees are the same as the ones in Bethany. I'm fairly certain the Durand Brothers Circus was based out of Cincinnati, so this must be a version of that city.

I gape at the crumbling mansion before me. It has to be Evangeline's house. The brooch must have taken me straight to her.

I reach for the doorknob but pause. The once golden handle is tarnished a mottled black. I do not need to use the doorknob. I can float through things here.

I glide through the splintering wood and into the house. The entryway is dark, as if somebody has turned off all the lights. A staircase spirals up into the shadows, and a stained wooden banister follows it. Ornate maroon and mint decorative paper peels off the walls in the corners.

There appear to be no souls here, which is not what I expected. There were many souls in the abandoned house I visited with Shiloh and Jonah.

A laugh floats down the stairs like a twinkling song from a music box, and I turn my head in the laugh's direction. Perhaps whoever made that sound will know where I can find Evangeline.

I glide up the curling stairs past the portrait of a frowning man with a mustache that looks like a caterpillar glued to his upper lip. When I reach the top, the laugh cuts out, replaced by gentle muttering which I follow into a sprawling trophy room that makes me slide to a stop.

There are no souls in here, but there are many bones. A worn-looking globe sits on the coffee table between long leather couches and bookcases lined with what look like warthog skulls. Long tusks stretch up the far corners of the room, and an enormous stuffed elephant head hangs over the fireplace. The elephant's trunk is drooping, a likely effect of this being the other side and not real life.

I stare into its lifeless eyes. I wonder if this elephant was part of the circus or hunted for sport. Elephants are supposed to be some of the smartest creatures in the entire animal kingdom. If I were being hunted for sport, I cannot imagine how afraid I would feel.

Composing myself, I turn my eyes away from the elephant and follow the voice into a circular salon.

Sitting in the middle of the room are two glowing souls on either side of a chessboard. I catch myself on the tail of a brass tiger. One soul turns his head to peer at me from underneath a bowl-like metal helmet. He is young, not much over twenty. Unlike the faceless man from the Monroes' farm, his face is intact. No gashes mar his smooth cheeks or the delicate chiseled point of his chin. His eyes are wide and sad, rather like Shiloh's, and he holds the strap of his helmet in his mouth as if he's lost in thought.

Across from him sits a luminous girl with large blue eyes and beautiful blonde ringlets tied back by a ribbon. Leftover baby fat is attached to her cheeks and jaw, suggesting she is close to me in age. A white blouse with puffy shoulders and rumpled fabric down the front hangs from her frame, tucked into a long floral skirt that falls to her mid-calf. Shiny black shoes are buckled to her feet. She blinks at me, and I momentarily forget how to breathe.

"Hello, there. What is your name?" she asks.

I open my mouth to respond, but I cannot come up with a

reply for far too many seconds. "Francesca," I say eventually, as if I have forgotten the word.

"Hello, Francesca." She smiles, and a tingling sensation sweeps across my face. "My name is Evangeline, and this is my older brother, Edmond. Would you like to join our game of chess? You can be on my side because Edmond always wins."

"I do not always win," Edmund protests. "Or rather, I *wouldn't* always win if you understood simple strategy and concentrated harder."

Evangeline rolls her eyes, and then blinks at me. "So?"

"I would like that very much," I say.

As soon as the words leave my mouth, something sharp digs into my pointer finger like a reminder that I have to hurry. It is as if my heart bursts into flames. I have little time before I drown in that helmet.

"But actually, I can't," I say. "Leonard Gailis sent me here to find you and return your soul to Earth."

The smile drops off Evangeline's face. "You can cross the veil?"

I suppose veil is another word for the barrier. I prefer it. It's airy and far prettier. "I am only projecting my soul, but Leonard would like you to return to Earth. Perhaps to make up for the mistake he made all those years ago."

"Oh." Evangeline flattens the rumple on the hips of her dress. "After my brother Paul passed, he told me Leonard was no longer alive."

"Well, he is."

"Then I would rather not see him again, if it's all the same to you. Please, would you tell him that?"

Evangeline speaks politely, but she seems quite sure of herself. Leonard's obsession with returning Evangeline to a new body has led me to assume that she would be keen to return to my world and see her friend once again. It did not cross my mind that he might be trying to bring her back against her will.

Edmund rushes straight at my face, spitting out the chinstrap of his helmet. "You ought to leave now," he growls. "Leonard

Gailis was a freak who never should have gotten his hands on my sister."

"He was misunderstood," Evangeline murmurs.

"Go on. Get out of here, now," Edmund carries on as if she had never spoken, as if Evangeline is no better than furniture and cannot decide things for herself.

"Please, Evangeline, will you take my hand?" My voice is little more than a whine. "I am so sorry to interrupt your game and to do this to you. But Leonard will not stop until he finds you."

Back in the material world, Leonard says something indistinguishable, his voice muffled by the heavy brass and the water that fills the helmet. I feel the pressure begin to leave my head. He must be taking the helmet off. He will be unhappy if I return without Evangeline. I imagine more of my fingers will land in the muddy water beneath the trees.

"I'm so sorry," I say, rushing past Edmund and closing my hands around Evangeline's delicate wrists. Her eyes widen in surprise as I feel a deluge of cold water pour over my shoulders and Evangeline's world flickers out of existence like I've been shaken from a dream.

I open my eyes.

Leonard grunts with the effort of holding the helmet and drops it onto the muddy ground. "So?" he asks. "Did you bring me Eveline?"

"I believe so." My tongue sits like a stone in my throat. "She had a hold of my hands."

Leonard's eyes raise over my head. All the malice drains from his face, and suddenly he no longer looks capable of killing. I can see the young boy he once was, bright and optimistic, knowing he may not be normal in terms of his time but thinking he will overcome it. I felt that way myself once, before I realized that you couldn't go around setting corpses on fire for reasons only you can explain and then expect the world to understand you.

"Hey there, Eveline," he says.

Behind me, there's a high-pitched feminine shriek.

Leonard's face wrinkles in hurt as he lunges over the top of me, dragging Evangeline's soul into my line of vision. "Hush, now. Why are you cryin'?"

"What is this place?" Evangeline asks as Leonard shifts the tarp off of Talulah's dead body. She raises a hand to her mouth and takes in a sharp breath when she sees her. Talulah's red curls are plastered to her face, and death along with the cold has turned her cherry lips a deep blue. Evangeline, in contrast, is still a soul, so the rain runs right through her. She is dry, and her ringlets are immaculate. She is the only beautiful thing in this place. "Who is that?"

"I'm savin' you, Eveline," Leonard says. "I'm bringin' you back so we can be together again. Like I said I would. You stay still, now."

Before she has time to reply, Leonard aligns her body with Talulah's and presses her down so that her pale outline overlaps with Talulah's, making the corpse appear to glow. Evangeline stares at Leonard with wide eyes, and I watch, unable to cry out, as she grows fainter, seeping through Talulah's pores until she has disappeared completely.

Leonard braces his hands on either side of Talulah's head, tapping her cheek. "Eveline? Hello?"

But Evangeline does not stir. Leonard taps her face again.

Please, wake up, Evangeline, I pray, the words faint in my pounding head. My eyelids are heavy. I cannot keep them open. I'd like to go to sleep now.

Talulah's eyes blink open, and I release a harsh sigh. Leonard's face blooms, and his smile widens. "Eveline, you're awake. I got you back this time." Evangeline moans against the duct tape covering her mouth, and Leonard yelps. "Hold on there, let me help you."

Leonard starts to remove the tape, but before he can get it all the way off her lips, a scream cuts through the woods.

I sit up against the chains. That voice belongs to Jonah. I heard him scream once before when he was sobbing over Miles's dead body, and while this scream is laced with more frustration than grief, it is unmistakably his.

And the sound is close.

Why is he screaming? The realization creeps in, turning my stomach to stone.

He must be in trouble. I have to help him.

Leonard sticks the tape back onto Evangeline's mouth and stands up, listening for the source of the scream like a hound sniffing out a scent. Evangeline groans, but Leonard is no longer paying attention to her.

"You girls wait here," he says. "I'll be right back."

He grabs a piece of rope from inside his plastic trunk and stalks off through the rain toward Jonah's scream.

I try to pull my wrists out of the cuffs, but they are too tight. Leonard left his plastic bin open. Perhaps there's a key in there. But the rope tied around my ankles prevents me from standing.

I thrust one leg out. My clog knocks into something solid in the puddle by my feet, and Evangeline's crocodile brooch emerges from the puddle, out of my reach.

Perhaps I can use that to pick the lock. I strain to reach the brooch with my foot, but it is too far away.

Reverend Guessford pokes his head out from behind the tree, his bottom lip quivering. "Is that demon gone?"

I get an idea. Squinting at Reverend Guessford, I imagine a large number of tiny hands reaching out, grabbing hold of him, and knocking him into the brooch.

Immediately, Reverend Guessford flies forward and the iron ball attached to his ankle crashes into the puddle, knocking the crocodile brooch into my shoe. I clench my teeth to bear the pain as I fit the small needle into the wide keyhole, moving it around until I hear a click as one cuff releases.

Untying the rope around my legs, I rush over to Evangeline and unlock her cuffs as well. "You must run," I tell her as I remove the tape from her lips. "Run away from here because Leonard is not a good man and he will hurt you."

She blinks, clutching at her wet clothes as her teeth clatter. "What happened to your hand?"

Her eyes are innocent, and it occurs to me that this world may be rather shocking to her. Fast-moving cars … mobile phones … I'm not entirely sure if she has any place to run to. I change my mind.

"Go somewhere into the woods and hide," I say. "I will come back for you, and I will try to take you back to where you came from."

Evangeline looks down at her new body and seems even more awkward in it than she had appeared to be in her own.

I offer her a reassuring smile before hobbling after Leonard toward Jonah's scream.

36

Shiloh

On the walk over here, I had pictured all the ways this plan could go wrong. Richie could stab me in the gut. He could cut Jonah's throat. Francesca could be hurt to the point where she couldn't use her abilities, and Miles might not have enough benmjöl to kill himself in time for her to bring him back. But running into a cop didn't even cross my mind.

Jonah lets out a long howl of frustration. "Are you *kidding* me?"

Officer Zweering barks a bunch of coded commands into his walkie-talkie. The blood runs out of my frozen hands that are braced behind my head as I cast a sidelong glance at Jonah, who presses his lips into a thin line. Even he's not mouthing off to the cop for once in his life.

"I *knew* there was something going on here." Zweering's eyes bug out of his head as satisfaction rolls off him in smug waves. "Noah said I was crazy. Lindsay thought I was obsessing about nothing. I even got in trouble with Schnebly, but I was *right*."

"This is not what it looks like." Jonah's voice is calm.

"Do not move or I'll shoot!" Zweering jiggles his gun. Jonah raises his arms higher over his head. "I swear I will. I said it before, and I'll say it again. When bad things happen, it's always kids like you who are behind them."

Miles sways on his feet, his cheeks bulging like he's trying to stop himself from throwing up.

"Are you feeling okay?" I whisper at him, not taking my eyes off Zweering.

"My mom's going to be so mad at me," he mutters.

My mom being mad is the least of my worries right now. When they hear about this, Babin and Finnegan will arrest me for attempted murder so fast that I won't even have time to tell my mom. Then when the gun comes back, they'll get me for actual murder, and I'll be spending the rest of my life in jail. All while Leonard walks free in Richie's body and kills Talulah and maybe even Francesca without the cops ever catching him.

Richie is regaining consciousness. He wriggles around at my feet, thrashing his head from side to side, struggling to get the plastic bags off so that he can breathe properly. There must be some air getting to him. Zweering stares like he can't decide whether or not to help him, because helping would require taking the gun off Jonah.

I glance to either side of the trail, trying to figure out which way to run. There are three of us and only one of him. If we run in different directions, Zweering won't be able to catch us all.

Jonah's standing too far for me to whisper anything that Zweering won't hear, so I raise my brows, trying to convey my plan.

He meets my eyes and gives me a small nod. For a second, I forget how hurt I was by what he said in front of his house. I can almost hear his words.

On three?

Jonah looks at Miles, who nods like he also knows what's happening. Every one of my muscles tenses, ready to run.

But before we can make a move, arms appear behind

Zweering in a flash of movement and wrap a rope around his neck.

Zweering lets out a cry and a gunshot splits the air. Miles ducks to the ground. I reach down to grab his hand. He grips mine so tightly that my knuckles throb. The gun goes off again before it falls from Zweering's hand. He throws his fist back toward his attacker, but the rope doesn't budge.

A gurgling noise escapes Zweering's throat. His mouth opens and closes like he's trying to form a word, saliva or rainwater stretching between his lips like a web. The rope doesn't slacken an inch. I clutch onto Miles, my heart thundering in my chest, and glance up at Jonah standing closer to the path that leads off into the woods.

"What do we do?" he says.

I don't know. Before I can form a response, Zweering's eyes roll back into his head, and he crumples to his knees and falls face-first into the mud. Behind him stands a short, pudgy guy with shoulder-length black hair and a dripping-wet maroon dress shirt. I have never seen him before in my life.

Miles lifts his eyes and blinks at the guy. "*Todd?*" he squeaks.

"Who the hell is Todd?" I hiss.

"My mom's teaching assistant," Miles explains as Todd pulls the rope from Officer Zweering's neck and throws it to one side. "He's getting his PhD in neuroscience and helps my mom with her research. He …" Miles stands up, rubbing his eyes with his palms. "What are you doing here?"

A low rumbling chuckle rolls out of Todd. He flexes his fingers to restore his circulation.

Coldness drops like a rock in the pit of my stomach. "Leonard," I say. "Francesca was right. You were never Richie."

The young guy brings his hands together in an ironic gesture of applause. He stands back for a second, his lips twisting into a sickly grin.

Oh no. "Does Todd come over to your house often?" I ask Miles.

"Pretty often," he says. "My mom missed a lot of class this week because of everything that's been happening with me, so he's been coming by to drop off papers and other things she asks for."

"Would he have come to the hospital when you got shot?" Jonah asks.

Miles thinks for a second. "Possibly. I mean, he works closely with my mom, so I'm sure he'd come if she asked him to, even to offer his support ..." Miles's voice trails off as he realizes the truth of what he's seeing. He turns to look at Todd, who is stepping over Zweering's body like it's garbage. *"You're Leonard?"*

Todd lets out his breath in a long, low hiss. "You think you're made out of brains, boy," he drawls like a theater kid doing a bad Southern accent. "But you ain't as clever as you believe."

"It ... *no*," Miles says. "It can't be you. The other day you came to my house, and you didn't talk like this."

"Goin' into someone's head can, uh, give you mem'ries of the way they talked. It ain't easy for someone who's spoken one way to speak another. It's a thing of willpower, but you can accomplish anythin' with 'nough willpower."

"But ..." Miles's voice is high. Panic pulses in his words. "You must have *taught* my mom's classes."

"I didn't teach nothin'. Your mom was gettin' awful frustrated at me for not takin' things seriously enough, but I didn't need to stay in her good graces for long. Just until I had the girl, and I have her now. You've got to thank me for savin' you from this officer." He nudges Zweering's body with his foot. Zweering is lying face-down in the mud, and I guess if Leonard hadn't strangled him first, he'd have drowned by now. I feel a pang of pity for him. He may have been a jerk to Jonah, but it's unfair he died just because he was in the wrong place at the wrong time.

But Babin and Finnegan are going to think I killed him. The growing knowledge of how much trouble I'm in makes my shoulders sag.

"I s-saw you this morning," Miles stutters. "You were at my *house.*"

"Who do y'all think sent the message to the girl?" Leonard asks. "I'll tell you, I'm not good with these new phones myself, but Riccardo here is." Richie groans underneath the plastic bags. "I asked him how to use it to write a message to someone. I used your phone while you were in the shower."

"It can't …" Miles stutters, still not believing him. "It doesn't —you *can't* be Leonard."

"How do you think I knew y'all were goin' to see Wilma?" Leonard asks. "Your mom told me. I was plannin' to go there anyways. Wilma made herself quite a tradeswoman, keeping a gosh-darned antiquities store in her old trunks, and she had some things I needed. But I wasn't plannin' on y'all asking her about me. It wasn't easy sneakin' in there without being recognized by your folks. I was going to talk to her after her act, but then she had to choose you to come up on stage, and she spent nearly forty-five minutes with you kids. By that time, the show was nearly over, so I had to kill her quick. I think that bendy girl saw me, but I'll be movin' on soon enough."

I realize with a pang that I have not heard a single word about Wilma's death since the day it happened. It didn't make the news. No police officers came to question me about it. Hundreds of people saw me running off the stage after her. Someone must have suspected me.

Knitting needles in her eyes. If that was killing her quickly, I'd have hated to see him kill her slowly.

"Wilma said you grew up together," I say. The memory of the Soothsayer's kind face wraps itself around my heart, and I knit my hands into fists at my sides. "Why did you kill her?"

Leonard smiles at the ground for a second, as if reminiscing about a pleasant memory. "The two of us had an old debt to settle. But I'll tell you, it surprised me to see she gave you kids the rest of that bone dust, but I was glad to find enough foolery to brainwash ol' Riccardo here." Without warning, Leonard kicks Richie in the head under the bag. Richie lets out a howl.

"You were supposed to kill them, not get yourself killed by them!"

"Stop! Please!" Richie begs, his voice high-pitched and so distorted that my heart aches for him.

"You brainwashed Richie?" Miles asks. "How?"

Leonard pauses mid-kick, the wrinkles etched into his forehead morphing into a self-satisfied smile. "Naegleria."

Miles thinks for a second. He's shaking as hard as the remaining leaves on the branches above our heads, as if his grasp on life is as thin as theirs. "Do you mean Naegleria Fowleri? The brain-eating amoeba?"

Leonard gives him a sick smile. "That's where it gets its name. There's none of them amoebas in the drug, though. Growin' up, we used to call the thing foolery, since it was close 'nough to its name. Say there, boy, do you know any more 'bout what Naegleria does?"

"It's a kind of amoeba found in warm freshwater," Miles says, like he's taking an oral exam. "It travels up through the nose into the brain and causes primary amebic meningoencephalitis, destroying the brain tissue and, in most cases, resulting in death."

Jonah blinks at Miles like he can't believe how nerdy Miles sounds. "Seriously?"

Miles rubs his arm. "I know a lot about brains."

Todd's mouth moves as Leonard digests the medical terminology. "I never knew anyone who died of the parasite, myself. All I know is that foolery makes you lose your mind. See, 'fore I met any of y'all, weren't nobody took notice of me. Not much of anybody wondered who I was, and none of 'em blamed me when kids went missin', cause the police"—he nudges Zweering's limp, curled hand with his boot—"they never found no bodies. But then y'all had to stick your noses in where they don't belong. I warned you what would happen if you crossed me." He points a stubby finger at me. "I warned you 'specially. I told you I'd give the cops that gun of yours if you didn't stop lookin' for me. And I did it." Leonard reaches down and pulls the garbage bags off Richie's mashed-in face. Richie recoils, but when he recognizes Leonard, his scream dies in his throat. "It didn't take much foolery to convince Riccardo here to get rid of y'all. His sister an' me, we're one in the same. I told him he could keep her, but Riccardo doesn't take no liking to any of you. I figured he'd have finished killing you by now, but I didn't expect him being so gosh-darned useless."

This explains the glazed-over look Richie had in his eyes when we were fighting him at the bridge, like he was not all there in the head. I was so sure he was Leonard—or Leonard was him. I remember what the Soothsayer said about the drugs they had in the circus:

We had drugs that turned you into a puppet, she had told us. *Elias gave them to the most difficult performers, those who said they wouldn't do what he wanted, and after that they did whatever he told them to do.*

I guess glazed-over eyes wouldn't be a concern if they were too far away for the audience to notice.

Leonard unties Richie's legs. In the corner of my eye, Officer Zweering's gun glints as the rain washes mud from it.

An idea pops into my head.

If I can get to the gun and shoot Leonard, then Jonah can still use the handcuffs to trap his ghost.

We can still end this.

But I have to hurry. While Leonard's still fumbling with the rope, I drop Miles's hand and run for the gun.

Leonard's head snaps up. He clamors for the gun, picking it up and pointing it at me.

"I wouldn't act all ugly, if I were you," he says, "unless you want to end up like your friend over there." He points the barrel over at Miles, who wraps his arms around his stomach. "Amazing how fast bone dust can take your body away from you, ain't it?"

Leonard places the gun by his shoe as he keeps untying Richie. He hums nursery rhymes under his breath as he slices through the duct tape with Richie's serrated hunting knife.

Hush, little baby, don't say a word
Mama's gonna buy you a mockingbird.

In the trees, I catch a glimmer of movement and see Francesca poking her head out from behind a tree.

Oh my God. She's alive. She presses a finger to her lips, and I chomp down on my lip to keep myself from crying out to her.

Francesca points to Zweering's corpse on the ground. Her eyes are enormous, like she's trying to tell me something.

But I have no idea what it is. She widens her eyes even more then points at Miles, who is staring into the storm clouds above us and muttering like he's reciting a prayer, even though I don't think he's religious. When Francesca jabs a finger at Zweering, what she's trying to say dawns on me.

Maybe not all hope is lost after all.

Leonard finishes untying Richie, who jumps to his feet, his glassy eyes darting around like a scared animal.

Leonard pats him on the shoulder. "There, there, Ricky-boy. It's all right. Here." He presses Zweering's gun into Richie's palm, and Jonah goes pale. "Go on, finish 'em off. You think you could do that for me?"

Richie looks down at the gun, up at Todd's face, and then back down at the gun. He nods.

"There's a good boy," Leonard says, like Richie is a dog that's learned a new trick. "Bye now, kids." Leonard saunters off into the woods back in the direction he came.

Richie trains his dead eyes on me. He's like a zombie, his movement slurred and uncoordinated, but I still barely have time to react before he pulls the trigger.

The bullet cracks past only inches from my face. Richie flinches from the noise. The dull metallic tang of gunpowder clings to the roof of my mouth like blood. Richie rubs his shoulder as if the first time he's ever shot a gun. I spring into action, running over to Miles and shoving him into the woods toward Francesca, ignoring his surprised sputters as he stumbles out of Richie's line of sight. Jonah takes off after him.

Richie fires at the space where Miles was a split second ago, but there's an expression of confusion on his face.

I wave my arms over my head to bring his attention back to me. "Richie, you stupid asshole, come and get me!"

Richie shoots at me but misses. Before he can shoot a fourth time, I run down the trail toward the labyrinth, lifting my face to the rain as I hear his heavy footsteps pounding behind me.

37

FRANCESCA

I hold back a scream. Richie hobbles after Shiloh, although he is too heavy on his feet to catch up with her right away. She rounds the bend and disappears. Richie fires at her, but the bullet thankfully lodges itself in a tree.

I emerge from my hiding place and run to Miles, who is steadying himself on Jonah's arm.

"Where did you come from?" Miles asks, his voice high and tinny.

"I escaped from Leonard," I say. Jonah opens his mouth to speak, but his words stick to his tongue like peanut butter. He glances in the direction Shiloh ran in. "Jonah, what are you waiting for?"

"But Miles—"

"Shiloh *needs* you." My voice nearly breaks with urgency. "She cannot defend herself against Richie alone."

A gunshot echoes from farther down the trail. A finger of terror runs up my back as I imagine the bullet shattering Shiloh's spine—or worse, bursting her head like a watermelon that's been hit with a hammer.

"*Please*, Jonah," I say.

This appears to get through to him, because he gives me a stunned nod before picking up Richie's hunting knife from inside a puddle and running down the trail.

"Do you have any more of your benmjöl?" I ask Miles.

Miles pulls out a crumpled plastic water bottle from his pocket, and the foggy liquid sloshes around inside of it.

"W-we have to help, t-too." Miles's words are sticking to his mouth on the way out. He must have taken quite a lot of benmjöl before he came here, as his pupils are so tiny that I can hardly see them in his murky brown eyes. The drug is wearing off, and the cold and rain are getting to him. His words are straining with the effort he's having to make to speak them through his stiff jaw. Enormous fluid-filled pustules have appeared on his cheeks which were not there the last time I saw him, and the surrounding skin is inflamed. They must be very painful.

"No, Miles, it's time for me to help you now," I say.

I tell him my plan. Miles makes a surprised bleat, but he listens carefully as he presses his thumb into the plastic of the bottle, making a soft and repetitive popping sound.

A high-pitched, feminine laugh weaves in between the trees as if riding the wind, ruffling the hairs on the top of my head. Goosebumps rise on my arms. That must be Evangeline. Leonard must have returned to the place he kept me prisoner and found her. Oh, rats. I promised to go back and rescue her. Why is she laughing?

My heart turns over. By now, Leonard has realized I'm gone, which means he will come looking for me very soon.

I gesture at the officer's body. "Could you help me turn him over?"

Miles and I roll the policeman onto his back, and I notice with a pang that he is very young. He must have been a bit intimidating while he was alive because of his uniform and his powerful profession, but death has a way of turning even the most fearsome of faces innocent. With his hair sticking up in many directions, he could be a twelve-year-old playing dress-up.

I try to swallow the tears rising in my throat as I scan the trees around us for his soul. But only streaks of rain fill the spaces between the trunks. Perhaps he faded away as soon as he died. Some souls do not stay souls for more than a couple of seconds. I believe that happened to my mother. By the time I learned of her death, her soul had already gone to the other side. I miss her dearly, but it would be silly to remain sad when I know I will see her again one day.

Miles is looking down at the benmjöl mixture with a thoughtful expression. He's looking at his own death in that crumpled plastic bottle, and he's trusting me with his life.

"This is going to work, right?" he asks. Wrinkles slice through the sheen of sweat and water on his waxen face. "I will overdose and die, and you promise you will bring me back?"

I wish I could tell him there was another way, but if we wait to transfer his soul into this new body, he will encounter the same problems as he did in his body. It has to be now. We have no other choice.

"I will be here with you the whole time," I say. "You will not be alone."

He looks through the trees toward the labyrinth as if it could provide him some comfort, but the trees are too thick for us to see through them. Miles takes my hand. His curled fingers are stiff, most likely because the benmjöl is wearing off, and they cannot fully wrap around mine.

"If something goes wrong, tell my parents I love them," he says, his bottom lip trembling. "Jonah, too. And tell Shiloh …" His face screws up around her name. "Tell her I wish we'd had more time."

I want to tell him nothing will go wrong. But the only thing I can promise is, "I will do everything in my power to bring you back, and then you can tell each of them this yourself."

"I'm scared."

"I know."

Miles's eyes pool. "I'm sorry for misjudging you for so long. You're a really good friend."

Friend.

My breath catches as I fight for something to say, but before I can think of anything, Miles drinks.

The liquid glugs as Miles gulps it down. Before he finishes, he gives the bottle a shake to make sure there is no sediment remaining on the bottom. He's a practical person, Miles. I have always liked that about him.

I shudder, the wind chilling me through my denim coat. Miles expels a long sigh. He puts the cap back on the bottle and sits back on his heels, glancing down at himself as if he's waiting for the drug to take effect. Or to hear something. Or to sense his impending death. I observe him, trying to pick out a sign that something is out of the ordinary from his features, but he looks normal—if a little nervous.

"It usually takes a minute or two to hit," Miles says.

Close to a minute goes by. I glance over my shoulder and scan the trees for Leonard, but I can see no sign of him.

Miles bends over his knees. "I don't … feel so good," he manages, before tipping onto his side in the mud.

I hurry across the officer's dead body to sit beside Miles. His hands are tightly wrapped around himself, so he does not reach out to take my hand again, but I push the hair out of his face because that's what I like to have done to me when I am sick. "I am here," I tell him.

Miles's breathing grows shallow. I want to help him, to save him, but I force myself to stay still. He must die. If I am going to bring him back, he has to endure this. I gently pull him onto my lap.

Miles's head rolls to one side. I steady his face in my hands as his breaths grow fainter and his eyes stare up at me, unfocused. Ms. Wilma told us that benmjöl is easy to overdose from. I'm sure it won't take long.

Only a little while longer, Miles, and everything will be all right.

"Francesca," a voice half-sings from deeper inside the woods. "Come on now, where d'you go?"

I straighten. Leonard's voice is coming from somewhere behind me, but one glance at the trees tells me he is not close enough to see me.

Miles's chest heaves, and a deep gurgling sound comes up from his throat as he vomits clear, goopy liquid onto my lap. I go to turn him onto his side so that he will not choke on the vomit, but I realize that I'm not supposed to be trying to save him. He needs to die—and quickly.

"Oh Francesca?" Leonard's voice sounds again, as if he is encouraging a dog.

"Please, die," I whisper to Miles as he convulses again, vomiting more liquid down the front of his shirt. A sour smell hits my nose, making my breath spill out onto my cheeks and twisting my voice as I try not to breathe in for a second. "Hurry."

I hear footsteps in the woods, treading on branches and squelching through puddles. They are getting closer. Miles is still breathing. Why hasn't he begun to choke?

Blackness tugs at my vision, threatening to pull the world away from me. I press my fingers to the fleshy part of Miles's neck. His pulse remains strong.

A heavy sob bubbles up from the depths of my stomach. I put my good hand over Miles's face, holding my palm over his mouth as my thumb and finger press his nostrils closed.

"I'm sorry," I whisper to him.

Color fills his ashen face. Blood fills his head, and his eyes open, wild and staring. A snore-like gurgling noise rattles in the back of his throat, and I force myself to press harder.

His breath hitches as he tries to breathe in, but my hand is stopping the oxygen from getting to his lungs. An animalistic scream scrapes against his voice box on its way out. He struggles to get away, gripping my wrists as he wriggles his weak frame. I climb on top of him and brace my knees against his shoulders, my tears falling onto his face and mixing with the rain and sweat. Miles's chest heaves like he's trying to vomit again.

"I'm so sorry, Miles," I say, lifting my eyes to the sky in prayer.

Please, dear God, let him die so I can save him. He must die for me to bring him back.

Miles's eyes turn backward into his skull. His chin tucks to his shoulder as his head rolls to one side, and I remove my trembling hand to see the imprint of my fingers on his face. I cover my mouth as I sob to stop myself from screaming. My chest feels as though it is being ripped in two.

"I'm so sorry," I whimper behind my hand. "I am so sorry, Miles."

Miles's body glows. Slowly, his soul sits up inside his body, looking around like he's trying to remember where he is.

"Miles," I say, my voice almost a gasp. I am expecting him to say hello. Or tell me he is all right.

Instead, he raises a hand and points at something behind me. "Uh, Francesca?" he half-whispers.

I twist around to find Leonard striding toward us in Todd's heavy frame. He's smiling like he's just won a prize at the fair.

Panic lights up my chest. I grab Miles's transparent wrist and yank his soul over to the officer's body. I struggle to line his quaking arms up with the corpse.

"Stay still," I whisper, stretching his legs down so they overlap the officer's. Leonard is running now. I only have seconds.

Gathering all my strength, I press down on Miles's chest, forcing him down into the body. Excruciating pain flares through me, as if lava is running through every one of my nerves. Miles grimaces but does not cry out like last time. He appears to be growing fainter. It is not happening fast enough. I shove him down, screaming as it feels like the skin is ripping off my arms. He fades into the front of the officer's uniform, but before he is completely gone, rough hands pull me off of him.

"Did you think you could run from me?" Leonard asks,

picking me up and throwing me again. Dizziness threatens to pull me under as I buckle over and deposit the contents of my stomach onto the muddy ground. My muscles feel sluggish, as if I am wading through cold honey. "Did you think you were so clever, gettin' away from me?"

Cleaning my mouth with my dripping wet scarf, I hobble toward the labyrinth. The trail bends under my feet in alarming ways. The dirt sways like the deck of a ship during a storm, surging and dipping over the waves. A tide of darkness tugs at my vision.

"You're comin' with me," Leonard says. "I have big plans for you and me."

I push myself off the tree and stagger down the trail, but the pounding in my head is too much.

"Shiloh!" I scream. "Please, help me!"

Leonard grabs me underneath my arms and drags me away. The last thing I hear before going under is his low, maniacal laugh.

38
JONAh

In the labyrinth, the rain's coming down so hard that it takes me a second to spot Shiloh. She's a dark blur ripping down the path. Richie's lumbering after her. He's big and uncoordinated, but he's hot on her tail.

The gun goes off. My stomach drops like a weight, but Shiloh keeps running.

If this asshole thinks he's going to shoot her, he's got another thing coming.

I run at Richie from behind. His brain's too dead to hear me, or maybe he's got a wax buildup. I gain on him fast. He crashes into the clearing in the middle of the labyrinth, and I leap onto his back, reaching around his head and gouging my fingers into his eyes.

"Gah!" Richie throws his shoulders from side to side, trying to get me off of him, but he doesn't drop the gun. His neck is as thick as a pylon. It's thicker than his head. I remember Moe telling Catherine something about never trusting a man whose neck is wider than his head. I definitely never trusted him.

I hang on tight. Richie shoves his meaty shoulder back and

knocks me off, turning on me like a hyena. Blood streams from his eye sockets, but I can't tell how much damage I've done. Not much, clearly, because he points the pistol straight at me and there's a second where everything slows to a stop, where even the raindrops seem to slow their descent as Richie squeezes the trigger.

But all the gun does is click. Richie gives it a little shake, then lets it hang uselessly at his side. He must have used all the bullets shooting at Shiloh when she was too far away for him to hit her.

A harsh laugh bursts out of my throat. "Wow, Leonard really wasn't kidding when he called you brain-dead, was he?"

Richie brings the butt of the gun up against the side of my head.

My laughter cuts out. Bright spots of light flash against the corners of my vision. Sharp pain flares up from my bad shoulder, and I realize I've fallen onto it and I'm lying on my side half curled up into a fetal position.

Richie yanks me from the ground and slams me back, but the soft mud absorbs the impact. I hear Shiloh scream, a sound that is clear and bright despite the rain falling into my ear. Richie straddles me and smashes the gun into my head again and then once into my nose. I struggle to push him off, but one of his knees is digging into my bad shoulder like he remembers that's where he cut me.

"Get off me," I try to say, but all that comes out is a garbled mess.

Richie pulls the gun back to hit me again. I spit blood at him, but it falls back onto me and is almost immediately washed away by the rain. I brace myself for the next impact.

All the weight is pulled off me. A tingling numbness fills my nose like it's been injected with Novocain. I try to prop myself up on my elbow, blinking through the throbbing pain in my temples that's making my head feel as if my brain has swollen to twice its normal size and is pressing against my skull. Long grass waves around me like a group of belly dancers to an unforgiving tempo. I hear a deep grunt and then a familiar squeal, which pulls me out of this unfocused state in time to see Richie smash the side of the gun into Shiloh's face.

Richie hits her again and again, not stopping or slowing down. Shiloh's legs go limp as she loses the ability to fight him.

Shiloh. I push myself onto unsteady feet and curl my hands around one stone that marks the path of the labyrinth. Worms and beetles crawl in the place where it sat.

I bring the stone down hard against Richie's head. If the stone had been any heavier, I'd have crushed his skull like an eggshell. As it is, Richie's spine straightens, and after a second he flops forward on top of Shiloh like he's hugging her. Something about the intimacy of their pose makes me want to smash his head in again. I wipe the blood running into my mouth with the back of my hand, grab a fistful of Richie's wet hair, and drag him off her. He's lying face up in the rain, one of his eyes forced inward where I'd grabbed him from behind, the other closed. I check his pulse. It's there, and it's steady. It would take something close to superhuman to kill Richie, and I'm surprised to feel a pang of relief that he's still alive. I wouldn't want to tell Francesca that I'd killed her brother. Leonard had brainwashed Richie into doing what he did, and although I never liked him much, it's still not his fault.

I turn to Shiloh and freeze in horror. She lies crumpled in the long grass, her nose bashed in and bent at an unnatural angle. Her blood is matting a clump of her blonde hair together, and the rain is spreading the stain across her face. Both of her eyes are closed.

I stare at her, unable to move. "Shiloh?"

I remember walking in on her and Miles a couple of hours ago, feeling a wave of gut-wrenching guilt wash over me because Miles was smiling for the first time since he'd learned he was going to die. Shiloh looked like she wanted to crawl up onto the bed and sit there with him, and I could do nothing but stare because that was the bed I'd kissed her on. She dropped Miles's hand and asked me if I was okay like everything was normal, and I couldn't do it. The impossibility of ever being with her hit me like cold wind in my face, and then she asked about my mom like she actually cared. Miles is good and kind. Shiloh has already been through so much. She deserves someone who's uncomplicated, not like me. I've got enough baggage weighing me down to drag both of us so far below the surface that we'd have no chance of ever swimming back up.

She's better off with Miles. I figured if I could hit her with a reality check, it would make her choice easier. But none of that matters. Not right now.

I crash to my knees, pulling her into my arms. Her neck falls back, but I cup the back of her head. Blood has glued clumps of her hair together. I move them out of her face, leaving crimson streaks on her cheeks. I run my fingers over the mangled skin on her skull, trying to feel for a dent, but there's so much blood that I can't tell.

"Shiloh." My voice sounds pathetic, not like my usual tone at all. "Come on, wake up."

Her eyes stay closed. This can't be happening. I could live with Leonard escaping. I could live with him bringing back Evangeline, and I could happily watch him bring back every one of his freak show friends. But I can't live with this. I feel around the fleshy part of her neck, trying to find a pulse, but unlike Richie, there's nothing there.

The blood rushes from my face.

I press her tightly against me, folding over her to shield her from the freezing rain that's falling on her without mercy. Her zipper snags against my lip as I bury my nose into the place where I was just looking for a pulse, and I still don't feel any sign of life. A heavy sob fights its way up through my chest and splits my rib cage down the middle on the way out.

"I'm sorry," I half-scream into the crunchy material of her raincoat. "I'm so fucking sorry."

Shiloh groans. The sound is so soft that for a second I think I made it up. But I lower her and find her blinking an eye open. The white of her eye is bright red like she burst a blood vessel.

"But … you were dead," I say, my voice straining with the effort of stopping myself from crying. "I couldn't find your pulse."

"Maybe you didn't look in the right place," she croaks, giving me the most radiant smile I've ever seen.

The sound of her voice fills me with such an intense rush of relief that I have no hope of hiding it. I gather her up in my arms, clinging to her like if I hold her tightly enough, I'll be able to stop anything bad from ever happening to her. I breathe in the smell of her hair—a mixture of blood, gunpowder, and rainwater.

Shiloh knits her hand into the front of my coat, pulling me closer to her. The simple gesture breaks down all of my walls, and I feel the hot tears spring from my eyes.

"I'm going to get you to the hospital," I tell her, wiping the tears away before she can notice them. "I'll call an ambulance."

Shiloh's half-red eye looks from one of mine to the other. She looks like she wants to say something, but whatever it is she can tell me later because she's bleeding a lot. If there's something wrong with her head, like a concussion or a brain bleed, we need to act fast. I dig my phone out of my pocket, wiping the screen off on my pants. The numbers swim in front of my eyes. I remember Richie hit me in the head, too. Bad enough to make me dizzy.

Richie lets out a dull groan. He's going to wake up soon, and there's no way we can be here when he does. I glance back down at Shiloh whose eye is fluttering closed like she's nodding off.

"No no no." I tap her cheek. I don't know much about concussions, but I know you're not allowed to sleep after hitting your head. "Come on, don't do that. You've got to stay with me."

Shiloh's eyes stay closed. I'm not supposed to move her, but somehow she's in my arms already. Who knows how badly Richie injured her head, but I'll carry her all the way to the hospital if I have to.

I grab the rock I used to knock Richie out with, ready to hit him again. But before I can get up, a sopping-wet figure emerges from the horizon, walking toward us along the labyrinth's path.

The dim light glints on the golden badge. Oh no. Zweering probably called for reinforcements before Leonard killed him. If that's a cop walking over to us, Richie's the least of our problems.

But when the officer comes into view, I rub my eyes to make sure I'm not seeing things.

Officer Zweering trudges through the long grass, wiping the raindrops from his brow to dispel them. This isn't real. He's dead. I saw him die.

Oh, crap. Leonard …

Did he change hosts again?

"Get away from us." I hold Shiloh closer. "She's worth a million of you. She is the best thing that's ever happened to me, and I will not let you touch her."

"Buddy, it's me," Zweering says in his usual grating voice, but his tone is not as sarcastic as it normally is. He points at himself like I should know who he is, then looks down at Shiloh in my arms. "It's Miles."

My brain short-circuits as he whips out a pair of handcuffs and fastens them around Richie's wrists before he can come to. Everything I said hits me all at once. I see myself through Miles's eyes, protecting Shiloh like a jealous lover, and try to swallow the lump in my throat.

"Miles?" is all I can say.

Zweering nods. "Francesca brought me back into his body."

I want to say that's crazy, because it is crazy, but it's also not crazy because Francesca has already proven that she can do that. The person in front of me looks and sounds exactly like Zweering, but I watched Zweering die, and if it isn't Leonard, who else can it be but Miles?

"Where's Frankie?" I ask. "Is she with you?"

Creases show up in Zweering's—or I guess Miles's—forehead. "Leonard has her. I saw him coming after her when she was bringing me back, but when I woke up in this new body, she was gone. I was looking for her when I heard Shiloh scream. Is she okay?"

I glance at Shiloh to see if she'll respond, but her eyes stay closed.

"We need to get her to a hospital," I say.

"But what about Francesca?" Desperation saws at Zweering's voice. "We have to save her."

Police sirens echo across the field. I freeze. They're far away, probably coming from the road leading down over the bridge, but they're getting louder. These must be the reinforcements Zweering called.

I glance down at Shiloh, limp in my arms but still breathing, then up at Miles who looks like he's trying to decide whether to stay put or run back to the trail and hide his own body before someone finds it and tells his parents, and then at Richie who is bleeding profusely from his head.

Miles stares at me, crouched in the rain holding Shiloh like nothing in the world is ever going to convince me to let her go.

The sirens get closer. Like a promise of approaching danger. Or safety. Or at least some shelter from the storm. Jail time, no matter what happens. Shiloh grips my hand, whimpering like she's having a bad dream. Miles glances down at our hands. One singular thought enters my head.

How the hell are we going to get out of this?

Wondering how Shiloh, Francesca, Miles, and Jonah will escape from the police and stop Leonard from bringing back more of his childhood friends? Claim your copy of *They Return*, Book 3 in the They Stay Series, using this code:

A Note from Claire

Thank you so much for taking the time to read *They Whisper* and for fighting Leonard with Shiloh, Francesca, Miles, and Jonah. I love this story. I hope you enjoyed reading it as much as I enjoyed writing it. If you have a second, I'd be SO grateful if you told your friends and considered leaving a review to help more readers discover the series. It really helps me get these books in the hands of more people who will enjoy them.

Can we keep in touch? Claim your free copy of *The Day I Lost My Job at the Bookstore*, a short story from Miles's POV, when you sign up for my newsletter:

Resources

Even though *They Whisper* is a work of fiction and to my knowledge nobody knows whether ghosts are real, the characters in this book deal with many challenges that teens and their families deal with in real life. If you or someone you care about needs information, resources, or someone to talk to, here is a short list of resources that could help.

SAMHSA's National Helpline
A free, confidential, 24/7, 365-day-a-year treatment referral and information service for individuals and families facing mental and/or substance use disorders.
1-800-662-HELP (4357)
https://www.samhsa.gov/find-help/national-helpline

The National Domestic Violence Hotline
A free, confidential hotline available 24/7 for anybody who is experiencing domestic violence or questioning aspects of their relationships.
1-800-799-SAFE (7233)

https://www.thehotline.org/

PACER Center's Teens Against Bullying
A website run by PACER's National Bullying Prevention Center created to help teens learn about bullying, how to respond to it, and how to stop it.
https://pacerteensagainstbullying.org/

National Suicide Prevention Lifeline
The Lifeline provides 24/7, free, and confidential emotional support to people in suicidal crisis or distress.
1-800-273-TALK (8255)
https://suicidepreventionlifeline.org/

RAINN National Sexual Assault Hotline
A 24/7 hotline that connects individuals who have experienced sexual assault, or who know someone who has, with a trained staff member in their area.
1-800-656-HOPE (4673)
https://www.rainn.org/about-national-sexual-assault-telephone-hotline

Acknowledgments

This book was so much harder to write than I was expecting. I had heard that writing a sequel was hard and, sure enough, it was so hard that it knocked me and my plucky can-do attitude on my butt many times and made me wonder whether I could do this. But I ended up being able to do it because of some pretty amazing people I'm going to talk about right now.

I want to thank Perry Iles. I couldn't have done this if it weren't for you. You are the best editor any writer could ever ask for, and even though this book was messy and my thoughts were scrambled and I was rewriting the book from scratch two months before release day, your confidence and enthusiasm for this story did not waver. You took my messy draft and helped me turn it into something that was alive, coming up with additions and ideas for directions the scenes could go in and suggestions for where the plot could end up. You helped me breathe life into each character in this book—especially the members of the Scooby Gang—and also led me the idea that allowed me to turn this into a five book series instead of a trilogy. I am so grateful to have had you to lean on during this process.

I'd like to thank Eve Porinchak for your kindness and guidance in the earliest stages of this journey. I was very unsure about the book when I sent it to you, but you helped me discover where the real story lies. Thank you for opening my eyes to the problems with the timeline and helping me conclude that the entire plot was flawed, prompting me to rewrite the story and turn it into the version I published. I am so proud of this book, and your help and insight were instrumental to it becoming something to be proud of.

I also want to thank my amazing beta readers. Amanda, Valorie, Jess, Monique, and Bhavana—this book would not be the book it is today if it weren't for you. This story was messy when you read it, and I can't thank you enough for spending time with my book baby before it was ready for anybody else's eyes.

Quick shout-out to my critique group for giving me some really excellent feedback on the opening chapters. You all are so awesome. I look up to you all as writers so much, and I'm so grateful for the opportunity to learn from you all.

I also want to extend my deepest thanks to Stephen, who did a fabulous job proofreading this book and getting it ready for everyone to read. I'm sorry I don't know how to use commas, and I'm so grateful that you do.

A huge THANK YOU to my enthusiastic ARC team. Before writing this book, I've never experienced the feeling of working on a story that other people are excited to read, and I'm filled with such deep gratitude for each one of you who messaged me telling me how pumped you are to continue the series, posted about the book on Instagram, or replied to my emails when I shared writing updates. I reached a pretty big sticking point with this book in mid-January, but because of the love you all showed my story, I was super motivated to finish writing it so you could read it. From the bottom of my heart: thank you for supporting my writing and me. You are all the best, and I'm so glad our paths have crossed.

Mila, thank you for working with me on such a beautiful cover design. I'm so excited about these covers and love how each one looks almost like a movie poster. They are so cool.

I kept my acknowledgements in *They Stay* pretty succinct because I figured the most important people in my life already know how I feel about them, but it doesn't hurt to get a reminder, so buckle in.

Papa, this book is dedicated to you, so I'm going to start with you. I'm so deeply grateful for everything you have done for me and for all the time I get to spend with you. My earliest memories of writing all have you in them—from reading you and Mum my Gladiator Girl stories to and having long conversations by the pool about the governmental system in the dystopian world I set *Imperfect* in. I'm thankful beyond words for the encouragement you gave me to follow my passion and be brave enough to publish my stories. I wouldn't be writing these books today if it weren't for you.

Mum, I also wouldn't be writing these books today if it weren't for you. Because of your wisdom and guidance, I had the opportunity to be homeschooled in high school, which gave me the time to discover this is truly what I loved to do. And as soon as I fell in love with doing something, you made it happen for me, opening up doors that let me expand my knowledge and dive deeper into my passion. Whether it was musical theatre, dog rescue, or writing, you helped me jump right in, which is the most amazing gift you could have given me. I'm so thankful to have had a champion who saw me both as the person I was and the person I wanted to be, and you helped me become the latter.

Tristan, you inspired this series. Not the ghost part, because that would be weird, but there's a reason that my first horror book featured a main character whose little brother goes missing. You are the coolest person ever. I am grateful beyond words that we're so close and that you're still down to hang out with me even though you're so cool and I go to bed at 8pm.

Andrew, you are the best boyfriend and teammate anyone could ask for. Thank you for supporting me and my publishing dreams from the very day we met back before *They Stay* even existed, and thank you for being there for me every time I need someone to talk plot points through. Our brainstorming sessions have made this world and these characters so much more alive.

I would have been a nervous wreck during this process if it weren't for my emotional support animals. Tuggles and Mocha, I know you won't read this, but I love you dearly.

Finally, I want to offer the deepest thanks go to EVERYONE WHO READS THIS BOOK! Thank you for giving my books a chance and for following this adventure.

Claire Fraise is the author of paranormal thrillers about sinister spirits and the brave ghost hunters who bring them down. She won the Grand Prize at the 2023 Writer's Digest Self-Published Book Awards for *They Stay*, and has written four more books in the completed series. When Claire is not sitting behind her computer writing about ghost hunting, you can find her hiking in the mountains, on the back of a horse, or teaching her rescue Chihuahua that it's not nice to bark at people. Even though it goes against every introverted bone in her body, she is on social media. Connect with her on YouTube at Write with Claire Fraise, Instagram and TikTok at @clairefraiseauthor, or visit her website at clairefraise.com.